ANDREW McGAHAN

The White Earth

First published in Australia by Allen & Unwin

First published in the United States in 2006 by
Soho Press, Inc.
853 Broadway
New York, NY 10003

Library of Congress Cataloging-in-Publication Data

McGahan, Andrew.
The white earth / Andrew McGahan.
p. cm.
ISBN-10: 1-56947-417-6
ISBN-13: 978-1-56947-417-4
1. Inheritance and succession—Fiction. 2. Cholesteatoma—Patients—Fiction. 3. Fatherless
families—Fiction. 4. Mothers and sons—Fiction. 5. Rural families—Fiction. 6. Family
farms—Fiction. 7. Land tenure—Fiction. 8. Queensland—Fiction. 9. Uncles—Fiction.
10. Boys—Fiction. 11. Psychological fiction. 12. Domestic fiction. I. Title.

PR9619.3.M3234W47 2006
823'.914—dc22   2005050415

10   9   8   7   6   5   4   3   2   1

For my parents, whose life this isn't.

Acknowledgments

Many thanks to Annette, Christa and Colette, and everyone else at Allen & Unwin, for all their hard work and patience with this book. The same goes for Fiona and everyone at Curtis Brown.

Special thanks to Michelle de Kretser for her demanding editing.

Thanks also to Professor Maurice French for his advice, and for the resource of his comprehensive histories. And to Jonathan Richards for some obscurer details.

And finally, thanks to my brother Martin for his medical information, and to my brother Peter, for a timely comment about water catchments.

Any factual mistakes and flaws are due to me, none of the above.

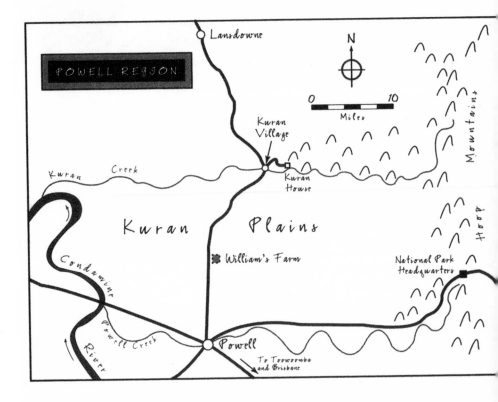

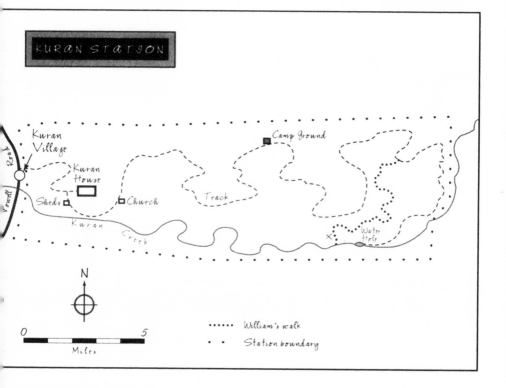

Prologue

ONE SPRING DAY IN LATE 1992, WHEN WILLIAM WAS HALFWAY between his eighth birthday and his ninth, he looked out from the back verandah and saw, huge in the sky, the mushroom cloud of a nuclear explosion. He stared at it, wondering. The thunderhead was dirty black, streaked with billows of grey. It rolled and boiled as it climbed into the clear blue day, casting a vast shadow upon the hills beyond. But there was no sound, no rumble of an explosion. Hot silence lay across the wheat fields, and the air was perfectly still. William said nothing, for there was no one to tell — his mother was in bed with a headache, and he knew better than to wake her. He sat on the edge of the verandah and watched. Ever expanding, the cloud began to drift, caught by some upper breeze. It loomed over the house, and great jets were arcing out from the main body, like the trails of slow meteorites. Down below, ash was beginning to fall, small black flecks spiralling in the air. Other particles were bigger, shrivelled and twisted embers, still glowing red as they settled. William was aware of the smell of burning ... but it was a good smell, a familiar smell. The smell of grass, of wheat, of the farm itself.

Suddenly he heard engines. There was a dirt track that ran past the house and out across the property, and now a flatbed four-wheel drive sped by along it, trailing dust. A car followed close behind. William didn't recognise either vehicle. This was odd. What were strangers doing on the farm? Looking out across the paddocks he saw an even more bizarre sight. A tractor — not his father's — was bouncing across the fields, as fast as he had ever seen a tractor go. And there was yet another four-wheel drive, right out amidst the wheat where there were no tracks, cutting a straight line through the crop. The farm was alive with movement. The phone had started ringing, and from the front of the house came the noise of more cars arriving, of doors slamming, and of women yelling. William climbed to his feet, studying the cloud. It was breaking up now, thinning to a misty orange. From its base stretched a long murky stalk of smoke, leading back to the ground. It seemed to touch down somewhere at the rear of the farm, where a haze hung around a small point of darkness.

There were urgent voices in the hallway. William's mother and two other women — he knew them, they were neighbours — dashed onto the verandah. They stopped, staring. His mother's hand went to her mouth.

'Oh God,' she said, 'Will ...'

And William knew that she meant his father, not himself.

It was outside all of his experience.

Only later would he understand what had happened, that the cloud was not from an atomic bomb, that indeed it couldn't have been anywhere near as big as a real mushroom cloud, no matter how large it loomed in his memory. Instead, it was the smoke from a seventy-acre paddock of wheat — ripe and tinder dry after the hottest spring in years — going up in flames. And somewhere in the middle of that field was the harvester which had set off the blaze. A big, bright red machine. Singed black. The fireball might have been started by an electrical fault, or an overheated bearing, perhaps, igniting some chaff that had gathered under the engine casing. William would never know. But in that harvester — or near it maybe, on the ground, for William was never told this either — were the remains of its driver. A man, suffocated probably as much as he was burned. Dead, either way. There was nothing anyone could have done. Dozens of farmers from the surrounding properties had seen the smoke, and knowing instantly what it was, they'd leapt into their farm vehicles and raced directly across the plains. All of them much too late.

After it was over, they gathered in the kitchen and in the dining room. Men grimed with ash and smoke, women busy making tea, or passing out iced water and solemn glasses of beer. William drifted through them, aware that something terrible had happened, but feeling outside of himself, confused by the attention the men and women gave him, and by their compassion. He caught passages of conversation. Plans. Offers of help. Of food. Of money. The police came and went away. An ambulance came, gathered up something from the shed, and went away. All the men went away too, and most of the women, leaving only a few to cluster around his mother. The afternoon lengthened into evening. William went and stood on the back verandah, stared out over the farm. The sky was clear again, as if nothing had happened.

When evening had turned into full night there came a final visitor, an old man who walked with a limp. He stood in the doorway to the kitchen, tall and grim. The women fell silent.

'Veronica,' he said.

William's mother nodded, dazed. She looked around the room until she saw William. He moved to her side, gazing up at the stranger. The man did not smile.

His mother said, 'William, this is your uncle John.'

William had never heard of any uncle.

He slipped away and hid in his bedroom. From there he could hear the talk in the kitchen. The women's voices mostly, but sometimes the man's voice too. It was low and dry and, unlike the others, it held no sympathy at all.

Later his mother came in, sat on his bed.

She said, 'I'm going to need your help from now on, Will. You'll have to be strong.'

'I know.'

'Do you understand what's happened?'

He nodded. 'I watched the fire.'

She echoed him distantly. 'You watched the fire ...' Her hands were twisted in each other. But then her gaze narrowed. 'What do you mean, you watched it?'

'From the verandah. I saw the cloud going up.'

'You were out there the whole time?'

He nodded again. Looked up at her.

She shuddered suddenly. Her arm lifted and she slapped him, her hand catching his right ear in a painful, piercing smack. Then she was crying. 'Stupid boy. You just sat there and watched? Why didn't you come and get me? Why didn't you do something? Your father ...'

And then she was gone.

William sat on his bed, his ear ringing. It was not the first time his mother had hit him and as always he knew she hadn't meant it, forgave her for it even as it happened. It was just the way she was. But he started to cry at last, because of the pain, and because of everything else. Finally he curled up, wanting to sleep. He lay there for hours, while out across the blackened fields the shell of his father's harvester smouldered under the stars. But the ringing in his ear wouldn't go away.

Chapter One

IT WAS THE WINTER OF 1993, DRY AND COLD, BY THE TIME WILLIAM and his mother said goodbye to their farm. They were going to live with William's uncle, John McIvor.

'He's not really your uncle,' William's mother warned. 'He's your great-uncle, on your father's side. That means he's not obliged to me and you at all, but he's doing this out of the goodness of his heart. So when we get there, I want you to behave yourself.'

William understood. They were now relying on charity.

It was not an entirely new sensation, for they had always been poor. Their farm was in the middle of the Kuran Plains, a region famous for its fertile black soil, but somehow their own property had never been a success. True, the last few seasons had been bad for everyone. The rains had failed two years running. Even so, the crops on William's farm seemed to wither or die more readily than those on surrounding properties. He had often heard his parents argue about the problem, and about money, and sometimes his mother would accuse his father of being no farmer. And maybe he wasn't. Would a good farmer have let his harvester accumulate so much dust within its engine compartment that a fire was inevitable? And would a good farmer have allowed the insurance to lapse, not only on the harvester, the farm's most expensive piece of equipment, but on his own life as well?

For when the ashes settled, his wife and child were destitute. The property was laden with debts, and there was no question of William's mother carrying on alone. She didn't work and never had — it was accepted that her health was not up to it. So the only option was to surrender the farm to the bank. William supposed that perhaps he had a right to be angry at his father for this — his mother certainly seemed to be — but he wasn't. He wasn't even angry at him for dying. That pillar of smoke in the sky had been too momentous a funeral pyre, too much like the hand of God in the heavens, for William to lay blame. And he had no wish to spoil the memories of his father with bitterness. Those memories were too few and too precious, the fading images of an untidy, gangling man with a lean, unshaven face and a smile that was always somehow sad.

Then there was the fateful harvester — one of William's favourite pastimes had been to ride in it with his father, high up in the cab, staring down as the wheat surrendered to the flashing blades of the comb. It was a fascinating process, the heads disappearing in a frenzy of dust and leaves under the rolling drum, sucked inwards to the guts of the machine, which rumbled and shook mysteriously, until naked grains poured out of a spout into the bin behind the cabin, and from the rear of the harvester shot a dirty fantail of stubble and waste. William couldn't imagine handling a machine so complex, and admired his father tremendously for doing so. There was no point in remembering that the wheat they were harvesting was always too thin, and that the harvester itself was too old, always prone to breaking down, and that the dust that would feed the fire had been gathering within the engine all the while. No point either in picturing how things must have been that day. There was so much to monitor while harvesting — the height of the blades, the level of grain in the bin, the rate and spin of a dozen different parts of the machinery — that one man could hardly keep track of everything. Maybe if William had been there in the cabin too, watching — but he wasn't, not on that afternoon. And so his father must have missed the first curl of smoke from below, and then the flames growing hungrily...

It was no part of love to think of any of that.

William's mother, meanwhile, had not received the grace of an early death and a martyrdom to fire, but his feelings about her had always been more complex. She was harder to love than her husband — physically harder too, a thin woman of angles and bones, with long wispy brown hair. If at his father's core there was a crucial weakness, a life of plans made but never fulfilled, then at his mother's core William sensed something fractured and brittle. It was never spoken about, but he had been aware from a very young age that she was delicate, in a special way. Headaches plagued her, and much of the time she was listless and exhausted. At other times she was wildly short-tempered, screaming weakly at William if he annoyed her, and stinging him with slaps. Afterwards she would lock herself in the main bedroom and weep. She took many pills, and frequently visited the doctor. On several occasions she had disappeared for up to a week. Resting, William's father would say, at a place where people went when they needed time away by themselves.

But when William played with children on the neighbouring farms, he could see that their mothers were different. They bustled with energy, they were friendly and welcoming, they helped their children with homework, they volunteered to serve on school committees and in the canteen, they had sandwiches waiting whenever William arrived. His mother did none of these things — she was always too tired, or her head hurt, or she was hidden in her room and William was forbidden to make a sound. It made him feel secretly ashamed of her, and he felt guilty about the shame. He knew that at least part of her behaviour was explained by the simple fact that life was more difficult for them than for other families. Their farm was not as prosperous, their car was not as new, their house was not as nice, and while these things did not seem to bother his father, they made his mother unhappy.

It was their house that displeased her most. It was very small and very old, a four-room cottage, with a back verandah, and a kitchen annexe to one side. It rested on wooden stumps that were driven deep into the soil — but never deep enough, for on the plains the bedrock lay far down below, and so the stumps were forever shifting, warping the floors and the door frames. Inside, the rooms were cramped and dark, and it was hot in summer, cold in the winter. William's father had promised that he would build them a new home one day. There was even a pile of lumber at the end of the yard, stacked up in a big square like a castle. But it had been there as long as William could remember, overgrown with weeds. His mother would harp on at his father about this, and William knew that she just wanted a nice home for them to live in, a place where she could invite people and host dinners, and not be embarrassed. Most of their neighbours had sprawling new homes made of brick, set on concrete slabs that floated upon the black soil like rafts. That's what his mother would really have loved, but his father wasn't so sure.

'Those slabs will crack one day,' he'd insist. 'And then all those bricks will just crumble. A wooden house is better. It might not look like much, but this old place will never fall down.' Then he would reach out to caress the crooked door frames fondly, the sleeves of his favourite green jumper all tattered and frayed at the elbows.

For William, the house was simply home and the centre of his world. Beyond the back door spread a bare dusty yard. His mother wanted a lawn, but his father was much more interested in one corner which he'd roped off and cultivated as a vegetable garden. Every year he planted ambitiously — tomatoes, beans, lettuces, melons, pumpkins — and yet nothing much ever seemed to grow. William's father blamed the birds. He shot at them with an old .22 rifle, or built scarecrows, but it made no difference. He planted trees too, oranges and lemons, the fruit of which William could never remember ripening. Then there was the chicken coop, which was supposed to supply them with roast dinners and eggs for breakfast. But foxes had got in some years earlier, and now the doors swung emptily and the wire fencing gaped. William had only one recollection of his father actually slaughtering a chicken — its head jammed between two nails on an old tree stump, until the axe came down and the bloodied, headless body leapt about. But then the gutting and plucking was a chore, and after half an hour of sitting on the back step, surrounded by feathers, his father lost patience, and from then on the family's chickens were store bought.

Beyond the coop was the farm's ageing shed, and it was one of William's favourite places to explore, big and dark and ramshackle, made entirely of corrugated iron. All the farm vehicles were kept within — the tractor, the harvester, the grain truck, an ancient Land Rover (army surplus from the Second World War, his father claimed) — but there was lots more. Huge workbenches loaded with all sorts of tools and engine parts. Old furniture, old cupboards, piles of old magazines and books. Mysterious blocks of metal, stacks of broken plough shares, air pumps, welding equipment, drums of oil, folded heaps of tarpaulins. All of it fitfully illuminated, for there were bullet holes in the shed's tin walls and shafts of sunlight would angle through them, highlighting the motes of the dust in the air. And everywhere there were nesting holes for rats and mice, an endless quarry, especially at night when

William hunted them with a flashlight, and the whole shed rustled and creaked with their movements, and their tiny eyes shone back at him from every corner.

Outside, at the far end of the shed, were the grain silos, two great rusty metal bins thirty feet high. And here was the best place of all, for ladders ran up their sides, and if William had the nerve to climb one or the other, he could sit on the peaked roof and see the whole farm at a glance, laid out like a quilt. It was a square mile exactly, six hundred and forty acres, perfectly flat, the fields marching right up to the back of the shed, alternately golden or green or black with fallow. Beyond their own property were those of their neighbours, and from there the view went on for miles, dozens of farms, hundreds, stretching out to a patchwork blur under an uninterrupted sky.

These were the Kuran Plains. They occupied, William knew, the northern part of a greater region known as the Darling Downs. If he looked south from atop the silos, he could see a smudge on the horizon that marked the town of Powell, with its ten thousand people; William caught a bus into school there every day. (An hour beyond Powell was the city of Toowoomba, the capital of the Downs. And beyond that again, over the mountains and down to the coast, lay the metropolis of Brisbane, where he had never been.) Turning east meanwhile, he could see, perhaps twenty miles away, the hazy blue ridges of the Hoop Mountains. They were an offshoot of the Great Dividing Range, and there was a national park up there, and forests and cool streams. Turning further still, to the north, he could see more plains, and then distant hills covered in scrub, where the Darling Downs came to an end at a little town called Lansdowne. And westwards? To the west was an open horizon that seemingly went on forever, bare of trees or towns or hills. Somewhere out there was a river known as the Condamine, and countless miles beyond that was the Outback, the desert, and the whole of Australia itself.

But at times, sitting on the silo roof on a still, hot, summer's day, the immense silence of the plains weighing down upon him, William would turn from compass point to compass point and find not a single thing in motion — not a bird in the air or a car on the Powell road or a tractor in the fields, not a single hint to let him know that the world lived and moved beyond his boundaries. There would be only himself, crushed and tiny on his lonely prominence, hypnotised by sheer scale into an exhausted lethargy.

And now he was leaving it all.

His uncle's property lay no more than a dozen miles away, and yet it sounded nothing like William's farm. It was a big place, his mother had told him, at least twenty times the size of their own, and it ran cattle, up in the foothills of the Hoop Mountains. It was called Kuran Station, and apparently it boasted a large home-stead called Kuran House. They should consider themselves lucky, his mother said, to be offered such a grand new home. And yet William found himself disturbed at the thought. He would have to go to a new school. And then there was his uncle. William hadn't seen him again, but he remembered the man with a limp, the measuring way he had stared at everybody, and he wondered what it would be like to live with someone so stern and so old.

It was school holidays when the time to move came. William helped as best he could with the packing, feeling more cold and reluctant with every day. Finally, on the last afternoon, he went out to say his farewells. The house had turned into a foreign place, half stripped of furniture and littered with boxes, but the farm was worse. The bank had already held sales and auctions, and almost everything moveable was gone. The shed was empty except for the workbenches and the old cupboards and magazines. There was no grain in the silos. Someone had even taken the pile of timber away from the back yard. Out in the fields there were only the rotting stubble of the last wheat harvest and the black stretches of fallow paddocks. And somewhere down the back of the property, where he had never gone since the fire, was a field of ash, an alien place that had afflicted the whole farm.

He stared east to the low humps of the Hoop Mountains. The weather was grey and chill, and leaden clouds rested like a sheet upon the range, but the wind rattled dryly and there was no sign of rain. To the northeast William could see a long spur of hills that ran from the mountains out into the plains. His uncle's property was up on that spur somewhere, he'd been told. It looked as far away as the moon.

Over a bleak dinner his mother attempted a smile. 'It hasn't been much fun for us, has it, Will?'

He didn't answer.

'It'll get better,' she promised, a little desperately. 'I know it's all hard to understand, but moving in with your uncle is the best thing for us, really. You'll see.'

'Yes, Mum.'

He went to bed, and could not sleep. He waited until the house grew silent, then sat on the back verandah, wrapped in a blanket, staring out as he had been the day his father died. It was dark under the clouds. A few pinpoints of brightness marked distant farm houses. Away on the southern horizon was a line of twinkling lights — the town of Powell, bright enough to cast a faint orange glow on the clouds above. He turned and looked towards the blackness of the hills and his uncle's station. There was a lone light visible up there. He waited, clinging to the blanket. The light was orange, not white like the farm houses across the plain. It quivered oddly. And it seemed to be moving. He watched it without real curiosity for some time. Then it flickered and blinked out, and everything up there was night again.

Chapter Two

IT WAS ANOTHER COLD, OVERCAST AFTERNOON. THE REMOVAL van lumbered out of the driveway, and William and his mother followed in their old blue station wagon. William was in the passenger seat, and the heater didn't work. He forgot to look one last time at his little cottage. Then the thought came to him that he hadn't sat in the back seat of the car since his father died, and never would now.

They turned onto the Powell–Lansdowne road and rolled north. Familiar landmarks slid by — the houses of neighbours, a disused railway siding, a line of old telephone poles, all leaning askew in the shifting soil. But after only a few miles William was already out of his home territory, for the focus of his life had always been south towards Powell, never towards the north. And so they soon came to a crossroads beyond which he had rarely travelled. Nearby rose heaped mounds of earth, surrounding a deep trench full of weeds and water, the mounds all grass-grown like ancient tombs. William's father had told him they were merely the remains of an abandoned drainage scheme. But they were still ominous shapes under the grey sky, sentinels beyond which all was strange.

They drove on slowly, the removal truck clearing their way. Some miles beyond the crossroads the road began to wind and angle away to the northeast. Ahead of them the long spur of hills marched closer, reaching out from the Hoops.

'See,' his mother said, pointing. She was an awkward driver, hunched small behind the wheel. Before the fire she had rarely driven at all. 'Up there in the trees. You can see Kuran House. It's not so far. We've hardly moved really.'

William caught a glimpse of stone walls and a dark roof; then it was gone. He didn't agree with his mother. They'd been in the car only fifteen minutes, but already it felt like another country. The farms were poorer here, as if the black soil was growing shallow as the hills grew near, like the ocean nearing a coastline. The road curved gently around invisible undulations, and before them the broad tip of the spur swelled out of the fields, cresting in a low hill. They crossed a bridge over a creek. Glancing down, William saw chunks of rock and a trickle of dark water. A sign announced 'Kuran', and then they were in a little village. Along the single street was a schoolhouse set in its playground, deserted for the holidays, then a worn weatherboard hall, and a string of small shop fronts, most of them empty. At the far end was a petrol station, a tin shed with pumps outside. No one was visible, and the half-dozen houses were closed tight against the cold, some of them looking as abandoned as the stores.

'We'll still have to do our shopping in Powell or Lansdowne,' his mother said, staring about. 'But the school looks nice, don't you think?'

William didn't answer. The schoolhouse looked tiny — a single classroom on tall stilts. It was over a week before the next term started anyway. Ahead of them the truck was turning off onto a side road, just beyond the petrol station. The new track climbed and wound about the hill, potholes catching at the wheels of the car. Scattered gum trees waited amidst dead grass, and a few cattle grazed behind fences. Then a stone gateway appeared, with iron gates swung wide, tangled in the bushes. They passed through, rattling over a cattle grid, beyond which were the remains of a stone building, its roof fallen in and only the hollow walls standing.

'That must have been the gatehouse,' his mother said.

The ruins slid away. The road curved further around the hill, and now they were crossing its southern face, looking out over the plains and back along the road by which they'd just come. William caught a glimpse of the chequerboard of farms laid out under the clouds, then the view was lost behind more scrub. They kept climbing. Finally they came to a long straight avenue lined with dark pines, their heads ragged and torn, almost black. At the end of the avenue was a high stone wall, pierced by an arched gate. It was open, but the removal truck pulled up, unable to fit through. William's mother hesitated, then passed on, under the archway. A fringe of low branches scraped against the windscreen. When the car cleared them, there was Kuran House at last.

A homestead, his mother had told him, and William had not really known what that might mean. Gazing at it now, his first amazed thought was of palaces and manors in somewhere like England, the stately homes of princes and dukes. Even in that initial moment he understood that the House wasn't quite on that scale, but still, it was easily the biggest home William had ever seen, built all of sandstone, two tall storeys high, with a roof of grey slate. Wide terraces wrapped around both upper and lower levels. A circular driveway with a fountain in the centre led up to the front steps, a cascade of them, climbing in turn to the porch and the double front doors that looked ten feet high. From there the House stretched out until it met two perpendicular wings that projected forward from either side, framing the driveway and the fountain. William stared up at carved stone. Was his uncle rich?

But then he was really *looking*, and the truth sank in. It was the roof he noticed first — the line of it sagged towards the middle, and dozens of tiles were cracked or sliding out of place. The gutters hung loose from the eaves, and below them, the high walls were draped in sullen vines and ivy. The upper verandah was ruinous, and within the shadow of the awning William could glimpse second-storey windows that were shuttered or smashed. The lower terrace was littered with junk — boxes, drums, a roll of wire, a dismantled bicycle — and the front steps were cracked and sunken. Splashes of white paint stained the sandstone walls, and some of the ground-floor windows had plywood partitions instead of glass. In another window an air-conditioner had been jammed, its grille streaked with rust. One of the front doors hung off its hinges, half open, and nearby sat a single metal chair, with some dirty plates and a coffee cup beside it, items that looked as if they might have been there for years.

William's mother was gazing through the windscreen, her hands tight on the wheel, a glint of dismay in her eyes. William looked at the House again, noting yet more signs of neglect. The fountain was full of grass, the driveway was deeply rutted with tyre tracks, and the garden was a wilderness of weeds.

'It's all right,' she said, voice quavering. 'It's all right.' She had papered on a smile. They climbed out of the car. No one emerged from the House to greet them, so they simply stood, staring up. 'It … it might look a little run down. But it'll be nicer inside. I'm sure.'

One of the removalists called out, asking William's mother what to do with the truck.

She glanced back and forth nervously, looked at William. 'Your uncle said that they're supposed to park around the back. I'd better go and show them. You stay here.'

She headed back to the gate. William heard the truck start up and rumble around to the rear of the building. Then silence settled again, and he was alone.

His new home frowned at him.

William turned his back on the House and took a few steps away from the car, the gravel crunching beneath his feet. The pebbles of the drive were white, or had been, before becoming mixed up with dirt and grass. The garden spread before him. There were hints that it had once been something grander. He could see pathways meandering between the weeds, some of them paved with fractured stone slabs. There was other stonework visible as well — the borders of garden beds, a bench, a bower in a far corner — all of it smothered in plants, or half buried in dirt. Lampposts were dotted along the pathways, but there were no bulbs in the sockets, and a washing line had been strung between two of the posts, pale laundry hanging there forlornly. Great shaggy trees loomed all around. And sticking up crazily at the very front of the yard, where the hill dropped away, a diving board perched on what must have been the rim of a swimming pool.

Nothing moved and no one came. Overhead the clouds hung motionless. The air in the garden was chill, cooler than down on the plain, and it smelled different too. William was used to the dry scent of grain and chaff, and the dusty breath of the black soil. This place had a dank odour to it, a complexity of plants and trees and weeds, a bitter forest smell, with an underlay of rotting wood. He noticed that there was a tall metal pole by the drive. A tattered flag hung limp at the top, patterned in blue and white, unrecognisable. A wave of loneliness swept over him.

He turned back towards the House. It might have been deserted. He walked towards the front steps, feeling very small as the weight of the walls rose up on either side, a vertigo of stone. He came to the fountain, peered in. Water hadn't flowed in it for years, and sand had gathered in the bowl, giving root to the grass. Its central pillar looked as if it had once borne a statue, but the column was snapped clean off, and only the enigmatic stump remained, a broken water pipe protruding.

'Ahoy there, boy.'

William glanced up. An old woman stood at the top of the steps.

'You'd be the nephew then,' she said.

She was a hunched figure, wrapped in what seemed to be multiple layers of dresses and cardigans. She had a dark, hawklike face, and scraggles of grey hair escaped from a woollen beanie perched upon her head.

'Your mother sent me,' she said. 'Come up here a minute.'

William ascended the steps silently. The old woman watched him with sharp eyes.

'How old are you?' she asked.

'Nine.'

A grunt. 'Your mother is with your uncle and the moving men.' She studied him some more. 'You know who I am?'

William shook his head.

'I'm your uncle's housekeeper. My name is Mrs Griffith.' She shuffled slowly about, taking him in from all sides. Her bony feet were encased in threadbare slippers, and her hands were twisted, curled in on themselves. She pointed to a plastic basket that sat near the front door. 'Well, go on, pick that up. You can help me get the washing in.'

William stared blankly.

'Come on,' she commanded, edging impatiently down the stairs, 'They don't want you under their feet while they get the furniture inside.'

He picked up the basket and followed the old woman as she journeyed slowly across the tangled garden to the washing line. Then he stood by, holding the basket to his chest. The house-keeper reached up painfully and unpegged the clothes, dropping them into the basket, item by item — grey shirts, faded dresses, shapeless underwear. For a long time she didn't speak, and neither did William. He stared at the House. None of this was what he'd expected. A housekeeper? Did that mean even more people lived here with his uncle? And yet the old man had seemed such a solitary figure on that long ago afternoon of the fire. William wanted his mother to return, but from around the back of House he could hear sounds of unloading, the voices of the men, and she would be busy there.

The old woman was watching him. Suddenly she stabbed a peg towards the House. 'You stay off those upstairs verandahs. They're not safe. You stay away from the upstairs altogether. It's no place for games.'

More clothes dropped into the basket.

She considered him again, sidelong. 'You don't think it looks like much, I suppose. I suppose you think your uncle should just throw in a few sticks of dynamite and finish it off.' She leaned down at him sourly. 'That's what he was told to do, you know, when he bought this place. The agent said he should just blow the House up and be done with it, before it collapsed and hurt someone. He offered to do it himself, before your uncle even signed the papers.'

The washing was all off the line and piled in the basket. The housekeeper began her slow traverse back towards the House, William trailing behind.

'But don't be fooled,' she went on. 'It's been here for one hundred and thirty years, and it's not falling down any time soon. Those verandahs are a mess, but that's just the woodwork. The stonework is fine. It'll still be standing long after we're all dead and buried. Even you, boy.'

William mustered a question. 'Does anyone else live here?'

'Who else would there be?'

They were climbing up to the front porch. The old woman paused at the top, turned to face outwards.

'Look out there,' she instructed.

From this height, William could see most of the garden, and there was indeed a half-guessed pattern to the overgrowth, the ghost of a formal arrangement long dead. The yard was bounded left and right by the stone walls, some sections dislodged into a jumble by tree roots, others leaning precariously. Directly in front was the swimming pool. He could see the outline of it, perfectly rectangular, the dusty gleam of tiles, the diving board, some metal handrails at one end. But the pool itself was empty and must have been for some time. There were sheets of rusty tin sticking up from within it, and the tops of tall bushes.

Beyond the pool, the southern flank of the hill rolled down and away, surprisingly steep. William could see brown grass and gum trees and old fence posts. And at the foot of the hill washed the plains, immediately flat. Close by the land was divided up into the familiar squares of cultivation, but as the eye leapt outwards the colours and shapes merged, fields and farms spreading all the way to the horizons. It was a far wider view than he had ever gained from his aerie atop the grain silos. He could see the plains whole. On the left marched the blue line of the mountains, and on the right, the land merely extended forever westwards.

'You see?' The old woman's voice was flat with displeasure. 'You see all that? Every single bit of it, every single thing you can see, all of it used to be owned by the people who built this house. Grand folk, that family. Can you imagine what a time that must have been?'

She was looking down at him now, shaking her head.

'Of course you can't,' she said. 'But I remember it. Your uncle does too. He was born here. That's something you should remember. You and your mother.'

She turned and edged through the half-open door. William waited a moment, confused, then followed her. He blinked as his eyes adjusted from the brighter light outside, taking in the dim image of a long shadowy hall and stairs ascending. Then movement caught his eye, a door at one end of the hall swinging shut with an echoing bang.

'There he goes,' said the housekeeper, 'back into his office.' She prodded the laundry basket that William still held to his chest. 'You keep out of his way.'

And she led him off into the darkness.

Chapter Three

JOHN MCIVOR'S EARLIEST MEMORY WAS OF SMOKE.

Smoke, and the smell of cooking meat. He was outside somewhere. A greasy cloud drifted against a blue sky. And he was crying, tears flooding down his face. His mother's arms were around him, tight and fearful. She was afraid, and so was he … but of what? The images were always elusive, at the very limit of consciousness, and behind them there was nothing at all.

They weren't important.

What was important was Kuran House. It was where he had grown up, and most certainly where he planned to die. But it wasn't where he had been born, not exactly. That had happened in one of the cottages at the back of the House, where the staff were quartered. The year was 1914. His father, Daniel McIvor, was away at the time, working somewhere up in the hills. Daniel was the manager of Kuran Station, with dozens of employees, thousands of sheep and cattle, and over one hundred thousand acres of pasture to administer.

The actual owners of the land, however, were the White family — a famous pastoral dynasty whose origins lay far back in England. At the time of John's birth the patriarch was one Edward White, but it was Edward's grandfather who had brought the family to Australia in the 1820s. Impoverished aristocrats, the White's had developed their wealth in the southern colonies by squatting on the fringes of civilisation, rearing thousands of sheep, and then selling out as the frontiers caught up with them. But the Kuran run was their biggest and their best, their crowning achievement, and it was meant to be the end of their wandering. When they took possession of the land in 1860 it spread out over three hundred thousand acres, from the Hoop Mountains in the east to the Condamine River in the west, from the fledgling town of Powell in the south to the campsite of Lansdowne in the north. A kingdom of their own.

But the Whites were not the original owners. Before them was a another squatter by the name of Heatherington. His agents had first roamed the Kuran region in the 1840s, a few lone men staking out boundaries in what was then an unknown wilderness. A few lone men … and yet they were part of a land rush, for after the first claims were marked out down near Warwick, almost one hundred miles away, it was only two or three years before the entire Darling Downs were taken up by squatters. The sheep took somewhat longer to arrive, and the men to tend and shear them even longer. There were no fences or roads or sheds or yards — only the wide open plains, and shepherds scattered in their huts, ex-convicts for the most part, ticket-of-leave men, as alone as anyone could be in Australia in those days. For its first fifteen years Kuran Station could boast little more then tents and huts by way of dwellings. It wasn't until 1859 that Heatherington himself arrived, and standing upon a hill at the station's very centre, conceived the plan of a great residence.

He wasn't the only one. The sheep barons of the Darling Downs (the Pure Merinos, as they were known) were all racing to outdo each other in mansion building, and stonemasons were at work on a dozen different stations. But Heatherington, with one of the biggest runs to his name, aimed for a house befitting his stature, and in doing so fatally overreached himself. Even though the land itself had been virtually free, setting up a station on the very edge of the known world was still an expensive business. Heatherington went deep into debt to commence his grand homestead, and was bankrupt before it was much more than a shell. His creditors resumed the property and Kuran Station's first owner disappeared into obscurity. Then the Whites stepped in. They took the framework of Heatherington's building, redesigned it, enlarged it with two great wings, surrounded it with a formal English garden, and finally Kuran House lifted its sandstone walls above the plains.

It was a triumph, 'the shining light of the Downs' as one socialite declared, an architectural marvel on the very frontier. For the next twenty years the Whites ruled supreme, one of the grandest of the Darling Downs squatter families, and their House was the political and cultural hub of the region. The village of Kuran grew up around the foot of the hill, a purely feudal community. But even in Powell, away on the southern rim of the property, the Whites were all-powerful. They owned many of the shops and hotels there and, most importantly, the votes of the townsfolk. There were barely a thousand registered voters in the whole of the northern Downs, and most of them relied on the station in some manner or other for their income. So it was with no great effort that the Whites got themselves elected to the Queensland parliament. There they joined their fellow landed gentry in a happy alliance that for several decades ruled the colony as its own private sheep run.

It wasn't to last. Towards the end of the century the cities and towns were growing, filling up with factory workers and shopkeepers who owed nothing to the pastoralists, and even out west, amongst the shearers and miners, the labour movement was abroad. Battles were fought and lost in parliament. Editorials cried out demanding land for the common man. The rents on pastoral leases, negligible in the early days, rose ever higher. And the Pure Merinos, land rich but cash poor, had no means to survive protracted bad times. The crippling recession of the 1890s cleaned many of them away forever. The Lands Department broke up their runs into smaller lots that were purchased by humbler graziers of uncertain political alliance, or into tiny blocks that were selected by yeoman farmers of Irish or German descent. By the declaration of Queensland's statehood in 1901, most of the grand runs were gone, and the great homesteads stood deserted.

But Kuran survived. Up on the northern edge of the Downs, furthest from the cities and major transport routes, it was the least attractive area for development. More importantly, the Whites fought tenaciously to hold it all together. Edward, the head of the family by then, had inherited his seat in parliament, where he ruled over a small pastoralist rump. When some resumption of the land became unavoidable, and outlying blocks of Kuran were carved up for selection, he was able to manipulate the Lands Department so that the prime land came back to him, either through direct purchase, or through friends and agents. And even those blocks that were sold to others were not necessarily lost forever. The small graziers and selectors often struggled to make their properties viable, and within a few years would sell out or simply abandon the land, after which Edward moved back in. It cost a fortune of course, which even the Whites could barely afford, but all in all, by the time John McIvor was born, Kuran Station was still almost half its original size.

John's father had entered the Whites' employ in 1902. Daniel, already middle-aged, had worked up and down Queensland in a variety of jobs, but he proved impressively capable on the station, and Edward promoted him rapidly. As manager, Daniel's duties extended beyond simply running the property. He also had responsibilities during election campaigns — mustering all the station workers and transporting them to Powell on polling day, dishing out free beer and food to the townspeople, delivering harsher encouragement to wayward voters when it was needed, howling down rival candidates in the streets, or quietly buying them off altogether. He was integral too in the array of schemes which kept most of the Kuran Plains under the Whites' control. He dummied for them at land sales, and organised others to do the same. He intimidated prospective buyers. And when people were rash enough to go ahead and select Kuran land anyway, Daniel and his men were not above burning down fences and crops and sheds to drive the newcomers away. He was regarded far and wide as a 'hard' man, and was known to carry a pistol with him at all times.

And yet after a decade at Kuran, Daniel understood, perhaps better even than Edward himself, that the station was approaching a crisis. Wool prices were fluctuating wildly, there were troubles with shearers and strikes, transport charges were high, and diseases stalked the livestock. The upkeep of the House alone was ruinous. And the government was forever muttering about the abuse of pastoral leases and the need for land to be released. As Kuran was the largest remaining property on the Downs, it provided a ready target. The townsfolk of Powell in particular were agitating for land reform. Without a formidable presence in parliament, and an iron hand on the station itself, the whole thing might dis-integrate. And yet Edward was getting old. If he died, who was to succeed him?

True, there was an heir to the White fortune, an adult son called Malcolm. Both Edward and Daniel, however, saw Malcolm for what he was — weak, indulgent, not a man to assume the reins. In any case, Malcolm himself wanted nothing to do with the station. His youth had been spent in Brisbane and Sydney, dissipated and wild and an embarrassment to his father. Finally he had been brought home in disgrace, on the condition that he would be supported only as long as he remained at the House. In sullen awe of his father, Malcolm acquiesced, but there was no hope he would ever learn the family business. His only useful contribution was to marry, and provide his father with an extension to the dynasty. But his sole child was a girl, Elizabeth, born in 1912. And a daughter was not what the Whites needed.

Yet her birth awoke an idea in Daniel McIvor. A life-long bachelor, he suddenly got married. He chose a lonely girl from the station staff — seemingly at random, certainly without any obvious affection. And a year after that, his son, John McIvor, was born. A son was all that mattered. For Daniel had devised a plan, and privately dared to hope an immense hope. A son of his own, a boy whom he could raise to be as hardy and able as himself, intimate with the workings of the property ... and Edward White's granddaughter, to whom everything must pass in the end. What could be a more sensible arrangement than to unite the two? The McIvor blood would give the White family the vigour it so lacked. And with vigour, the survival of Kuran Station could be guaranteed.

For young John McIvor, it was the greatest of expectations. His father never spoke of it directly, but the understanding was there, in Daniel's every look and word. Thus the seed was sown, and John grew up secretly believing that Kuran Station would one day be his. The thought filled him with pride, and as a boy he learnt every inch of the run, every corner and crest, from far out on the plains to high up in the hills. And over the years he grew into everything that his father had hoped — tall and handsome and sure of himself, quick, capable and strong. Even Edward White was impressed, and congratulated Daniel on the blessing of a son who could follow in his father's footsteps, perhaps even assume the mantle of station manager one day.

Meanwhile, the life of Kuran House and the White family went on before John's eyes, familiar, yet tantalisingly out of reach. The prisoner Malcolm lived in high state. His wife was a local beauty, the daughter of the Mayor of Powell, and since they could not go themselves to the bright lights of society, they had instead created their own imitation. The weekend party was in vogue, and at Kuran House there was no paucity of bedrooms or food or drink, so dozens of people wended their way west over the mountains and across the plains. Malcolm's parties were not exactly the scandal of the Darling Downs, perhaps, but they were certainly exotic, and the guest list, at times, was infamous. Away in Brisbane Malcolm's father scowled and complained, and when the old man came home between parliamentary sessions, Malcolm was wise enough to banish his friends. But then when Edward was gone again...

John watched it all from beyond the garden wall. The parties in the afternoon, women and men all in white, strolling across the lawns, or lounging about the swimming pool, while servants moved eternally amongst them bearing drinks and food. Or at night, when the House would be lit to a blaze, and music and laughter came from inside. John would sneak about the windows and peer into rooms where dancers writhed before gramophones, where men smoked and shouted over billiards, or where gargantuan meals were spread across the sixteen-seat dining table. And later, when all was dark and he tried to sleep in the bedroom of his parents' cottage, he would hear the shrieks and cries from the upper halls of the House, and the sound of running feet and slamming doors, never knowing whether he was hearing fear or pleasure or pain.

And yet he knew that there was more to the House then just people and lights, for it was the centre of something larger — the whole great expanse that was Kuran Station. John had seen the wide plains and the dark hills and the men who worked and sweated on them, struggling to keep the property alive. Those men, their wives and their families, and the people of the villages and towns all looked to the House for authority, for judgment, for leadership — not just parties. When his day came, he vowed, he would act with more gravity. The coming of that day depended on Elizabeth, and so John watched over her carefully, contemplating their mutual future. She remained oddly distant however, a lone figure moving about the House and the garden. She had no friends, as far as he could tell, and it seemed to him that she should have been grateful for his company, for the presence of another child who was her equal. But on those occasions when she noticed John at all, she treated him almost as if he were no different from any of the other staff children.

He was seldom allowed *inside* the House, apart from rare visits accompanying his father, but there came one late summer's afternoon, when Malcolm and his wife were absent on a visit to Powell. The building lay drowsing in the warm sunlight, empty and inviting, and John, eleven years old, could not resist the chance to explore it alone. Slipping through the back gate, he stole across the lawns, the air hazy with pollens and the buzz of insects. The front doors stood open, as they always did in summer, and in a moment he was inside. There was no one about. He walked from room to room, wondering at the height of the ceilings, at the tall windows diffusing the sunlight through lace curtains, at the fireplaces big enough to stand in, at the furniture glowing with its deep red grain and at the floors polished to shining. It was all beautiful beyond anything he had ever seen, but his favourite room on the lower floor was Edward's office. This was a huge chamber in a corner of the west wing, with leather-bound volumes lining the walls and a desk six feet wide. Velvet hangings covered the windows, and an intoxicating aroma of whisky and tobacco flowed from every corner. John's father worked here at times and John had often imagined what it would be like to sit behind that desk, and call it his own.

But in the central hall was the grand staircase, climbing to the second level, and that was where he had never been before. He crept upwards now, listening for any sound, but none came, and he arrived, hushed, at the upper landing. It was even more airy and spacious up there. Tall glass doors opened out onto the upper terrace, and they flooded with light a long gallery that ran away into the east and west wings. John ventured westwards, passing door after door, and catching glimpses into bedrooms. One was decorated in red and black, with white paper screens that made him think of pictures he'd seen from China or Japan. Another had bright multi-coloured hangings and was arranged with roughly carved wooden statues from somewhere like Africa or New Guinea. And the beds were gigantic, mysterious four posters, draped with curtains. This was where the adults roamed at night, playing in their magical rooms, and crying out in the darkness.

And then, at the end of the hall, in the right-hand corner of the west wing, he came to one last open door. This room was all white, and shone with an ethereal glow from arched windows hung with billowing gauze. It felt almost empty, with only a small, single bed in the corner. And sitting before one of the windows, in a winged wicker chair, was a slim, dark-haired girl, her legs drawn up beneath her and her face turned away as she studied the pages of a book. John froze. It was only Elizabeth, and yet she seemed no more real than the room around her, a painting or a statue in perfect repose.

Then she sensed him and turned, her brow creased at the interruption. *You shouldn't be up here*, she said. *Go away.*

John stood there, a million things to say in his head, but none of them emerging. The crease turned to a frown, and she seemed ten years older than him, not two.

Go away, I said.

And John went, his face burning, fleeing down the hall.

How had she done that, frightened him so, when he was not afraid of anything? And how was it possible that they would be together one day when he couldn't even speak in her presence? But he had recovered by the time he was back outside. She'd caught him off guard, nervous about breaking the rules, that was all. Their mutual destiny was many years off yet, there was plenty of time, and he would show her soon enough, when he was older.

But the memory of that afternoon remained. And from then on, whenever he thought of Elizabeth, he would see her in that abstracted pose, framed by light, lost in her thoughts, and seemingly unaware that a boy named John McIvor, her husband to be, even existed.

Chapter Four

I⊤ WAS A WEEK SINCE THE MOVE, AND WILLIAM HAD NOT YET SEEN his uncle.

'Don't bother him,' his mother sighed in response to William's questions, rubbing her head, a familiar sign that she had a migraine. She was still only halfway through the unpacking, working at it in irritable fits and bursts. 'When he wants you, he'll call you. Go outside and play.'

William did not go outside. It was too cold. Bitter sheets of cloud crept continuously across the sky, high and rainless. So he stayed inside and explored his new home, searching through the hallways with a growing dread in his heart, and the smell of age and rot in his nostrils.

As bad as the House looked from the outside, the interior was worse. It was a dim tangle of cramped rooms, narrow passageways and dead ends. It did not feel like anyone's home; instead, it reminded William of a derelict hotel. He finally concluded that there had once been four separate apartments on the lower floor, an old subdivision that had broken down into a labyrinth. There was no centre to it, no core of warmth, like a single living room or kitchen. Instead, there were four kitchens, all of them small and dark, and three of them unusable. There were four of everything, in fact, a maze of bedrooms and bathrooms and sitting rooms that could have housed a dozen people and more. All they housed now, however, was rubbish. William had to pick his way amidst tattered furniture, leaning cupboards, mouldering boxes of clothes and decaying heaps of newspapers. Everything seemed shabby and cheap. The walls were thin fibro, stained with age and punctured with gaping holes, the carpets were worn bare, and the linoleum in the kitchens had curled up at the corners.

And yet he could see that it had not always been this way — here and there he found indications that larger, richer rooms had pre-dated the apartments. Beneath the peeling linoleum lay wide wooden boards with a smouldering red grain. In other places the fibro had fallen away to reveal dark panelling that gleamed dully. In some corners were the remains of giant stone fireplaces, the mantelpieces stripped away and the hearths bricked in. The windows too, despite being either painted over or hidden away behind wardrobes, still boasted tall, arched frames. But it was the ceilings which really spoke of the scale on which the House had been originally designed. Sagging and dilapidated those ceilings might be, lost in cobwebs, but they still soared high above everything else, ornately plastered, making the little rooms seem absurdly narrow and tall. Often the apartment walls did not even reach all the way up to them. Sad wires dangled down, ending in naked light bulbs; but the mountings from which they had hung were solid, and at one time, surely, they must have borne chandeliers.

Day by day, William mapped out the House. It was shaped like a giant H, as seen from above, with the east and west wings forming the vertical strokes. The front doors looked south, positioned in the middle of the horizontal bar. Behind them was the shrunken version of the original entrance hall, dominated by a once-grand staircase fashioned from a deep red wood that was now scuffed and splintered. The stairs doubled back on themselves, and at the halfway landing a partition had been thrown up, an ugly white barrier made of fibro, pierced only by a small door that was securely bolted and padlocked. This door marked a limit on William's explorations, for the upper floor was forbidden to him. It was forbidden to everyone, Mrs Griffith had warned tersely, pointing out the way the ground-floor ceilings bulged and hung low. Condemned as unsafe, especially for little boys. There were other staircases, William found, in each of the wings, narrow flights that climbed straight up. But these too were blocked off.

William and his mother occupied the rear apartment in the east wing, and William suspected that this whole section of the House had been abandoned for some time. The air was stale with mould, and there were marks on the carpet where large boxes and cupboards and other, unidentifiable items had obviously lain for years. Even with their familiar furniture installed, the place still felt gloomy and cold to William. His mother set out the couch and the television in the living room, and plugged in the little electric heater she had brought from home; but the warm air simply rose to the ceilings high above, and the deep chill of the House remained. William's own room was in the back corner of the apartment. It was narrow and high and dark, and its windows looked out on a jungle of ivy and bushes.

Mrs Griffith was quartered in the same wing, in the front apartment, and her private rooms were strictly out of bounds to William. However, as her apartment had the only kitchen with a functioning stove, it was here that hot meals were prepared. Attached to Mrs Griffith's kitchen was a dining room where William and his mother and the housekeeper ate their dinners.

William's uncle was never in attendance. His territory, apparently, was the west wing, but in fact the old man had not emerged from his office since the day of William's arrival. Day after day, the door was shut fast. His work, William was told, must not be disturbed. But did that mean he would stay in there forever? Did he even sleep in there? For although William had tentatively explored the western apartments, and had come across several bedrooms, none of them showed any signs of habitation.

He was sure of one thing, however — he was the first child to have lived in the House for years. There were no toys anywhere, nothing bright or for fun. And when he ventured outside into the cold, the garden was no better. Thorny weeds clinging to him, he wandered down the remains of formal pathways. He peered into the pool. The bottom was cracked open and naked earth showed through, a foundation for the long grasses and bushes that smothered the concrete. The wooden diving board was rotting on its springs. At the rear of the House, William found a gravel parking lot. It held his mother's car, a rusting horse trailer on flat tyres, and an old farm utility. Attached to the back wall of the main building was an annexe that must have been the original kitchen, and a path led from it to the staff cottages, which were lined up outside the garden wall. None of these roofless, crumbling structures were habitable now, except for one which held firewood. And beyond the cottages were only more grass and trees and scrub rolling away under the bleak sky.

There were circumstances in which William might have found his surroundings enticing. If he'd had a friend to explore with him, perhaps, or if he had been visiting for a weekend. But he was alone, and this was no visit, so the act of discovery seemed hollow. He crept around the dark rooms, noting everything silently, but feeling no urge to delve into the boxes or to dig through the piles of old equipment he came across. None of it was his, or had any relation to him. It would be trespassing. And though he guessed that the outbuildings would be crawling with rats and mice, he couldn't imagine going out there at night with a torch to chase them. At night the blackness outside seemed unbreakable. And inside, the House was at its worst. Many of the rooms had no lights. Even when they did, to navigate between them meant braving the shadows that waited in the hallways and corners, and in whole suites that lay deserted. And it was at night that the cold sank in deepest, as if flowing from the walls.

William piled on jumpers, pulled a beanie down over his ears, and slept under layers of blankets, but still never felt the sort of warmth he remembered from his bed at home. Other comforts were missing, too. The television reception was bad, fogging all the shows with static. The showers leaked only a dribble of water. And mealtimes were cheerless, especially dinner. Breakfast and lunch weren't so bad — William and his mother had their refrigerator from home, and could at least make toast or sandwiches in their own kitchen. But each evening they were forced to gather with Mrs Griffith, the three of them zig-zagging in from their respective corners to meet in her dining room. It was a long, narrow chamber containing a large table which reached almost to the walls, barely leaving space for a mixed collection of chairs. There was a sideboard at one end, laden with yellowing china and decorated with plastic flowers. The tablecloth was plastic as well, a creamy white, upon which salt and pepper shakers and bottles of sauce sat always in the one spot, leaving faint grimy circles when lifted.

Each night the housekeeper served out four meals. She would place the fourth on a tray, and then, with much muttering, shuffle off laboriously towards the office to deliver it. Upon her return she would sit, dour and silent, at one end of the table. She dined as if she was still living alone, gazing ahead fixedly. William and his mother faced each other over the middle of the table. They barely spoke, not in Mrs Griffith's inhibiting presence, and there was only the clink of cutlery as they worked their way through the roasts and stews that were the housekeeper's standard fare. They were not hearty meals, always on the verge of going cold, the vegetables pale and drained of colour. Dessert usually consisted of tinned fruit and custard. And when dinner was done, the old woman's muttering would begin again as she retrieved the tray from the office, then cleared the table and finally disappeared back into her kitchen. At first, William's mother had offered to help. She could wash up, she suggested, or she could cook, or maybe William could deliver the tray, to save the housekeeper the long walk. Mrs Griffith refused her with a glare. It was her job, she insisted, and her kitchen. She had been cooking for John McIvor for over twenty years, and wasn't going to stop now.

To William it was plain that the housekeeper considered them unwelcome guests. Maybe she even hated them. So was this what their new life was going to be like, hidden away in a musty apartment, with an angry old woman standing between them and something as simple as cooking their own dinner? Was that what the death of his father really meant? William watched his mother uneasily as the first week crept by, waiting for her to say something about their future. But she never did. Her moods swung between the short temper of her headaches and a drowsy apathy. The state of the House, the meanness of their reception, nothing seemed to register with her. Perhaps she had exhausted her reserves just to get herself and her son installed. But occasionally William would catch a certain expression on her face, as she studied the desolation around her. In those moments she looked suddenly appalled, as if a mask had slipped and she had seen the truth.

'Mum,' he asked in one of those instants, 'are we staying here forever?'

Denial immediately clouded her eyes. 'Why? What's wrong with it?'

William could only stare around at the walls in answer.

'Where else would we go?' she pressed, her voice rising to an edge, defensive and frantic all at once. 'Where's the money going to come from?'

'I don't know...'

'I've done all I can, Will. You just have to make the best of it. There are things you don't understand, and I don't want you ruining them.'

'What things?'

'It all depends on your uncle.'

His uncle — the greatest mystery of all. The old man's presence hung over everything, but he remained hidden, heeded and obeyed but never seen. At times, roaming the hallways, William could hear his voice within the office, loud and hectoring, as if he was talking on the phone. At other times there was the sound of a typewriter clacking furiously in there, or a different, unidentifiable noise, like a machine rolling and rattling. There was a radio too, usually turned up loud, but not playing music, only news reports or talkback, the voices indistinct. William asked his mother if it was really such hard work, running a property like Kuran Station. She only shook her head. 'He has a manager for that. Your uncle does other things now. You're not really old enough to explain.'

Even so, William found himself loitering near the office, striving to hear what was happening inside, dreading that the door might open and his uncle emerge in a rage, but hoping for it as well, if only to solve the enigma. But why, he wondered, did he envisage his uncle in a rage? He had seen him only the once, after the fire, and the old man had said nothing harsh that day, done nothing cruel. He had offered his House to a homeless mother and her child, surely an act of kindness. But still William guessed that the tall, limping figure would be a man of anger. Maybe it was just the hammer of the typewriter keys. Or perhaps it was the tone in his mother's voice when she spoke of his uncle, or the way the housekeeper doggedly went about the duties of serving him. There was no kindness suggested in any of these things. And so William wondered if he really wanted to meet him, or might it be better that the old man remained a ghost, a brooding captain of an ancient ship, whom the passengers never saw.

Towards the end of the week, however, William discovered several boxes piled outside the office. They were stuffed with sheets of paper, all fresh and new and smelling of ink. Hovering as close as he dared, he saw that the sheets were stapled into bunches, and covered with dense print. Behind the office door the typewriter and the other machine had fallen quiet. Instead there were voices, not the radio, but two people were talking. To his amazement William realised that one of them was his mother. William couldn't hear what she was saying to his uncle, but he was sure he heard his name mentioned. He stole away again before he was discovered, and the next day the boxes were gone and the west wing was silent, as if the old man had completed his labours and now, finally, rested.

Thus the days inched by. At the end of each one William would retreat to his bedroom, which was no refuge at all, and try to sleep. It wasn't easy, with the great weight of the House pressing down around him. Sometimes a chill, dry wind blew outside, but at other times there was only a ringing quiet in which every tiny sound stood out. The settling of timber, the rustle of small creatures in the creepers outside his window, the lowing of cattle far off across the hill. And footsteps, always footsteps, muted, as his mother, or Mrs Griffith, or perhaps even his uncle, moved around on the old floors, until the House sounded full of restless, wandering feet. Only above him, on the second storey, was there utter silence. Nothing and no one moved up there, not even rats or possums. He would stare at the invisible ceiling, and think of the weight of masonry and timber that hung above him, a rotten pile ready to fall and crush him in his bed.

Chapter Five

Two days before school was due to resume, William was called to the office. His mother went with him. She seemed to have been expecting the summons. 'This is important,' she warned, and William readied himself to finally meet his uncle. But instead, waiting at the doorway was a fat man in a baggy corduroy jacket. His face was mottled, and he held a black bag in his hand.

'Ah,' the stranger said, fleshy eyes wrinkling. 'So this is the boy.'

'William,' his mother announced, 'this is Dr Moffat.'

The man was quite old, with thin wisps of hair combed across a shiny red pate, and he wore big dirty gumboots. He smiled at William genially.

'I'm your uncle's GP. He's asked me to have a look at you.'

William glanced up his mother, confused.

'It's a check-up, that's all. Just do what he says.'

'That's right,' the doctor chimed in. 'Nothing to worry about.' And he ushered them into the office.

The first thing William noticed was a fire, and the smell of smoke. Then he was struck by the size of the room. It was easily the largest he had seen in the House, taking up an entire corner of the wing. A thrill of recognition ran through him, because this was right, this was what the House was supposed to look like; even the high ceiling seemed in proportion here. In fact, on closer inspection, William realised that the office, like the rest of the building, had once been subdivided into several smaller rooms. The partitions had left ugly marks on the floor. But in an act of restoration the fibro walls had been removed, the fireplace cleared and the mantelpiece re-installed. Winged leather armchairs now clustered about the hearth. There were high windows in two of the walls, with deep bookshelves between, and at the far end of the room stood a huge carved desk, thickly cluttered with magazines and documents, and there were three other tables, chaotically piled with boxes and newspapers and mysterious shapes that bulked under plastic sheets.

The only thing missing was the old man himself.

'I thought John would be here,' William's mother said.

'He's resting. That newsletter always takes it out of him. It doesn't matter. I can find my way around.' Dr Moffat was busy at a small cabinet that held multicoloured bottles. He filled a glass with something golden, then settled himself noisily in one of the leather chairs before the fire. 'We discussed it all over the phone,' he said, eyeing William benignly across the rim of the glass. 'A quick examination.'

William looked at his mother. 'But I'm not sick.'

'Just go on over. It won't take long.'

Baffled, William crossed the room. The doctor swigged from his glass, then dropped a hand on either of William's shoulders and pulled him close, studying his face. Returning the stare, William could see the enlarged pores on the doctor's nose, and the white stubble on his cheeks. The man smelled of old clothes and alcohol, and his puffy eyes were etched with red.

'How old are you again?'

'Nine.'

The doctor turned to William's mother. 'Has he ever been sick with anything serious? Spent any time in hospital? Any broken bones?'

'No.'

'Hmm.' He held up a stubby finger. 'Follow this with your eyes, Will.'

The finger waved back and forth. William watched it. It made his eyeballs ache.

'Stand on one foot. Your left foot.'

William did. It was difficult to keep his balance.

'Touch your nose with your right finger.'

William touched his nose.

'All right. Good. Now take off your clothes for a minute.'

When William was in his underwear the doctor began to prod and probe him, making his muscles twitch. A stethoscope appeared from the black bag and was applied, freezing, to his back and chest. A small hammer was knocked against his knee. A clammy hand scooped his testicles briefly as he was asked to cough. The examiner hummed and muttered throughout.

'Okay, you can get dressed.' Dr Moffat returned to his glass for a moment. Then he addressed William's mother. 'Well, he seems perfectly healthy to me.'

'That's what I told his uncle. He's fine.'

The doctor mused. 'You know what John wants.'

'But what about school?'

'A few months off doesn't matter at Will's age.'

'Isn't there a law about missing school?'

'Not if you have a medical certificate. I can take care of that.'

'A certificate saying what?'

Dr Moffat pondered some more. 'How about glandular fever? Kids are always missing a year here or there because of that.'

William was dressed again by now, and had listened to the exchange in bewilderment. 'Is something wrong with me?' he asked his mother.

She sighed. 'Of course not. This is just … an arrangement.'

'You're going to have a holiday,' the doctor added. He was pouring himself another drink. 'For the rest of the year.'

'Why?'

'Why not? Most kids would jump at the chance. And this way you'll have time to get to know the place. And your uncle too. Without having to run off to school every day. It'll be fun.'

'Oh.' William wasn't sure how he felt about the news, only that he didn't understand it. Then he remembered something. 'My ear. I forgot. It hurts sometimes.'

His mother glanced at him. 'You never told me that.'

William said nothing. There was an ache that came and went, but he hadn't told her about it because it was the ear she had hit, on the night of the fire.

Dr Moffat beamed. 'We'd better have a look then, hadn't we?'

He pulled an instrument with a pointed eyepiece from his bag and inserted it into William's ear. William winced.

'Doesn't hurt that much, does it?' The doctor was squinting into the eyepiece, and the smell of alcohol was cloying.

William steeled himself. 'No.'

'Well … it's a little red and inflamed in there.' He was talking to William's mother. 'Probably just a bit of an infection, kids get them all the time.'

But as he spoke he pushed the instrument a little further inwards, and suddenly an incredible pain ignited deep in William's ear, making him gasp and pull away.

'Whoa,' said the doctor. 'All right. I've finished.'

William's ear throbbed and twitched hotly, and his vision swam with black dots. He needed to sit down. It felt like someone had stabbed his eardrum with a needle.

'Does it need antibiotics?' he heard his mother ask, sounding strangely far off.

'Keep an eye on it. If it gets any worse ... Look, I'll write you a prescription. You can fill it whenever you like.'

William walked away gingerly, and sat in a chair near the desk. Why did he feel so dizzy? Was that what an ear infection did?

Dr Moffat was packing his bag. 'I'll drop Will's medical certificate down at the school sometime next week. I have to visit there anyway to give a few inoculations.'

'I thought you were retired.'

'Oh, I am. But I still do little things like that.'

'Where was your practice?'

'In Lansdowne. That's where I met John.'

'You're part of this organisation of his, aren't you?'

'Oh yes. Have been for years.'

His mother and the doctor talked on, but William's attention wandered. He gazed around at the walls. Old photographs hung there, brown and faded under their glass. It helped to fight the dizziness if he focused on them. Faces stared out of the frames, men and women posed stiffly for the camera. People from long ago — William could tell from the clothes. One picture showed a breakfast scene on a sunlit porch, a husband and wife and child seated around a table. Another showed a crowd sprawling across a manicured lawn, the trees behind them hung with streamers.

'...three or four hundred members by now.'

'And he runs it all by himself?'

'Well, there's a committee that helps. I'm on it myself. But he's always been the driving force.'

'And the money, that comes from him as well?'

'There're the membership fees, of course, but they don't cover everything.'

'I didn't think so...'

The dizziness wasn't going away. William's eyes moved from the photos to a large framed map that hung beside them. The paper was yellow and looked brittle with age. William studied lines and boundaries that meant nothing to him, until at the bottom of the map, in ornate writing, he saw the word 'Powell'. Landmarks began to fall into place. The Condamine River came winding along the left-hand side of the map. On the right side were the Hoop Mountains. Towards the centre of the frame crept the line of a creek, and along it was a small representation of a building, labelled 'Homestead and Village'. And across the entire empty centre, in letters so big he hadn't even noticed them at first, ran the words 'KURAN STATION'.

'…this place does better than most, even with things dry as they are. John has money, don't concern yourself about that.'

'But the House, it's so … Why does he keep it this way?'

'Ah, well now. He did restore this office, when he first moved in, and he certainly planned to do the rest. But then there was the business with his wife.'

'I only heard rumours…'

Another map hung beside the first, this one on clean white paper. It showed the same region, only now the map was crowded with lines. Roads and railways struck out in all directions, unerringly straight, and between them was a dense spiderweb of thinner lines, marking out numbered allotments and farms of all shapes and sizes. Kuran House was merely an anonymous dot, but a sliver of land around the House had been shaded with pencil. It was long and narrow and ran back towards the mountains.

'…very sorry to hear about your trouble, of course. Must have been hard.'

'Yes, it was.'

'Fire is a horrible thing.'

'Thankfully we could come here.'

'Well, I know he's taken a keen interest in the boy…'

William's vision blurred and he felt he might vomit. When his eyes cleared he saw an amazing thing upon the wall. He'd thought that its splotched look was due to age, but now he realised that in fact the surface had been used as a giant canvas. The images depicted there had been clouded by years of grime and smoke, but he could make out the suggestion of a white horse, and then others, their legs stretched in a gallop. The horses bore ghostly riders dressed in faded red coats. One of the men held a horn to his mouth. Painted fragments of dogs swarmed. And in the background were green patches of countryside, rolling hills and hedges, and something that looked like the ruins of a castle. William understood that he was looking at a painting of a fox hunt. In England.

'...and you really don't feel you can cope without it?'

'It's just been too much, since the fire, with William and everything else.'

'I understand. I'll write you out a script.'

'I wouldn't ask, I usually go to the clinic in Powell, but since you're here.

'Of course. Prothiaden, was it?'

'Tryptanol.'

William turned his head and looked at the wall behind the desk. It took a moment for his eyes to adjust, like staring at a magic picture puzzle, but then he saw another painting, as indistinct as the first. There were white blobs that he thought must be dogs again, but no, this time they were a flock of sheep. Horses grazed on long grass nearby, their riders leaning easily upon their backs. The colours were different too, brown and muted, and instead of rolling hills and castles in the background, William could discern the vague outline of the House itself. This wasn't England any more. And off in one corner of the painting, so faded as to be almost invisible, was a collection of shapes recognisable as people only because of their white eyes and teeth. Black men, looking on from the shadows, their expressions impossible to read. Hostile? Fearful?

Phantoms. He blinked and the vision was gone. So was the dizziness, and the pain in his ear had receded. He looked around, feeling as if he had slipped back from a dream. The doctor was scribbling on a prescription pad. He finished with a flourish, then tore off two sheets of paper that he handed to William's mother.

'Thank you,' she said, oddly fervent.

'A pleasure.' Dr Moffat glanced happily at William. 'Glandular fever. That's what you've got, that's what I'll tell your uncle.'

'If anyone else asks,' his mother added, 'you're too sick for school.'

'Glandular fever,' William repeated, testing the words. He understood that none of this was quite the truth. But on the other hand, why had he felt so dizzy? And what was he supposed to do for the rest of the year, if he wouldn't be at school?

Then he saw that both Dr Moffat and his mother were gazing at the ceiling.

'Are you going up to see him?' his mother asked.

The doctor shook his head, laughed uneasily. 'I don't really like it. Those floors aren't safe. With my weight I'd probably fall through.'

'So why does he stay up there?'

'God only knows.'

Chapter Six

WHEN JOHN MCIVOR REACHED HIS TEENS, THERE WAS SOMETHING
disturbing he came to understand — many people did not like his
father. The sentiment was unspoken but ever present, not amongst
the station staff, who would never have dared, but amongst people
outside Daniel's sphere of influence. John sensed it in some of the
older and wealthier inhabitants of Powell, for instance — the
town councillors, the local solicitors, the editor of the newspaper
— and it was as simple as a reticence in their conversation, or a
hesitation before shaking hands. A faint revulsion. He had no idea
what it might mean. It couldn't be a question of class. His father's
origins were humble enough, but they were perfectly respectable
— he had even been a police officer once. His famous pistol was
a keepsake.

Perhaps it was just resentment. Kuran Station had loomed over
Powell for decades, dominating its politics and strangling its access
to land, so the station manager undoubtedly had enemies. In fact,
lately even Edward White's position in parliament had come under

threat. He was a grey widower by now, an old man who rarely ventured beyond Brisbane. The newspapers called him 'The Last of the Pure Merinos', and it was not a complimentary title. Edward was seen as out of date. The Darling Downs, the papers said, needed fresh blood, younger men committed to a future of bustling shops and thriving farms of wheat and cotton, not relics of the squatter past tying up thousands of acres with their sheep. But Daniel McIvor had long closed his mind to such talk. Unlike Edward, he was still as hale as ever, and bestrode the plains like a colossus.

Indeed, his own great scheme was ripening. For some years now he had been whispering in Edward's ear, pushing John's suit for Elizabeth. At first the old man had resisted. His granddaughter, after all, could surely do much better than the son of his station manager. But Daniel pointed out the deeper problem. Certainly, Elizabeth might marry someone of her own status ... but could anyone guarantee that her new family — perhaps city folk — would choose to keep a property that was already unprofitable, and likely only to get worse? And if Edward wanted to find her a husband from a pastoral background, then where was he to look? The other Darling Downs' dynasties were in poorer shape than his own. No, what Kuran needed was someone born to the place, and passionately dedicated to its survival. Who better than John? And as the years went by, Daniel could see that Edward, growing ever more feeble, was coming round to the idea.

John himself left school at fourteen to take up station work full time, and at fifteen he was maturing into his role. The rest of the staff already looked to him as his father's successor, and the daughters of Kuran village were making their interest known. But John had no interest in these girls. He was focused on Elizabeth. She spent most of her time now at boarding school in Toowoomba, but he watched her closely during her visits home. He thought she was beautiful, in a remote way, and he certainly desired her; but she worried him too. She remained so aloof.

He found it difficult to imagine actual intimacy between them. Did that matter? Perhaps not. He looked at his own parents, and saw no great love between husband and wife. It was the station that mattered, not intimacy. Elizabeth's prime role would be to confer ownership upon him. And in this, John trusted his father. After all, Edward was almost persuaded, and where her grandfather led, Elizabeth would surely follow.

But then Edward White died.

It was during the 1929 election campaign for state parliament, which in truth had not being going well. Edward was up against a much younger man from the Labor Party, and while the senior White might style himself as a grand old man of the plains, in reality he was just old. Critics had universally attacked his conservatism and denounced his vested interest. Daniel McIvor was there at his employer's side as always, and yet there was only so much he could do. One afternoon the campaign cavalcade drove out to the little town of Kogan, where Edward was to address a meeting. Not long after they'd crossed the Condamine River, the candidate, who'd been sleepy and vague all day, went into convulsions. Daniel ordered the car to a halt, lifted Edward from the back seat, and, in an attempt to ease the fits, laid him out alongside the road. Edward White expired there in the scrub, several miles beyond the borders of his beloved station.

He was buried at the Kuran Station cemetery, in accordance with his wishes, and the funeral was an event. It was considered that his passing marked the end of an era. The little station church couldn't cope with the crowd, so the ceremony was held under a great marquee surrounded by extra chairs for the overflow. After the service, a grand wake was held in the gardens of the House, presided over by Malcolm. It was the biggest party he had ever thrown, but there was no joy in it for him. It wasn't that he mourned his father. If anything, that death had come too late, for Malcolm was no longer young, and he was in ill health. But now, instead of the release he'd been waiting for all his life, he found he was trapped in a new and unexpected fashion.

Hasty arrangements had been made behind the scenes, and a furious round of meetings had taken place between Edward's allies in parliament, his political staff and, of course, Daniel McIvor. Unlike the other mourners, none of them considered the death of the old man to mark an end, although it was certainly an inconvenience. However, the pastoral cause had to go on. But who was to take Edward's place on the ballot? The committee settled on Malcolm. He was incompetent, yes, everyone admitted that. But he had the family name, he was the son of the great man, and Kuran Station was, after all, his now. With a properly managed campaign he might still win. Malcolm himself was not invited to any of these discussions, and when told of the decision, he refused in horror. Undeterred, Daniel locked himself and Malcolm in the office one evening, and after a torrid night of persuasion, abuse and (it was rumoured) even physical violence, Malcolm emerged chastened and prepared to accept the nomination.

He announced his candidacy at his father's wake, to tumultuous, if well-rehearsed, acclaim. It proved to be the sole highlight of his campaign. No matter how gifted his speechwriters, there was no hiding the unwilling candidate's almost complete ignorance of political matters. Then his incipient alcoholism bloomed under the stress. Crowds laughed at him for his red face, his reedy voice, his swaying walk. Newspapers derided him as the last rotten fruit of a decaying aristocratic tree. His opponents mocked him as an idiot son better left hidden in the attic, where his father had sensibly kept him. And on the streets of Powell, Daniel's free beer and intimidation could no longer turn the tide. It was a different age, a different mood, and the result of the election was never in doubt.

For Malcolm it was the last and greatest in a long line of humiliations. He left the station in Daniel's hands and escaped to

Brisbane with his wife. There he drank ruinously for a month and died — exhausted, insensible, coughing up endless gouts of blood — in his hotel room. He was fifty-one years old, and left an unpaid bill of close to a thousand pounds. The death was not noted. His body was transported back to Kuran and quietly buried in the family plot. There was no need for marquees or extra seating, even the little church was not quite full. And so Kuran Station passed to the last remaining member of the White dynasty. Elizabeth had only just turned eighteen, and since leaving school had been occupied with little else but burying her grandfather and watching her father slowly suicide. And in all that time John McIvor had barely spoken a word to her.

Indeed, in the space of a few bewildering months John's world had been badly shaken. Kuran Station and its owners had always seemed as immutable as sunrise and sunset, but now he awoke to the uncertainty of the station's future. It was the dark year of 1930, and the economy of the Powell region was plunged into gloom. They were calling it a depression; even worse, some said, than the depression of the 1890s. Streams of men came wandering over the plains in search of work. Daniel had none to offer. He was locked away in the office, growling in frustration as debts grew and commodity prices plummeted. He began to speak of drastic measures, of scaling back on the livestock, and of cutting down on wages and staff.

To John, the fragility of the station's future only made the place all the more precious. He loved the wide golden spread of the plains, and the hills that swept up smoothly in the east. He loved the herds of cattle and the mobs of sheep straying lazily in front of his horse. He loved the days spent working out amongst the men under the open sky, or camping with them at night, beneath an arch of faultlessly clear stars. He loved the fury of the shearing shed and the way the wool bales piled up, great square blocks of prosperity. Most of all, he loved Kuran House. So solid and secure and rooted in the earth. The tragedy was that, since Malcolm's funeral, the great stone building had stood empty. His wife and daughter had returned to Brisbane, and so the station lacked what it needed most — a living, beating heart.

It was a full six months before Elizabeth returned, and strangely she came alone. John's father was immediately summoned to meet with her. Daniel, sensing that the fate of the station would be discussed, took John with him. She was waiting for them behind the desk in the office. She seemed older, much older than John remembered. She was only eighteen, after all. But he saw now a tall girl with a serious face and unreadable eyes, sitting straight in her chair, and she wasn't really a girl anymore. She was — and this was the first time John had properly considered it — the owner of Kuran Station. There was no grandfather to direct her, no father to hinder her, Elizabeth was all on her own.

It should have been at this moment that she reached out to John and his father for support — John had imagined exactly how it would happen — but instead her greeting was cool. Daniel, however, seemed unconcerned. He poured himself a drink, made himself comfortable in a chair by the empty fireplace, and got straight down to business. He'd sent Elizabeth plenty of reports, she knew the situation and how much there was to be done, so here was what he thought...

Elizabeth cut him off. She had an announcement to make.

She was selling the station.

It was a simple statement, but in that instant John felt the whole fantasy of his life shudder and sway.

Daniel's first reaction was complete disbelief. What on earth was she talking about? No one was going to be selling anything. But Elizabeth only shook her head and explained it all patiently. Her lawyers had been in talks with representatives of the state government and a deal had been brokered. She had agreed to surrender most of the pastoral lease, and as compensation the government had agreed to grant her a perpetual lease on the House and fifteen thousand acres surrounding it. Once the legalities were finalised, she would sell that land and return to live in Brisbane.

That was when the anger came, that was when Daniel loomed out of his chair. Who the hell did she think she was? He had worked for her family for almost thirty years, he and he alone had kept Kuran alive. Sell the station? It was impossible! But watching Elizabeth, John could see that she was unimpressed and unafraid — the determination never left her eyes. How could he have been so wrong about her? How had he ever imagined that she would need him or agree to place herself under his care? His face burned with humiliation, and still he said nothing.

Elizabeth produced a sheaf of documents. It was all there, the signed contracts and lease documents. The thing was settled. She had returned only to inform the staff of her decision and collect some personal items. The furniture would be sent for later. Daniel was shaking his head, refusing to hear, refusing to credit that any member of the White family could defy him. Did she really expect him to cooperate with all this? To divide up the station and disperse its assets, to throw away his life's work? No, Elizabeth replied. It was no longer any business of his at all. As of this minute she was terminating his employment.

At that, a cataclysmic fury seemed to boil behind Daniel's face … but Elizabeth only stared back at him, a smooth-skinned teenage girl, waiting with the imperturbable certainty of youth. And something broke in the station manager. The girl had fired him. It was her right to do so. It was inconceivable that she would have the *nerve* to do so. But she had. All the strength in him drained away, useless. And even through his shock, John understood that he was witnessing something acutely personal. Elizabeth hated his father. Why, he didn't know, but he could see in her the same repugnance for Daniel McIvor that he had seen in so many other eyes, only naked and magnified. She said, *You were only ever an employee, Mr McIvor.* And for the first time in the interview her gaze flickered over John as he sat by stupidly, and he saw that her contempt embraced him as well. *Your son was only ever an employee. I think you might have forgotten that.*

It was finished, all in a matter of minutes. John had spoken not one word of protest as his inheritance was ripped away from him. In the last moments he could only stare at Elizabeth, and out of his shame there flamed a terrible admiration for her. Then his father had hold of his arm, and was dragging him backwards through the office door.

Chapter Seven

WILLIAM WAS ROUSED FROM SLEEP BY A HAND ON HIS SHOULDER and a voice whispering his name. He opened his eyes drowsily. A figure was hunched over the bed, a face leaning down close to his. Was it a dream? And then he came fully awake, rearing back against the pillow.

'Quiet,' his uncle hissed.

William stared in amazement. The old man was right there — a bony, angular face, glowing weirdly in the beam of a flashlight. His hair was dishevelled and he was clad in wrinkled pyjamas underneath an old bathrobe. He looked like a prophet, come in from the desert.

'Get up. Quickly.'

The figure withdrew. William obediently climbed out of bed, and searched around for his shoes. It was cold, and a deep silence reigned over the House. The old man waited by the door, a shadow behind the torch.

'Outside,' he said, and led the way.

His mind fogged, William stumbled through hallways that were inky black. Finally they came to the front doors, which were wide open to the night. His uncle switched off the torch. William paused on the doorstep, for all the clouds had blown away and the sky was stunningly clear, the stars blazing. But his uncle had already limped on ahead, following a path through the garden, his robe flapping in the darkness. William hurried after him carefully. They circled the pool, its broken floor lost in shadow. Then they were on the decking that jutted out from the garden walls, where the hill dropped away below them. South and west stretched the plains, a silky grey sheet, as featureless as an ocean. Powell was no more than a sprinkle of pinpricks on the horizon, mirroring the stars. A faint breeze slid across the hill, the air was freezing, and the entire world was asleep.

'Watch,' his uncle instructed.

The old man was gazing at the sky, standing stiff and unmoving, his face a pale blur. William was wide awake now. He studied the stars. And suddenly, as he stared up, a greenish fire streaked across the sky and was gone.

There was another streak, and perhaps a minute later, another. To William they seemed both close and infinitely far away. Shooting stars. He had seen them before, of course, but never so many at once, nor at such a lonely hour. Was this what his uncle did at night, watch the sky? He wondered if he should speak, to express amazement or thanks. But the old man appeared to have forgotten he was there, so William stood waiting, his head craned back as the ghostly scintillations came and went.

'I saw one hit the ground once.'

The words caught William unaware. His uncle's face was still set to the heavens.

'It was out there on the plains, years ago, when I was a boy. It came down about a mile from our camp, a big flash and a clap of thunder. When we looked for it the next day all we found was a ring of dirt, like a ripple in a pond, and a little hole at the centre. No matter how long we dug, we couldn't find anything. The black soil had swallowed it up. It's deep, the soil out there. Forty feet, sixty feet, eighty. No one knows for sure. There's bedrock underneath it somewhere, but in my time I've seen whole houses sink down into the earth and vanish without a trace. They might still be there even now, resting on the bottom, if you knew where to look.'

It was a rich, dry voice, rolling in the darkness. William waited, disturbed and uncertain. The old man sniffed at the air.

'There are strange things in the world. Another day, we were camped out there during a storm, and in all the rain and wind something huge passed by. The horses went mad and the tents were blown away. Afterwards we followed a track through the grass, where the earth had been scoured bare a hundred yards wide. We followed it for miles, this way and that, and then suddenly there was nothing — it had lifted itself back into the clouds. The soil had been gouged away a foot deep, and polished so that it almost shone. That storm had signed its name in the ground.'

There was another streak overhead, and for an instant William glimpsed his uncle's face, tinged with luminous green, narrow and severe, with dark holes for eyes.

'You live long enough in one place, there's nothing you won't have seen.' The old man tilted his head southwards, a shadow against the stars. 'I even saw the smoke, the day your father died.'

William swallowed, his mouth dry.

'What about you, Will? What have you seen?'

William didn't know what to say. What had he seen? He thought back to his life on his parents' farm … but there had only been small things. Little dust devils, dancing across paddocks. Icicles hanging from gutters on the roof, on deep winter mornings. Flights of crows, trailing after the tractor to pick at the freshly turned earth. But he divined that his uncle wanted something more. Something to match a night of shooting stars, or a tornado.

'No wonders?' the old man inquired, looking down William now, his voice alert and testing. 'No floods or droughts? No swarms of locusts or plagues of mice in the wheat?'

William shook his head, and in the sky a meteor flared and sputtered out.

His uncle nodded towards the eastern horizon, where shadows humped, a wall against the plains. 'Have you been to the mountains?'

'Yes,' William whispered.

'I was told a story once, by an old man. He said he was one of the first to climb those hills. It was all forest then, thick and dark, and he hunted an animal up there that he had never seen before. He didn't give it a name, but he said that when it bellowed in the night, the other creatures, the birds and the insects, would all go quiet. It left footprints by the creeks, and slept in caves under the cliffs. One night he cornered it in a gully, and it almost crushed him as it fought its way out. Huge and shaggy and wet, he said it was, with a stink like old mud. And a great head with wild, white eyes. He never saw it again. He thought maybe it died, when the loggers came and cut down most of the forest. I was one of those loggers, as it happens. And once I saw some enormous prints, by a creek, like an elephant had stomped past. And I saw marks in the sand of a cave, like something big had rolled there. And I heard something one night, crashing through the undergrowth, and I could smell mud even though there was no mud anywhere near.'

The shadowed face studied William once more.

'Did you ever wander off into forest? Did you ever see the terrible bunyip?'

Again, William could only shake his head. And even though he knew there were no such things as bunyips, he heard no humour in his uncle's question, only that hard edge, examining.

William felt cold. The old man turned towards the brow of the hill upon which the House rode. A tangle of trees waited at the top amidst the silvery grass, tall gums with white skin and pleading arms.

'You won't find any monsters down here in the foothills,' he said. 'But I've seen packs of wild dogs around here, and the bodies of sheep and cattle, torn apart. Sometimes they used to come down to the House on clear nights like this, howling at the moon like wolves, always one big dog in the lead and the others slinking behind. It was a horrible sound they made, and sad too. We shot as many we could. And then there were feral cats, big and mean, squealing in the night, just like the sound of a baby crying. People who didn't know better nearly went mad searching out in the bush for abandoned children. But there were never very many people in these hills. There was no gold to find here, no timber to cut. Just scrub and grass.'

He paused, drew in a breath of the cold air.

'I'll tell you something. Maybe a dozen people have owned this property before me. The land has been cleared and grazed for almost one hundred and fifty years. There have been cattle and sheep here, dogs and cats and foxes and hares and a hundred other creatures that don't belong. Foreign weeds too, lantana and black-berry and worse. You'd think there would be nothing left of what used to be here before they came. But I've walked this property from one end to the other, year after year. And there are still places where I don't think a foot has ever set down apart from my own. Places where nothing has changed. But you need the eyes for it. You have to be able to see. Not everyone can.'

William looked away from the hill. Out on the southern horizon a light had detached itself from the small galaxy that was Powell, and was moving north, a vehicle driving along the Lansdowne road. It was still many miles away, but such was the clarity of the night William could see the two headlights, and a fringe of smaller yellow lights above them. A truck headed who knew where, its driver hunched hollow-eyed over the wheel. William thought of his bedroom back at his old home, and the sound of trucks passing by on the road late at night, like thunder in his dreams.

'How long have you been here now?' his uncle asked.

'Ten days.'

'Long enough. Forget about your little farm. Tell me what you've seen *here*.'

William searched for an answer. He was failing the exam-ination, whatever it was. And he could feel sleep stealing over him again, sullen and irresistible. 'The House,' he said.

'Ah.' The old man turned and faced the building — the broken-back roof slumped against the sky, the ivy-covered walls black in the starlight. 'Mrs Griffith tells me you're not impressed.'

William could hear the taint of mockery.

'She's lived here all her life, you know. Ever since she was a little girl, no older than you are now. She was a maid here once. Owners and managers have come and gone, but not her, she always stayed. In the end, in fact, she was the only one left. For a long time she had this place all to herself. So she's not fond of intruders. She doesn't even like me. She was furious when I moved in. I'm sure she's sworn to outlive me, just so she'll be alone here again.'

Suddenly he crouched down at William's side.

'But you now ... She'll be worried about you. She can't outlive a boy.' The white face hovered close for a moment, a cryptic blur. 'What do you think?'

William shivered. He didn't even understand the question. Above him, the meteors had died and the faintest hint of dawn was paling the east. From far off he could hear the drone of an engine. It was the truck, plunging on into the night. It was the most desolate, lonely sound imaginable.

'Time will tell, I suppose.' The eagerness in the old man's voice had faded. He climbed stiffly to his feet. 'I've kept you long enough. You should go back to bed.'

Instantly, sleep came sweeping over William. He followed his uncle numbly, back around the pool and through the garden, to the doorway yawning black to swallow them. Inside it felt airless, almost warm, and the smell of age and rot assailed William's nostrils. Then his uncle's voice came, disembodied in the dark.

'Don't waste what time you have here, Will. You're no use to me if you just hide away in the House.'

The torch was switched on, dazzling, and thrust into William's hand. His uncle limped up the stairs, the sway of his robe casting great winged shadows ahead of him. On the landing, the little door in the partition was wide open. His uncle bent to go through, then paused, glanced back down.

'Explore. See what there is to see out there. But remember, you're not to go beyond this door. There's nothing up here for you.'

The old man pulled the door shut behind him, and for a moment William heard his slow footsteps climbing higher. Then they receded, and William was left to grope his way back to his bedroom.

Chapter Eight

NEXT MORNING IT WAS HARD TO BELIEVE THAT THERE HAD EVER been stars in the heavens, let alone streaks of fire. William gazed out from the front porch and the sky was a crisp blue, the winter sun shining brightly. Had he really stood with the old man, over there by the pool, and talked in the darkness? It all seemed so different now. But there was one thing he remembered clearly. His uncle had told him not to hide away in the House. And it was true, the time had come to venture further afield. The fine weather demanded it, and the whole station was waiting.

He said nothing to his mother. There was no need. Now that the unpacking was finally complete, she spent most of her afternoons on the couch, watching the shadowy TV screen or sleeping, and he was under instruction not to bother her. She wouldn't even notice he was gone. At least she seemed less irritable, ever since the doctor's visit. He waited until she had settled down after lunch, then slipped quietly into the hallways. On the way he caught a glimpse of Mrs Griffith gliding through a doorway ahead of him, silent and shrouded in black, and for an instant the night of stars rushed back. But then William was through the front doors and out into the day.

He turned left from the porch, crossed the garden and came to the eastern wall. The stonework had tumbled outwards in several places, and he climbed over into the grass beyond. Pausing there, he looked up at the knot of gum trees on the hilltop. They would be his first target. He began striding upwards, although the grass was deeper than it looked, brown and brittle tussocks that came up to his waist. He thought of snakes suddenly. And what about the cattle? He couldn't see any, but what if there were bulls in these paddocks? Would they charge at him? He pushed on towards the trees. But when he reached them, he saw that what he'd thought was the top of the hill was actually only a subsidiary rise. Beyond it was another broad grassy crest.

Looking back, William realised he was already quite high. The House was below him now, and he could see right across its swayback roof. It was an ugly perspective. Some of the chimneys had collapsed, littering bricks across the slate tiles, and in places the tiles themselves were missing, patched over with sheets of tin held down by rocks. Under this tattered brim, the House looked squat and fat. But he could also see more of the lower hill from here. At its foot wound the line of a creek, and clustered beside the creek was a motley collection of sheds and silos and stockyards — the working heart of the station. A tractor was parked out in the sun, a man in overalls half immersed in its engine. The distant sound of something being hammered wafted up from below.

The scene reminded William a little of his own farm, but he didn't think he could ever go down there to ask for rides on the tractor, or to investigate the sheds, as he'd done with his father. It wouldn't be the same. For a moment a cold sensation of loss swept through him. He turned and stomped on through the grass. The brow of the hill flattened out, then at last the land dropped away, and there before him was a small, shallow valley. Beyond it another hill rose to the east, wider and broader, and beyond that he could glimpse yet more hills, receding away under the sky.

It all seemed to be the same sort of country, scrub and trees and grass, and there was no guessing how many miles it ran, but below him he could see a gravel track. It curled around the slope on which he stood, and then climbed away eastwards. No doubt it came from the sheds and stockyards, and from there it must wander its way into the depths of the property. But what really caught William's eye was a structure nestled beside the track on the far side of the valley. It was a church. Tiny and white, with a little steeple. And beside the church, fenced in iron, was a cemetery.

This was something! He tramped down the hill, and then up again. As he approached the church he saw that its weatherboard walls were actually a scabrous grey. The building was just another ruin. Grass grew high around the foundations, the window frames were empty, and the tin roof had fallen in at the far end, where the green leaves of some plant poked out. William studied it all in disappointment. He had never been inside a church, but he had a dim conception of pews and altars, of candles and statues and priests in robes. There would be none of that here. The front steps were broken, and the doors were padlocked shut.

He moved on to the cemetery gate and edged through. He remembered another graveyard, in Powell, a spreading green lawn where his father lay buried under a rectangle of black stone. William could still see the coffin as it sank into its hole, neat and smooth. This place was different. It was small and very old, the iron fence tangled with bushes, the headstones barely visible amidst tall, shaggy weeds. There were only five graves. The first two were side by side in one corner, marked by leaning headpieces, the writing worn away to a blur. The third grave must have been more recent. It stood alone, the slab cracked and sprouting grass, but the name on the headstone was still legible. 'Malcolm Jeremy White'. The dates below told that the man had died in 1930, but there were no other messages or clues about him.

The last two graves were the biggest, with pillars and carved angels to stand guard over them — except that the pillars were broken and the angels had been vandalised, their wings snapped off, their faces staring blankly without noses or lips. But here too the names on the tombstones were still visible. The less impressive of the two read, 'Marjorie Anne White, Beloved Wife of Edward'. The larger said simply, 'Edward Thomas White, of Kuran Station'. William pondered them both. Who were all these Whites, and why were they the only ones buried here? He saw a large hole in the earth, leading down under the two stones. It tunnelled away at an angle, rutted by rain and trailing roots. But it was also smooth in places, as if an animal had burrowed there. He remembered the wild dogs then, his uncle talking about packs of them, howling at the moon. The graveyard no longer felt like a place he wanted to investigate. The day remained bright and warm, and the House was only a few minutes walk away over the rise, but it was so quiet, and he was all alone.

He left the graves, made his way to the sunken steps of the little church and climbed up carefully. He saw now that the padlock on the doors was broken, hanging loosely on the bolt. William pushed and one of the doors gave a little, scraping against the floor. With another good shove he was able to slide inside. He found himself in a small, empty room with narrow windows and a rubbish-strewn floor. Broken glass crunched beneath his shoes. Something scuffled and scratched above him, and looking up he saw that there was no ceiling, only the open framework that supported sheets of tin. Birds had nested up there. He could see tufts of straw and mud in the corners. The floor below was layered with feathers and droppings, and William felt a sudden itch in his scalp, thinking about lice.

And yet there were clear signs that people had been here.

Empty beer bottles. Soft drink cans. Cigarette butts. Bits of news-paper and magazines, and even what looked like a mouldering toilet roll. In one corner was a crude barbecue made out of bricks and a sheet of tin, with a pile of ashes beneath it. In another corner lay an old mattress, filthy and flattened and stained. Near it were a pair of crumpled track-suit pants, and a single sandal. And here and there around the walls, jagged graffiti had been carved into the wood, initials and names and dates and dirty words. It all reminded William of an empty shed near his school in Powell, where the bigger kids had gone after classes to smoke and have fights. Maybe the children from Kuran village had once done the same thing up here at the church. But everything, the cans, the bottles, the mattress, was layered with dust and bird droppings. Even trespassers had long abandoned the place.

At the far end of the church the floor had fallen in, grass had grown through the hole, and in the middle of it, leaning against the rear wall, was a tree. The limbs had reached up and unseated the sheets of the roof, so that a mottled green daylight was visible through a fringe of leaves. But within the church itself the tree looked dead, a leafless tangle of branches that had sought its way across the wall in search of light. Again, some creature scuttled momentarily in the roof. A bird, perhaps, or a possum. Or a rat. A tremor ran through William. This was worse than the cemetery. Would everything on his uncle's property be the same, defaced and decayed and torn apart by the slow creep of branches and roots? If so, then what was the point of exploring any of it?

He backed away, out of the church and into the daylight again, leaving the door open. But the afternoon no longer seemed bright and welcoming. He gazed around, apprehensive, and eager now to get back home. He could follow the gravel track, but that would be the longer way, and meanwhile there was the knot of gum trees up on the hill, his landmark. He set off through the grass. But when he reached the trees, confusion rose. The land fell away into another shallow valley, and he couldn't see the House. Looking about, he realised that there were several groups of trees, and his landmark could have been any one of them.

He considered going back down to the track, but then decided that the House simply had to lie to the west. He walked towards the sun for a few minutes, but there was only more grass and trees. Finally, to his bafflement, he found himself on a hillside that faced north, gazing out over rolling country which was completely foreign to him. On the maps in his uncle's office the property had looked only a few miles wide — why was it proving so difficult to find his way? He set off again, and descended into a gully, the bottom of which was dense with scrub and already in shadow from the westering sun. He stopped, seriously worried now. Surely he couldn't be lost? He had walked barely fifteen minutes to reach the church in the first place. He turned around again and aimed towards the highest land in sight. But when he reached the spot, he saw no sign of the House *or* the church. Tears started in William's eyes. What if he was still out here when it got dark?

He thought about wild dogs again, and other things his uncle had said about the hills, how parts of them were still unexplored. The dark gully behind him, was that one of those places? He plunged off in the opposite direction. Should he yell for help? Was he close enough to the House for anyone to hear? Or was he heading further away all the time. Then he tripped over something in the grass. He fell, the rough blades scratching at his face, and glimpsed something white. Scrambling to his feet, he saw a bone, a long, curved rib, sticking up from the earth. He realised there were more. Brown skin clung to some of them, and they joined at a half-buried spine. The skull lay to one side, its jaws stretched open in one last soundless cry. Ants crawled and picked at dark shreds that lay within, and there was the faintest scent of rotting in the air.

It was only a cow, he told himself, only a dead cow. But he was horrified, stumbling away in tears, unable to stop the panic growing. They were an awful place, the hills. At home on the plains he had been able to see everything, it was impossible to get lost, but the hills were deceitful, they tricked and misled and were full of dead things, gravestones and creeping trees on walls and empty eyes set in skulls. Why had he ever left the House? And then all of a sudden there it was, rising before him. He gaped at it. He *had* come the wrong way round, because now he was approaching the House from the rear. He could see the tumbled ruins of the outbuildings, and beyond them the familiar grey slate roof. But even through his relief, the House looked grim and cold and ugly. He remembered the interior of the church, and it came to him that the upper floor of the House would be the same, dark and filthy, and that his uncle slept on a stained mattress in some derelict room.

But it was his home now. Exhausted, he picked his way through the last of the grass and climbed through a break in the back wall. All he wanted was the safety of his own room. He tramped across the red earth of the car park, and then around to the front garden. And there he stopped short.

His uncle was sitting on the porch.

He could have been waiting there just for William, or for no purpose at all, an old man merely watching the afternoon sky. He looked nothing like the wild-haired prophet of the night before. He was wearing work pants and boots, and a flannel shirt with the sleeves rolled up, revealing the gnarled bones of his forearms. Tufts of white hair were visible on his chest, and he cradled a teacup in his hands. William hesitated, knowing that he wasn't quite safely home after all.

The old man regarded him levelly.

'You look a bit done in. How far did you go?'

William lowered his eyes, feeling guilty for no reason he could name. 'The graveyard...'

'Only the graveyard?' His uncle fixed him with a frown. 'Something give you a fright, did it?'

William could feel that his face was flushed. Even worse, his eyes were still swollen with tears. Yes … it was obvious to anyone. The little boy had got lost, and started to cry.

'Hmm.' The old man drained his cup, then stretched out his bad leg and kneaded the muscles before rising to his feet. 'Well, never mind. We'll make a proper start tomorrow.'

William looked up. 'A start?'

'It's a big place, this station. I should have known. No use you blundering about on your own. We'll go for a drive tomorrow, you and me, and I'll show you the whole property.'

William blinked in confusion. He could still feel the itch of grass against his skin, and he could still smell the dead cow's flesh clinging to bone. He hated Kuran Station, every inch of it.

But the old man was smiling. 'At least that way we'll know what we're talking about.'

Chapter Nine

FOR JOHN MCIVOR, BANISHMENT FROM KURAN STATION WAS LIKE an amputation. One moment he had been whole and young and full of hope. The next, a limb had been lopped away and the blood was draining out, leaving him cold and pinched. Elizabeth White had wielded an axe upon his life.

The last days on the station were almost too painful to remember. The House was stripped bare, the stock was sold off and most of the workers were dismissed. After swift negotiations, the property was bought by a grazing consortium from interstate. The McIvors were homeless. John's only hope lay in his father. Kuran Station might be lost to them forever, but Daniel had savings, so why shouldn't they buy some land of their own somewhere else? It would be a more humble place, no doubt, but the family could start all over again, secure this time in ownership.

Instead, his father cashed in everything, borrowed more, and purchased a hotel in Powell. The station manager would become a publican. John was amazed. What did his father know about the hotel business? Cattle and sheep, that was their life. But Daniel's sacking had turned him bitter and stubborn. He would not, he declared, be chased away. For thirty years he had been the strength behind the White throne, the most important man in the district, and nothing about that was going to change. Accordingly, the Royal Hotel was one of the grandest buildings in Powell, a two-storey affair, with wide balconies fringed in wrought iron. By early 1931 the purchase was complete, and the family flung the doors open for business.

John, working behind the bar, saw that the enterprise was doomed from the start. The publican trade was nothing like the pastoral industry. There was no store of wealth behind a hotel, no resources of land and stock to see it through troubled times and keep the banks patient. A hotel needed cash, it needed a regular turnover, and for that it needed customers. But nobody came to the Royal. There were logical explanations for this. The depression was raging, and Powell, with a population of only four thousand, had over twenty other pubs. But John, roaming about the town in lonely anguish, saw that there was another, uglier reason for the lack of custom. Powell, in fact, was enjoying Daniel McIvor's downfall. Now that he had been stripped of his power (and by a mere girl, no less!) the townsfolk finally had him at their mercy. Old accounts were being settled.

But there was more to it than that. John could read it in faces and overhear it on street corners. The familiar pattern of whispers and looks, of half-caught insinuations about his father, had asserted itself again. Some dark slur lay behind it all, both maddening and mysterious, and ultimately unanswerable, because, as ever, John had no idea where the core of it lay. Nor was there anyone he could ask, for he was as much a pariah in the town as his father, the son of a marked man. Still, after only a few months of poor trade and mounting debts, he could foresee the inevitable. He pleaded with his father to sell the hotel again, quickly, before all was lost. They could still start over, as long as it was away from Powell. Daniel only shook his head, a mania gleaming deep within his eyes. Powell *owed* him, he insisted. The whole region owed him for the things he had done. He would never leave. But he was drinking much harder than he ever had before, and even in defiance he seemed shrunken now, suddenly an old man.

John could think of nowhere else to turn. His mother had always been a silent stranger to him, and anyway, she had no influence over her husband. And his little sister — born in 1927 — was just a child, merely another mouth to feed. So John gave up in disgust. His father might be bent on self destruction, but there was no need for his son to stay and share the humiliation. John was almost eighteen now, old enough to stand on his own. He packed his few belongings and struck out along the dusty roads, westwards, to seek his fortune.

He had assumed he would find employment on cattle or sheep stations. But the properties in the far west proved to be nothing like Kuran. They were vast, scorched, empty things, with low homesteads squatting away alone in the scrub. John knew nothing about such arid country, and owners and managers alike laughed when he talked about his pastoral experience back east. To them, Kuran Station, for all its grandeur and history, was no more than a gentleman's hobby farm. Their own properties were ten times the size, and fifty times harder to run. In any case, no one was hiring. Even if they were, there were always twenty other men after the job. The roads were choked with wandering souls. It was the same story with the railways gangs and the drovers and shearers. If there was any work at all, it went to men with wives and children to support, not striplings on their own.

Disillusioned, John moved on, a swagman. From the far west he travelled north through the mining country, labouring for a day here and there, and then east to the coastal towns admidst the mangrove swamps. Last of all he tramped his way southwards to

Brisbane. But wherever he went, all he found were thousands of unemployed, as desperate as himself. It was John's first look at greater Queensland, and his first true indication of just how alone he really was. He hated the cities with their crowds and squalor, he hated the coasts with their sweltering heat and tropical jungles, and the great emptiness of the west, naked and red, oppressed him. Most of all he loathed his own helplessness and poverty. No one knew his name. No one understood what great things he had been promised. No one cared that the prize had been torn so cruelly from his hands.

It took John a full year to accept that he had made a mistake and that his father, even in madness, had perceived a kernel of truth. The most important thing was to keep to your own country. The Kuran Plains was where he belonged. His name might do him no favours there, but even prejudice was better than crushing anonymity. So from Brisbane he turned westwards, up the Great Dividing Range to Toowoomba, and then out through the rolling hills until they faded away into black soil. The horizon etched a curve before him, and he was back in Powell. The town had been battered by the depression, but John had seen a hundred other towns far worse off, some of them stricken to the death. Powell would survive. The same could not be said of the Royal. The hotel was dirty, neglected and empty of guests. His father was incoherent with alcohol. His mother was as powerless as ever, his sister a face he barely recognised. It took only a glance over the books for John to see that the money was all gone.

So he refused to stay at the Royal. The important thing was to stand apart, to create his own name, free from his father. He slept on the banks of Powell Creek, amongst the tents and shanties which had sprung up there. Eventually he was hired by a farmer to help with the filling and carting of wheat bags during the harvest. It was John's first experience of grain-growing. Nothing about it appealed to him, but he did see that, if necessary, wheat could be a means to an end. More importantly, the farm, a few miles north of Powell, was situated right up against the old southern boundary of Kuran Station. John could stare over the fence to his former home, where only two years previous open grassland had extended away forever. Now the land had been surveyed and the blocks marked out with pegs, three hundred and twenty or six hundred and forty acres in size. Here and there the new owners had already moved in, ploughing up the grass and planting crops. Shacks had been built, and sheds, and fences. In some places the pasture still grew undisturbed, but to John's eye the plains had taken on a painfully moth-eaten appearance.

The irony was that there were still plenty of cheap blocks available. The depression had stifled demand. All he needed, John mused, was a little capital. True, he'd heard that most of the farmers who had taken up selections on the Kuran run were already going broke. Apparently the land was less fertile than predicted, and there were mysterious barren patches amidst the grass, confounding the newcomers. But John had known every inch of the land, good and bad, since he was a child. If he ever chose a farm for himself out there, it would be in the right place and it would succeed. But of course he had no capital. In the end, he would always lift up his eyes from the plains to the distant spur that jutted out from the mountains, unable to see Kuran House, but knowing exactly where it stood. And the familiar despair would rise in him, and the yearning, and the anger.

For the House was still empty. The new owners had gone bankrupt only a few months after taking possession. The property had returned to the bank, and there had been no buyer for it since. A caretaker staff remained in the cottages — but the House itself was completely shut down, its gardens already running wild. In these times, it seemed, no one had any use for a mansion. And for John that was the most terrible thing. He could almost feel the great homestead calling out to him, giant and deserted. The thought of it burned. The House should have been his. It should be his, even now. If only he could raise the money to reclaim the place as his own. What a moment that would be, what a revenge upon Elizabeth! But it was impossible. The work on the wheat farm ended with the harvest, and once again he was stalking the streets of Powell with a bare few coins in his pockets. From where was this great fortune to come?

Early 1933 found John labouring in a sawmill on the outskirts of town. The pay was miserly, and it was a dreary life, toting wood and choking on sawdust and bloodying his hands with splinters. Then, one summer afternoon as dust hung stifling about the mill, John saw a small party of men approaching. They were walking slowly along the road that led down from the Hoop Mountains, and they bore a roughly hewn stretcher on which a shape lay, covered by a sheet. Flies buzzed hungrily about it, and a man walked at the stretcher's side, brushing them away. The group paused in the shade of tree. Word passed around that they were timber-getters, a logging team from the mountains, one of several that supplied the mill. Usually they came to town only every few months, for supplies, or to besiege some hotel bar until their money was gone. But that day one of the loggers had been crushed by a falling tree. His comrades had carried him down in search of medical aid, but he had died before reaching it. Knowing he had a wife and family in Powell, they had elected to carry his body all the way home.

John studied the men. They were lean and wiry, with strangely pale faces and watchful eyes, their forearms densely muscled. Even standing about idly they radiated a profound assurance in themselves, so different from the sawmill workers, or the thousands of unemployed John had seen on the roads. Their home was high in the hills, where even the depression, it seemed, had not touched them. Now they were a man down. Something stirred inside John. He lifted his eyes eastward to the Hoop Mountains. They stood clean and high against the sky, a tumble of green and grey, a country of cool airs and misty streams, a thousand miles away from the heat and grime.

John was decided in an instant. He walked away from the sawmill, to where the men waited with the corpse beneath the tree.

Chapter Ten

THE OLD UTILITY RATTLED ALONG BETWEEN THE PINES OF THE driveway. It was another fine blue morning and William sat in the passenger seat, glancing warily across at his uncle. The cabin was redolent of earth and diesel, and mould from the seats. All pleasant smells, and sandwiches had been packed for the tour of the station ... and yet William remained uneasy. A whole day with the old man. For the moment, in the sunlight and with his arm on the window, his uncle looked as benign as someone's grandfather. But William remembered the prophet, stern and testing, from the night of the shooting stars.

His mother had emphasised the point. 'Pay attention to what he says today. He's not doing this just for fun.'

So William waited, alert, but right now his uncle was only whistling amiably. They turned off the driveway onto a track that swung south down the hill, past the sheds and silos that he had seen the day before. His uncle showed no interest in the buildings. At the foot of the slope the track turned back east, to run alongside the creek. William peered over the dashboard, trying to see if there was any water in the channel.

The old man broke off whistling. 'Kuran Creek, it's called. It starts up in the mountains and runs along the whole southern side of the spur.'

'Can you swim in it?'

'Well ... there's only a few puddles these days, with the drought. Further up in the hills you might get a bit of water flowing, but not this far down.'

The track curved away and crossed into the next valley. There was the church and the graveyard on the far slope. It was so close, William marvelled. How was it possible that he had become lost between here and the House? Then he remembered the names he'd read on the gravestones.

'Who were the Whites?' he asked.

His uncle frowned. 'They owned the station, long ago.'

'The graves are all broken.'

A shrug. 'Just goes to show, doesn't it? There's better things to leave behind than headstones.' The utility was rolling past the cemetery, and the old man eyed the tombs. 'I'll tell you this — when my time comes, I'm going on the bonfire.'

They topped the next rise. A jumble of hills spread out before them, the spur receding all the way to the blue line of the mountains.

William's uncle straightened enthusiastically behind the wheel. 'Now, from here on we're into the station proper. Ten miles it runs from this spot, two or three miles wide all the way.'

William stared across the broad slopes, their hides brown with grass and dotted with trees. A brief memory came of what it had been like the previous day, when the countryside had seemed so bewildering — but in fact he hadn't even made it beyond the home paddock!

His uncle's smile was knowing. 'The first thing to learn is, always be aware of exactly where you are. So get it right. These hills are the westernmost spur of the Hoop Mountains, and the Hoops themselves are a spur of the Great Dividing Range. Think of a map of Australia. Think of the east coast. The Great Divide runs the whole length of it. We're about halfway down, on the western side of the range, a hundred miles inland from Brisbane.'

They were moving downhill now, into another small valley. The track was rutted and overgrown in places, slowing them down, but in any case, his uncle seemed in no hurry.

'It's interesting though. Go back a few hundred million years. Right here where we stand, there was nothing back then but ocean. The continent that eventually became Australia was somewhere else entirely — it was wandering about between the equator and the south pole. It wasn't even the same shape as now. You wouldn't be able to find the station on it, you wouldn't even be able to find the hills or the plains. None of them existed. You see what I mean? It's one thing to know where a piece of land is. It's another to know where it came from.'

The old man's eyes were searching the horizons appreciatively.

'Away across in Western Australia — now there you've got some old country. You've got rock that's been exposed for age upon age, and it's as lifeless as the moon. But this country, it's pretty young. The only old thing around here is the bedrock, down there under the plains. Millions of years ago it was the bottom of an inland sea. Then the ocean levels dropped and you had a sandstone plain covered in swamps and bogs. It dried out finally, but meanwhile in the east volcanoes were erupting and the mountains were formed and the plains were drowned again, in lava and ash this time. Over the centuries the lava and ash broke down, and that's where the black soil comes from. But do you know why there aren't any trees out there?'

'No.'

'The black soil won't support them. Not big ones, anyway. In droughts it cracks open and snaps their roots, in the wet it turns liquid and trees just topple. So there's only ever been grass out there. A treeless plain. And because of all that grass, people came. With sheep. And then with wheat. You've heard of Allan Cunningham? He was the first European to lay eyes on the place, in 1827. He battled his way north from Sydney through forests and mountain ranges and suddenly he saw this open, rolling country. Perfect for grazing. He named it after the Governor of New South Wales — Lieutenant-General Ralph Darling. And so here we are today.'

William nodded. He knew that Cunningham was a famous explorer — but that was only history. He was more impressed by the station unfolding before him. They couldn't be more than a mile along the track, but to William it already felt wide and empty. Old fences ran alongside the road, and a few grazing cattle lifted their heads as the utility drove by, but there were no buildings, no ploughed paddocks, no telephone poles or power lines. Just the hills and the blue sky above.

'Of course, what Cunningham saw was only the southern edge of the Downs. That's miles south of here, down near Warwick. He never saw the Kuran Plains or the Hoop Mountains. That was left to the first settlers. The grass was so tall that it came up to the shoulders of their horses. But along the spur here, this was all eucalypt forest. It took them years to clear it for grazing.'

They hadn't cleared it entirely, however. There were still plenty of trees on the open slopes, where the grass grew brown and stiff, and cattle rested in the shade. Tall graceful gums with smooth white trunks, or grey ones with the bark peeling away in hairy strips. Trees that flung out wide canopies and had fat red trunks like rusty iron, trees that were hunched and contorted, with rough, jagged bark. There were gullies too, with a denser scrub of bushes and ugly, tangled vines. William saw crows take flight as the utility approached, heard their harsh croaks over the engine. He glimpsed a hare darting off the road in alarm. And once he was startled by three wallabies rearing out of the grass and bounding away. But mostly the hills were a sleepy, shaggy place, an old country baking under the sun. His uncle said it was young, but that was impossible to believe.

'Hardly anyone comes here now,' the old man said, as if reading his thoughts. 'Only the cattle, and not so many of them, not with the drought. We're running about a quarter of what we'd have in a good season. At mustering time I'll have men up here with horses or motorbikes, but otherwise there's no reason for anyone to be around. And that's the way I want to keep it. Some stations out west get tourists in. They set up campgrounds and picnic areas, and people wander all over the place. Not on my land, though. I'd never let that happen here.'

William could hear the pride in the way his uncle said 'my land'. It had never occurred to him to be proud of his little farm back home. How could you be proud of a square mile of dirt? But the station was something much more, a great bulk of land that rolled and reared. The hills rose steeper, and the crests of some them were tumbled with boulders. The banks of the gullies grew more precipitous, the scrub within them more dense and forbidding. Now they were passing into an altogether wilder, darker country. The House and its gentle hill seemed far behind, and it was easy to imagine packs of wild dogs roaming up here, and century-old trees lurking in forgotten corners. The only modern structure William could see was a rusty windmill, standing at the foot of a tall slope, a water tank tethered to its side, with a trough for the cattle. The grass was beaten down around it, and from the windmill a narrow path curled back and forth up the hill. The top was half hidden by trees, but staring up William thought he could see — somehow disturbingly — a ring of stones there, jutting from the grass.

'In the early days,' his uncle continued, 'these hills were a lonely place. The only thing up here was an old shepherd's hut.

When I was boy I used to hear stories about how two men were stationed there, way back in the 1850s, when there was no House or anything. Supposedly, both of them went mad, alone for so long. One of them killed the other with an axe. Only bits of the body ever turned up. People said his friend ate him. I don't know if that's true. But the hut was still standing when I was young. And believe me, the place felt weird. Now though, it's just a few old posts. You'd pass it right by without even knowing.'

And on they went, the old man's talk carrying them further and further into the hills. Finally, they began to climb out of a narrow valley, and William's uncle dropped the utility into its lowest gear.

'Almost there now,' he said. 'Our first stop.'

They were ascending a steep hill. A single tree, bent by years of wind, marked the crown. And beyond that seemed to be open air.

The utility coughed to a halt beneath the tree. William was aware of a wide view all around, as they climbed out. The air was cool and still, and they were much higher up than he had expected. The first thing he saw were the Hoop Mountains. They had appeared from nowhere, immediately to the east, leaping up in a series of tall ridges, blue and crisp in the winter light, a thousand metres high. From his father's farm on the plains, these same mountains had been a faded blue line on the horizon; now they seemed close enough to touch. He could see individual trees standing upon the crest of the central range. Thick forests swept down the flanks, but in the shadowed glens a tantalising darkness waited, naked cliffs of stone where the mountainsides had collapsed, while in other places again the peaks were worn and rounded and bore only grass, like great hairless heads. But the closeness was an illusion, he realised. The main ridge was still some miles away. In between, he could see now, were the higher foothills, a rugged tumble of them, cast out by the mountains and descending in waves until they lapped at the foot of the rise on which he stood.

'Well, this is all of it.' The old man had his hands in his pockets, as he stared out at the world. 'Everything that Kuran Station ever was. Twenty-five miles north to south along the tops of the mountains here, and then another twenty miles out into the plains, all the way to the Condamine River. Five hundred square miles all told.'

William turned slowly to take it all in. The Hoop Mountains strode away in a great curve to either side, and the plains washed up against the foothills like a yellow sea. The spur was a wide, hump-backed spear of land jutting far out into that ocean. Its last hill, where Kuran House sat, remained hidden away at the western extremity. And beyond that was a great swathe of farmland, blurring with distance, until the horizon waited in an arc against the sky. William turned full circle, and confronted the mountains again. It was dumbfounding to think that it had all been one property once.

His uncle was shaking his head. 'It was too big, of course, even from the beginning. Ridiculous to think it could all hold together. They started breaking it up almost straight away. The mountains were the first to go. By the time the Whites took over, the boundary had been pulled back to the foothills. There were already loggers up there, and then people from Powell started using the mountains for camping trips. Later on the government turned it all into the national park.'

William was searching the mountains for landmarks he could recognise from visits he had made with his parents, but the angle was wrong. He could see no sign of the road that climbed up from Powell, or of the little resort village and camping grounds that he knew were nestled up there, next to the park. But he remembered guided walks with the rangers, and listening to lectures about the forest, craning his neck to see the tops of the giant trees — the famous bunya pines, and, of course, the hoop pines which gave the mountains their name.

'The mountains don't matter to us,' his uncle said. 'They're the old Kuran Station, and we'll never get that back. Now there's only twenty-odd square miles left, and that's what concerns you and me. What we're standing on right now. The land I own.'

William looked west again.

'Do you see?' His uncle crouched down at his side. 'It's nothing like the farm you grew up on. Your farm was a machine, a factory to grow wheat. But this isn't anything like that. This is a piece of country. It's not just about heads of cattle per acre. This place is alive in its own right. It has a history. It's growing and changing all the time. It breathes.'

Glancing at the old man's face, William saw a warmth there he wouldn't have thought existed. It wasn't directed at him, it was directed outwards, to the hills.

'It even talks, to the right person. And that's the thing — finding the right person. The truth is, land has to belong to someone to really come alive. It needs a human being to hear it and see it and to understand everything about it — where it came from, where it's going. Otherwise it's just a piece of ground. And when I die, I won't be leaving a hole in a cemetery or my name on a gravestone. This is what I'll be leaving.'

He was studying William now, his gaze intent.

'Do you understand what I'm talking about?'

William couldn't bear that gaze for long. It felt as if the old man saw deep within him and found only a lack, a little boy who didn't understand anything. He dropped his eyes.

His uncle sighed, climbed to his feet.

'Anyway,' he said after a time, 'this is as far east as we can go. From here we head south.'

William turned and looked down. At the foot of the hill was a line of winding trees that marked another creek — or possibly a different part of the one that ran past the House. A fence stretched along the near bank.

'Cross over the creek,' his uncle said, 'and you're into the national park.'

Something caught William's attention. 'What's that?' he asked, pointing.

His uncle peered down. On the far side of the creek, barely visible amidst the trees, was the red flash of a tent. And yes, there were men moving about down there.

'So you've got eyes after all.'

'Who are they?' William asked.

The warmth had departed from the old man like an eclipsed sun. 'I don't know. But we'll find out soon enough.'

Chapter Eleven

THERE WERE TWO MEN BY THE TENT, AND THEY WERE CROUCHED over what appeared to be a chart spread out upon the ground before them. Their heads lifted as they heard the utility rolling down the hill. When they saw that it was stopping by the fence, they rose and came to the far edge of the creek, then, after a pause, made their way across. Their feet splashed as they came, for this close to the mountains an inch or so of clear water was still trickling across the stony bed.

William and his uncle climbed out to meet them.

'G'day,' said the first man, lifting a finger as he came up. He was tanned and unshaven, and dressed, William noted with interest, in a faded ranger's uniform.

His uncle returned the greeting watchfully.

The ranger nodded across the fence. 'This your property, is it?'

'That's right.'

'Well, good.' He leant on a fence post and pulled out a cigarette, eyeing William for a moment as he lit it, then turning his attention back to the old man. 'Might be lucky we ran into you.' He stuck out a hand. 'I'm Ken Coates. National Parks. And this is James. He's a PhD student I'm showing around.'

William's uncle shook hands with them both. The second man wore ordinary clothes and looked much younger than the first, despite a bushy beard. Across the creek the tent sat brightly beneath the trees. There seemed to be a lot of gear stashed about it, and the ashen pile of a fireplace waited nearby. It was a pleasant, shady valley, with the creek running through, but it was far from the campgrounds up on the main range. And William knew that the national park rules were strict. You certainly weren't allowed to camp just anywhere.

'Yeah, been here since last night,' the ranger was saying. 'And it's cold too, once the sun goes. So what do you run here? Cattle?'

'Mostly.' But William's uncle didn't seem interested in cattle. 'You're a long way down.'

The ranger tilted his cigarette towards his companion. 'The boy's doing some research, and I've been roped in as a guide.' He flicked ash into the grass. 'This your grandson, is he?'

'Nephew. What sort of research?'

The young man spoke up. 'I'm writing a history of the Hoops.' He was gazing over the fence. 'This is Kuran Station, isn't it?'

William's uncle ran a measuring eye over him. 'Yes.'

'I thought so. I've read a bit about this place. From back when the mountains were part of the lease. Huge bloody place it was.'

'This is as far as it goes now.'

'The original owners — they were quite a famous family. You're not descended from them, are you?'

'No.'

'Pity. I bet they'd have some stories to tell.'

'No doubt.'

'They don't seem to have left any personal documentation,

which is a shame. Is there any of that family left in the district? I should look them up.'

'Not that I know of.' The old man shifted his feet. 'I think they left back in the '30s, long before I got the place.'

The young man shrugged. 'Oh well.'

'What sort of history is it, exactly?'

'I'm mainly interested in presettlement times. Indigenous occupation, the relevance of the mountains to their culture. Mostly I've been up on the range, where the big corroborees were held, trying to pinpoint localities.'

The ranger was smiling wryly. 'The kid's had me crawling all over the place. Looking for bora rings and shinning up bunya pines … but all we've found so far are a few old logging huts.'

The student nodded. 'There were gangs all over the mountains, from the 1860s on. And you can still find some of the roads the loggers cut, and those chutes they dug in the mountainsides to slide the logs down to the bottom. Of course it was all in decline by the First World War, and pretty much finished with by the Second. The hoop and bunya pines were logged out, and the red cedar too, except for a few left in the national park, but that was out of bounds by then.'

William's uncle said nothing.

The ranger had finished his cigarette. He stubbed it out on the post, then drew a tobacco tin out of his pocket and stashed the butt away. He glanced at the old man. 'Grew up around here, did you?'

'Out on the plains mostly.'

'Familiar with the mountains at all?'

'I've been up there.'

The student broke in again. 'So what about these bunya pines? You got any theories?'

William's uncle regarded him blankly. 'Theories about what?'

'You know, the scars. On the big old trees, the ones that are a hundred and fifty, two hundred years old. Some people say they were made by Aborigines with stone axes, cutting footholds into the trunks so they could climb up to get the nuts. Other people reckon that's rubbish and that they're natural, just marks where branches have fallen off. You ever hear anything, one way or the other?'

'I've heard both.'

'What about the balds? Any thoughts?'

'No.'

'How about any other old stories? You know, stuff you might have heard from your grandfather about the early days. Strange happenings in the mountains, people stumbling into hidden gullies, that sort of thing.'

The old man only shook his head. There was a repressive pause. William was standing by, silent and wondering. He could sense that his uncle was being purposely uncommunicative, but didn't understand why. What about all the tales he'd told William? Didn't he like the men? He'd said that he didn't want visitors or tourists on his property, but these two weren't trespassing. They were in the national park. And one of them was a ranger.

'What are balds?' William asked at last.

The ranger grinned at him. He turned and pointed up to the mountains. 'See those bare patches on some of the higher hills, where there's only grass, no trees? They call them balds. No one knows why they're like that. They weren't cleared by logging or anything, and the soil is fine, but for some reason there were never any trees there, even though there's forest all around.'

'They might have something to do with the indigenous inhabitants,' the student said. 'Or they might not. It's one of the things I'm investigating.'

'You been up in the mountains, son?' the ranger asked William.

'Sometimes.'

'Ever eaten a bunya nut?

'No.'

'Bloody beautiful. Fry 'em like potatoes. Fatten you up in no time.'

William's uncle had stood by austerely through all this. 'There aren't any balds down around here,' he said. 'Or bunya pines.'

'No,' the ranger admitted. 'We're after something else, along the creek.'

'Yes?'

'Water holes, actually,' the student said.

The old man frowned. 'On this side of the range?'

The ranger sighed. 'I know, that's what I told him. We're in the wrong place. The only decent water holes are in the eastern catchment.'

'It's there in the oral sources though,' the student insisted. 'There was supposed to be a sizeable pool on this side, a water hole that you could rely on, even in droughts. It was pretty important in cultural terms, apparently, so there might be artefacts or other significant finds around it.'

The ranger was studying the creek. 'We've been tracking all the west-flowing streams, up and down the mountains. Haven't found a thing so far. That's what we were wondering. You know this area. Nothing you can tell us?'

William's uncle scraped a hand across his chin. 'Never heard of a big water hole this side. And anyway, it wouldn't be so low down. You should be looking higher up.'

'We have been,' the student said.

'Maybe you heard wrong. What are these sources?'

'Well, there's people's letters and journals — early settlers, the loggers, the odd explorer. And old maps, though you can't always rely on those. But oral sources, I'm talking about older stuff there, like Aboriginal legends. Tribes from all over southeast Queensland gathered here when the bunya nuts ripened, so the mountains feature in the tales of quite a few different tribal groups. All gone now, but I've talked to a few old men and women in places like Cherbourg, and they remember a thing or two. Part of my funding comes from their local land council, actually. There's been some pretty good studies of Aboriginal history in the Darling Downs area, but nothing all that specific about the Hoops.'

'National Parks are funding him too,' the ranger said. 'There's talk of an Aboriginal cultural centre up in the park, if we can get enough information.'

The young man smiled ironically. 'Might be more than that, once these new laws come in. With enough historical evidence, who knows, the land council might put in a claim over the park. It's Crown land, after all.'

'Hmm.' The ranger shifted his cap unhappily. 'We'll see.' He turned to William's uncle again. 'So, this creek, it ends up running through your property?'

The old man nodded. 'About a mile from here it turns west and crosses the boundary.'

'Yeah, we went that far. No holes, I suppose, along your stretch?'

'No.'

'Wouldn't be the water for it, I guess.'

'Most of the time we hardly get any flow at all.'

The ranger shoved away from the post. 'I guess that's that then.' He gave the student a look. 'It's back up into the hills for us.'

'Fair enough.' The young man addressed William's uncle. 'Thanks for your help.'

'Yeah,' the ranger added. 'Good of you to stop. What brings you up this way anyway? Lost a few beasts or something?'

'Showing the boy around.'

'Ah. Good. Nice-looking piece of land it is, too. Bit dry, of course.'

'It's the times.'

The ranger tipped his cap, and the two men turned away.

'Let's go,' William's uncle said coldly.

They went back to the utility and climbed in. William remained silent while his uncle started up and drove along the fence for a while. The track curved away from the creek finally, and began to climb another hill. Halfway up the old man slowed the vehicle, then turned it around, the wheels jolting on the rough ground. He switched the engine off. William stared about curiously.

'Why have we stopped?'

'Shut up for a minute.'

His uncle was gazing intently through the windscreen. Abashed, William looked too. They were facing back towards the creek. Far off through the trees, William could see the red splash of the tent, and the men moving about it. His uncle was watching them, his hands gripped tight on the steering wheel. William's head was full of questions, but obviously his uncle wasn't in the mood to answer them, so he waited. Eventually the tent was taken down. The ranger went to the creek and dipped something into the water. Was he filling a water bottle? Then the two men set off eastwards. They were visible for a while, as they began to climb upwards, but after a few minutes they were lost in the trees.

William's uncle seemed to relax slightly. Without comment, he started the utility, turned it round once more and continued up the rise. They crested the hill and came down the other side. William saw the creek again. It was flowing west now, having left the national park behind. The banks were fringed with long brown grass and overhanging trees. The track took them down to the waterway, and they drove alongside it for maybe half a mile. Then they came to a flat shelf of sandstone, where the land fell away. A stone bench sat there, looking as old as the rock itself, shaded by the long leaves of a willow tree.

'End of the line,' his uncle said. 'We'll have lunch.'

As the old man unloaded the sandwiches and drinks, William ventured onto the stone shelf. The creek came winding down from his left, its bed rocky between the low banks, the water the merest trickle. On reaching the shelf it spread into a small pool that was maybe a foot deep, before spilling through a worn lip in the stone. William stared over the lip in amazement. For the water fell in a sudden drop, a dozen feet perhaps, into a miracle. Nestled in the dry hillside, hidden by trees and high rocky banks, was a water hole. It was long and wide and, judging by the darkness of the water, deep. The stone bench had been set right on the brink of the shelf, and William crouched there, gazing down. Around the edges of the pool he could see rocks that lay just below the surface, and the ghostly limbs of trees that had fallen in from above. At the far end he could tell that the pool became shallow again, before ebbing over another lip of stone, and winding away along the creek bed once more. But in the middle, and directly below him where the water dripped over the shelf, the depths were pitch black and the bottom was invisible.

His uncle was standing beside him, staring down at the pool, some unreadable emotion in his eyes. William looked up at him in questioning confusion.

'Well,' the old man said, 'you wanted somewhere to swim.'

Chapter Twelve

DANIEL MCIVOR DIED DURING JOHN'S SECOND YEAR IN THE mountains. The message came up to the logging camp via a human telegraph line of bullock drivers and timber-getters, and it told John that the burial would be delayed until his return to Powell. He put up his axe, walked down out of the mountains, and caught a ride into town. He found that his mother and sister had been evicted from the hotel and were staying with cousins from his mother's side. His father — officially bankrupt — had seen out his last weeks in a ward at the Powell General Hospital, dying from a disease of the liver. The only thing he'd left to his son was a chest of personal belongings. John glanced through it once, puzzled over some of the contents, then shut it up and stored it away in a warehouse.

The funeral was small, just the immediate family and a few of the old workers from Kuran Station. There was no representative from the White family, nor any message of condolence. John had no doubt that if his father had died only a few years earlier he would have been buried with honour in the Kuran graveyard, alongside the Whites' grandiose tombs. Instead, he had a mean plot in the Powell cemetery. Watching the coffin sink, John wondered what it was he should be feeling. Grief? It wasn't there. His father had failed completely, and his last years had only displayed the shame of it in public. Better that he was dead. As for John's mother and sister, when he said goodbye after the funeral, he had no expectation of ever seeing them again.

He hitched a ride back to the mountains. If he belonged anywhere now, if there was such a thing as a home in his exile, it was in the Hoops, high in the logging camps with his fellow timber-getters. There amidst the forest they laboured from dawn to dusk, chopping and sawing, their tents set up in clearings stamped out of the undergrowth. And despite the annoyances of ticks and leeches and damp, it was a strangely satisfying life, following its own patterns and laws. The loggers were quiet men, for the most part, like John himself. They could even be called lonely, but there was nothing small or defeated about them. They measured themselves against the giant trees every day. Not even the drovers or shearers of Kuran Station had impressed John so much, and within his own small gang he felt an irresistible sense of acceptance. There was no hint of the boy about him any longer, he was full grown and strong, an equal amongst independent men.

His closest friend through the following years was a fellow logger named Dudley Green. They were the same age, but whereas John was tall and dark and silent, Dudley was short, sandy-haired and smiling. He was the second son of a wheat farmer — one of those very farmers who had taken up a claim on the old Kuran land. But Dudley had no interest in wheat and so had set out to make his own way. He and John formed a team, alternating axe blows or working at either end of the huge saws. At first, John found his partner's quick tongue and innate cheerfulness almost grating. But in time he saw what lay beneath — a hardy spirit bent on confronting a grim world, and no less determined about it than John himself. Dudley talked more than John, and drank more and swore more and fought more, but each of them recognised the same resilient quality in the other, and admired it.

It was something new for John. He'd never had a close friend before, never shared the pains of his life with anyone. He even found himself telling Dudley about his youth on Kuran Station — about what had been promised, and what had been taken away. And Dudley listened, shaking his head with a ready sympathy, but also with an indifference that spoke more than commiserations. After all, what needed to be said? Everyone had been through difficult times with the depression — why should John be any different? At least he was making his own honest living now, wasn't he? So what more acknowledgment did the great tragedy need than a rueful shrug? In response, John felt an awakening breeze blow through him. His friend was right. The events of his childhood, the grand betrayal ... how trivial it all sounded when told aloud over a campfire.

For a time he lifted his gaze from himself, and regarded the world afresh. It was then that the mountains began to captivate him. Despite years of logging, much of the area was still relatively pristine, especially where the national park had been declared, and it was a place utterly unlike the plains of his youth. Down there it was a flat and featureless world, a great empty space beneath a wide sky. In the mountains the sky was something that was only glimpsed through treetops, or observed as a narrow shard of blue between the hills. There was no horizon. Clouds loomed without warning at any time, sweeping up from below in misty reverse avalanches, or swooping above the mountain tops, their dark bellies pregnant with rain. It was a world of smells. Pine and eucalyptus. Damp earth, rotting leaves, campfire smoke. It was a world of colour too, the deep glistening green of ferns and creepers in the rain forests, dappled with sunlight, the dusty khaki of the bush on the lower slopes, the startling red of a parrot, the raw crimson of split and bleeding wood, the fine white shimmer of a waterfall.

And more than anything else it was a world of noises. The roar of wind as it swept over the hills and set the trees thrumming. The piping of birds, crystal in the high air. The bubble of streams, and the distant rush of water plunging into chasms. The thumps of wallabies as they leapt through the undergrowth, and the scrabble of bush turkeys, clustering around camp sites. And echoes. There had been no echoes out on the plains. But the mountains rang with them, and sounds seemed to travel fantastic distances. The forests reverberated with distant axes at work, the steady clock of steel striking wood or the hungry rasp of saws. Bullocks snuffed and groaned as they laboured in hidden gullies, their drivers' shouts rising, punctuated by cracks of whips. Trucks whined on the lower mountain tracks. And every once in a while there would come the deep, rumbling rush and crackle that signified the felling of yet another tree, and for a moment the entire range would stand still, hushed, as the echoes rolled back and forth. John would never find another place where sound would seem so three dimensional, so crisp, and so suggestive.

It was a world of secrets, too. On the plains, everything could be seen and only the very curve of the earth could hide you. In the mountains, the land turned in on itself, concealing, and yet revealing something new with almost every step. New vistas, new perspectives. Dark gullies where the sun never shone. Sheer cliffs that dropped away without warning right beneath your feet. Granite boulders that lay piled in creek beds as if torrents had once gushed there. Caves that had been scooped out of bluffs by the wind and rain. Giant strangler fig trees that had trunks hollowed out like spreading tents. Dead tree stumps full of water, alive with swimming creatures. Bizarrely shaped fungi, feeding off the rotting limbs of fallen trees. Spreading fogs that blanketed the hills for days, and sent creeping tendrils under the forest canopy.

The strange warmth of the rain forest even in deepest winter. The sheer amazement of snow on the exposed peaks, as alien and impossible as it was fleeting, melting within hours.

The beauty of it all washed cold and cleansing through John, but it was the deeper mysteries of the mountains that called most strongly to him, and awakened some dormant part of his soul. There were the balds, for one thing, here and there on the hilltops, soft grassy pates, often littered with granite boulders and stones. They offered the only unobstructed views of the plains far below, and later, lookouts would be built there for tourists, but for the first wanderers in the mountains, they were strange, windswept, inexplicable places. Were they made by Aborigines in some earlier time? The old timers said they weren't, but John, circling the clearings and probing the soil with his feet, was not so sure. Maybe they weren't man-made, but something about them spoke to man all the same.

Then there were the bunya pines. They were tall, straight trees that opened to a conical dome, often rising far above the rest of the forest canopy. For the loggers they promised many thousands of feet of timber, but for the Aborigines, in earlier times, they had promised food, because they bore large, smooth cones that made a superlative meal. These 'nuts' ripened every three years, when Aboriginal tribes from far and wide would converge on the mountains to gorge themselves in a great festival. The loggers did the same, roasting the cones and feasting on the almost over-rich, buttery kernels. And whenever they came across one of the old leviathan pines, they would see, running up its trunk to where the cones grew, a ladder of footholds, seemingly cut out by a stone axe, perhaps as much as two centuries earlier. All across the mountains there was no other clear sign that people had been there before white men — no dwellings or middens or cave drawings. There were only these notches hewn in the tree trunks, slowly disappearing.

It wasn't that John cared about the Aborigines themselves.

They were gone and wouldn't be coming back. But he walked the hills and pondered all he saw, the bunya pines, and the grassy hilltops, and it seemed to him that there was something about these places that those earliest inhabitants must surely have recognised in their turn. Maybe they had not made the clearings; but sensing the atmosphere of those places, had they positioned the stones? Likewise, there were caves, and certain rock outcrops and waterfalls that spoke to John of a long human presence. Of being important to that human presence. He could not define it, but it was there. He talked with men who had lived all their lives in the Hoops. They claimed to remember the last tribes who had roamed the hills, and even to have seen the last of the bunya nut festivals. But according to these old men, the blacks had never lived in the mountains — supposedly they'd believed the upper hills to be haunted by spirits. So they had climbed the range solely in the daytime, to harvest the pine cones, and then had withdrawn to the lower slopes to hold their festivals by night.

John heard the same history wherever he asked, but it left him dissatisfied. The truth was, up until this time, he had regarded land purely as an inanimate thing. As a boy, riding the plains with his father, he had seen all that sweeping expanse of grass and thought almost exclusively in terms of sheep and weights of wool. He had come to mountains in the same frame of mind — he was a timber-cutter, and the Hoops were a source of trees, nothing else. But the more time John spent in the hills, the more he seemed to perceive the land around him as something powerful in its own right — to hear a voice in it, meant specifically for human ears. And yet the sensation would slip away again, just as soon as he thought he had grasped it. He wondered, eventually, if this was because, even after several years, he was still a stranger to the mountains. He had not grown up there, nor had anyone in his family. Maybe it took a lifetime to get a piece of country into your bones; and maybe other lifetimes as well, your father's and grandfather's.

Nevertheless, John was happier in the mountains than he had ever been. And yet, both he and Dudley were acutely aware that the logging industry in the Hoops was winding down. Its heyday had been two generations earlier. The remains of that busier time were everywhere, huts and mills and chutes, all sinking into ruin. Now there was perhaps a decade or two of logging left, increasingly limited in scale. The future lay in the cattle that grazed the lower slopes. John and Dudley discussed these things at night, waiting for sleep, when a velvet blackness enfolded the rain forest, and moths and other insects swarmed around their campfires. Perhaps, when they'd saved up enough, they could buy a property in the foothills. Beef cattle, or maybe dairy. And one day, not too far ahead surely, when the roads were better, tourists would be flocking to the national park. There would be other opportunities then. Guest houses. Camping grounds. Guided walks. And who knew the mountains better than they did themselves?

They were fine nights of talking and dreams. Strangely, John seldom thought about Kuran Station any more. Occasionally, he would find himself on some high point, gazing westwards at the wide world of the plains. Where once there would have been an unbroken sea of tall, swaying grass, John now saw a patchwork of cultivation and roads. Even as he watched he knew invisibly small men and horses and tractors were at work down there, and the last remnants of virgin pasture were disappearing under the plough. He was surprised at how little he cared. He would look northwards then, to the long spur that ran out into the plains, and he would remember Kuran House, and the hills he had explored in his childhood; and he would remember too the vow he had made to regain it all one day. But had that vow actually meant anything? After all, could a grown man remain bound forever by his youth? Then he would breathe in the fresh forest air, and think of a future where he stayed in the mountains for the rest of his days, building his own life, not seeking vainly for one that was gone.

Chapter Thirteen

'DON'T FALL IN,' THE OLD MAN WARNED.

William was clambering along the rocky shelf above the water hole. Small flakes of stone disturbed by his progress slipped over the edge and dropped into the pool with low plunks. The tone of the warning was serious, and William glanced back over his shoulder. His uncle had seated himself on the bench beneath the willow tree, the sandwiches unopened at his side

'It's deep. And cold in winter. Too cold for swimming.'

'How deep?'

'No one knows. Maybe it's bottomless.'

William's eyes narrowed. 'Really?'

'I used to swim here as a boy. And *I* never touched the bottom. Oh, most of it is shallow enough. But the deepest part is right under the waterfall, and when you dive down there it's very dark and very cold. There's an overhang and a sort of cave that goes back and downwards. Deep down, into a hole. But it's freezing in there and your lungs shrivel up…'

William stared down. Most of the pool reflected the sky, but under the overhanging shelf a blackness waited.

'There's always water here,' his uncle continued. 'No matter whether it rains or not. In a long drought the creek will stop flowing and most of the pool will drain away, but it never goes completely dry. There's a spring, down in the cave. The water oozes up from the rocks. I suppose it comes from under the mountains somewhere. Maybe that's why it's so cold.'

William left off his exploring, came back along the shelf. 'Isn't this what those men were looking for?' he asked.

His uncle gave a measured nod.

'But why didn't you tell them?'

'What do you think would happen if I did?'

William shrugged. 'They'd come and look at it.'

'Yes. But they wouldn't be the last. And that's the thing. Right now, apart from you and me, hardly anyone knows about this place. Of course in the old days the station staff used to come up here for picnics. That's when this bench was put in. But that was long ago, and those people are dead and gone. It's a secret now, this place.'

William gazed over the water hole. A secret.

The old man began to unwrap the sandwiches. 'It's better that way. Places like this need to be protected. I don't even let the cattle into this part of the property. But if I told those men this was here, that student fellow would write about it. Then lots of people would know. They'd want to come and look. Others would want to come in the summer to swim. Some of them wouldn't even bother to ask, they'd just sneak onto the property.'

William tried to remember what the two men had said. Wasn't there an important reason they wanted to find the water hole?

'It could get even worse,' his uncle said. 'The shire council or the government or someone else might try and take the water hole away from us. That student might say it's too important to leave in private hands. That's the problem with people like him. They stick their noses into everyone's business. Maybe the council would want to add this bit of land to the national park. Then there'd be picnic tables and rubbish everywhere.'

William was staring at the pool. It was so still, and with the high banks and the overlooking trees, it looked so hidden that it might never have been visited before.

'I won't tell anyone,' he said.

'Not even your mother?'

William hadn't thought of that. 'I can't tell her?'

'We'll see. Maybe we'll bring her up here one day. But until then, it might be better to keep quiet. Things like this ... it's a man's business.'

William selected a sandwich and both of them ate in silence for a time.

His uncle spoke finally. 'You know, this water hole — it's the source of the biggest river in Australia.'

'Is it?'

'Well, in a way. You take the creek. It starts behind us, up in the mountains. But it doesn't always flow. This is the first permanent water source, right here, so this is really the beginning.' He nodded towards the far end of the pool, where the water eased over the lip in the rock and wound away. 'From here the creek flows along the spur, and then out west across the plains. Eventually it joins up with the Condamine River. You've seen the Condamine, haven't you?'

William nodded dubiously. It was only a shallow, sandy watercourse, the Condamine. Surely that wasn't the biggest river in the country.

His uncle smiled. 'I know. The Condamine isn't so big. But it flows down into New South Wales and eventually it becomes one of the headwaters of the Darling River. Now the Darling is something. It's narrow and muddy, but it's very long. It flows all the way through western New South Wales. Hundreds of miles. Through desert, for a lot of it. Darling River, Darling Downs — they're named after the same person, of course.'

The old man mused for a moment, chewing on another bite from his sandwich.

'There used to be steamboats on the Darling, when there was enough water. You could travel by boat from the ocean right up into the middle of Australia. That's how they used to get the wool out from the big stations, before trains and trucks came along. Sometimes the Darling would flood and spread out across the plains, fifteen or twenty miles wide. Those little steamboats would get lost and then, when the floods passed, they'd find themselves stuck in the bush, ten miles from the river.'

He wiped crumbs from his mouth.

'Anyway, the Darling flows into the Murray, way down south, on the border with Victoria. The Murray, well, it's already big. It starts up in the Snowy Mountains. In fact, between them, the Murray and the Darling drain just about the whole of inland eastern Australia. And after they join up they run on together westwards, all the way into South Australia. This is thousands of miles away by now. Until finally the river reaches the sea. Way down near Adelaide. The other end of the country. Of course, the Murray is nothing like the Amazon or the Mississippi or the Nile. Those rivers are even longer, and have ten times the water in them. A hundred times. But that's Australia for you. It's big ... but it's *thin* too. Million and millions of acres of land, but most of the soil is just dust, there's not enough rain, the rivers haven't got any water, and the mountains are so old they've worn away to nothing.'

The old man stretched a hand out over the water hole.

'Okay, maybe this isn't the real source of the Condamine. That's down near Warwick. But the Condamine flows up here in a big loop before it heads south, and this creek is the northern-most tributary on that loop. So you and me, we're sitting right at the very top of the entire Murray–Darling system. Those rivers, they keep Australia alive. All that vitality and wealth — the wellspring for it is right here, in this little pool.'

William was gazing along the creek bed, a rutted channel amidst the trees. He tried to picture it winding away to meet great rivers and deserts and snowcapped mountains and southern oceans, but imagination failed him.

'That's the sort of thing you have to know about a piece of land, Will, if you're going to own it. You have to know where it fits in. You don't just buy a few square miles and put up a fence and say, This is it. Every stretch of earth has its story. You have to listen, and understand how it connects with other stories. Stories that involve the whole country in the end.'

William looked up and found the old man's eyes on his.

'I asked you before what stories you could tell me about your old farm. Wasn't there anything you learnt from your father?'

From his father? William thought of laughter over the dinner table, or the two of them tinkering about in the shed, or walking through the wheat, looking for wild oats and turnips and other weeds. But his uncle wanted something big and broad, and William's father had never told him anything like that. There hadn't been enough time, before he was gone.

'It's not you I blame,' his uncle said. 'Your father was the problem.'

William lowered his head, felt resentment stir within him, like a cloud passing above.

'Do you know exactly how you and I are related?' the old man asked.

'I know you're not really my uncle.'

'Right. I'm your great-uncle. I had a little sister, you see. She grew up in Powell and got married and had a son — your father. I only met him once, at my sister's funeral. He was a mail clerk for the town council then, and had just married your mother. Didn't

have two cents to rub together, poor fool. I'd no idea he wanted
to be a farmer. But then who he was, what he did, that was no
concern of mine.' The old man's indifference was chilling. 'I'm
sure he was a good enough person. But the fact is, he had no
feeling for the country. He certainly didn't know much about
growing wheat. If he had talked to me first, I would have told him
never to buy that property.'

'Why not?'

'That land was never any good, that's why. It's a bad patch.
There's a few of them out there. Back when it was all sheep
country, you saw pretty quick that although the plains look like
they're dead flat, that isn't the case at all. When it floods, for
instance, the water doesn't just sit there. It flows, east to west. And
it's not just one big flat sheet of water. It flows in channels —
some bits of land stay dry, others go a foot under water. The smart
farmers, they get their land professionally surveyed and then
arrange their paddocks into contour banks. Your father didn't do
that, neither did anyone who owned the place before him. So that
farm had lost a lot of its best soil to erosion. But that wasn't the
big problem. The big problem was that there wasn't much good
soil there in the first place.'

William looked up, disbelieving. Not much soil? That was
ridiculous.

His uncle held up a hand. 'I know: how can you run out of
soil when it's sixty feet deep? But it's not the same everywhere.
There are shallower, sandy places. I don't know where they came
from, but when it was all pasture you could see the bad patches
plain as day. Big yellow stretches that died off first in the summer.
The sheep wouldn't go there. And no farmer should have either.'

'Our farm was one those places?'

The old man nodded. 'When they divided all that land,
they didn't bother about which bits were good and which bits
weren't. The Lands Department just cut it up into squares and

sold it off, no questions asked. Most of the farms were fine, but a few, like your father's ... Family after family just went bust on them.'

'Then why did Dad buy it?'

'That's what I'm trying to tell you. He didn't know what he was doing. He wasn't a farmer. But for some reason he wanted to be one. So he buried himself in debt to raise the money, then went looking for a property. The banks are to blame too, of course. They'd lend money to any idiot, back then.'

'But if our farm was no good...'

'Your father couldn't see that. It was a bumper year when he went looking. Perfect rain, perfect weather. The wheat was two tons to the acre. And so he finds this piece of land that's for sale, smack in the middle of the Kuran Plains, the best grain-growing region in the state, and it looks wonderful, he can't believe the owner wants to sell so cheap ... You see what I mean?'

William thought of his father's gentle, smiling face, and the way he had been so happy with his little property, and so baffled at its failure.

'Why didn't someone tell him?'

'Who? The fellow who was selling? The banks? Why would they?'

William felt his face growing hot with shame.

'Why didn't *you* tell him?'

'By the time I heard about it, it was all signed and sealed. They were doomed on that farm, your parents, fire or no fire. Some people are just doomed, period. Your dad without a clue, and your mother ... well, you know your own mother.'

William could hear the unspoken thoughts behind his uncle's words. But nothing was ever supposed to be said about his mother's condition. Not out loud.

'The thing is, people like your parents, sometimes they hunger for a piece of land, because they've never had anything of their own before, and they think a few hundred acres will make all the difference. But nine times out of ten it's a disaster.'

The shame in William finally turned to anger. How could his uncle talk this way? 'Is your farm making money?' he demanded, seeking to wound back.

The old man laughed. 'It makes money, boy. *I* know what I'm doing.'

'Then why don't you fix up the House?'

Something flashed in his uncle's eyes. 'That House would just be rubble by now if it wasn't for me!' Then it faded, and he sighed. 'But you're talking about millions of dollars there, to fix it up properly. Once, maybe, I could have done it. I certainly planned to.' The old man dwelt on some regretful memory, then waved it away. 'I could have been rich years ago, if that was what I wanted. I *was* rich. But buying this place was never about money.'

'What was it about then?'

His uncle spread his arms to the surrounding hills. 'It was about everything I've been saying to you. About knowing where you belong and taking responsibility for that place. This is where I belong. It's where I was raised. I was taught all about it by my father, and he spent most of his life here too. But you now...' He paused to regard William again. 'You don't know anything because your father didn't know anything in his turn. But the important thing is you're still young. You can still learn, if there's someone to teach you.'

It was that searching, testing look that William had felt before. But there was something expectant in it too, something hopeful.

'I'm old, Will. I have no family, no children to raise. What will happen to all this when I'm gone? What will happen to the House, to the property, to this water hole here? Lately I've been wondering. Then I see a fire out on the plains and discover I've got a great-nephew. A boy with McIvor blood in his veins. A boy who might have what this place needs.'

Again, William felt that his uncle could see right through to the centre of him, probing his heart for some vital quality. And although William had no idea what it was, or if it was there inside him, he finally grasped what his uncle was offering, if it could be found.

'Do you understand me, Will? Do you understand what I'm looking for?'

'I think so,' he said.

'You think so?' The old man's gaze held a moment longer, and then wandered away, brooding and dissatisfied. 'You think so...'

The moment was over. The day seemed to have grown colder. A wind stirred in the trees and ruffled the surface of the pool, and leaves spiralled down to land on the black water.

His uncle glanced up. 'Not a cloud in sight,' he said, resigned. 'This is as much water as we'll see in the pool this year. Come summer, it'll be barely half the size.' He shook his head. 'It's time we headed home.'

They packed up and walked back to the utility. William gazed about at the surrounding hills. It was the same country, the grass and scrub and leaning fences, but it was as if a whole new colour had swept across the property. For the first time in his life, William drank in the sight of a land that one day, somehow, unbelievably, might be his own.

'I'll be away for the next week or two,' the old man said. 'On business. You want to know where my money goes? On more important things than fixing up the House, that's where. But think about what I've said. And when I get back, if you're ready, I'll show you what my real work is all about.'

Chapter Fourteen

By that night, despite all the revelations of the day, William's mood had darkened strangely. He found that he was thinking about his father. Cold thoughts, and cruel. In just one afternoon, his uncle had shown him so much. But in all the years of William's childhood, his own father had never told him anything about drifting continents, or about people who lived and died in earlier years, or about rivers that flowed away to far ends of the earth. His father should have known these things, but he hadn't. Worst of all, he had never sat William on his knee, pointed out across the wheat fields, and promised, *One day, son, all this will be yours.*

Like John McIvor just had.

Then there was his mother. William told her about his afternoon and about what he had seen, but he could tell she wasn't really interested in the station. Not the hills or the trees or the grass, or the men from the national park. (He made no mention of the water hole.) It was only when, hesitantly, he reported the final conversation with his uncle that attention lit in her eyes.

'Tell me exactly,' she commanded, 'what did he say?'

'He ... he said he didn't know what would happen to the station, after he died.'

'What else?'

'Nothing...' For what had seemed so certain when William had first heard it, didn't seem so certain when he came to retell it. And so instead of a statement, he found he only had a question to ask. 'What *is* going to happen?'

His mother chewed a ragged fingernail. They were sitting in the dimness of their living room, the little heater blowing warm air on their legs. She hadn't changed out of her bathrobe from the morning, and her hair was mussed and tangled from sleeping on the couch.

'I don't know,' she said tensely. 'Your uncle told me we can stay here until Christmas at least. So that he can get to know us. Get to know you. But after that ... It depends.'

'On what?'

'Remember how I told you to do what you're uncle asks?'

'I remember.'

'There's a reason for that. Because you're right. One day — maybe not so far away — your uncle is going to die. He's an old man. And he needs someone to leave all this to.' She searched hopefully in him, smiling as she finally said it out loud. 'It might be us. It might be you.'

It was true then. He hadn't misunderstood. The great prize really had been offered to him. William felt oddly disappointed. He realised that this was because his news was no surprise to his mother. Instead she might have been waiting for it, impatient even that it was so long in coming. Had she known all along? Was this the only reason that she had brought them to the House — to tender William to his uncle? And was that a bad thing anyway? Surely she only wanted what was best for them both. But he remembered the way his uncle had spoken of her. *People like that sometimes hunger for a piece of land.* It had made her sound hateful. And watching his mother now, seeing the eagerness in her, William felt an ugly sense of confirmation.

'You mean, if Uncle John likes me, we can stay?'

She nodded, reaching out to stroke his cheek. 'If it all works out, we can stay forever.' Her fingers felt hot against his skin. 'What do you think? Do you like it here?'

'I don't know.'

'It's important that you do, Will.'

Her hands lingered on him, and he fought the urge to pull away. A touch from her was a rare thing, but now the fervour was unsettling.

'Do *you* want to stay?' he asked.

'We've got nowhere else to go, sweetheart. Look, this has been hard for me too. We've got no money, I can't work, you know that. We'd never have another place of our own.'

William looked away, unseeing. He felt the future sway coldly in front of him, and a terrible weight of responsibility settle.

She wasn't finished. 'You can't be a little boy about this. I know you don't like the House, but that isn't the point. You think I like it either? But if your uncle left it to you, we could do what we liked. This property is worth a lot of money — we could sell it and move away to somewhere nice.' She was solicitous now, stroking his hair. 'It all depends on you, honey. Your uncle doesn't care about me. It's you he's interested in. Do you see?'

He nodded.

'You'll have to grow up fast. You have to do this for me.'

'I will.'

But he was relieved when her hand finally dropped away.

His uncle left the next day, driving off in the utility. William had no idea where he was going — but at least some things were clear now.

The way his uncle had appeared from nowhere after the fire, the hushed conversations with William's mother, the doctor's visit, the summons to watch the shooting stars. It was all for the one reason — the old man was alone in the world and needed someone to follow after him. And yet, again, William felt a suspicion that it wasn't that simple at all. His uncle had used the word *might*, so the station was not a gift that would be simply handed over. It was something that William had yet to earn, and he had until Christmas, it seemed, to do so. And if he failed ... What then? The more William thought about it, the more overwhelming it seemed. His mother had made it clear that it was all up to him — but it wasn't his fault that his father had died and that they had nowhere else to go. Those were adult problems. And it was one thing to promise to stop being a child. How did you actually do it?

For the next few days William loitered about the House, gnawed by inadequacy. It didn't help that he found himself under the watchful eyes of Mrs Griffith. Now that his uncle was gone, the housekeeper patrolled the hallways with a special vigilance, wrapped in her cardigans. There was nobody to contest her authority, it was *her* House again, just as it must have been years ago when the place was abandoned and only she remained, a forgotten caretaker — before William's uncle arrived and stole it from her. And if she resented the old man's presence, then what would she think of his nephew, a mere boy, becoming her lord and master? No ... William could read it in her frowns and cold hostility. She wanted him to go away. She wanted his uncle to go away too, or to die. Even then, the House would never really be hers. But she would be alone once more.

Dinners were the worst times, when William and his mother confronted the old woman over the grimy tablecloth. The meals were eaten in heavy silence as always, but William could feel undercurrents in it now, the swirl of hidden motives and threats. And one night finally, he had to face Mrs Griffith alone. His mother was suffering one of her headaches and had no appetite. William wasn't hungry either, but his mother, stretched upon the couch with a wet towel across her brow, waved away his objections. So he crept through the darkness and came to the table, where the housekeeper waited.

'Mum's sick,' he told her.

The old woman glared briefly at the third plate, where pale slices of roast beef waited with mashed potato and vegetables. 'And what about you?'

William sat down at his place, aware more acutely than ever of her gaze on him. They ate without speaking for a time. But for once Mrs Griffith could not keep silent.

'Your mother's often *sick*, isn't she?'

William stared at his food.

'Sickly, the both of you. What is it you're supposed to have?'

'Glandular fever.'

'Ha!' She worked at the meat with her knife and fork. 'Don't think I don't know about it. Or about those pills Dr Moffat gave your mother. I know what they're for.'

William tasted cold potato like ash in his mouth.

'She was always that way, even as a girl.'

He glanced up in surprise, caught the malice in the old woman's smile.

'Oh yes. I knew your mother's family. Everyone in Powell knew them. White trash, down there in the caravan park. Not that I ever met your grandfather. A drinker, they said. And worse besides. The police knew him plenty, I'll tell you that.' Mrs Griffith was relishing some private memory. 'And Veronica — she was a dirty little thing. Thin as a scarecrow. Hungry, I suppose. Took after her father too. How she wanted those pretty dresses in the shops. No wonder there was trouble. Stealing! But anyone could tell there was something not right about her, even back then. She was always a little touched, a little...'

The housekeeper searched for a word, and William was staring at his plate again, frozen. *Crazy*, she was going to say that his mother was *crazy*.

The old woman shrugged. 'God knows how she made a catch of your father. He could have done better. Either way, her type never changes. Now she's gone and found another man, hasn't she, with a big House, up on a hill.'

It was enough. William shoved back his plate.

'You haven't finished, boy.'

'I'm not hungry.'

'All right. Go on then.' But as William rose, she grabbed his arm and held him. 'It'll never happen, you know. You'll make a mistake. And your uncle will see what sort of child you are, and what sort of family you come from.'

William wrenched his arm free and fled outside, into the night.

Lies, it was all lies. The appalling old monster, she was trying to hurt him, that was all, to scare him away. He looked up to the sky, where the stars blazed, the air freezing on the red flush of his face. His anger cooled, and was replaced by a piercing loneliness. Lies or not, it didn't matter. Nothing was the same any more. His uncle's tantalising promise ... everything had become twisted by it. The memories of his father, the actions of his mother, and now the housekeeper's hatred unveiled. And there were months yet of the old man's probing and testing to come. Mrs Griffith might be right, he might make too many mistakes, his uncle might decide he was unworthy after all. It was too much. It was unfair. He was only a boy.

Grow up, he heard again.

William turned to the House. It loomed grey beneath the stars. He stared up at the ivy-covered walls and the sagging line of the roof and the two great wings reaching out. He studied the deep archways of the doors, the wide sweep of the verandahs, the shadows of the windows on the second storey. And there in the darkness, amidst his fears and shame, it seemed that something did change and grow older inside him. His doubts faded away, and he felt an odd sensation of expansion. It was the House, calling to him. And the House didn't lie. It was solid stone, it was permanent and unchanging. It had the sort of strength that he could never possess...

Except that he could.

The realisation shook him. He thought of the dark hallways within, and suddenly it was as if he could see through them, to panels of polished wood. He thought of chandeliers sparkling from the ceilings. He thought of flames raging in great fireplaces. And dwelling on these visions, he could see an image of himself as an adult, a man, moving through those golden hallways. Tall and assured and invulnerable. Alone in the House. His own House.

The sense of expansion widened, thrilling in a deep, physical way, as if ownership was something that enlarged the veins and enriched the blood. For there was not only the House, there was Kuran Station as well, a sleeping giant of a thing, native and alive and half wild. His mother had said they could sell the property if they wanted. But she hadn't even seen it. William had. He had felt the reality of it, earth and rock swelling beneath his feet, he had smelled it, and listened to the silence of it. If it was his, he would be able to walk the hills just as his uncle did, knowing them, having learnt all the stories and secrets that there were to learn, a master of wisdom inaccessible to anyone else. The power of that! The certainty of that!

William suddenly felt a need to shout or laugh or run. It didn't matter what the housekeeper said. It didn't matter about his mother. It didn't matter that everything depended on him alone. For in that moment, he made up his mind. He *did* want the station. And whatever it took, he would show his uncle he was worthy.

Chapter Fifteen

AT THE AGE OF TWENTY-FOUR, JOHN MCIVOR HAD KNOWN FEW
women. Indeed, there had been only one romantic interest in his
life so far, and she had remained a stranger to him, right up until
the day she banished John and his father from her presence. Was
he still in love with Elizabeth White? All John knew was that no
woman he'd met since was comparable to her. They were either
too frivolous or too coarse, their conversation bored him or their
broad accents grated in his ear. They had, to sum it up, no stature.
They stirred nothing inside him to match the memory, so
repressed he was barely aware of it, of a girl curled in a cane chair,
white curtains billowing gently behind her.

Harriet Fisher changed all that.

She was the daughter of Oliver Fisher, who was the owner of
the sawmill for which John and Dudley and the rest of their gang
cut timber. Oliver was a self-made man of some wealth, fifty-five
years old and with the stocky frame of a labourer who had served
his own time felling trees in the forests. Now he lived in an

impressive residence halfway between the Hoops and Powell, on the main road. It was Oliver who had plucked John from unemployment back in 1933. However, he had never introduced any of his workers to his daughter. In honour of his wife, who had died some years before, he had raised Harriet for finer company than timber-getters.

Luck cast them all together in early 1938. One mid-summer afternoon, John and Dudley were on their way into Powell, bearded and ragged after a long stint up in the mountains. As they tramped along the road, greenish-grey thunderheads were building in the west. The two friends watched the storm's approach in weary resignation, but as the first warning breezes stirred the dust, they spied the Fisher house ahead of them. They would not normally have thought to intrude, but now they sprinted the last few hundred yards. By the time they knocked on the front door, the wind was rising, the sky was black and the first drops of water were smacking the ground. Oliver, recognising them as two of his own, welcomed them in. From the back verandah they watched as rain and hail hammered down, and the surrounding paddocks turned into white lakes. The Powell road, still mostly unsealed, would be an impassable quagmire until the next day at least. Oliver, in a fit of generosity, declared that his two loggers should stay for dinner, and then the night.

The men washed and shaved and emerged transformed, drying off in the kitchen while the Fishers' elderly cook prepared the meal. Edging awkwardly into the dining room, they found Harriet and her younger brother waiting. Matthew was fifteen, a solid, youthful version of his father; John and Dudley had already caught sight of him about the sawmill. But Harriet, just turned nineteen, and matron of her father's house, was an entirely pleasant surprise. Indeed, it had been so long since John and Dudley had sat in a well-appointed dining room, with fine china and crystal glasses on the table, that the evening seemed almost magical. Oliver was a genial host, the wine settled deliciously in his guests' veins, and, more than anything else, there was the pleasure of female company. Harriet was nothing like her brick of a father. She had been born into wealth, polished at respectable schools, and had inherited a slender shape and natural style from her dead mother. Yet for all her education and grace, there was nothing aloof about Harriet — she was perfectly at ease entertaining two of her father's workers for an evening. Her conversation was bright and bantering, and even John, with his innate reserve, found himself caught up in the good cheer.

So the party carried on far into the night. When it finally broke up, Oliver, actually quite drunk, announced that the two men must feel free to visit the house whenever they might happen to be passing. Thus the courtship of Harriet began. Of course, neither John nor Dudley, in those early days, considered himself a serious proposition for Harriet. Nor did Oliver Fisher. He liked the two men well enough, but he also knew how little they earned (who knew better?) and two timber-getters of slim means, without a home to call their own, were hardly the most eligible of suitors for his daughter. Still, he made no serious objection to their visits, not even when they started escorting Harriet to the occasional movie, or to picnics, or to the local dances. He even let · John and Dudley borrow his car to drive Harriet around. Perhaps he looked on the two men as older brothers to his daughter, a rough and ready influence, but a benign one. It would have been a different story if either man had tried to date her alone, but as it was, there was always the one to chaperone the other.

To John, Dudley and Harriet, however, it gradually became clear that they were more than just big brothers and sister. For the two loggers, time away from the mountains became increasingly focused around the Fisher house, while for Harriet, the days spent with her boys from the hills became the most precious of her engagements. Did they seem more vital and alive than anyone else she knew? They had nothing in the world but themselves, but did that make them freer, more fiercely individual? Whatever moved her, she played no favourite between them. Dudley was the laughing one, the better talker, and the better dancer. Harriet responded in kind, but there was more to her than conviviality. Perhaps the early death of her mother had matured her, for there was a side to her that appreciated the gravity in John, and which shared, in part, his wariness of the world.

After a year it became accepted between the three of them that Harriet would choose one or the other eventually. Her father remained blissfully unaware of this development, but she no longer even pretended to be interested in other men. It was with Harriet in mind, then, that John and Dudley began to seriously assess their futures. They had saved alarmingly little from their time in the mountains. In truth, the work was intermittent. There were often long periods when there was no demand for timber, and the gangs had to wait idly in their camps until new orders came in, surviving as best they could. It might be years before either of them would have any real financial security. They arrived at an agreement, therefore, that neither would press his suit until happier and richer days. It seemed that Harriet tacitly acquiesced. And maybe it was better that way, for it delayed a painful choice.

Not that John had any doubts about whom Harriet preferred. Admittedly, he was rarely alone with her, but he was convinced that in those moments he could detect an emotion from Harriet that was meant uniquely for him. It was as simple as an intensity in her eyes as she probed at his long silences. Dudley, all on the surface, she seemed to understand effortlessly, but John could see that in comparison he himself remained a mystery. She was intrigued — and that was a heady thing to sense from a woman. Especially one so smooth and elegant, and now amazingly within his reach. But what would happen when she actually made her choice known — how Dudley would react when he lost — that was something John couldn't bring himself to contemplate.

Fate took it all out of their hands, in the shape of a falling tree. It was the spring of 1939, and John, Dudley and the rest of their gang were at work high in the mountains. They were sawing through the trunk of a hoop pine, deep within a rain forest gully. John was standing by, well out of the line of fall, but when the tree began to topple, its upper limbs became caught in the canopy, and the trunk revolved perversely on its own base. Men scattered as the tree lurched this way and that, but when the whole thing came down, it was John who failed to get clear. He received a glancing blow to his left leg. It shattered his knee and snapped his shin in a compound fracture.

His work mates quickly rigged up a stretcher and got him down the mountain, from where, via an agonising ride on a sawmill truck, they took him to the hospital in Powell. Infection set in, and for a week John hung in a delirium of pain, fever and repeated surgery. When his head finally cleared, a doctor told him that they'd managed to save the leg, though he didn't think it would ever be much use again. On the brighter side, the doctor added, at least John didn't have to worry about joining the army now. The army? John didn't know what the man was talking about. Oh, the doctor replied, hadn't John heard? Australia was at war with Germany, and had been for four days.

When Dudley came to visit he was full of the news. John listened without much interest. He was in pain, and Europe was a long way away. So it was a complete shock when Dudley announced that he planned to enlist as soon as possible. He talked on about duty and the old country and the evils of Nazism, and went so far as to offer sympathy because John would be unable to join up too. But even through his disbelief John knew full well that, leg or no leg, he would never have enlisted anyway. His experiences at Kuran Station still bit deep. True, the Whites were no more English than John himself, but he had glimpsed the mother country behind their prejudices and arrogance. They stood for the Empire, the Whites, and they had rejected him. So the Empire's wars were no business of his.

They weren't Dudley's business either, and John told him so. How could he throw everything away just for the sake of rallying around the Union Jack? If Australia insisted on sending an army to Europe, well, there were hundreds of thousands of unemployed men who would welcome the food and the pay. They didn't need Dudley. Oliver Fisher agreed. The sawmill owner could see lucrative military contracts in the offing — it was no time to be losing his timber men. Why be rash, he told Dudley, why run off to war? Nothing was actually happening in Europe yet anyway. When Harriet echoed her father, Dudley relented. He turned his back on the recruiting stations and returned to the mountains.

Relieved, John began the long, painful process of learning to walk again. At the end of several months, the best he could do was shuffle along with the aid of a stick. The stick, hopefully, could be disposed of one day, but he would always limp, and when he was tired the knee was liable to give way entirely. Oliver gave him some part-time duties around the sawmill, but John was forced to acknowledge that he would never cut timber again. And things weren't really settled with Dudley. John and Harriet were aware of a restlessness in their friend as he pored over newspaper reports and listened to the radio. His ears were pricked for the sound of faraway gunfire.

When Germany finally invaded France, there was no holding Dudley back a second time. They resolved to send him off as best they could. Even as the evacuation of Dunkirk was being carried out on the other side of the world, Dudley's enlistment party was held at the Fisher house. John spent the night full of a cold foreboding. The war was assuming an ominous tone. It was obviously going to be long and bloody and world-altering, and however deluded Dudley might be, he was going to fight for his country and John wasn't. It would change things between the two of them forever. He'd seen it amongst older men who had lived through the Great War — the unbridgeable gulf between those who went and those who stayed. Whatever their individual stories, those left behind had ever after been judged the lesser men. And it would be the same this time around.

At the end of the night, John and Dudley and Harriet sat out on the back verandah. They knew it was the end of something. They were caught up in a bigger history now, vulnerable to its currents. *We'll all come back here,* Harriet insisted as they sat there, the night cool and dark about them. She clutched their hands, looking back and forth. *When it's all over, we'll meet up right here, and everything will be the same.* Her eyes searched into each of her two men, affirming and questioning at the same time. John and Dudley exchanged glances over her head, understanding fully what she meant. And afterwards, when Harriet had retired, it did not need to be spoken again. Everything was to be held in abeyance until after the war was over. It was the only thing to be done. They shook hands, more than six years of friendship and trust behind them, and then withdrew, each to his sleepless bed.

Chapter Sixteen

IT WAS TWO WEEKS BEFORE WILLIAM'S UNCLE RETURNED, AND when he did, he immediately set to work in his office and spoke to no one for three days. William hovered hopefully outside the door. He could hear the clatter of the typewriter, and again, the rhythmic thump of the other machine. It was all very frustrating, and it wasn't until the fourth day that he was invited inside. He found his uncle ensconced behind the desk, still poking away at the typewriter. He looked tired, his face hollow above the collar of a faded woollen jumper. Stubble pricked his cheeks, and under the desk William could see a pair of bony feet jammed into slippers. But the old man's eyes were alert, and his fingers stabbed down vehemently on the keys. Coffee-cups and dinner plates littered the desk, and papers were scattered everywhere, some printed, some handwritten, some crumpled up into contemptuous balls.

'Take a seat,' his uncle said, typing on.

William selected a chair near the desk and waited. His glance fell on one of the tables, where a hulked shape had been unveiled from beneath its dust sheet. He realised that it was an old printing machine. A crank handle stuck out from its side, and William knew exactly the sort of noise it would make — he had heard it clanking away for the past three days. The smell of ink was in the air, and beside the contraption sat several thick piles of paper, freshly printed in smudgy purple lines.

The old man hit an emphatic full stop, then dug around in a drawer. He retrieved a sheet of paper, and slid it across the desk.

'Have a look at that.'

It was a small poster, and it showed a flag, slightly furled as if blowing in a wind. The flag was blue, and bore a white cross with a star at the tip of each arm and a star in the centre.

'You recognise it?'

William shook his head.

'You should. That flag has been flying on the flagpole out front ever since you got here.'

William had never seen the flag outside do anything but hang limp against its pole. He studied the poster again. There were bold capitals above the picture — THE AUSTRALIAN INDEPENDENCE LEAGUE. His uncle held out a hand.

'Are you telling me you've really never seen that flag before?'

William gave the poster back. 'No.'

'Not even at school? You've never heard of the Eureka Stockade?'

William lowered his eyes. Was this another of the old man's tests? William had resolved to be as adult as he could, but what was he to do when there were just things he didn't know?

'Good Lord,' the old man mused. Then he straightened in his chair. 'Eureka was one of the first movements for independence in this country. There was a group of gold miners, during the gold rush down in Victoria, in the 1850s, when Australia was still a colony ruled by England. The miners were digging away and trying to scratch out a living, and suddenly the colonial government came along and inflicted huge licence fees on them. Fees that would ruin most of the miners. It wasn't just the money, there were other issues too, but basically people were sick of being at the beck and call of the lords and ladies back in England. What right did England have to charge fees over Australian soil? So the miners revolted. They threw up barricades and flew the Southern Cross flag and declared their own republic. There were hundreds of them, and the whole state of Victoria went into a panic. These were volatile times. Australia was a brand new place, and when rebels talked about republics a lot of people got excited. The colonial government didn't muck around. They mustered all the troops they could and sent them in. It was a full-scale battle, and the miners lost. But they won too, because nothing was the same after that.'

His uncle picked up the poster again, turning it towards William.

'This is their flag. You could argue that it's the first truly Australian flag, not like that monstrosity with the Union Jack. But these days the Eureka flag gets used for any old thing. People fly it to sell used cars and hamburgers, or stick it on margarine labels. They think it just means something patriotic. Other people use it as a protest flag. Even the Australian Communist Party waves it around sometimes — as if the miners were socialists, for Christ's sake, and Peter Lalor was our answer to Karl Marx.' He dropped the poster on the desk. 'But I use it because of what this flag really stands for. Independence. That's the key word. You know what it means, don't you?'

'I think so,' said William.

The old man laughed. 'Then you're a rarity, Will, because not many people do.'

William blinked in bafflement. His uncle sobered and returned his attention to the sheet of paper in the typewriter. William noticed now that the sheet was a waxy stencil, and that the letters were actually holes, punched through by the typewriter keys. Satisfied with what he read, the old man pulled out the page and stood up. 'So what did you do while I was away?'

It sounded a casual question, but William knew otherwise. This was what he'd been waiting for. 'I looked around,' he answered, very serious. 'A lot.'

'Ah.' His uncle was smiling. 'The old place doesn't seem so bad now, does it?'

William shook his head gravely.

'Good. Maybe you'll understand what's at stake then.' He moved over to the printing machine and began fixing the stencil to an ink-stained drum on top of the device. 'This property — it's mine, isn't it? I own it. If I don't want anyone knowing about that water hole, for instance, then that's my business. Right?'

'Right.'

'Well, there are things happening in this country that will take that choice away, if people like me don't put a stop to it.'

'What things?'

'Government things. Same as always.' He inserted a sheaf of blank paper into a tray at the rear of the machine, then stood back. 'You see these old paintings?'

He was pointing at the smoky images upon the walls — the fox hunt on one hand, and on the other, men riding amidst sheep as the golden plains rolled beyond.

'They were done in the 1860s, when the House was built. The Whites spared no expense in getting the artist. They wanted the finest of everything. But don't go thinking Kuran Station was always like that. Go back to the 1840s, when white men first came here. This was a wilderness, far beyond the colonial frontier. There was no civilisation, no law and order — that was all a thousand miles behind, back in Sydney. So those first men were completely alone, a law unto themselves. Something like that is unimaginable these days. It would scare most people to death.'

The old man was moving along the wall, peering at the faded scenes of Kuran's bygone days. The more William stared, the more he could see — the painting growing almost luminous and three-dimensional, the grassland extending away into the distance.

'They marked out their properties, drove great mobs of sheep up here, all by themselves, and set up their station houses. Not the mansions that came later — just little shacks in the middle of nowhere. There were no roads, no tracks, and it was maybe twenty miles to the next sign of life, and all you found there anyway was another man, just as alone as you were. For the first ten years there weren't more than maybe two dozen white people on the whole of the Darling Downs. Now there's two hundred thousand at least.'

From the murky wall the horse-riders stared out, their faces white blurs, stoic and impassive. William's uncle strode amongst them.

'It was a hard life. And then there were the sheep to watch. No fences, of course, only a shepherd. I told you about shepherds. They lived wild, often without even a shack to call home, just a bit of canvas for a tent. In the meantime the blacks were spearing the sheep, or just as likely the shepherds. Nothing you could do if they did — no police, no hospitals, no one to help. A man had to look after himself.'

The old man rested his hand briefly on the dark figures gathered in the lower corner of the painting.

'*That's* independence for you. It means hard work and self-reliance. And that's how Australia began. It took those men years and a lot of them died, but slowly they built up their stations. Built better houses. Built stockyards and shearing sheds, brought their wives and children up from down south. It was the end of the earth, but they made it work somehow.'

He had turned to the other wall and was frowning at the men in their red coats, with dogs at their feet and the misty castle floating in the background.

'And that's when, and only when, the government finally took some interest. If people are making money somewhere, the government always wants to know. The Darling Downs were officially placed under colonial jurisdiction. And from that moment on, the rights of people up here started getting stripped away. Suddenly they owe the government money for the land they've settled. They've got to sign leases, pay rent, go through all the red tape. Suddenly there're laws about what they can and can't do with their properties. And more people come up. Agents and civil servants and shopkeepers and schoolteachers and priests and all sorts of fools who think they want to be farmers. And all these people want land of their own, so the government starts taking it off those that got there first and did all the hard work.'

The old man gazed intently into the depths of the painting, and then seemed to relent slightly. He turned away, back to the printing machine.

'All right, maybe it was always going to happen, they could hardly keep it all to themselves. But those first men, the ones who did it all — can you imagine what sort of nerve it took? There aren't people like that any more. We're a weaker lot now. We sit in our suburbs and do what we're told and wait for the government to make us happy. And that's *not* good enough.'

He took hold of the handle of the printing machine and turned it just once. The machine clanked, the drum rolled, and a single printed sheet slipped into a tray at the front. The old man lifted the paper, inspected it carefully.

'So this is my newsletter, my own way of trying to stop things getting worse. Twelve issues a year, and this is our twelfth year running.' He glanced at William. 'One day I should get a computer. This Mimeograph is as old as the hills. Still, it should never be too easy. Otherwise every idiot would be doing it.'

He was cranking the handle steadily now, and the smell of ink was pungent. A stream of pages was emerging. 'It's a big job. We have three hundred and sixty-odd full members in the League, mostly from Queensland, but from the rest of the country too. Most newsletters run five or six pages long, so that's at least two thousand pages. It's more actually, because I always print five hundred copies of each issue. I take the leftovers with me when I travel and leave them in shops, pubs, wherever. We're always recruiting. Not a cheap business either.'

'Is it a club?' William asked.

His uncle shook his head. 'It's a league of concerned citizens. People who are worried about what's happening to this country. I'm the president, and there's a central committee that meets four times a year. I'm the editor of the newsletter too. Members send in their own articles sometimes, but mostly it's all written by me. That's where I've been the last two weeks, travelling around Queensland to see what's happening, talking to people, researching stuff in Brisbane. These are grim days. Dangerous things are in the wind.' He took up a printed sheet from one of the piles across the table. 'See — we're getting ready.'

It was a map, hand-drawn and rough, but William could see that it showed the Kuran Plains, and gave directions on how to reach Kuran Station. There was even an inset which depicted the village and the House. Arrows pointed the way along the driveway, leading past the House and onwards into the heart of the station. A black square had been marked there and labelled 'Campgrounds'. William stared at it, confused. He hadn't seen any campgrounds during their drive.

The old man said, 'We're having a rally in about a month. I expect we'll get a couple of hundred people. It'll be held over a weekend. People can bring their tents and vans and camp out.'

'A rally? What for?'

'That's what this edition is all about.' He lifted another sheet from one of the piles. 'Here's the front page.'

Andrew McGahan

Rally Called to Discuss Native Title

In the wake of the Mabo judgment, the federal government is currently drawing up plans for sweeping Native Title legislation which it plans to introduce before the end of the year. This will alienate land to the black minority, and affect us all directly! It is vital that we meet to formulate an action plan and ensure our voices are heard before it's too late. As president, I am happy to offer my own property as a meeting ground, and a date has been set for...

The article went on, talking about the federal government and about legislation and the prime minister, Mr Keating. There were many words William didn't understand.

'It's all right,' the old man said. 'I'll explain it all in time. Now, do you think you can crank this handle while I get going on the envelopes and addresses?'

William nodded. He set his hand to the handle and began to turn. It wasn't hard, and freshly printed pages slid into the tray, one by one.

His uncle patted him on the shoulder. 'Just keep going till the paper runs out. Five hundred copies. Call me if they start to smudge too badly.'

William cranked and watched the pages stack up. So this was what his uncle did, this was his secret work. He felt vaguely let down. The old man had said that something dangerous was happening, but it actually seemed rather dull. And yet maybe that was what being an adult was all about. It was important, in any case, that he did what his uncle asked. Then he remembered the rally. Two hundred people, and camping up in the hills. At least that sounded interesting. Maybe he would get to sleep in a tent.

His eyes settled on the page he was printing. Under the words 'Our Charter' was a series of statements.

We reject the monarchy and the two-party system of parliament.
We reject the United Nations and any other body that seeks to limit
Australian sovereignty.
We reject government interference with basic individual rights.
We reject excessive immigration and the dilution of traditional
Australian culture.
We reject excessive control of Australian resources by foreigners.
We reject special and preferential treatment of elite minorities.
We reject the alienation of Australian soil to elite minorities.

We believe in a republican and proudly independent Australia.
We believe that all Australians are equal and should be treated as such.
We believe in an Australia run by all Australians for the benefit of
all Australians.
We believe that the rights of the individual cannot be interfered with.
We believe in the inherent value of Australian culture and traditions.
We believe in One Flag.
In One People.
One Nation.

William blinked and looked up. His uncle was watching him from
behind the desk.

The old man smiled. 'Not bad, hey?'

Chapter Seventeen

IT TOOK WILLIAM AND HIS UNCLE THE REST OF THAT DAY AND most of the next to assemble the newsletters. First the pages had to be stapled together. William went back and forth along the separate piles, gathering up the sheets. Then each newsletter had to be folded and inserted into an envelope, and finally the envelopes had to be stamped and addressed. That was his uncle's job. The old man had pulled a large black ledger from the desk drawer. Laboriously running his finger down the pages, he found the address of each member, then wrote it out by hand. It was slow work, but William enjoyed it. On the second day the weather grew cool again, so the fire was lit, and it felt good to be shut away in the big dark office, with bright flames burning. To William's delight, Mrs Griffith even brought in his lunch on a tray, next to his uncle's. The housekeeper shot him a foul look, but for once he wasn't afraid of her. He felt warm, secure and useful.

His disappointment over the old man's secret work had long since faded. The newsletter was an impressive piece of work, and his uncle was the president of an organisation with hundreds of members. A few hundred didn't sound much, but after all the stapling and folding, William appreciated just how many people that really was. And it was a serious business — amazing to think that his uncle was battling something as large and powerful as the entire Australian government.

'But what *is* Native Title?' he asked at one stage. It seemed to be the central issue, but nowhere in the newsletter was it fully explained.

'A disaster,' the old man replied, head buried in the ledger. But when he saw that William was waiting in puzzled silence, he put down his pen. 'The truth is, at this stage, no one has a clue what Native Title is. That's the problem. The government is still drafting the legislation. But all indications are that it will be terrible for people like us.'

'Why?'

'Why?' His uncle leant back in his chair, sucking his lips at the vastness of the question. 'Well, one of the things it means is that someone like me won't have a say any more about what happens on my own property. It's already pretty bad. Right now I can't do things like clear trees or build a dam without the government wanting to know about it. Native Title would make it even harder. But that's not all. The worst of it is that I might not even *own* the land any more. Not outright. Other people could come along and say they owned it as well. People who haven't had anything to do with the place for centuries. And I wouldn't be able to do a thing without their say-so.' He leant forward again. 'There are lots of aspects to it and you'll hear all sorts of rubbish about this and that, but don't fall for it. Deep down, it's purely a question of property rights.'

William wasn't sure what property rights might be, but the idea that someone else could claim his uncle's station, that seemed disturbing. Especially now.

'What people?' he asked.

'Minorities. Elites. Activists.' The old man regarded William's confusion for a moment, then sighed. 'Aborigines, of course. Who else would it be?'

William got back to work. Aborigines? He thought of deserts, and dark-skinned figures with spears, but he had never met a black person. There weren't any even in Powell, as far as he knew, so it was hard to see what connection they might have with Kuran Station. Then he remembered what the men in the national park had said about marks on bunya pines, and about the clearings on the hilltops. But that was long ago, surely.

The big radio that sat in a corner was kept switched on, and they listened to it as they worked. The old man preferred news broadcasts or talkback shows. Most of it was of no interest to William — wars overseas, or peace talks, or stories about the economy and the unemployment rate — but he took cues from his uncle, paying attention to the items that induced angry mutterings or nods of approval. These reports were mostly about rural issues. Between the drought, and low prices for grain and livestock, and high interest rates, it seemed that things were bad everywhere.

But the old man's deeper rages were reserved for the reports that dealt directly with the government. William learnt quickly that his uncle hated the prime minister, Mr Keating. That was no surprise. Mr Keating had won the federal election held earlier in the year, and William knew that this was considered an awful thing in the Powell district. Nobody liked the prime minister. But his uncle didn't seem to like the opposition leader, Dr Hewson, either. That did surprise William, for there was no one else from whom to choose, was there?

Late on the second day his uncle tuned to a station that was actually playing a live broadcast of parliament sitting in Canberra. It had an empty, echoing sound over the radio, and seemed very dull, but the old man rocked testily back and forth in his chair as the politicians declaimed.

William ventured the question: 'Who did you vote for?'

'I didn't vote.'

'I thought everyone had to.'

'That's the law, but to hell with them. They can't make me choose sides.' The old man lifted a copy of his newsletter. 'I'm on my own side.'

'But...'

'But what?'

William let it drop. He could sense displeasure threatening in the old man. He went back to sorting the pages. He was down to the last few. But his uncle continued watching him, and then reached out a hand to switch off the radio.

'Don't ever be too impressed by the authorities, Will. Politicians, police, the courts, the councils. I know they sound big and important, and they'll try to make you do all sorts of things throughout your life. But it's all just noise. You have to make your own decisions in the end.'

William nodded dutifully.

'Don't you nod at me!'

Startled, William glanced up. The grandfather figure of the last two days had vanished in an instant. The prophet of the shooting stars sat there, glaring coldly.

'You have absolutely no idea what I'm talking about! What have you been thinking? That one day I'll just hand all of this over to you, and that'll be that?'

'No...'

'You'd better believe I won't!'

William looked away, shocked.

But his uncle rose angrily to his feet. 'Now you listen. No one handed me anything. I should've had this property sixty years ago. Instead I had to fight my whole life to get it. But you know what?

It's better that way. Because things like this station can't just be given to you. You have to earn them, like I did.'

The old man strode across the office. He came to the fireplace and, grabbing the rusty iron bar that served as a poker, jabbed at the logs.

'Governments! I used to vote, yes, and all they ever did was make up laws that got in my way. Whitlam was the one who started it — I watched that man give away money to any fool who asked for it. Suddenly it was okay not to work, the government would pay you anyway. They'd pay you to waste your time at university. They'd pay you to smoke drugs and march on the streets, they'd pay you to rip your own country apart. And they laughed at idiots like me. They hated us. Even though all the time we were the ones footing the bill.'

The flames leapt up, so that William saw his uncle as a dark shape before the fire, surrounded by ruin and rubbish, the rage rising in his voice with the flames.

'We threw Whitlam out and Fraser came in — but nothing changed. No one gave a damn about you unless you were waving a placard. You had to be a migrant, or black, or homosexual. But God help you if you were a normal Australian, let alone a farmer like me. We used to be the backbone of this country. But not to those people. To them, we were the biggest problem. We were fascists. We were destroying the environment. We had to be controlled. Fraser went and Hawke came in, and things just kept getting worse. That's when I gave up voting. Why bother? Parties, politicians — they're all exactly the same.'

The firewood was sparking and spitting, and the old man stamped at the embers on the floor.

'They don't even like the way people like me *talk* any more. You can't say a thing without someone calling you racist or sexist or some other sort of bigot. No one cares that farms are going broke right across the country, that people are dying of misery out here. You have to speak nicely, lie nicely, that's all that matters. Now we've got Keating, and he's the worst yet. If he gets his way, rural Australia is finished forever. So yes, I'll fight him and his Native Title. No one is taking one square inch of my land away. I've kept this station alive despite everything the world has thrown at me. And I did it alone.'

The old man turned from the fire at last, the iron bar still gripped in his hand.

'And you! You spend a few weeks here and you think all you have to do is wait for me to die! Well, it won't be like that. You have to earn the right. You haven't earnt anything. So don't you *ever* nod at me like that!'

William didn't move. The flames crackled and writhed, but everything, the fire and the room and the shape of his uncle, was blurred by the tears in his eyes. He'd been doing his best, to help, to grow up. What had he done that was so wrong?

'Don't cry, for Christ's sake.' The old man dropped the iron bar, took a few random steps about the room, stopped again. He waved a hand at the desk. 'Look. Just finish off those newsletters. And clean up some of this mess. I'll address the rest of the envelopes tomorrow.'

He turned towards the door, hesitated. 'You have to understand. Nothing is easy ... and I can't leave this station to someone who'll just give up when things get too hard.'

And with that he was gone.

William blinked away his tears. He sniffed, then unfolded himself, remembering the handful of pages he carried. He took them to the stapler, and then numbly worked his way through the last few copies of the newsletter, stapling and folding and sliding them into the envelopes. He didn't feel useful any more. He felt cold, even with the fire bright behind him.

The work was done. William looked about the office, littered with crumpled papers and torn envelopes and scraps from the sheets of stamps. He gathered them up and placed them in a bin behind the desk. All he wanted to do now was creep back to his wing of the House and hide in his bedroom. But then he saw that one of the desk drawers was open. Something gleamed in there, amidst piles of old cheque books and ink pads. It was a large keyring. William stared. It held half a dozen keys. In his mind was a picture of the door on the landing of the central staircase, the door that led to the second storey. And the doors on the other staircases, at either end of the House. Locked doors. Without even thinking, he lifted the ring out, slowly, so as not to jangle it.

This was wrong, he knew. He had no business in his uncle's desk, stealing keys. He certainly had no business going upstairs. The housekeeper had told him that on his very first day. His uncle had repeated the order. William held the keys before him, dreadfully fascinated. He almost put them back. But an anger was stirring in him now, at what the old man had put him through. And if he was supposed to grow up, if he was supposed to be strong and make his own decisions, then why should he always do what he was told?

Directly overheard, he could hear noises. The sound of something heavy being dragged, and footsteps, pacing back and forth on an echoing floor.

William put the keys into his pocket. He slid the drawer closed and, already afraid, slipped away into the halls.

Chapter Eighteen

By 1941, JOHN WAS BACK AT WORK IN THE HOOP MOUNTAINS. With the war stimulating demand for timber, Oliver Fisher had expanded his sawmill operations and needed a supervisor up on the hills. Manpower was short, so John, even with his bad leg, got the job. Dudley, meanwhile, had been assigned as a gunner in the Eighth Division AIF. His formation had shipped out for the battle-fields of Libya, but along the way they had been diverted to garrison duty north of Singapore. Dudley, in his letters, sounded fit and healthy, and somewhat bored.

It seemed to John that maybe hostilities would pass his friend by. But then the Japanese armies rolled down the Malay peninsula, the Allied forces retreated in disorder, and Singapore fell. Suddenly Japanese bombs were dropping on Darwin and Townsville. Panic gripped the country, and there was no question of standing aside now — John volunteered immediately. He was rejected and sent back to his duties in the mountains. All he could do was join the militia, and with other timber-cutters he formed a troop that was designated as a guerrilla force. In case of invasion, their job was to hide out in the hills and, using their local knowledge, disrupt any enemy activity in the area. But even with the war raging all about, the Powell region seemed a sleepy and unlikely battleground.

What made it all the more galling for John was that even Harriet had donned a uniform, enlisting in the Australian Women's Army Service. She was posted locally, however, so at least the two of them were still able to meet from time to time. Their chief concern in those days was the fate of Dudley. The Eighth Division had been routed, and the survivors had passed into Japanese captivity — but was he one of those survivors? There was no mention of him in the casualty lists, but nor did his name appear on the Red Cross lists of those in the prison camps. He was simply missing in action. John and Harriet vowed to each other that they would not give up hope, but as the months went by without word, their talk of Dudley took on the tone of mourning. And in mourning him, they were steadily drawn closer together, and closer to betraying him.

Still, it was a shadowed courtship, for without Dudley around there was less laughter, less joy, and there were days when Australia itself seemed destined to fall. But in those grim months, at least John felt that there need be no more doubts about himself and Harriet. It was only the two of them now, and things like financial security or her father's approval no longer seemed to matter. It was just a question of waiting until a decent time had passed in honour of Dudley, and until perhaps the war situation improved. And indeed, as 1942 progressed, things looked brighter. In the Pacific, the Japanese fleets were in retreat, and in New Guinea their troops had been brought to a halt at last. The threat of invasion receded. It was time, John decided, to speak.

But then came word from the Red Cross — Dudley was alive after all! He had finally turned up in a prison camp. There was no report on his condition, and frightening stories were already circulating about Japanese treatment of the POWs, but it was still the best possible news. Harriet was overjoyed — and yet John found himself confused by his own reaction. Relief, yes, but he was also aware of a sudden fear. Had Dudley been the one Harriet was waiting for all along? Had she turned to John only out of grief? They had spoken no direct words of marriage, after all. So what would happen when Dudley returned home, aglow with the glamour of war? What would her choice be then? John strove against these suspicions, but they refused to go away. More bitterly than ever he was convinced that, after the war, the world would belong to the men who had fought it. The world, and with it the one woman he wanted.

He arrived at Harriet's house one hot summer day to find her restless, full of a cheerful energy that nagged at his heart, because he knew its source. She chatted about Dudley and her war work, optimistic that it might all end well. John was unresponsive, for there was nothing to say about his own work, and he didn't want to talk about Dudley. It was a torpid afternoon, and they were slumped in chairs on the back verandah. Eventually, Harriet gave up. A vagrant boredom seemed to creep over her, and she stared out silently, fanning herself as heat shimmered across the paddocks. John could sense her disappointment with him, and with his brooding quiet.

Finally, her patience at an end, Harriet suggested they go swimming. With an effort, John roused himself and agreed. Perhaps cold water would dispel his resentment. The question was where to go? There was a public pool in town, but it would be crowded with children, the water tepid and reeking of chlorine. And then, for the first time since his childhood, John remembered the water hole on the borders of Kuran Station. Of course! It was deep and cool and never ran dry. A vision of it sparkled darkly in his memory. Suddenly the afternoon was too close and too oppressive to bear. He could already feel the water on his skin, and taste it on his tongue, icy, with the faintest hint of decaying leaves and earth. Inspired, he instructed Harriet to don her swimming costume. They would take Oliver's car. Petrol was rationed, but Oliver had stored away a secret supply of his own. They could be at the water hole within the hour.

However, it would mean passing through the station itself, and there was a part of John that knew he might find this a disturbing experience, after so much time. But in the sweltering heat, and with Harriet in a fey mood beside him, that didn't seem to matter. It was an instant to be seized, a single afternoon away from the war. Anyway, what was there to fear? The Whites were gone. Elizabeth was gone. So under the glaring sky, and with the car seats burning the backs of their legs, they cut across the plains to the Lansdowne road, and then drove northwards to Kuran Village. The hill loomed behind it, and John steered up through the first gates and along the avenue lined with pines. He should have turned off there, taking the track that led to the water hole. But on an impulse he continued straight ahead, and so arrived at the second gate. And there, waiting for him, was the House.

It was one of the worst moments of John's life.

He had known, of course, that things would not be exactly the same as he remembered. Twelve years had passed, and a succession of failed owners had come and gone. He'd heard that the workers' cottages were no longer fit for use, and that the current landlord had converted the lower storey of the House into flats. But even so, he had not expected *this*. The great homestead had become a shabby hulk. Paint was peeling away from the verandahs, creepers were growing raggedly up the walls, and tiles were askew on the roof. Some of the upper-storey windows had been smashed, others were shuttered. The lawns were long dead and the flower-beds were dust bowls. Chickens wandered freely in the yard. There was no water in the fountain, or in the pool. Heat radiated from the bare earth, and there was not a living soul in sight.

But the ghosts — the ghosts were everywhere. Visions of men and women dressed in white, strolling over green grass and reclining in shady recesses or by sparkling water, visions of a stern old man in a panelled office aglow with firelight, and, irresistibly, of a girl in white with curtains floating behind her. But with the visions came a terrible sense of dislocation — for how could any of it have happened in this barren place? It was all so dirty and shrunken and drab. John was hardly aware of Harriet at his side, peering through the windscreen. *What a pity*, she said, *it must have been a nice house once.* And an enormous throb of outrage swelled in him. A pity! It was far more than that. The dust, the blank windows, the front doors yawning emptily.

He put the car in reverse and pulled away. Even that felt like desertion, as if the building was crying out to him for help. But what could he do? He steered back down the driveway, turned off towards the water hole. But his despair only deepened as he drove. Everywhere he saw the same forlorn signs of neglect. Fences that leant or had fallen, piles of rubbish that had once been sheds and stables. When they came over the first hill, he saw that the little church too was sinking into ruin, the graveyard overgrown with grass. He didn't give a damn about the cemetery — let the Whites rot and their headstones tumble — but everything else cut with a pain that was almost physical. Bad enough that he had lost everything when it should have been his, worse still to find that no one else even wanted it! He drove the rest of the way in a furious silence, while Harriet gazed all un-knowing out the windows.

But when they reached the water hole, something strange happened. For the pool, at least, was unchanged — nestled beneath the sandstone shelf as always, shaded by overhanging gums and the willow tree. Even the old stone seat was still there, by the lip of the trickling waterfall. Harriet was delighted, and set about exploring. John followed more slowly. He studied the dark water, then raised his eyes to the foothills that swelled all about, and beyond them to the high line of the mountains. As a boy, those mountains had been a different world. Now he knew them intimately, every ridge and gully and cliff, just as he knew this water hole, and the hills and plains of his youth that stretched out behind him. And standing there, John felt a sudden merging of two inner parts of himself, his childhood and his adult life, the station and the mountains. They all came together here in this spot.

The anger in him burned away. It was as if the land was speaking to him directly, pulsing up through the stone at his feet. He *belonged* here. Not in the mountains or on the plains or in the towns, but here, on this one piece of country. It was the focus around which he had always circled. And look how it had suffered in his absence. As he suffered himself, incomplete, and doomed to be so, unless he returned. And in that moment, he knew. It was no pleasant fantasy or hope, it was an utter conviction, an acceptance of truth — no matter how long it took, he would get the station back. Indeed, as he turned upon the spot, drinking in every sight and sound of the landscape, he knew that this was the instant in which he took possession. Not legally, not financially, but essentially. The strength of the revelation filled him with a fierce pride, a vitality that flowed into him from the hills themselves, as if all of their age and power was his.

He was suddenly keenly aware of Harriet's presence. She had already stripped down to her swimming costume and slid into the water. Afire with the joy of ownership, John ripped off his shirt and joined her in the pool. It was deliciously cool, and for a time the two of them swam about, splashing each other, laughing, revelling in the secret of water and stone. Then as the heat of the afternoon drained away, a languor stole into their limbs. They drifted, talking. The sun sank, and insects buzzed and skipped across the surface. Finally they fell silent, circling each other slowly. John felt a deep serenity, more at peace than he had ever been, and he could tell that Harriet had seen the change in him. He was a man who knew exactly who he was. An intensity seemed to build between them, drowsy and hypnotic. Then Harriet abruptly shook her hair, and without a word climbed out of the pool. John remained in the water, watching her. She picked her way slowly amongst the rocks, and then settled on a smooth sheet of stone, warmed by the last beams of light that filtered through the trees. Stretching herself out, she opened her arms and closed her eyes to the sun. John hung in the water, observing her in repose for one long unguarded moment. Then he kicked his legs, and dived deep.

The water was colder below the surface, and clear. He saw the sandy floor dipping away from him as it ran back towards the shelf. Fallen tree limbs littered the sides of the pool, but under the shelf there was darkness. He kicked towards it, sinking, his mind ablaze with the image of Harriet spread across the rock, water beading on her skin. He longed for her as if she was the crowning symbol of everything that had just been revealed to him, everything that in the future would be his — could be theirs together. And then, unbidden, there came a vision of Dudley returning triumphant from the war, and of Harriet's body, pale and smooth, surrendered to him instead. John was in the depths of the hole now, far under the overhang of the shelf. A slow current seemed to flow from the blackness, broken only by the white glimmer of sticks and branches that had sunk there, deep beyond his reach. His lungs began to ache, the water was freezing, and still the thought of Harriet set his skin alight. But when Dudley returned, John would be dispossessed of her. Just as he had been of everything else.

Expelling air at last, he turned and kicked upwards, spearing towards the far end of the pool. He surfaced in the shallows, and lifted himself clear of the water. Dripping, he climbed over the rocks, until he stood above her, drawing breath. Harriet was aware of him only dreamily for a moment, but then opened her eyes, shading them as she looked up. And who knew what she thought in her heart about her two men, and whether the choice would have been John or Dudley, if they had all been reunited one day. But there had always been a mystery within John, a man never fully revealed, and that man stood over her now, a figure she barely recognised, half naked, almost wild, almost frightening, but un-masked for her alone. For his part, John saw Harriet sit up with something that might have been alarm, but which in fact had no defence about it, no rejection, only a sudden willingness. At the last moment she seemed to catch herself, and drew her knees to her chest. But by then John was kneeling before her, his face was close to hers, and his hands were on the straps of her suit.

Chapter Nineteen

IT TOOK WILLIAM ANOTHER TWO DAYS TO MUSTER HIS COURAGE
and use the keys. The chance came when his uncle carted the
newsletters away to mail in Powell, rattling off down the driveway
in the old utility. That left only his mother and Mrs Griffith to
worry about. His mother was no problem, but the housekeeper
could appear anywhere, silent as a ghost on her patrols. For that
reason William decided not to use the central staircase. It was too
exposed. It would have to be one of the stairwells in the east or
west wing. The west wing would have been the best — it was the
furthest from Mrs Griffith's flat. But the landing there was blocked
by dusty piles of boxes and papers.

Which left only one choice. William retrieved the keys from
under his bed and made his way to the eastern stairs. They were
narrow and unadorned, a stark passage climbing upwards. He
ascended the first flight, the old boards creaking faintly under his
feet. Then he was on the landing, and examining the fibro
partition. It was unpainted, and fitted only roughly from wall to

wall, a makeshift barrier thrown up temporarily perhaps, and then forgotten. The door had obviously been salvaged from somewhere else — it was old, with streaks of garish green paint adhering to dark wooden panels. Below the knob a bolt had been installed, held shut by a padlock. William began trying the keys, one by one. The third slotted in perfectly. But then there was a long struggle, first to turn the key and open the padlock, stiff with age, and then to draw back the rusty bolt. He paused when he was done, a little breathless and with aching fingers, certain that he made far too much noise. But he heard no movement from anywhere else in the House. Gingerly, he turned the doorknob, and pushed.

Hinges groaned, and a gulf of darkness opened. William hesitated until his eyes adjusted to the gloom and he could see the stairs, ascending away dimly. Then he stepped through and pulled the door closed behind him. Resuming the climb, he became aware of a smell. It was familiar from the ground floor — the scent of mould, of rotting wood, of inescapable age. But while downstairs it was an undertone, up here it was ripe and pungent, making William's nose itch. It was colder too. He grimaced, rubbed his nose, and then he was at the top of the stairs.

Cold, dark … and empty. That was his first impression. He was standing at the end of a long hallway, a gallery far higher and wider than anything he had seen downstairs. It ran away off into the shadows before him, dappled with pale shafts of illumination, and seemed to extend the entire length of the House, from the east wing to the west. William stared in awe. It was a vast space, bare of furniture or ornament, and he realised that the upper storey, unlike the lower, had never been subdivided. He was seeing the House in its original scale and shape. But not in anything like its original glory. The ceiling was draped with cobwebs, and whole slabs of it sagged in great, soggy bulges. The walls were streaked with mould, naked latticework showing where chunks of plaster had fallen away. And the floor was blackened and warped, the boards marred by the abstract stains of water damage.

The hall was lined with tall, vacant doorways. Feeling as if he had strayed into some fairytale giant's castle, William began to creep from room to room, peering in. The eastern wing was made up of four huge chambers, two on either side of the central gallery. The rooms were identical, with large windows, great stone fireplaces and double doors opening out to the upper verandah. All of them were empty. Holes gaped in floors, the fireplaces had been stripped of their mantelpieces, and the windows were boarded over. They must have been bedrooms, William decided, but bigger than any bedrooms he had ever seen. So silent and desolate. He hadn't known what he expected to find upstairs, only that he expected to find *something*, not this gaunt emptiness.

But this was no place to linger. He was standing above Mrs Griffith's flat. He stole westwards along the hall, into the narrower central section of the House. Here were another four rooms, two on each side. They were smaller than the first four, although still very big. One was floored with black and white tiles, and pipes stuck out of the walls in several places, so perhaps it had been a bathroom once. But all these rooms too were dark and deserted. He moved beyond them, into the centre of the House. The main staircase was on the right, climbing up to meet him. On the left was an open space leading to wide double doors, opening directly onto the front verandah. William paused, studying the stairway and the partition thrown across the landing below. This was the route his uncle used ... but where did he go when he came up here?

William crept on. The western half of the House was a mirror image of the east wing. William was counting. Eight rooms at each end: taking away the bathrooms, that left fourteen bedrooms. But surely they couldn't have needed that many. What sort of people had they been anyway? He'd heard their names, but that told him nothing, and the bare rooms revealed nothing about them either.

He paused and listened. The floor creaked subtly beneath his feet, and from time to time he heard faint rustlings in the ceiling. The great hall stretched away from him, a cavern of shadows. Were there memories here? Voices? Faces? No ... There was no such thing as ghosts. He ventured on, into the west wing proper. And finally, here was something different. The doors to the last two rooms on either side were both closed. And one of them was padlocked.

This was it then. Whatever crime William had committed by coming up here, it would be doubly serious if he opened these doors. But he was beyond hesitation now. He tried the unlocked door, the last on the right-hand side. It swung open without a sound. White light enfolded him. He blinked, amazed. Curtains were the first thing he saw, white curtains that drifted in front of clear, sunlit windows. And high white walls that reflected the light back, so that William felt for an instant as if he was swimming in a bowl of illumination. It might have been a different House entirely. A bed stood out from one wall, iron framed and sheeted in white. There was a stately wardrobe, and a dresser of the same design. Old-fashioned leather armchairs surrounded a low table in front of the fireplace and there were silver candlesticks on the mantelpiece. And beyond the verandah doors were two winged cane chairs, facing out to the hills, like a vision of some bygone age.

So this was where his uncle slept! William had always imagined his uncle's bedroom would be the darkest and coldest of all the chambers in the House, but this ... this was all sunlight and air. And yet there was no doubt about it — he could see the old man's slippers by the bed, and his tattered bathrobe and pyjamas cast across the sheets. It was as if William had looked into his uncle's stern heart and found there something delicate and beautiful. No wonder the old man had forbidden him from the second storey. This was a true secret. Admittedly, closer inspection revealed that the room had not entirely escaped the effects of time. The floor was warped like everywhere else, and the white

plaster of the walls was flecked with cracks and old stains. But still
— it felt strangely like a woman lived here, not a man. The cane
chairs on the verandah, for instance, the gauzy white curtains.

Then William remembered the other room, the one with the
padlock. He went back into the hall, and peered at the last door.
This room would be directly above the office. He looked at the
keys, aware of a reluctance to go further. The hall was hollow and
bleak after the warmth of sunlight, or perhaps it was a premonition
that he would discover nothing so wonderful as the white bedroom
behind this door. But he tested the keys in the lock, and the second
turned easily. There was no excuse, so he swung the door back.
A smell assailed him. Not the musk of age and damp, but an oily,
metallic scent, with a sharper tang beneath it. William was reminded
fleetingly of his father's shed, back on their farm, but it wasn't
quite that either. He advanced into a darkness that was weirdly
crimson. Heavy blinds hung across the windows, but he could see
that the walls were painted a blood red. Against one wall stood a
tall cabinet, faced with glass, and tucked into a corner was a large
wooden trunk. Against another wall ran a long workbench,
littered with tools. But what really caught William's eye was the
angular shape that loomed against the window at the back of
the room.

It was a telescope — a brass tube on an iron stand, a device
possessed, somehow, of a watching, predatory intelligence. It was
not the modern sort of telescope that people used to study the
stars. It was an older instrument that spoke of sailing ships and the
sea. Is that what his uncle did up here, alone, night after night?
William could almost picture the old man hunched to the
eyepiece, sweeping the dark ocean of the plains, a captain in search
of land, or of a sail upon the horizon. But to what end? What
would he really be looking for? It was another glimpse into his
uncle's soul. A disturbing one, this time, such an instrument
lurking in that red space.

Unnerved, William turned his attention to the long table against the wall. There was a vice attached to the edge, and a toolbox sitting beneath a lamp, but it wasn't an ordinary workbench. In a frame above it hung three rifles. Their steel barrels gleamed, polished with oil. And upon the bench itself sat boxes of ammunition, and a spray of bullets, shining dully. William recognised, at last, the elusive smell that had bothered him all along. It was gunpowder. It was no surprise that his uncle would have a collection of rifles. He had talked of shooting dogs, and everyone knew that, in droughts, farmers sometimes had to shoot their cattle. But William didn't like the rifles. They deepened the sensation that he should not be in this room.

He moved on to the glass-fronted cabinet. It contained five shelves, but each shelf held only a single object. There was an old pair of spectacle frames, without any lenses. There was a tarnished metal compass with a broken needle. There was what looked like a fob watch, all blackened, the face missing and the inside caked with dirt. There was a red leather-bound notebook, faded and stiff, its cover scuffed and scratched. And last, and most unsettling of all, was a single boot, tattered, torn and rotted. What were these things? All of them appeared worthless — why were they kept in a fine cabinet? A brief image came to William of his uncle bowed before the objects, as if the room was a hidden chapel. It made no sense, and yet he felt that this was where the real John McIvor was to be found, not in the room of light across the hall. His unease grew stronger, and he turned away.

There was only the chest now, waiting in its corner. It was an unadorned wooden trunk. William told himself that there was no need for it to be opened. He could leave this last mystery unexamined, and escape the red walls and the watching eye of the telescope. But he knelt before it all the same, pried back the clasp and lifted the lid. He smelled mothballs, and saw that the chest contained nothing but a folded suit and a military-style hat.

Fascinated beyond fear, William lifted the hat out gently. It was very old, threadbare and shrunken, something like an army officer's cap. He studied the gold braid around the crown, then tested the cap upon his head. It was heavy, and too large, but not uncomfortable. He reached into the chest and carefully pulled out the jacket of what he now realised was a uniform. It was so faded it was hard to tell what colour it had originally been, but there was a stripe on the lower sleeve, and a cloth patch sewn high upon the arm. Whose uniform was it? His uncle's? Had the old man fought in a war?

Then William noticed that something bulged in the front pocket, and he withdrew a velvet-lined box. Medals, he thought, it would contain war medals. But when he lifted the lid he saw only a badge, a golden shield, embossed with a crest that had letters arranged around the rim. He took off the cap and examined the front. Yes, there was a darker patch there. He pinned the badge to it. That was better: the hat looked official and important, and when he placed it on his head again, the extra weight felt right as well. He was a commander of ... well, of something. Strangely satisfied, William dug around in the chest again. His hand touched cold metal beneath the uniform trousers. He lifted out the object, surprised at its heaviness, and was amazed to discover he was holding a pistol. It looked ancient. It wasn't a six-shooter, like the guns he had seen in old Westerns; it was black and angular and appeared almost home-made. But it was a pistol, sure enough.

William cradled it wonderingly. And with the hat on his head, and the gun in his hand, he felt a power working in him. He was still somewhere where he didn't belong, the red walls still frowned down about him, but he had donned a uniform now, and held a weapon in his hand. He stood up. He felt taller. Older. He turned to the cabinet, and saw himself reflected in the glass. The badge gleamed on his brow, and the gun hung potently from his hand.

He was only a boy, but he could see the shadow of a man. He lifted the gun slowly, took aim along the barrel.

Another shape loomed in the reflection, white-faced and silent. William turned to find Mrs Griffith above him, her eyes blazing. And before he could speak or move, her hand slapped painfully down on his own, and the gun fell, clattering, to the floor.

Chapter Twenty

WILLIAM HAD COMPLETELY FORGOTTEN ABOUT THE HOUSEKEEPER and her stealth. How had she known? Had she heard his movements? Had she found the unlocked door on the stairs, and crept up to investigate? Or, somehow, had she just been aware of him? It didn't matter, he was discovered. His hand was stinging, and now Mrs Griffith shoved him roughly backwards, away from the gun. It lay on the floor like a dangerous snake.

'Did you load it?'

William shook his head. The housekeeper was an impossible confusion of grey hair and cardigans, but there was strength in her, strength and surprising speed.

'Was it already loaded? Did you look?'

He shook his head again, bewildered. He had found the gun at the bottom of a chest, covered by old clothes. Why would it be loaded?

'Idiot boy.'

She bent to the gun — not crouching, but splaying her legs and leaning down with an angry grunt. Holding it gingerly out before her, she lowered it onto the bench. Then she turned to William and slapped him across the face, sending the army hat flying. He stared up at her, stunned.

'There'll be more than that,' she hissed, 'when your uncle finds out. How did you get in?'

He attempted a lie. 'The doors were open.'

'Rubbish. You had keys. Show me.'

Shamefaced, William pulled the keyring out of his pocket.

The housekeeper plucked it from his hand. 'Where did you get these keys?'

'The office.'

'Stole them! From your uncle's desk!' She secreted the keys away under her clothes, then peered about. 'What else have you stolen? What else do you have in your pockets?'

'There's nothing.'

'We'll see. We'll see when your uncle gets home. We'll wait right here so that you can't go and hide anything. I'll lock you in this room. How would you like that?'

'I don't have anything,' William cried, turning out his pockets.

'Hmm.' The old woman studied his empty hands. 'You've been in that chest, though. What was that hat doing on your head?'

'I was only trying it on.'

'Your uncle won't be pleased. His father left him that chest.'

'I'll put it back...'

'No you won't. You'll leave everything just as it is.'

The housekeeper had hobbled over to the cabinet now, and was examining the objects within, hoping for further evidence of wrongdoing. She was a witch, William decided. And she'd been waiting all along for him to make a mistake, just as she had promised she would.

'Count your blessings, boy,' she said, prodding the cabinet. 'If you'd fiddled with anything in here, I don't know what he would've done. Do you know what these things are?'

He shook his head sullenly.

'Not so smart, are you? They belong to a dead man, that's what.'

William felt his skin crawl.

'Oh yes,' she said, shuffling back towards him. 'They were taken from his grave. He's buried here, right under our feet. This House was built over him.'

He shrank away from her, and the relish that lit her face.

'Remember that, when you want to go sneaking where you shouldn't. There's a dead man in this room. This House is his tombstone.' She fluttered her hands at him. 'Get out. Go back to your room, and wait there until you're called.'

William fled, all the way through the empty halls and down to his own flat. But then there was his mother to be faced, and there was no hiding his distress — he was forced to tell her what had happened. She was furious, yelling at him shrilly. What on earth did he think he was doing? His uncle had set strict rules, William's job was to obey them, not to steal keys and open locked doors. Didn't he understand what was at stake? Didn't he understand what his uncle might do? Did she have to explain everything to him again? William shook his head hopelessly. He would never do anything like that again, he promised. But in his heart he knew that it was too late anyway. His uncle was already disgusted with him. This would surely be the last straw. When his mother was done, he retreated to his room and curled up on his bed, waiting for the inevitable summons.

It was a long time coming.

Eventually William heard the muffled sounds of the utility arriving, and of his uncle's steps within the hallways. There followed a tense half-hour of silence, during which he knew the housekeeper would be making her report. And finally his mother appeared at his bedroom door: his uncle wanted to see him, in the front yard. William rose and went, a boy walking to his execution. Outside, the late afternoon was turning cool. His uncle was sitting on the lip of the empty fountain, gazing out over the plains, something cradled in his lap. It was the army hat, William saw. The evidence. He reached the old man's side and stood there for a time, silent and penitent.

'The winter crops are up,' his uncle said at last.

William looked warily. Out across the plains the chequerboard pattern of farms was flushed a dusty green in places — the new wheat. In a few months the wheat would be golden and ripe, which would mean that his father would have been dead for a year.

'Those farmers have taken a gamble, with things the way they are. If it doesn't rain soon, none of their crops will make it.' The old man was scanning the empty sky. 'If you ask me though, it's not going to rain. Not this spring. Not this summer. We're in for terrible times.' He lowered his gaze, cleared his throat. 'Mrs Griffith tells me you've been exploring.'

Now it would come.

'There were reasons I told you not to go up there,' his uncle said, frowning. 'Those floors aren't secure in places. I know my way around, but you, you could have fallen through or brought a wall down on yourself. It isn't safe.'

'I'm sorry.'

The old man stared levelly at him. 'I'm not too impressed with this stealing of keys, either. I don't lock doors for the fun of it. Especially where guns are concerned. Guns aren't toys. That's why I keep those rifles well out of the way, and behind a padlock.' He paused, started to say something, but then gave a rueful half-smile. 'That pistol though, I'd forgotten all about that.'

William waited in surprise.

But his uncle was stern once more. 'You shouldn't have touched it. That thing is over a century old. It wasn't loaded, but you didn't know that. Mrs Griffith was right to be angry. You had no business there at all.' Then the smile hovered again. 'But Mrs Griffith doesn't think anyone has any business in this House, except her. Not even me.' He clapped William lightly on the shoulder. 'No harm done this time. But don't go up there again, not unless I'm with you.'

William hardly dared believe it. 'You're not mad?'

'You helped me with the newsletter, so let's call it square.' The old man glanced at him awry. 'I suppose you're wondering about the things you saw in that cabinet.'

'Mrs Griffith said they belong to a dead man.'

'Did she? Well, it's true enough.'

'She said he was buried under the House.'

His uncle laughed. 'She's trying to scare you.'

'It's not true?'

'Oh, it might be.' He twisted around and studied the fountain, its broken stump rising bluntly amidst the weeds. 'Actually, his statue used to be the centrepiece here. He was an explorer. His name was Alfred Kirchmeyer.'

William looked blank.

'No,' his uncle agreed, 'He's not one of the famous ones. But if anyone can be said to have discovered Kuran Station, it was him. He was certainly the first white man to set foot here.'

'I thought...'

'Yes, yes, Cunningham found the Darling Downs, but I told you, he never came this far north. That was left to Kirchmeyer, and the three men with him, ten years later. Not that you'll find them in any history books. Alfred was no great bushman, he was just a smalltime Sydney surveyor. God knows why he wanted to go exploring. Maybe he dreamt of finding the infamous inland sea. But he and his party were so slow about getting up here that they barely beat the first settlers.'

The old man gazed pointedly out at the southern horizon, where the sinking sun had cast great shadows across the fields.

'It was pathetic. The blacks stole half their food and drove off all their horses, so the four of them were blundering about out there on foot. Then Kirchmeyer headed off on his own one morning — no one knows why — and was never seen again. The others looked for him for a while, but then gave up and headed back to Sydney. Kirchmeyer's maps and his journal had vanished with him, so there wasn't even anything to report. Settlers had reached the southern Downs by then anyway, and the whole expedition was forgotten in the land rush. And that might have been that. But a year or so later, a squatter named Heatherington sent an agent up here, to stake a claim. The agent crisscrossed the plains until one day he came to a hill. He climbed it, looked all around and thought, yes, this is the place.'

William caught a look in his uncle's eye.

'Here?' he asked.

'Exactly. But that isn't all. That night, while the agent was setting up camp, he came across a skeleton lying in the grass. He knew it was a white man from the clothes. And in the pockets of the clothes were other things. Glasses, a compass, a watch, a journal...'

And one boot, William thought, understanding.

His uncle was nodding. 'The journal was enough to make an identification. The initials A.K. are carved into the cover. One other thing — the skull was smashed in. Kirchmeyer hadn't just wandered off and died, he'd been killed. It was the blacks, of course. They weren't stupid, they knew the white man was bad news. I suppose he came up here for the view, all alone, and they cut him down.'

The old man pondered this a while.

'Anyway, the agent buried the body, but kept the things he'd found and took them back to Heatherington. Years later, when Heatherington decided to build a House on his station, he chose this hill. Maybe he thought even a failed explorer deserved at least that much in his memory.'

'So it's true? His grave is under the House?'

'Supposedly. No one really knows. The funny thing is,

Heatherington didn't name the station after Kirchmeyer, but after the Aboriginal tribe who killed him. Still, it's hard to say who really won in the end. The Kuran people are long gone — shot, or killed by disease, or carted away. And Alfred — no one around here even remembers his name. Heatherington put up this statue, before the Whites took over, but it fell down years ago. Now there isn't a single memorial to Kirchmeyer anywhere on the Downs. Not even a street named after him.'

The old man was staring up at the House, the southern face of which was all in shadow.

'The worst of it is, he was still one of the first people to cross this part of the country. He might have named a creek after himself, or a peak in the Hoop Mountains. If he'd got back alive, the names might have stuck and he'd be remembered. But when his journal was found, it'd been out in the weather so long that nothing in it was legible. So no one knows what he saw or discovered. An awful thing, that book upstairs.'

William looked up to the dark windows of the red chamber. 'Have those things always been in that room?' he asked.

'No. That was my idea. It seemed the decent thing to do. The Whites just kept them in a bag in a cupboard somewhere. I don't know how they came to my father, but he left them to me in that chest. I'm probably the last man alive who knows the whole story.'

'Is it a secret?'

'It's a lesson.' The old man regarded William seriously. 'Discovery isn't enough. Doing something great isn't enough. Someone has to know about it, for it to mean anything. Whatever you do in this world, you have to leave someone behind who remembers.'

And contemplating this, William thought that he understood why his uncle had forgiven him so easily, and why their argument in the office had been forgotten.

The old man was hunched low now, rolling the army cap between his fingers.

Andrew McGahan

'Was that his too?' William asked.

'No. This was my father's.'

'Was he in a war?'

'It's not from the army — it's a police hat.'

William studied the cap, and remembered the jacket he had pulled from the chest, reeking of mothballs. 'The police...' he said, doubtfully.

His uncle rubbed at the badge. 'It's from late last century. My father was in the police then, when he was young, long before he came to the station. It was only for a few years. But the police had different uniforms back then, that's why it looks strange.' The old man caught William eyeing the cap, and abruptly he reached out and placed it on his nephew's head. 'You like it, do you?'

William repositioned the hat, lifting the brim from his nose, and nodded.

'Isn't it too big for you?'

'No.' William discovered that he wanted to keep the cap. He felt that he'd earned it for having braved the locked doors and the empty hallway and the red room. 'No, it fits okay.'

His uncle was smiling. 'Well, it's only rotting away up there. Keep it if you want. So long as it stays in the family.' Then his face grew sober. 'But the guns ... You stay away from them. If you want to play soldier, use a stick or something.'

William nodded again, amenable to anything now.

The old man lifted himself from the edge of the fountain, rubbing his back as if it was sore. 'Thanks again for the newsletters, Will. I mailed them all today.' He glanced out at the afternoon one last time. 'Now we just have to wait a month, and see who turns up at the rally.'

'Do we really get to go camping?'

'That we do. Amongst other things.'

The old man headed inside, but William hung back, sitting on the fountain. He took off the cap and examined it once more, frowning. A police hat. Studying the badge, he could make out the letters QMP embossed around a coat of arms. Did the P stand for Police? But there was nothing very interesting about the police. He decided he would wear it as an army cap, no matter what his uncle said. A captain's hat. William settled it back firmly on his scalp. He liked the way it felt. The badge seemed to cast a glow of authority before it, the way the torch on a miner's helmet casts light. He gazed out over the plains as if he commanded an army gathered there. Not that there had ever been anything like an army on the Kuran Plains, or any great battles, but he could always imagine.

And his uncle liked him again.

When William went to bed that night, he hung the cap on the bedpost. He would wear it all the time now, wherever he went. It was a sign of his uncle's favour, it was good luck. He tossed and rolled for hours, reflecting on the day.

He was hardly aware that his ear had started to ache again.

Chapter Twenty-one

IN THE HOOP MOUNTAINS THE SUMMER OF EARLY 1943 WAS HOT
and dry. Creeks dwindled to dust, and even the rain forest took on
a brittle tinge. It was bushfire season. John McIvor organised the
mountain militia into a fire-fighting brigade, and for weeks on
end they were kept busy, patrolling up and down the range,
extinguishing small outbreaks. The whole time, John's thoughts
were filled exultantly with memories of the events at the water
hole. He had claimed Harriet now, irrevocably. But far more, he
had regained purpose to his life. To think, he had almost
abandoned his dreams for Kuran Station. His childhood dis-
appointments had blinded him. The Whites. His father. All along
he should have realised that none of them mattered — only his
profound link with the property itself.

In the meantime the fire danger left him no moment of
leisure to seek out Harriet again. Instead, late one searingly hot
afternoon, as a blustery west wind was scorching across the hills,
he received a visit from her father. John had set up camp that day

on the western slopes of the range, not far, as it happened, from the borders of Kuran Station. He was resting his leg at the tents, his men fanned out through the scrub below, when he looked up to see Oliver approaching. John was surprised, for the sawmill owner rarely came up into the hills any more. But there were no greetings. Oliver was red-faced, breathless and furious. Harriet had broken down and told him the news just that morning.

She was pregnant.

In the first instant, John was actually thrilled. For what could be better than Harriet carrying his child? What could bind her closer to him? (And when he had climaxed into her, his skin still cold from the water, had he hoped for this?) But he understood a father's feelings, and hastened to explain that, of course, he and Harriet fully intended to marry. And yet Oliver's rage only grew. Marriage? To a timber-getter without prospects, without home or property? To a cripple? He would never allow it. Or was that why John had stolen Harriet away to a secret spot in the first place? To entrap her? And what was really happening here anyway? Was it her money he was after? Was he that sort of a man?

John was stunned. *I don't need her money*, he managed to get out.

Fine, Oliver retorted, because he wouldn't be getting any of it. From this moment on, he was banned from the Fisher household. And what was more, he could consider his employment terminated. Harriet would not be blackmailed. Pregnancies could be terminated too.

It might have come to blows at that point, with the hot wind gusting through the trees around them. But they were interrupted. Night was falling and the other men were returning to the camp. John and Oliver retreated from each other. Darkness arrived with its sudden mountain swiftness, and a carefully watched campfire was lit to prepare dinner. Silent and hostile, John and Oliver haunted opposite ends of the clearing while the rest of the men watched them warily. Then there was nothing to be done except go to sleep. But the tension remained, and the west wind blew on, spattering the ground with dead leaves from the trees, and filling the dark with dust and noise.

John lay awake, brooding far into the night. Shocked as he was by Oliver's reaction, he had no intention of heeding the instructions. The sawmill owner could dismiss him, sure enough, but that was nothing to do with Harriet. John would spirit her away and marry her before anyone could stop it. He'd find other work too. There was no shortage of work now, not with the war. Maybe he'd take Harriet as far as Brisbane. John had heard promising things about Brisbane. It had turned into a wild, overpopulated garrison town, stuffed with troops and transient workers and money. He and Harriet could disappear from her father's eyes completely there, until the baby was born.

But the indictments still burned A cripple! And worse, the accusation that he was after Harriet for her money. That was beyond belief. Harriet's wealth had never even entered his thoughts. And yet, perversely, now John did find himself thinking about money. He had so little, and if Oliver cut them off, then he and Harriet would be alone in the world. A vision came to him of the two of them in a few years time — living in a rented room in Brisbane, trying to raise their child on a labourer's wages. He had no schooling, no qualifications. Even as a labourer, his leg would tell against him. Could Harriet live like that? Or would she begin to yearn for her luxurious house back in Powell? Would she look at her husband then with new, disappointed eyes?

John's imagination ran on horribly. It wasn't just that he would have a family to support. How was he ever going to raise the sort of funds he would need to regain Kuran Station? He had decided that it must happen, but *how* was it to happen? He rolled back and forth, tortured. Could it actually be true? Had he been assuming, all along, that the wealth from the sawmills would be his to collect one day, through Harriet? That Oliver would welcome him as a son, and inevitably raise him into a partnership? Was that the reason he had fixed upon Harriet in the very beginning?

He slept finally, but the doubts plagued his dreams, and so he was the first to wake in the camp. He realised at once that something wasn't right. His watch told him it was nearly dawn, and yet there was a thick rolling blackness in the sky. The wind had risen to violent gusts that set the forest dancing. Was a storm coming? He climbed to his feet, sniffed the air for the heralding scent of rain. Instead he smelled burning. In an awful instant, he understood. There was no storm. The blackness above was smoke, underscored with red, and he heard now a deeper roar above the wind. He cried out and the other men started up from their beds in alarm, but it was already too late.

The wall of fire came rushing up the hill. There was no time to do anything, no defence to be prepared, no line to be drawn and held. Men simply scattered as the flames bore down, the trees behind them exploding in fiery expectoration. The only safety lay on the far side of the ridge. John laboured upwards as best he could, his bad leg singing. Ash and flaming cinders rained down about him and smoke whipped along through the trees ahead, black and choking. He scrambled through tinder dry undergrowth, until suddenly he was out of the trees, running over grass and rock. Above him the ridge crested in a bald crown against a pale dawn sky. Turning on his heel, he looked back and beheld a terrible thing. The entire mountainside was aflame, but worse, in the gully below him, lost amid the smoke and raining debris, a single figure staggered.

It was Oliver Fisher. He was grimed black with ash, and his hands were cupped over his eyes in a vain attempt to see as he coughed and retched. John yelled out, but his voice was tossed away by the wind. Smoke obscured Oliver for a moment, and then he was visible again, on his knees, his head turning blindly.

John gauged the progress of the fire. Were there ten seconds before it swallowed them, were there thirty? Was there time to get down to Oliver, to drag him back up the slope? Could he even manage it, with his bad leg, and Oliver disorientated and perhaps unconscious by then?

The instant of hesitation seemed to last forever. And then John saw a monster step out of the smoke. It was a tornado of flames, a giant eddy in the firestorm, crowned with the white-hot sparks of detonating leaves. The whirlwind howled, swayed this way and that in search of prey, and then curled gleefully to engulf Oliver where he crouched. John stayed stricken for one last second, long enough to see his employer rear up, a flailing, burning shape of arms and legs. Then the whole slope below was one torrent, gushing upwards. He fled. Fire licked his heels, singed the hair from the back of his head and set his shirt smouldering, but he dashed across the hilltop, leapt over a low cliff on the far side, and fell to the earth. A great sheet of solid flame streamed into the sky above him. It roared in frustration for a time, and then, deprived of fuel at last, it fluttered, wavered, and died.

Two other men were lost that morning, besides Oliver.

It was the beginning of the worst fire the mountains had seen in decades, and no one knew who or what had ignited it. Either way, it was only after another week of fire-fighting that John, still scorched and blackened, made his way down from the mountains and called on Harriet. Her father's body had preceded him. There wasn't much they could say to each other. John was exhausted, and Harriet was devastated. It meant that the two of them never discussed Harriet's pregnancy. It was simply swept up in events, and accepted. Nor did John ever tell Harriet that he'd witnessed her father's last moments, or that he and Oliver had argued so violently about her, only the night before.

His own behaviour in that crucial moment, the hesitation

between action and inaction, was something that John long refused to examine. It was only later that he would wonder if, underneath his horror of the fire, he had felt a surge of exultation when he'd seen Oliver trapped in that gully — an excited certainty that Oliver would die, and that with him every obstacle between himself and Harriet and her money would disappear. And later still would come a darker conviction. For the fire had in fact begun in the easternmost reaches of Kuran Station, before sweeping up into the mountains. And so John would return to the memory — the rushing flames, and a frenzied, burning figure — and savour it as a gift both precious and awesome. For his secret belief was that, in his hour of greatest need, the hills of his station had ignited by themselves that night, and so devoured his enemy.

Within a month, John and Harriet were married. In accordance with Oliver's will, his estate was split between his children — two-thirds to Matthew, one-third to Harriet. The money involved was something of a disappointment, however, especially to John. It turned out that Oliver had squandered much of his wealth on the stock market and at the racetrack. Still, John and Harriet began their married life in comfort at the Fisher residence, and John and Matthew took over management of the sawmills. Two years later, as the war drew to a close and the timber supply in the Hoops approached exhaustion, they decided to shut down the mills and sell off the equipment. They sold the Fisher family home too, and Oliver's legacy was complete. John and Harriet's share was no grand fortune, certainly not enough for John to consider buying Kuran Station. It was, however, enough to purchase a wheat farm on the Kuran Plains.

At the age of thirty-one, thus, John McIvor finally became an independent landowner. The pride of it filled him to the brim. He had studied the available properties carefully, and chosen a six hundred and forty acre block, one square mile, consisting of the deepest and darkest black soil. It was not Kuran Station by any comparison — but the hill upon which the House sat was clearly visible, seven or eight miles away across the plains, and John knew that this was all the start he needed to reach it.

He was a father now too, of course. Harriet had given birth to a healthy, dark-haired girl, whom they named Ruth. And little Ruth was in Harriet's arms when John and his family went to the Powell train station to greet Dudley, the soldier finally returning home from war.

Chapter Twenty-two

For William, the month leading up to the rally took forever to pass. It was the biggest event the Australian Independence League had ever attempted, and his uncle seemed to have a thousand things to organise. There were marquees to be hired and erected on the site, portable toilets to be installed, cartons of toilet paper to be ordered, firewood to be cut and stockpiled, lighting and a public address system to be set up, and then an electric generator to power it all. Delivery trucks left great piles of gear at the House, or went directly up into the hills to the campground.

Amidst all this excitement, William's only concern was his ear. The ache was never acute, but it was ever present, a throb that seemed to penetrate deep within his skull. Finally he mentioned it to his mother. She had Dr Moffat's prescription filled, and over the next ten days William swallowed antibiotics. The pain seemed to fade slightly, but to be honest, he wasn't sure. Nevertheless, he told his mother that he felt better. Both she and the doctor had appeared to regard an earache as a minor annoyance, something that every child had to put up with, and he didn't want to sound weak. Besides, it would be a disaster if the rally arrived and William was banished to his bedroom just because his ear was hurting.

Meanwhile, through all the preparations, he'd quite forgotten that the great event wasn't just a party, that it also had a serious purpose. One night, however, about a week before the big day, he was in the living room after dinner, curled up quietly on a chair while his mother watched a current affairs show. William was paying no attention, but then he overheard two familiar words. He looked up at the television. On the hazy screen he could see a man being interviewed in the studio. The man was answering a question, and the topic, it seemed, was Native Title.

'…so let me tell you about terra nullius. Part of the theory is that the Aborigines didn't work the land, they just left it as they found it, and so therefore they had no rights of ownership. But that isn't quite true. They did what they could, with very limited resources. Australia was no paradise. It didn't have any native plants suitable for large-scale farming — no wheat or barley or cotton or any of the rest. It didn't have the right sort of animals for domestication either, no sheep or cows. It wasn't until Europeans brought those plants and animals that you could farm the way we do now, with paddocks and fences. In the meantime the Aborigines farmed the only way that was viable…'

William glanced at his mother. Normally she would have switched something like this off. But she only stared at the screen, glassy-eyed and far away.

'…then the High Court led the way with the Mabo judgment. It recognised finally that terra nullius was always a lie, and now the government is responding to historical reality with the Native Title legislation. This country was Aboriginal land and it was stolen from them without compensation. That was unfair. For a century and a half Aboriginal people have been herded into missions or deserts or urban ghettos and forgotten about.

That's unfair too. They've had no proper access to education or health services or employment — many of them couldn't even vote until the '60s. All of that's unfair, and the effects will last for generations, but Native Title is at least the first step in righting the wrong...'

William watched attentively. It was strange. He had listened to the radio for hours with his uncle, and heard all sorts of discussions about the new laws and how bad they would be. This was the first time he had heard anyone who seemed to think they were a good thing.

'...but if your land is freehold, Native Title won't touch it. It shouldn't even touch pastoral leases. In fact, the whole point of the legislation is to *protect* pastoral leases. Okay, a very few of them might still be open to claim, but only if there has been an ongoing Aboriginal presence on the land — and that's going to be hard to prove. And even if a claim is successful, all the lease-holder will have to do is share some access with the traditional owners, and consult with them about any major works which might affect cultural sites on the property. It's hardly stealing farms away...'

Strange and puzzling. It didn't even sound like the same law that made his uncle so angry. William looked at his mother again. Was she listening? He had never asked her what she thought about his uncle's business. Or even about the rally.

'Mum?'

She blinked at him, her eyes slowly focusing. 'What?'

'You know what the rally is for, don't you?'

'Your uncle is spending a lot of money, that's all I know.'

'But those new laws. Do you think they're a good thing or a bad thing?'

She rubbed her forehead. 'Christ, Will, it isn't up to me.'

'Uncle John says...'

'William, not now! Whatever your uncle says, that's fine with me. Just keep on his good side. All right?'

William let it go. But the next day he told his uncle what he
had heard on television.

His uncle raised an eyebrow. 'You saw that, did you? Well, I
always told you, some people are for these new laws. Not that they
really understand. Or did you think he was right?'

'I don't know … no. But…'

'Hmm.' The old man considered his nephew for a long
moment. Then he rose from his desk. 'Tell you what — I was
about to go and check on progress out at the campground. Why
don't you come along?'

William agreed, happy for the chance of a drive, and they
climbed into the utility. It was a fine blue day. Spring was well
advanced now, and the sun was warm again. But his uncle's mood
grew serious as they wound their way along the track into the
hills. Dust hung in the air. No rain had fallen and fields looked
parched. If it stayed this dry, the old man noted grimly, then desperate measures might need to be taken, like selling off even more
of the cattle. The creek was empty, and the Condamine River,
he'd heard, had stopped flowing. What about the water hole?
William asked. Wouldn't there still be water there? His uncle
nodded. The pool would be sunken, but yes, the spring in the cave
meant there was always water, in that one place at least. Perhaps
when the rally was over and they had some time to spare, they
would even go swimming.

They drove on to the campground, a cleared space at the foot
of a broad hill. William remembered the windmill that stood there,
with a water tank beside it, and a trough. A cardboard sign directed
visitors towards a large parking area marked off with orange plastic
tape. Beyond that, on the lower slopes of the hill, and shaded by
widely spaced gum trees, was the camp itself. There were stacks of
firewood here and there, and fire pits carefully marked out with
stones. Still higher up the slope were several mounds of folded
canvas, and a mess of ropes and pegs. It was here too that makeshift

lampposts had been erected, and already light bulbs were hanging from wires that stretched between them. And finally, up above it all, on the crown of the hill, William could glimpse, as he had once before, a circle of standing stones, dark amidst the trees.

The whole site looked thrilling. It was a circus before the crowds arrived, but even better, it was William's own circus, away off in the hills and bush, which only a secret few knew about. His uncle drove directly through the camping area, up onto the shoulder of the hill, and parked by the folded tents. They climbed out and took in the view — the brown hills rolling away to distant wheat fields out on the plains, and the mountains marching along the eastern horizon. The sun was bright, a gentle breeze blew and the air smelled of eucalyptus and cattle.

'Well?' his uncle asked. 'You think it'll do?'

William nodded fervently.

The old man indicated the piles of canvas. 'We'll get the marquee set up a day or two before the weekend. If by any chance it rains, we'll want somewhere under cover to set up the PA and hold the sessions.'

'What about our tent?' said William.

'We might not need one. Just sleep out under the stars.' He smiled at William's disappointment. 'No — we can set it up wherever we like. We'll have first choice, which is lucky. Believe me, the whole ground will be full, by the time everyone arrives and gets unpacked.'

They stood there for a time, listening to the deep quiet of the hills. Two crows glided between the trees below, calling out their strangled laments.

The old man stirred. 'We could have held the rally near the House, you know. It would have been simpler. But there's a reason I chose to have it here.'

'Why?'

'Come on. This is what I want you to see.'

He turned and led William up the slope. At the top of the hill there was a wide belt of trees that formed a ring around the crown, tall gums with reaching limbs and smooth white bark. Deep shade fell between them, but beyond, upon the actual hilltop, there was a wide empty circle of sunlight. And here were the standing stones that were half-visible from below — although up close William could see that the rocks were not really free-standing. The brow of the hill was weathered away, and a jumble of boulders and rocky protrusions had emerged from deep in the soil, like broken teeth. The larger ones formed a roughly ovoid pattern about a central grassy space.

William's uncle strode to the very centre of the oval, and spread his arms to the rocks. 'As long as it doesn't rain,' he said, 'this is where we'll set up the PA and hold the meetings.'

William looked around, dubious. The hilltop felt claustrophobic somehow. The sky was blue above, and yet the air felt stuffy, with the grey trees leaning inwards all around and the stones looming. It was difficult to imagine lights and people here, let alone loudspeakers.

'You'd almost think someone built this, wouldn't you?' said his uncle. 'In fact, it's a natural formation. But even so, this is a special place. A meeting place. I think people have held meetings here for centuries.'

'What people?'

'You know what people.' The old man selected a boulder to sit on, waved William over to a place by his side. 'Now, you're going to hear a lot of things talked about at this rally, just like you did on TV last night. There are going to be some angry people, and some hard opinions. A lot of the discussion is going to be about Native Title, and that means a lot of it is going to be about Aborigines. You'll hear some pretty nasty things said. But there are a few points I want you to understand.'

William waited.

'The first thing,' his uncle said finally, 'is that I don't hate Aborigines. Some of the people who are coming to the rally do … but not many, and I certainly don't agree with them. That isn't what the League is all about. Personally, I have a great deal of respect for Aborigines and the way they used to live. They were here before us, after all, and they survived for thousands of years. They understood a lot of things. Like this circle. I don't have any proof, but I'm sure that they used to gather right here.'

William studied the stones. 'What for?'

'I don't know. Corroborees, maybe. Initiations. Important rituals. It doesn't really matter what they came here for … what's important is that this is where they came. Look around. Can't you feel something?'

William could. It was faint and hard to catch, like something from the corner of his eye, but it was there. A circle of stone within a circle of trees.

'They wouldn't have missed a spot like this,' his uncle insisted. 'There's something powerful here. They would have sniffed it out and used it.' He tilted his head to look at William. 'Have you ever heard of bora rings?'

'No.'

'The Aborigines used to mark out rings, away in the bush, in places that were special to them. Powerful places. They were sacred. And I think this is one of them. You wait until you're up here at night, with a big fire burning. You'll see what I mean. I've had a few smaller meetings up here before. And something is present on this hill. Something comes alive.'

Fire … a fire burning amidst the stones. A memory chilled William, from months ago. He had been sitting on the back verandah of his old house, on the night before he and his mother left it forever. He had seen a point of light out in the darkness, up in the hills. Recalling it now, William turned and gazed through the trees to the plains below. His old farm was down there

Andrew McGahan

somewhere, and from there he might have been looking up to this very spot. So had he witnessed some earlier meeting of his uncle's? But no ... the mysterious light had flickered in and out of view. It hadn't been stationary like a campfire, William was sure. It had been moving.

'Now there are some people who would find it stupid to meet in an Aboriginal place. They don't think the blacks ever did anything worthwhile. But I don't want you to think that, no matter what you hear. The Aborigines may not have made this place, but they recognised it, and it's partly out of respect for them that I chose it for the rally.' The old man straightened sternly. 'But the ironic thing is that because of laws like Native Title, I have to keep this place secret. And it *is* a secret, Will.'

'Like the water hole?'

'Exactly like the water hole.'

'But why?'

'It's dangerous information in these times, that's why. This is my land now, I know you understand that. Whoever might have lived here once, they're gone. But the people who support Native Title, they don't accept that. They think that the Aborigines can be brought back somehow, given back their old land. I think that's madness. It's far too late to undo the things that were done, not without making an even bigger mess than we already have. But take this bora ring. If the government or some Aboriginal land council knew it was here, they'd be swarming up this hill in no time. They'd say these stones were proof that the blacks lived here, that they used this land for their rituals, and that therefore I should give it back to them. Obviously I don't want that to happen, so I don't tell anybody that the ring is here. And that's what these new laws will make people like me do. Keep all sorts of secrets we wouldn't have to otherwise.'

'But lots of people will be here next week.'

His uncle laughed. 'We don't have to worry about them. They

won't tell. But I wanted you to think about it. You see, I chose this place partly out of respect, but partly as a protest too.'

'A protest?'

The old man nodded, sombre again. 'There are folk out there who believe that the Aborigines are the only ones who understand the land, that only the blacks could have a found a place like this and appreciated what it was. They think that the blacks have some magical connection that whites can never have, that we're just stumbling around here without any idea, that we don't understand the country, that we just want to exploit it. But that's not true. We can have connections with the land too, our own kind of magic. This land talks to me. It doesn't care what colour I am, all that matters is that I'm here. And I understand what it says, just as well as anyone before me, black or white. I found this ring, didn't I? So I deserve respect too.'

He fell silent. William pondered the stone circle. Here was another secret he had learnt about the station. And that was a good thing. The more time he spent with his uncle, the more was revealed to him. He was getting closer all the time to knowing the land in the way the old man knew it. A magical connection, his uncle had called it — knowing about places like the stone ring and the water hole, or the story of the explorer who lay buried under the House.

Knowledge, William decided, that was the issue. Knowledge was the essence of ownership. The black men, it seemed, had held the knowledge when they had owned the land. His uncle held it now. And when William had the knowledge, when he knew everything about the station there was to know, he too would be ready to be own it in his turn.

The old man was standing again. He reached down and ruffled the army cap upon William's head. 'Just don't let anyone tell you that the League is racist.'

Chapter Twenty-three

Two days before the rally began, four members of the League's central committee arrived to help with final preparations. William was posted as guard on the front steps. His job was to greet the guests and direct them to his uncle's office.

The first to arrive was none other than Dr Moffat. He pulled up in his old car and climbed out, as round and red-faced as ever. He waved an airy greeting, then proceeded to unload two cartons of wine from the boot, toting them breathlessly up the stairs into the entrance hall.

'And how's that glandular fever of yours?' he wheezed.

It was a moment before William even remembered. 'Okay.'

A wink. ''Course it is. Back at school next year, hey?'

William nodded uncertainly. With the doctor right there in front of him, he almost said something about his ear. But what if he was sent to bed and told to stay there? And he remembered how agonising it had been when Dr Moffat examined him the last time. So he said nothing, and in any case, the doctor was already heading for the office.

The next guest drove up in a big, silvery four-wheel drive, and the man who climbed out was just as big and broad. He wasn't young — he had thinning hair, a creased, sunburnt face, and a huge belly bulging through his shirt — but he seemed hale and fit all the same, smartly dressed in jeans and boots. He stomped up the stairs, eyeing William cheerfully. 'Standing sentry are we?' The man raised a hand to his forehead, saluting. 'What are you under that hat? Captain? Major? General?'

William was caught off guard. 'It's not really an army hat,' he admitted. 'It's a police hat.'

'Bullshit. Used to be a copper m'self. Never saw a police hat like that, not in my whole career. You'd be this nephew I've been hearing about?'

'I guess so.'

'Good lad. So where's your uncle?'

The man's name was Terry Butterworth, and it turned out he really had been a policeman once, although he was some years retired. He ran a business of his own now, in Toowoomba. Something to do with installing locks and burglar alarms. He was large and loud and rough, but William liked him, and was impressed enough to practise saluting for a while, when he returned to his station on the porch.

Another four-wheel drive appeared, this one painted with safari stripes. It was all dented and covered in dust, and sported a huge bull bar and spotlights. The driver, however, was small and wiry and old. He was dressed in a faded khaki uniform, his skin was tanned a leathery brown and his face was lost in a wild tangle of beard, from which dangled a smouldering cigarette. Coming up the front steps, he was as bow-legged as a crab. Emboldened, William tried out his salute. The old man reared back momentarily, the cigarette stiffening in astonishment.

'I'll be buggered,' he said. He returned the salute with a single finger to his brow, then headed off towards the office without another word.

Abashed, William was left to study the vehicle. On the side were emblazoned the words 'Lost Reef Outback Tours — Proprietor Henry Lasseter'.

This meant nothing to William, but later his uncle explained all about the legend of the prospector Harold Lasseter, and the giant deposit of gold he claimed to have found, but then lost again, out in the desert. *Henry* Lasseter meanwhile, tour guide, was no relation to the original. What was more, his tours operated only in western Queensland, nowhere near the region in which the reef supposedly existed. But Henry hadn't let such minor details stand in his way. William got the impression that his uncle didn't think much of the old tour guide, or the tourists who hired him, or indeed the whole Lasseter legend in general. 'But if people want to be fooled by old stories,' his uncle said, 'then one fraud deserves another.'

The last committee member arrived around sunset, rolling up the driveway in a sleek red sedan. Attached to the rear bumper of the car was a bicycle, the sort that was built for racing, and the driver was much younger than the other guests. He had neat dark hair and a clean-shaven face and, most startling of all, he was wearing a suit and a tie. For a disturbing instant, William was reminded of the undertakers who had buried his father. He forgot to salute. The newcomer pulled a briefcase from his car and stared up doubtfully at the crumbling walls, the clinging ivy, and the sagging verandah of the upper floor.

'Is this John McIvor's place?' he asked with a frown, his eyes coming to rest dubiously on William's hat.

'Yes sir.'

'Good Lord.'

His name, it emerged, was Kevin Goodwin, and he was from Brisbane. He was an accountant, and because of that, William's uncle had appointed him as League treasurer, even though he was a relatively new member. But William decided he didn't like him much. The man appeared to think that a boy wearing an army hat was something silly.

But that was the sentry duty accomplished. William returned to his own wing and settled down to toasted sandwiches in front of television. Occasionally there came distant yells and a hubbub of voices from the office, where his uncle was entertaining the men. It grew very late, and William was nodding off in the chair when his uncle appeared in the doorway.

'First meeting,' the old man said. 'Come on.'

The committee had gathered in the dining room, ranging themselves around the table as a naked bulb burned above. They each had drinks in their hands, beer or wine or scotch, and cigarette smoke was already thick in the air. William sat in the corner, and watched wide-eyed as his uncle — seated upright at the head of the table — opened the proceedings. But there were all sorts of formalities to be attended to, and minutes to be read, and William soon grew bored. His gaze drifted towards the ceiling. Great cobwebs floated dreamily in the corners. He watched them drift, growing sleepy, and then blinked suddenly. The meeting proper was under way.

'I've seen the maps,' Terry Butterworth was declaring, fingers jammed under his straining belt buckle. 'No matter who says what — half the country is open to claim. The pastoral industry, the mining industry, they'd both be paralysed. And take Henry there — the places he runs his tours through are all either leasehold or Crown property.'

'I'd be screwed,' the tour guide rasped. He was hunched forward over the table, scribbling in a ledger that lay open before him, taking the minutes. 'Suddenly it's black land and sacred sites and whites aren't allowed in. Look what's happened in the Northern Territory. They have independent bloody countries up there, you need fucking passports to go anywhere.'

'It's a legal fiction anyway,' the policeman remarked. 'Either the whole country was stolen, in which case the entire continent's up for Native Title claims, or none of it was. You can't just say that freehold is somehow magically immune. Even the blacks are pissed off about that. Freehold, pastoral leases — they reckon it's all theirs regardless.'

William's uncle spoke. 'Freehold means city properties. The government knows that if they touch the cities there'd be a revolution. They're not that stupid. But pastoral lease-holders are a tiny minority, so they don't matter.'

'They?' This was Kevin Goodwin, looking puzzled. 'Aren't you one of them?'

William's uncle shook his head. 'The original Kuran Station was all pastoral lease, of course. But when it was broken up the government ceded fifteen thousand acres to the Whites as part of the deal. That land was converted to something called perpetual lease. From a legal point of view, I'm told, it's just as secure as freehold.'

A spray of documents surrounded the accountant, and a pen twirled constantly in his fingers. 'So you've got nothing to lose, even if the legislation passes?'

'The principle of the thing is what matters. A man's land won't be his own. We all lose if this law gets in.'

'Agreed. But as I see it, the problem is finding a base from which to fight. The League is all very well as a lobby group, but we've got no direct political power. Isn't it time we rethought things and actually ran some candidates in the next election?'

William's uncle was firm. 'We are not going to sign up and join in with the system. It's the system that's the problem. As soon as we start running candidates we're tacitly approving the way things work, and before we knew it we'd be as rotten as any other party.'

'Christ, son,' said Terry Butterworth, 'we're not here to run candidates. Our job is to preserve some true Australian values, so that when everything finally falls apart, there'll be people like us to pick up the pieces.'

The accountant was unruffled. 'And what if things never fall apart?'

Henry Lasseter glanced up from his ledger. 'They will, lad, quicker than you might think.'

'Maybe so, but right now we need broader support if we want to stop things like this legislation. Sooner or later we'll have to build a base in the cities.'

'Fuck the cities,' said Henry. 'If I had my way, the bush would just cut the cities loose and declare independence.'

The policeman laughed. 'Shit, if the blacks can have their own countries up north, why can't we? If worst comes to worst, we can set up our own state out west somewhere.'

'Why the hell not?' Henry puffed himself up. 'The federation isn't fucking inviolate. Western Australia is always on the verge of pulling out. It never wanted to join in the first place. North Queensland would jump too, if things got bad enough.'

William's uncle rapped the table dryly. 'We're getting a little ahead of ourselves…'

The debate rolled from one end of the table to the other, and William slumped further down in his chair. The air was heavy with the scent of alcohol and tobacco, and he was getting drowsy again. He knew that the topic was important, but he wished that these preliminaries could be finished with, and that the rally itself would begin. He yawned, forced his eyes open.

'The legislation will pass in the lower house,' his uncle was saying. 'We all know that. But the government doesn't have the numbers in the Senate. They'll be relying on the minor parties. Question is, how do we make sure those minor parties vote against it?'

Kevin Goodwin responded. 'We have to alert the country to the dangers, make people see how much they have to lose. If there's a popular outcry against the legislation, the Senate will back off. Problem is, the people in the cities don't feel threatened, they think their back yards are safe. So how do we ram the point home? Should it be some sort of legal angle? Maybe the whole idea of Native Title is unconstitutional.'

'Bugger the courts!' The old tour guide was scornful. 'They started this mess.'

Terry Butterworth shifted his bulk and sat forward. 'Direct action is what we need. Protests, blockades. I saw enough of them in my days on the force, and the thing is, they work. I reckon we choose one of our members who owns property out west, property that's under pastoral lease and open to claim if the laws get in. And we set up a picket line around it. We declare that we refuse to accept Native Title, no matter what the government decides, and that we'll stay there forever if we have to, to protect the boundaries. In fact, we publicly dare any blacks who think different to try and bust through, and just see how far they get. Make a big stink about it, get the newspapers in, and the TV. They'd love it — a struggling farmer and his family, terrified of being kicked off their land, land they've worked for generations. And in the meantime we're screaming at the cameras — You could be next! The government is lying! Your back yards aren't safe! Your parks aren't safe, your beaches and your rivers aren't safe! Native Title will steal the lot!'

The accountant whirled his pen. 'It might be difficult to set up the right sort of confrontation. We'd have to select a property that was extremely important to the Aboriginal claimants, one they'd be prepared to physically fight for if we denied them access — that way we'd get the sort of violent exchange and publicity you're hoping for. Black hordes invading white family's home, that sort of thing. If we mustered enough outrage along those lines, then the Senate would have to take notice. John?'

A thoughtful pause. 'It's got possibilities...'

It went on and on. William set his head back against the wall and let his hat slip forward over his eyes, the weight of the badge on the front heavy and reassuring. His ear throbbed, and hot red colours seemed to dance through his mind.

'Some training could be useful,' Terry Butterworth was musing now, 'if it gets down to blockades and things turn nasty.'

'We should form a proper militia,' Henry suggested. 'It's one of the duties of a democracy, being prepared to fight for the bloody thing. And most of our members already have guns.'

Kevin Goodwin sounded dubious. 'An armed militia mightn't look good on TV. We're supposed to be the good guys.'

'This is bigger than just Native Title,' the policeman stated. 'This is about national security. You think the Australian army could defend this country if the Japs ever come back, or if the Indonesians ever invaded, or the Chinese? We'll need citizen troops, lots of them and well armed, people who know their local areas. The League should be ready to contribute. We could set it up easily enough. What d'you think, John?'

'I've got nothing against organising a militia. I was in one during the war. As long as that's all it is. I'm not having the League turned into a military body.'

'No, no, just an associated militia. Like Henry says, it's part of our responsibility as Australians. We can put it to the general meeting. Kevin?'

'Well … I suppose it can't hurt to see what the members think. And I'd be interested to see what sort of force we could actually muster.'

William's uncle was insistent. 'Our main business this weekend is formulating a response to Native Title.'

'Of course, of course,' said Terry Butterworth. 'But it can still go on the agenda. I propose the motion that we float the idea of an organised militia to the members.'

'I second,' said Henry Lasseter.

William's uncle sighed. 'All right then, it's passed.'

There was a babble of excited talk from the others.

'We'll have to think of a name.'

'How about the Australian Independence Militia. AIM — that's to the point.'

'What about a uniform?'

'Uniform?'

'Okay, not a full kit. Just a badge or something. So we all know who's who.'

'Like Will over there, with his hat. Hey, Will, you wanna join up? We can make you a field marshal...'

The men laughed, but William's head was on his chest. He stirred restlessly at the sound, lost in a half-dream of fire. Then the laughter subsided, and the men got back to their business.

Chapter Twenty-four

By 1950, THE KURAN PLAINS WERE BOOMING AT LAST, RIDING ON the back of wheat prices that had never soared so high. New grain varieties had arrived, resistant to drought and disease, and there were new fertilisers too, new pesticides, new tractors and harvesters and trucks. Sealed roads spread out from Powell, and telephone lines and power cables. The population skyrocketed, the humble shacks of the old selectors disappearing, replaced by sturdy farmhouses crowded with children. Only twenty years earlier the plains had all been open pasture, wide and lonely. Now the lights of a hundred homes glowed there every night, and the dust of a hundred ploughs rose by day.

And yet, frustratingly, all this prosperity seemed to elude John McIvor. He worked away diligently, planting wheat or barley in the winter, corn or millet in the summer, but he was learning that even in good times, things could go wrong. One year a late frost blighted his wheat just as it was ripening. Another year a sudden hail storm battered his corn. He suffered plagues — of weeds, of mice, even of locusts. And once, during harvest, it stayed wet and dreary for five weeks on end, and his barley rotted in the paddocks. The list went on, and somehow, bumper crops never quite seemed to eventuate. The farm was certainly profitable in a small way, but John needed much more than that.

He had no intention of tilling this little square of dirt all his life. His plan was to expand, to buy a second farm with the profits from the first, and then a third, and so on, until the day he could sell it all and acquire Kuran Station. But here he was struggling to save a few hundred pounds a year. It was too slow. He could always go to the banks for a loan, of course, but John harboured a deep aversion to the idea of borrowing. The old Kuran Station had been laden with debt, and it was that which had doomed the property, more certainly than anything the Whites had done. Whatever John owned, he wanted to own it outright, not under mortgage. Possession was meaningless if it wasn't absolute.

The fact that he now had a family only made his impatience for Kuran all the greater. He wanted his children to grow up on the station. Surely his daughter deserved as much as Elizabeth White — the fine bedroom of floating curtains, the clothes, the education. Indeed, he wanted Ruth to have more, to be better than Elizabeth ever was. What more fitting proof could there be that the station had been his by right all along? And one day he would have a son to carry on the McIvor name. He wanted no uncertainty for the boy, none of the doubts and disasters that had afflicted his own youth. His son must grow up knowing without question that Kuran Station was his to inherit. Then he would look to his father with gratitude and pride, not disappointment.

But the years passed, harvest after harvest, and not only did Kuran Station remain far beyond John's grasp, no son arrived either. Harriet fell pregnant again in 1946, but miscarried. She miscarried again in 1948. And after that, there were no more pregnancies. Ruth remained their first and only child — the product of that one encounter amidst the stone and water and hills. John looked at her anew then, and took fresh heart. Her very existence was mingled with the station, after all, so perhaps it was a matter of destiny. He began taking the little girl out with him across the farm. She was quick and clever and unafraid, and far happier, it seemed, with her feet and hands in the dirt than when she was at home playing with dolls or dresses. And yet John continued to worry, for by 1950 Ruth was already seven years old. How was he to secure Kuran Station before she grew up?

And then there was Dudley Green.

The soldier had came home a forlorn shadow of the man who went away. He was living with his parents now, on their farm. His older brother had died in the war, so he was all they had left. But of Dudley's own wartime experiences, John and Harriet knew little. His unit had been encircled during the early battles on the Malay peninsula. After capture, he was interned in several makeshift prisons, until he was finally reunited with the rest of the division in Changhi. He was sent out again to the work camps, the Burma–Thailand railroad among them, yet of all those years of labour and hunger and brutality, Dudley seldom spoke. His body was testimony enough — after enduring long bouts of dysentery, beriberi and malaria, he was permanently shrunken and stooped. His lungs were especially affected, making him readily susceptible to influenza and pneumonia. He was also afflicted with biting arthritis and skin rashes.

But it was the emotional changes in Dudley that pained John and Harriet most. The camps had leached the brightness out of him, broken something inside. He had become strange and distracted — haunted, it seemed, by his own memories. Upon his return he had taken up none of his old pursuits, and retreated even from contact with his fellow POWs. His solitary social pleasure became to visit John and Harriet's house — only a few miles from his own — where he lavished shy attention on little Ruth.

He openly adored her. And if he resented John and Harriet for what they had done in his absence, he never showed it. So it was that John found himself waking to a clear and damning sense of shame. All through the war he had envied Dudley, and feared his homecoming. He had betrayed their pact out of that fear. But here was John, who had stayed at home, secure now with a farm and a wife and a child. And there was his friend, who had gone to war, with nothing and no one to show for it.

Dudley's mother died of cancer in 1951. A year later, worn out with labour and worry, his father followed her, leaving him completely alone on the farm he now owned. In isolation, his nervous condition began to deteriorate. John and Harriet could only watch on helplessly. He neglected the routine work upon his property. His house became cluttered with rubbish. He grew lax about bathing and washing his clothes, and ceased shaving. Nor was he eating properly, so that the weight he had gained after coming home began to fall away again. And his drinking, only social before the war, turned hard. He took to sleeping all day, and drunkenly roaming his untended farm by night. John began to hear the names he was called by the neighbours. All they saw was his long hair and tangled beard, his dirty clothes and evasive eyes. *Poor Dudley,* they said, with resigned shakes of the head and mutterings about shell shock. Or *Old Dudley,* even though he was not old. John suspected that the names were worse out of his own hearing. *Mad Dudley,* perhaps. *Crazy Dudley,* just as likely.

One day in 1953, John arrived at his friend's house to find him naked and unconscious on the living room floor. Dudley's body was appallingly thin, laced with faded scars and the pale blotches of poorly healed tropical ulcers. It was some hours before John could rouse him or help him dress. Dudley reeked of rum, but John divined that this was more than just drunkenness. The man was close to starvation. John packed him up and took him home. Harriet prepared a meal and they both watched while he ate.

Then they set up a camp bed in John's office, and sent him off to sleep. They kept him there the next day as well, and the day following. With food and attention he seemed to improve, and there was no real decision to make. They didn't even consult Dudley. They simply never took him home again. And Dudley, for his part, never asked to go back.

It was a penance, both John and Harriet knew. There was no question of sending him to an institution for care by strangers. He would never go. Nor could they just abandon him to his fate. Hadn't they already done that once? They weren't to blame for his condition, they knew, and yet the guilt remained. But it was far from easy. John had to take over the running of Dudley's farm, even though he could barely spare the time from his own. And at home Dudley could be difficult. He remained haphazard about his personal hygiene, so the smell of him was everywhere. Often he refused food for days at a time, angrily if they tried to force it on him. And there was no denying him the solace of alcohol. When drunk, he was prone to outbursts of weak rage, and in his sleep he raved incoherently with nightmares. But they dealt with it all as patiently as they could, because of who he was, and because, in his better moments, he was patently so happy to be included in their lives. He still regarded John as his unfailing best friend, and remained utterly devoted to Harriet.

But it was Ruth who had really captured his heart. She turned ten during his first year in the house, and seemed to be maturing effortlessly into adolescence, an unaffected girl, very much her father's daughter, dark and handsome. Dudley trailed after her faithfully, and outside of school hours she watched over him and helped with the small tasks he was still able to perform around his own property. She called him her uncle, and didn't seem to mind that he smelled bad, or that his breath stank of rum, or that his wild beard was often stiff with grease or with phlegm from his constant coughing. He was a member of her family, that was all, and she was not the sort of girl, John noted with pride, to be put off by a little ugliness.

Indeed, John had long since ceased regretting the lack of a son. Ruth was as good as any boy. And while she had inherited her father's looks, she had none of his grim temperament. She was happy and keen, and repeatedly a look or a word from her could melt the winter in John's heart with a confused rush of love that was acute in its nakedness. But his dreams for his daughter — Kuran House and the station with it — remained as elusive as ever. The truth was, John had begun to despair of the farming life. The longer he laboured, the more wealth and fortune seemed to recede before him like a mirage. There was a string of poor seasons though '53 and '54, and the harvests were mediocre.

Even the plains themselves began to oppress him. There was no space any more, where once everything had been open sky and clear horizons. His neighbours too grated on him. They rode proudly on their tractors and called themselves hardened folk, country folk, but to John they looked as soft as any city-dweller mowing a quarter-acre lawn. Where were the bold pioneers that he remembered, the stockmen, the shearers? Lesser men had inherited the earth, and John knew that he alone was different, that an older and more vital blood flowed in his veins. So it was a source of immense dissatisfaction to him that he couldn't rise to the level which that blood demanded. In the darker moments of the night he would lie in bed next to his sleeping wife, gazing bitterly into a future that might see him die there on his little farm, amongst his inferiors. The same as them, in fact.

Then in 1955 Dudley's health began to fail seriously. The drinking, the fasting, they were a mortal strain upon a body already severely debilitated. An attack of influenza prostrated him for several months, racking his worn-out frame with shivers and aches, and even long afterwards he suffered from a persistent whooping and wheezing like emphysema. By his forty-first birthday Dudley looked like a grandfather of seventy. John and Harriet could see what the end of all this must inevitably be. But John was still unsuspecting when Dudley came to him one afternoon with some legal documents. The first gave John power of attorney over all Dudley's affairs. The second was his last will and testament, in which he left his farm to John and Harriet.

John didn't know what to make of it. Was it even proper? For instance, Dudley had relatives. There was an aunt, the sister of Dudley's father. Shouldn't the farm stay in the family and go to her? Dudley disagreed. John and Harriet and Ruth were his family, he insisted. The farm was the only thing he had, and he wanted to give it to them, in gratitude for everything they had done. That way, Dudley concluded, he could die in peace. There was no need to talk of death, John protested, no one was about to die ... but Dudley only smiled, completely his old self for once, and John fell silent.

So the documents were allowed to stand. And if from that moment on John threw himself more eagerly into the management of Dudley's farm, and even came to view the property with a certain propriety air, there was nothing sinister in his motives. It was all really for Ruth, anyway. Ruth was the one Dudley loved most, and it was her future of which Dudley was surely thinking. Even so, John felt that a weight had been lifted from him. It was progress at last. At a stroke he had effectively doubled his land and his revenue. And like magic, as the winter of 1955 advanced into spring, the rain and sunshine came in perfect balance, the pests and diseases stayed away, and a bumper crop of wheat began to ripen in the paddocks of both Dudley's farm and his own. For a time John even dared to believe that Kuran Station was not so impossibly far away after all.

Strange, then, that it was around this time that the dreams began.

Chapter Twenty-five

THE DAY OF THE RALLY FINALLY DAWNED. WILLIAM WAS UP AT FIRST light, and then had to wait impatiently for everyone else to get out of bed and finish their breakfasts. His mother was staying home, and his uncle was occupied with some last-minute work in the office, so William rode out to the camp site with Terry Butterworth and Henry Lasseter in the big safari truck. The morning was already bright and warm, and everything was in order. The toilets had been delivered, the generator was primed, and the great marquee, all red and green and strung with ropes, had risen like a giant fungus out of the yellow grass. And high upon the hill, within the circle of stones, a flagpole had been raised. From down below William could just see the tip of it, rising over the surrounding trees. But there was no flag upon it yet — that would be part of the opening ceremony, after everyone else had arrived.

Terry and Henry got busy with the final touches around their own camp. They were easily William's favourites from the central committee — Terry because he was so loud and cheerful, and Henry because he was all crusty and bad-tempered on the outside, but quite harmless underneath. The two men had adopted William in turn, addressing him as 'Captain Bill' because of his hat, and including him in everything they did. They had even found a little nylon tent for him, and set it up next to theirs — a great big canvas tent that you could stand in, flanked by tables and chairs and a barbecue and, most importantly, two giant metal bins full of ice and beer. The site was high on the hill, and once everything was organised and the first bottle of beer opened, the three of them sat back to watch the cavalcade roll in below.

The first car came bumping along the track about an hour before noon, trailing dust. By the time its occupants had climbed out, another car had pulled in, and then another. From then on there came a steady stream of vehicles of all shapes and sizes — farm utilities and family sedans; four-wheel drives, big and small, some covered in mud and dirt, others pristine; sports cars, low to the ground and picking their way carefully around the rocks; campervans and minibuses; and two huge prime movers, devoid of trailers, that rumbled up the hill together like glistening behemoths, their air horns blaring bravely. There was even a gang of motorbikes that roared up the track in formation, all noise and dust and chrome, the riders clad in black leather — the effect spoiled only a little by the two old station wagons that wheezed along behind them, toting their wives and kids. William counted each arrival, but after fifty he lost count. There must have been over one hundred cars by the end, and over three hundred people.

They swarmed over the hill, setting up camp. There were young men and old men, wearing wide-brimmed Akubras or oily farming caps, some in checked shirts and boots, others in loose shorts, colourful shirts and thongs. There were young women and old women, country and town, their outfits ranging from cut-off jeans and bikini tops through to floral sundresses and straw hats.

There were children of every age. And lastly there were the dogs, entire packs of them, of all different breeds. Every family seemed to have brought one. They ran about everywhere, barking madly and adding to the chaos. Mothers yelled at children, fathers yelled at each other and engines growled as latecomers hunted for parking spots. By early afternoon there were campfires burning right across the hill and tea was boiling in fifty billycans. Smoke drifted through the trees. Men stood about drinking beer, and music from half a dozen radios and portable stereos competed back and forth across the slope.

For the first hour or so William stayed close to Terry and Henry's camp. When they lit the barbecue, he ate a hamburger. But the two committee members seemed very popular and soon he was lost in a crowd that had gathered around their tent. William set off on his own. He could see that his uncle had arrived and was moving about the hill, as well as Dr Moffat and Kevin Goodwin, but he didn't try to intersect with any of them. He joined an admiring circle of children that were standing around the motorbikes. The riders were drinking beer and tinkering lazily with their engines, revving one occasionally, shooting out clouds of blue smoke. William studied their jackets, impressed by the pictures of skulls and fists, and wondering about words like 'Vietnam', and various enigmatic acronyms stitched on the backs.

From there he trailed the other kids as they headed over to inspect the two prime movers. They all gazed up at the huge chrome grilles and massive bull bars, and some climbed up on the steps to peer into the cabins. A lucky few even got to sit behind the wheel and play with the CB radios. The big trucks were veritable homes on wheels, with beds and fridges and televisions, and the two men who owned them were almost as gargantuan as their rigs, red-faced giants with huge bellies spilling forth from their blue singlets. They were drinking beer and regaling their young audience with tales about wild pigs and crocodiles and roads so straight you didn't have to turn the wheel for a hundred miles. The whole of Australia was their home. Why, only this morning they'd been up north near Gladstone, hundred of miles away, fishing on the Great Barrier Reef at dawn. To prove it they revealed a battered old esky and plucked from it, to everyone's astonishment, several mammoth crabs and crayfish, horribly alive with their legs waving in the air.

The day rolled on. Under the marquee, a serious group of men gathered to discuss League matters, William's uncle among them, but the bulk of the crowd was bent on fun. An impromptu sports carnival began down towards the bottom of the hill, with younger children running various races. Some of the older boys and younger men started kicking footballs around, and then a game of cricket was organised. William watched it all but took no part. He felt perfectly happy by himself, roaming about with his hat settled firmly on his head. His only worry was that his ear was still aching. And he'd become aware of a bad smell. It was fleeting amidst the smoke of campfires and barbecues, but it came and went persistently throughout the day. The smell of something rotten. It reminded him of a dead animal. Oddly enough, it was strongest when he crawled back inside his little tent for a moment. But he searched the surrounding area, finding nothing. And no one else seemed to notice anything at all.

Finally, towards four o'clock, there came the sputtering sound of the generator kicking into life. Shortly afterwards, the public address system echoed out from the top of the hill. Distorted as it was, William recognised Terry Butterworth's voice. 'Ladies and gentlemen, boys and girls, the national anthem.'

People all across the hill paused what they were doing, and stood waiting. Strains of familiar music began to waft down from above, faint at first, and scratchy, but then, after several squawks and screeches, ringing out load and clear.

Once a jolly swagman camped by a billabong,
Under the shade of a coolabah tree;
And he sang as he watched and waited 'til his billy boiled,
'Who'll come a-waltzing Matilda with me?'

William stared — it was the wrong song. He knew 'Waltzing Matilda', of course, but it wasn't the national anthem. And yet no one else seemed to think it was a mistake. Some people were singing along, and others had their drinks raised in salute. The thin voices sounded weirdly sad, out there under the blue sky, with the hills and bush all around. And now all eyes were turned to the top of the hill, to where the flagpole stood. A banner was being raised — the white Southern Cross on a blue background. And the song was coming to a close, the swagman drowned and the troopers foiled.

And his ghost may be heard as you pass by that billabong,
'You'll come a-waltzing Matilda with me.'

A breeze took the flag, fluttered it out proudly, dark blue against the paler sky. There was silence for a long moment, and then the PA spoke again, solemn.

'Welcome, all, to the inaugural rally of the Australian Independence League.'

Everyone broke into cheers and applause, and the rally was officially launched. Then there came a string of announcements — new members were to report to the registration tent, could parents please ensure their children didn't wander off into the bush and get lost, did the owner of a yellow Holden Commodore know that his lights were on, and everyone should remember to gather at the top of the hill at eight o'clock sharp, once dinner was out of the way. The crowd milled about happily, and William drifted up towards the marquee again. He spotted his uncle off to one side, alone for the moment, sitting on a log and taking the chance to eat a hamburger.

William went over. 'That wasn't the national anthem,' he said.

'Wasn't it?' The old man was in good humour, smiling over his food. 'Says who?'

'It was "Waltzing Matilda".'

'That's right. Banjo Paterson, 1895.'

'But it's wrong.'

The smile lingered. 'It all really happened, you know. Out in western Queensland. The swagman, the troopers, the squatter, the lot.'

William was surprised. 'He really drowned himself?'

'Doesn't make sense, does it? Stealing sheep was hardly a hanging offence. So when the troopers came for him, why didn't he just go along? But no, instead he cries out, "You'll never catch me alive!" like he's some sort of famous bushranger, and jumps into the water and drowns.'

'Why?'

'Well ... the truth wasn't really much like the poem, although a man certainly died. It was during the great shearers' strike of 1894. The shearers had unionised, you see. They were demanding better conditions, and the station owners hated that, so the two sides were at each other's throats and the entire outback was at a standstill. It was like Eureka all over again. The government was sending in troops to support the squatters, thousands of men were unemployed and shearing sheds were burning down. Then one of the union leaders was found dead by a water hole. Murder, suicide, no one knows, and it doesn't matter. Paterson wasn't writing a news report. He was making a point, and the point was that the little man had had enough. Enough of high-handed governments that only worked for the rich, enough of penny pinching squatters who controlled everything, enough of the police always siding with landowners, enough of hunger and misery and all the injustice of those days. So Paterson has his swagman say, That's it. A little man can't win, so to hell with you all. And he jumps into the water. But it's got nothing to do with stealing a sheep. It's all about oppression. It's a protest song.'

The old man rose from the log, wiped his lips.

'And you're right, it's not the national anthem. But the real national anthem tells you nothing whatsoever about Australia, whereas "Waltzing Matilda" has got something important to say. It gets right to the heart of everything that can go wrong in this country, if we don't watch out. Everything that these people here are fighting against. So that's what we sing. I'll see you up at the bonfire.'

He strode off to rejoin the discussion in the marquee.

Nonplussed, William sat on the log himself, watching people come and go. He thought about shearers and swagmen and squatters for a while. Hadn't Kuran Station been like that once? Did that mean there were dead bodies in billabongs here too? He stifled a yawn. A moment later he heard what sounded like gunshots. People stared about, startled. The shots continued, from somewhere up over the hill, and men were shouting. But they were laughing too. The crowd relaxed, began to move towards the sound. William followed. On the far side of the hill he found a group of men with rifles, firing at tin cans and plastic bottles, set up along a fallen tree trunk about thirty yards away.

Terry Butterworth appeared, beer in hand. 'All right, you kids keep well back. You can watch, but I don't want anyone in the line of fire.'

'You still got your old police special?' someone yelled to him.

Grinning, Terry dug into his pocket and pulled out a handgun. There were appreciative murmurs. Terry turned, took aim, and blazed away at the targets. He didn't hit anything, but there were cheers all the same.

Other men were arriving now, with more guns. William sat and watched the shooting, fascinated. There were so many different weapons. Some of them made light cracking sounds that you hardly noticed, but others, like the shotguns a few of the motorbike riders brandished, made sharp echoing booms. Sometimes the cans skipped and spun when hit, sometimes they exploded. The bottles might fall apart in large pieces, or shatter into dust. Eventually Henry Lasseter came up the hill, struggling under the weight of something big. The crowd craned heads with interest. It was a weapon unlike any other they'd seen so far. It was long and thick, with protruding sections, and had to be set up on its own low stand. William heard the words 'machine gun' and 'M16' being passed about. Finally a circle was cleared, and Henry lay down behind the gun, took hold of the stock, sighted along the barrel, and let fly. The noise was shattering, it seemed to drill painfully right into William's bad ear. The targets shuddered and jumped and flew away, and the tree trunk itself splintered into chips. The crowd was applauding.

The men all began taking turns with the M16. Terry Butterworth was one, laughing uproariously as the gun chattered in his hand. William was amazed to see that even Kevin Goodwin had a go. The accountant, who had looked ill at ease all day, appeared even more uncomfortable now, as he hunkered down on the ground, and squinted earnestly along the barrel. But the gun hammered away regardless when he pulled the trigger, and when Kevin rose, flushed and grinning, William hardly recognised him. It was as if the gun could perform magic on a man. And others were lining up for a turn. There was no talk in the crowd any more, just an awed hush between firings.

The air grew heavy with smoke and gunpowder, and the noise seemed to work its way into William's head, until the throbbing in his ear became a headache. But he couldn't turn away. The men, who had appeared so aimless and amiable earlier in the afternoon, had somehow become a pack, a tightly knit gang clustered about the weapons, full of importance and power.

It was only when William noticed orange flashes of flame at the muzzles of the guns that he realised it was getting dark. He stood up then, swaying, aware of sudden pangs of nausea. He took a few steps away from the crowd and smoke. Looking up to the crown of the hill, he could see the looming stones, and amidst them, alone, his uncle standing beneath the flagpole. The old man was watching the crowd, and even from that distance William could sense his disapproval. It all felt strange, the sunny afternoon with its flag fluttering brightly, gone forever. William's head thumped furiously. Dogs crept about in the fading light, growling with hunger. Somewhere, someone was banging a billy can like a gong. Campfires glowed, and behind him the gunfire petered off to a few last shots, then died away to silence.

Chapter Twenty-six

NIGHT STOLE OVER THE RALLY. WILLIAM LOITERED ABOUT HIS camp, where Terry and Henry were entertaining their friends. They had the barbecue alight, blue flames hissing under the grill. William could smell sausages frying, and steak, and onions, and yet he didn't feel hungry. His nausea hadn't gone away. And maybe it was only the smoke from the campfires hanging in the air, but there seemed to be a haze over his vision. The world looked distant and flat. When Terry offered him a sandwich crammed with sausages and onions, William turned it down.

'You okay, champ?' the policeman wanted to know.

'I guess so.'

'Maybe you should lie down for a bit, before things get started.'

William nodded and went to his tent, curling up on his sleeping bag. But whatever was wrong, it wasn't making him sleepy. He rolled about, restless. The noises from outside the tent — people talking and laughing — sounded jarring and strange.

And the rotting smell was back, as elusive as ever, but undeniable. Eventually, Terry poked his head inside and announced that the meeting was about to start. William got up. Lying down wasn't working anyway — the more he kept his eyes closed, the dizzier he felt. He emerged from the tent. All across the hillside shadowy figures could be seen making their way towards the top. William followed them. There was a muttering of conversation, but the speakers were faceless in the dark, and no one spoke to him. He felt very alone. Below the voices and the other sounds of movement, he was aware of the steady clatter of the generator, and below that again, all around, there was the deeper silence of the bush. He cast his eyes to the sky, but there was no moon and the stars were a blur. He blinked and blinked, yet his vision refused to clear. Then the stone circle loomed upon the crown of the hill. The rocks and trees formed black shapes against a leaping brightness. A bonfire had been built at one end of the circle, and was blazing brightly, casting back the darkness. Shadows jumped and danced, and within the ring hundreds of people were gathering, their voices low, their faces reflecting red from the flames.

William felt he had stepped into another world. He could see his uncle now, framed against the fire, standing next to a microphone. A few paces behind him, side by side, stood the other four members of the central committee. The crowd was organising itself in a wide arc about them, settling down on the grass or on blankets or in folding chairs. William remained at the rear, his back against one of the stones. It felt cool and solid, reassuring, and he needed a foundation, for the dizziness would not go away. The crowd, the fire, it all pressed upon him, noisome and stifling. He looked outwards, off to the south. The treetops hung white and grey in the flickering light. Beyond them, dying campfires sprinkled the hillside, and further below still was the wide blackness of the plains. Pinpricks of light shone out there, from farmhouses and sheds where people worked and moved, and far off on the horizon was the glow of Powell, with its ten thousand souls going about their lives. But that was the normal world, impossibly distant, and it had nothing to do with what was happening up on the hill.

William's uncle stepped to the microphone.

'Welcome,' he said.

Even amplified and crackling, his voice was quiet, and a hush fell over the circle. He glanced at the sky and smiled.

'Well, we've a fine night for it.'

The crowd murmured appreciatively. William looked around at each of the stones, and they too waited, listening.

'Many of you won't know this,' his uncle said, 'but hundreds of years ago, I'm sure that Aborigines used to meet on this very spot. It was a sacred site to them. Now, we're going to be hearing a lot about Aboriginal history and sacred sites in the coming years, and it might seem strange that we, of all people, should gather at one of their special places. But there's a message in this. The Aborigines are gone. And that's the point. This is my property now. This is all your properties, your farms, your houses, your yards — this hill represents them all. We must be prepared to defend what we own.' The crowd bent forward, approving, and the old man's voice went low. 'Australia — every square inch of it — is *our* sacred site.'

Then Terry Butterworth was clapping, firm and slow, and after a moment all the other committee members joined in, followed by the crowd. The applause swelled into thunder, and William's uncle waited for the noise to die away.

'There are those who want to deny the truth of history. Those who want to divide this nation up into camps, black and white, and tell us where we can and can't go in our own country. Apartheid is what they're talking about. Rights for some, but not for others. Our government in Canberra is at this very moment debating ways to deny all of us here the basic entitlements of ownership over land, and security in that ownership. Which is why it is so important that we are here, in this place that we have claimed. To meet. To talk. And to make our battle plans.'

More applause, and more cheers.

And so the meeting was underway. Yet for William, nothing felt right. It all looked distorted, and his empty stomach rolled queasily. He sank down against the stone and held his head in his hands. Meanwhile, his uncle gave way to other speakers — first Terry Butterworth and then Kevin Goodwin. They spoke of things with which William was already familiar. The government and Native Title and the rights of people over their own properties. But through his misery, none of it mattered. And on the edges of his sight, away from the fire, the night seemed to be crowding in, heavier and heavier, and utterly black. Then there were other speakers at the microphone, people William didn't know, and then men and women who simply stood up from the crowd to say what they wanted.

'...we're the ones who suffer, not the city people...'

'...what do they know, they've never owned a property, worked it for generations...'

'...black and white always got along out here, everyone knew their place, but now the blacks are getting cocky, they think they're gonna end up owning everything...'

'...they don't even have to pay for it like we do, they just get it handed over...'

'...and no one's listening to us, no one gives a damn...'

They were angry words, and angry people. Their mood reeked of frustration and stale sunscreen and beer. Then Terry was up at the microphone again, discussing the committee's plan to find a property that would be threatened by the new laws, and to set up a barricade around it. Hands were raised, volunteering to man picket lines, while half a dozen people offered their properties for selection. The debate surged back and forth. William felt he was growing seasick on an ocean of talk.

Someone raised the question of whether the men on the barricades should bear arms. Suddenly Kevin Goodwin was up again — still swollen, it seemed, from his moment with the machine gun. He declared that the only answer was an organised militia. William's head was whirring. A militia? Hadn't that been Terry's idea, or Henry's? But the crowd was inspired.

'...a hundred men right here...'

'...do it now, before the bastards take our guns away...'

'...show them armed men can defend their rights...'

'...defend our fucking borders, you mean, no one else is doing it, might as well put out a bloody welcome mat...'

'...it's open house, it's Asians and Arabs and God knows who else, and it's a proven fact, those people bring all their old problems with them...'

'...you saw it, all of us, today, that was the real Australia for you...'

'...and what's so wrong with it, why should *we* feel guilty...'

But then William's uncle was at the microphone, his hands raised for calm. 'Let's not stray too far. Immigration is certainly an issue, but it can wait. As for a militia, if people want one, well and good, but that's a long-term thing. A response to the Native Title legislation is what we're here to organise.'

But William could sense an impatience in the crowd now. An ugly stubbornness. What had happened to everyone? He stared about, trying to focus on faces, but recognised no one from the sunny afternoon. This was a different collection of people, here in the ring and the firelight.

More voices were yelling.

'...Kevin's right, they just ignore us now...'

'...but once we're armed they'll listen. Any fucking blacks come to take my farm, I'll...'

'...they'll only ruin it anyway, they don't know how to run a property, they never did anything with this country...'

'…the old settlers knew it, they didn't get all weepy about it, they just did what had to be done, and if it took a gun…'

'…pity of it is, they didn't finish them off when they had the chance…'

'…you know they were cannibals, they were barely even…'

'No.' It was William's uncle once more, standing sternly at the microphone. The crowd grew quiet sullenly. 'This is not what we're about. We are not now, and have never been, a racist organisation. This is not about Aborigines. I've got no problem with them, not as a race. But there's no turning back the clock. That's why I'm angry about this legislation. Not because of the Aborigines. But because the legislation is stupid. It ignores reality. It tries to make criminals out of honest people who have worked hard for their land, it tries to say that we stole this country, when in fact we earned it. The new laws will tie us up in a sentimental mishmash of impossible rules that pretend history never happened, that somehow we're back where we were two hundred years ago. We're not, and the laws are wrong. But I will not have racist talk here!'

The crowd wasn't convinced. More disagreements broke out. People demanded that Kevin Goodwin be given the microphone. Through the veil of his nausea, William saw his uncle and Kevin arguing fiercely, but he couldn't hear the words. Nearby, a child on its mother's lap was crying. Everywhere William looked he saw red, angry faces, or others that were bewildered. He couldn't stand it any longer. It was as if the sickness in his head had spread out across the gathering. He lurched away from the stone and out of the circle. His eyes turned skywards for a moment and he saw the flagpole spearing into the night, but the light from the bonfire didn't reach the top, and the flag that hung there was black.

William reeled on, gravity propelling his legs down the hill. He passed right through the empty campsite and across the car park. And onwards still, into a welcoming darkness. The ground levelled out and trees rose thickly about him. It seemed that he had descended into a fold between the hills. Finally he came to a rutted channel in the dark, a gully along which water would flow when it rained, though now it was dusty and dry. And here he cast himself down, grateful, his face to the heavens. Yet even with solid earth beneath him he still felt he was spinning. The stars wheeled above, his skin was sweaty, and his head ached and throbbed. But eventually the vertigo began to fade. He lay very still, listening. From far off he could hear the whine of the generator, and the sound of voices from the hilltop, but it was very quiet there amongst the trees, and for a time he simply let himself drift, his mind empty of thought.

Gradually, however, an awareness came over him. The quiet had been a relief at first, but the longer William lay there, the more it seemed to weigh him down. There was still the distant clamour of his uncle's rally, but he could sense the silence as a greater thing, hanging above. It enfolded the entire hillside. It spread far into the sky and out across the night. It *was* the night. It reached back along the spur and up into the mountains, to where dark and empty chasms plunged. It spread westwards too, to where the House loomed above its ruined garden. And further, all the way across the plains, across endless miles of paddocks and crops, where nothing moved or made a sound, and where the darkness clustered around lone farm houses, and people hid away from it, huddled in front of their televisions.

The air had turned cold.

William sat up, hugging his arms around himself. *It was coming.* A moment, a thing — he was suddenly alert to its approach. His limbs ached, and the pain in his ear was piercing, but he found that he could see everything around him with chill clarity. Every tree, each individual leaf, was a crystal-edged shadow. The black bulk of the hills rose against the paler darkness of the sky. A thousand stars blazed noiselessly high above. And yet everything might have been frozen, the trees, the hills, the stars, paused in an instant of expectation. Even the insects that crawled in the grass had fallen still. The small animals that burrowed in the earth or hunted each other across the ground had ceased their activities. The night birds that stood sentinel in the trees, black eyes shining, had become stone. Every creature was motionless. Up on the hill people argued and fires burned, but all around them the land stood deathly still in anticipation.

And in answer, something came to William out of the night.

At first he saw only a glimmer of light. It was a flame, somewhere off to the east of him. It was hidden by the trees … No, it was moving amongst the trees, passing from shadow to shadow between the trunks, a flame that flickered and flared. It appeared to be some distance off, and it wasn't moving quickly. It was as if someone was carrying a fire as they walked, unhurried, picking their way alongside the dry bed of the water channel. But the flame was unearthly too. It wasn't focused around a single point, but seemed to change in shape, to swell and shrink and remould itself endlessly, and yet hint at something familiar. And he could hear no crackle of wood. The fire was utterly without sound.

An unreasoning fear shook William. He'd seen this thing before. It was the light he'd glimpsed moving in the hills, all those months ago, from down on the plains. And it wasn't anything to do with the rally on the hilltop, or with the bonfire in the circle of stones. It was something else entirely. Something, William was certain, that trod the night even when there was no one else there. He was shivering now. He stood up, ready to flee, but in the same moment, off through the trees, the flame paused in its progress. William hesitated, holding his breath. It was aware of him. Whoever or whatever carried the flame, it had seen him now. William hung motionless in the darkness, staring. And then the flame shifted slightly, and resolved into a shape, and finally, irrevocably, he saw. It wasn't a man carrying a fire, as he'd first thought — it was a man *on* fire. And yet the figure didn't scream or struggle, but stood perfectly still. William could discern arms and legs wrapped in flame, a torso that streamed silent fire. And a head, tilted calmly to one side, as if to ask a question while it burned.

He was running then. Blindly, away from the water channel and back up the hill, through the campsite and onwards, to where people and safety lay. The thing didn't pursue him, but he knew that if he glanced back it would be waiting. It had looked as if it would wait forever. What question it might have asked he did not know, nor want to. He kept running. And as he approached the hilltop, he felt the air stir at his back. A wind was gathering, from out of the west. It gusted, ebbed, then blustered again, so that if there had been a cloud in the sky, William would have thought a storm was on its way. But there were no clouds. Up over the hilltop the wind tumbled, blowing William with it. And then he was amongst the circle of trees and stone, and in the light of the bonfire.

But the bonfire was guttering, and the crowd had broken into milling, arguing groups. Men were shouting, and women and children were drifting away, and dust, whipped up by the wind, streamed between the stones. Dogs snarled and snapped at each other. William couldn't see anyone he knew. Not Terry or Henry, or even the accountant. Where had they all gone? And then he caught sight of his uncle amidst a knot of people, saw the anger on his face, the wild gestures of his arms. It was as if he had been set upon by his followers. Had a madness come with the wind? William ran to the old man, tugged on his hand.

'Uncle John,' he begged. 'Uncle John…'

His uncle tore his hand away. 'Not now, damn it.'

'But I saw … down there … I saw…'

'I don't care what you saw!'

'There was a man on fire!' William wailed.

John McIvor stared down at his nephew then, and for an instant William saw a stunned recognition in the old man's eyes. But it was only for an instant, for suddenly, to William's horror, there really was fire. It came rushing up over the brow of the hill. He shrank back, transfixed by the sight of a great burning cross towering into the night. It flared hungrily in the wind, and the men who held it aloft were all robed in white, their heads covered with hoods, black holes of emptiness cut out for eyes. They cried and yelled with alien voices, and the crowd drew apart from them, aghast.

'No,' pleaded a voice, freakishly loud. William's uncle was at the microphone one last time, his face livid in the light from the flames. 'Not this. This isn't the way. This isn't the Australian way. This is from somewhere else...'

But the men in robes howled him down, pushed him aside. Some people in the crowd were cheering now, while others were fleeing down the hill. Gunfire was ringing out again, shots fired wildly into the darkness, and white sheets seemed to dance everywhere, in and out of the stones. Amidst the chaos William caught a glimpse of his uncle, sprawled on the ground, his face contorted in pain. William tried to reach him, but was shoved this way and that, and fell to the ground himself. He rose to his knees and gazed up. The burning cross loomed directly above him, bright and crackling with angry noise. Even as he watched, the timber blistered and bubbled and turned to ash, and clouds of grey smoke billowed off into the wind, obliterating the night sky.

Then the cross toppled to the ground, showering sparks, and everything was over.

Chapter Twenty-seven

JOHN MCIVOR WOKE, SWEATING FROM THE NIGHTMARE.

For a time he lay frozen, his eyes wide to a full moon shining through the bedroom window. What had woken him? Was it the dream? The moon? Or was there, from some other part of the house, the stealthiest sound of movement? He listened. But Harriet lay fast asleep at his side, and the night was silent. Sweat cooled on his limbs. The dream ... it had come to him before, several times, but never as bad as this. In the past it had just been dancing images of flames, and a creeping sense of dread. But tonight he had actually seen it — a hand reaching out, wreathed in fire, and then a human shape, all ablaze, and yet standing motionless as it burned.

What did it mean? Who was on fire, and why? A memory skittered through John's mind, a vision of Harriet's father, and the way he had died. Was that it? But it was thirteen years since the bushfire, and in all that time John had slept undisturbed. Why was he dreaming about Oliver now? He stared at the baleful moon, the bedroom awash with silvery light, wondering. Was it even

Oliver at all? Surely, if Harriet's father had returned to plague him, the fiery shape would be vengeful, or agonised, crying out for help. But the dream wasn't like that. He sensed no emotion in the burning figure. It was just there, wrapped in smoke and flames, but patient also, waiting.

The hammer of his heartbeat had faded away. He felt clammy and cold. Harriet stirred in sleep, then rolled towards him. She was frowning in her own dreams, and John studied her face in the moonlight, noting the dark lines of age on her brow. She was thirty-seven years old. He was forty-two himself. Neither of them was young any more. Was that why the nightmare felt like an obscure intimation of mortality? Was he burning his time away? Would death come before he'd achieved any of the things he wanted? But no … the situation was looking better than it ever had. The season past had seen bountiful crops on both his farm and Dudley's, and grain prices were excellent. Kuran Station beckoned ever closer.

But still the ephemeral fears awoken by the dream chased through him. He watched Harriet as she slept. And he realised, with a certain amount of shock, that he had never really explained his plans for the future to his wife. True, Harriet knew about his childhood on Kuran, but amazing as it seemed now, he couldn't remember ever telling her that regaining the station was the central purpose of his life. He was a private man, used to harbouring his own thoughts, but still, in thirteen years of marriage, to have never spoken of it — what did that say about the two of them? And with another shock he realised that, for all Harriet knew, this little farmhouse was all they would ever possess.

Could she actually be content with that? John's own days were spent away from home, and Harriet's private time was largely an unregarded mystery to him, but she didn't appear to be bored or dissatisfied. She ran the house, and cared for Ruth and Dudley. She served on several committees for Ruth's school, and was a member of the Country Women's Association, and had made friends with their neighbours. Indeed, she had put down roots, there on the plains. John had never bothered, knowing he would be moving on to better things, but suddenly, as Harriet slumbered, her hair tousled about her face, he saw a humble farmer's wife. A woman at peace in her little cottage, a woman, in fact, who might be lost in the vastness of a sandstone mansion.

The nightmare chill went through him again. And then John really did hear it, the sound of movement somewhere in the house. All his other thoughts and preoccupations fled. He threw back the covers, swung his feet out of bed, and crossed to the bedroom door. The hall was filled with the dusty blue glow of the moon and there was nothing to be seen, only shadows. He crept along to the next doorway, which was Dudley's bedroom. The narrow camp bed was empty. Was that all it was — just Dudley up and wandering about? And yet doubt nagged him. Dudley was prone to sleeplessness, but normally he switched on the lights if he was up, and clattered around the kitchen, coughing and muttering to himself. There was none of that now. Only the furtive whisper of *something*.

John moved on, peering into the living room, which was as empty and cold as the rest of the house. Then he heard a definite thump, and a stifled voice. It came from Ruth's bedroom at the far end of the hall. John stared for a moment, then moved quickly down to her door. It was closed. That was normal — Ruth had been keeping it closed for years now. She was twelve, she wanted her privacy. But beyond the door something seemed to shuffle and groan, and then, unmistakably, there came a choked, frightened cry. Galvanised, John threw the door open and saw, on Ruth's bed, a confused, moonlit tangle of limbs. For an instant he had no comprehension of what he was seeing, then he flicked on the light and the room was starkly illuminated.

Hideously so. The next thing he knew, he was heaving Dudley off his daughter, loathing, all at once, the grimy feel of the man's skin, the sight of his pale naked body racked with scars, the glimpse of his penis, gleaming red and erect. Ruth was stretched across the bed, her nightdress rumpled up, her eyes wide and terrified, her mouth bruised where Dudley's hand had been clamped down. Then John was kicking and screaming at a figure that lay huddled on the floor, arms up over its head, and suddenly Harriet was in the room, their daughter was sobbing, and someone was crying, *Stop it! Stop it!*

John stopped. He stared down dully. The figure uncurled, and there was the familiar face of his friend, with his wild hair and matted beard and shining, hopeless eyes. It was only Dudley. Only sad, pathetic Dudley, stuttering that he was sorry, that he was so, so sorry...

It was then that there were choices to be made.

The first thing was to get Dudley out of the house. John bundled him into the car, drove him several miles through the night, then left him there, sniffing and moaning by the roadside, to walk the rest of the way to his farm. He didn't care if Dudley got lost. For the moment, John didn't care if he never saw Dudley again. Returning to his own house, he found that Harriet had bathed Ruth in his absence. Now the two of them were curled up in the main bedroom, holding each other as Ruth cried and Harriet stroked her hair and whispered comfort. Not needed, he wandered the house vainly until dawn, when Harriet emerged with the news that Ruth had finally fallen asleep.

Thus the two of them breakfasted and considered their options. They couldn't call the police. It would only shame Ruth further, and besides, they both knew that there was nothing to be gained now by revenge. There wasn't even the desire for it. They were perfectly aware of what a ruin Dudley had become, and of how little he was responsible for his own actions. It was *their* fault. They were the ones who had rushed so thoughtlessly to welcome him into their home, never even considering whether he might be a danger. And to think that in trying to atone for one sin they had only inflicted another upon their daughter, an innocent — that was unbearable.

There was one small mercy at least. Ruth had told her mother that this was the only time Dudley had invaded her room. But should they send her to a doctor? There was no point, Harriet announced bleakly, not yet. A few weeks, and then they would know. The more urgent question was what to do about Dudley himself. He had to be kept away from Ruth, that was clear. But where to send him? For a while, perhaps, they could leave him at his own house, but sooner or later someone in authority would notice that he was incapable of surviving alone. In the end, he would be committed to an institution. So perhaps, Harriet suggested, they should begin to look for a place now. To make sure he was cared for properly, in decent surroundings, while he still had some choice in the matter.

It made sense, John knew, but something in him quailed at the thought. Later that morning he drove over to the other house. He found Dudley huddled on the floorboards of the front verandah. He'd spent the night out in the cold, because he had no keys. And despite everything, it still wrenched at John to see him that way, his knees drawn to his chest like a child. It all came back, his memories of Dudley from before the war, the energy and humour of him, the clean, perfect health of his body, the force and intimacy of their friendship. All gone, ravaged by prison and loss. And now it had come to this — an assault on the one person Dudley himself cherished most.

John opened the house, made up one of the beds, and put Dudley to sleep. He would have to come back again that night with some food. But for the time being he sat on Dudley's front step, and wondered despairingly about what they were all going to do. There was, of course, a deeper consideration other than

Dudley and Ruth. It had risen to John's mind during the previous night, as he waited for the dawn. It had seemed a cold and clinical thought then, and he had tried to suppress it, but there was no denying it now, as he stared out over the paddocks of Dudley's farm. If they did send Dudley away to an institution, what would happen to his property? John could go on running it — the question was, would he have the legal right to do so? There was still Dudley's aunt, for instance.

John knew very little about her. She lived far away in Warwick, and she might not be at all interested in Dudley, or his farm. But the thought of her burned at him. She was Dudley's closest relative, his only family — if he was committed, then she was bound to be informed. She would look into his affairs and discover the bequest he had made. What if she then argued that he had never been in any fit state to sign away his property? The bequest might be made void. The more John thought about it, the surer he became. The aunt would interfere, she would challenge the will. Dudley's farm, and all the work that John had put into it, would be stripped away. And with it would go the careful plans John had made, the path he had laid out for himself and his family, leading all the way to the front door of Kuran House. That must not be allowed to happen. So the conclusion was that they could never commit Dudley. Not for his sake, and not for their own.

John drove home again. His resolution faltered when he saw his daughter. Something within her had been maimed, a spirit that had been carefree and joyful. She sat silent at the kitchen table, mechanically eating her lunch, and wouldn't meet his eyes. Did she blame him? Even though he was the one who had rescued her? But then came the bitter reminder — he'd arrived too late. In the safety of her own bed, her childhood uncle had raped her while her father slept. But he forced himself to think. What was done was done. Surely it could only be made worse by depriving her of a secure future. And that was all that would be accomplished by sending Dudley away.

He discussed the situation with Harriet that night. At first he spoke only of how Dudley needed their help, not the punishment of an institution. If they assisted him with cooking and cleaning, maybe he could survive at his own house? Harriet didn't agree. Dudley was beyond their help. The events of the previous night had proved it. He was becoming dangerous — not just to Ruth, but maybe to other people as well. Dudley, in his right mind, would never have wanted that. He needed professional care. Faced with this, John struggled internally for a moment, then came to a reluctant admission. It wasn't that simple, he said. And he outlined his concerns about Dudley's property.

Harriet stared at him, disbelieving. And so was revealed, finally, the immense gulf that lay between them. They debated far into the night. No matter how he tried, John was incapable of making Harriet appreciate what Dudley's farm might mean to their fortunes. In his extremity he revealed his hopes of reclaiming Kuran House one day, for all of them. *That old ruin?* she said, amazed. What did they want with a derelict mansion ten times bigger than they could ever need? And so John saw that his suspicion was right — Harriet was content where she was, and that far from wanting the House, she was repelled by it. And for her part, Harriet was appalled to discover what really lay at the core of her husband — a man so cold and calculating that his main concern wasn't for their daughter's safety, or even for Dudley's, but for property and money and a crumbling old homestead.

In is heart, perhaps, John knew she was right.

But then it came to him.

What if they sent Ruth to boarding school?

It was the perfect solution. They had always planned to send her to Brisbane for the final years of her education; this would simply mean her leaving a few years earlier. She'd be safe. She wouldn't have to see Dudley, or even hear anything about him. But with her gone, John and Harriet would be free to give him all the care he needed, without recourse to the authorities.

Harriet was utterly against it. Their daughter needed to be at home, not away living with strangers. But John remained adamant, knowing that time was on his side. Weeks went by, and there was no pregnancy. Dudley remained in his own house, yet in need of constant care. As John refused to seek outside help, Harriet found that she was being called upon to run two households. It was too much work. And it was disturbing Ruth. She no longer saw Dudley, but she knew where her parents spent so much of their time. Eventually, Harriet could see no other choice. And it was true, boarding school was always their intention for Ruth. She was unhappy at home now anyway. It might be the best for her, after all. It really might. But deep down she knew she was merely acceding to her husband's will, and that in this matter he was deeply and forever wrong.

She began to hate him then.

And Ruth, upon hearing the news, could only wonder that her father, whom she had always adored, had not only failed to save her that night, but had now convinced her mother to send her away. And worse, that although she had done nothing wrong, committed no crime, it was Uncle Dudley who was being allowed to stay, and she who was being punished with exile.

Chapter Twenty-eight

WILLIAM WOKE TO FIND HIS MOTHER PACING ABOUT HIS ROOM, muttering angrily to herself. Then she saw he was awake.

'Your uncle is in hospital,' she announced. 'He's had a heart attack.'

William stared. 'Is he all right?'

'Who knows!' She relented a little. 'They say he's stable, for now.'

William sank back into the pillow. A heart attack? That was awful. Confused memories of the previous night tumbled through his head. He felt sore all over. And drained. But the dizziness and nausea were gone, and the throb in his ear had dwindled.

His mother was unable to keep still. 'What on earth was he doing out there, running around like that at his age? And you! They had to carry you home at three in the morning.'

'I was sick.'

'I know.' She waved the issue aside. 'Terry said you ate a bad burger or something.'

A bad hamburger? Could that be right? He had felt so ... disjointed. Even now, events were hard to recall clearly. He thought of white robes flapping, of fire and smoke, and of a wind, blowing up over the hill. He could hear that same wind now, moaning outside his window, and feel faint quivers shake his bed as the House's old frame bent and stretched.

'Is the rally over?' he asked.

'Of course! Everyone's gone. It's a complete mess.' Outrage flashed again in her eyes. 'The old fool, he might have died.'

William suddenly understood why his mother was upset. And it wasn't because of the chaos at the rally, or because her son had been sick.

'He might still die yet.' She was biting at one of her fingers as her eyes flicked back and forth. 'And what happens to us then? Has he written anything down on paper about you? Because if he hasn't, then what's the point of any of this?'

William felt a coldness inside. 'I've tried to make him like me ...'

She glared at him. 'Not enough to make if official. And you won't even be allowed to see him again, unless he gets better. So you know who'll have to do everything now, don't you?'

William blinked at her in confusion, and she was gone.

Five days later, his uncle returned from hospital.

It was sooner than the doctors wanted, apparently, but the old man had insisted. An ambulance delivered him to the front door, and two men helped him up the stairs to his bedroom. William caught a glimpse of the trio as they ascended, and was shocked. His uncle looked terribly frail and small, dressed in pyjamas many sizes too big, with his hair tufted wildly and his arms hanging limp around the ambulance men's shoulders. Where was the stern prophet, or the wise grandfather? But it was only a glimpse, and the old man did not notice William or speak to him. He was still very sick, everyone said, and not to be bothered. William didn't need the warning. The door on the landing remained open, but nothing could have drawn him upstairs anyway. He was haunted by the idea of a thin, feeble stranger lying up there in the white bedroom, possibly waiting to die.

The westerly winds blew on. Indeed, it seemed to William that, over the following weeks, they never ceased to blow. They were remorseless, hot and dry, and everyone knew what such weather meant — this was the scalding breath of summer, come full grown and early. Temperatures across southern Queensland soared into the 40s, and on television the faces of the weathermen turned grim. There was no sign of rain, they said, no hope of it ... and this was the third rainless year in a row. Inland, the winds whipped over deserts and dusty fields, and by the time they reached the eastern regions they drove clouds of clinging topsoil before them. Farmers and graziers hunched their shoulders, despairing as the cattle starved and the rivers died. And on the coasts, city-dwellers squinted unhappily at the haze-filled skies, spraying their gardens in guilty defiance of water restrictions.

The Kuran Plains were not spared. The wheat shrivelled up, and the black soil cracked open into chasms. Kuran Station suffered too. The wind thrummed and beat about the House, tugging at loose tiles on the roof and rattling the windows. The old building creaked and strained, and William felt that he was adrift in some wrecked behemoth of a ship, caught by storm. But there was no ocean outside, only the scorched hills, where the trees bent and shuddered, and where the last faded tints of grass shrank away to crusts. Inside, hot gusts rummaged through the hallways, layering everything with grit and dust, until the front doors were shut fast despite the heat. Locked away thus, William, his mother and the housekeeper all waited, prisoners in the darkness, sharing the old man's death-watch.

For William, there was nothing to do and no one to talk to. He waited vainly for visitors to come and call upon his uncle. He was expecting someone like Terry or Henry or Kevin, but none of them appeared. Only Dr Moffat called, and occasionally the station manager, Mr Drury. Neither had any time for William. The doctor, when he came to check on his patient's progress, seemed gloomy and preoccupied. And Mr Drury was a dour, middle-aged man whom William had hardly ever seen. Now his news was all bad; the pastures were empty, and the few remaining cattle were surviving on fodder. He made his reports to the old man upstairs, and received his orders, but he spent no other time in the House. Which left William only his mother for company.

His mother, however, suddenly had other business. One afternoon William heard her arguing with Mrs Griffith about who should be looking after the old man. So far the housekeeper had been doing it, labouring painfully up and down the stairs a dozen times a day. But now his mother was insisting that Mrs Griffith was too old to be climbing about like that. What if she fell? What if the old man needed help quickly? Mrs Griffith was denying that it was any trouble for her at all, but the housekeeper sounded shaken, unsure of herself and, amazingly, William's mother prevailed. From that moment on, by sheer force, she shouldered the old woman aside and took over the care of the invalid — cooking for him, washing his pyjamas and sheets, and sitting by his bed through the long days.

William could scarcely believe it. What about his mother's headaches? What about her eternal fatigue? What about her hours in front of the television, empty-eyed and wrapped in her bathrobe? And it wasn't that her health was any better than usual — in fact, so many demands only strained her nerves to breaking point. The bottles of pills proliferated, and at the end of each day she would shuffle back to their flat, exhausted and barely aware of William's presence. But gradually he came to understand. She had said it herself — he no longer had access to his uncle. In his mother's eyes, that meant he could no longer press his claims for the station. So instead, *she* had been compelled to take on the role. By caring for the old man, she was trying to secure their place in his heart. And William would just have to look after himself. For the time being, he was of no use or interest to her at all.

At least he no longer had to fear Mrs Griffith. In fact, the housekeeper's decline had begun long ago, on the day she caught William upstairs in the red room. He had been rewarded for that, instead of punished, and ever since Mrs Griffith had been sulking over her defeat. Now she was diminished even further. She stopped eating dinner with William and his mother, retreating instead to her own rooms. When she did venture out, she seemed bereft. William spied her at times standing at the bottom of the central staircase, peering up into the darkness where his mother tended his uncle, her expression a black mix of envy, anxiety and dismay. But she never ascended. William found that he could even pity her. Her sole excuse for being in the House was to care for the old man — yet here was John McIvor bedridden, and there was nothing she could do, supplanted by a younger woman.

But she was no company for William either. Loneliness enveloped him. The winds rattled interminably outside, but inside, all remained depressingly quiet. There was no phone ringing, no radio booming in the office, no typewriter clattering away. But, of course, all that activity had been before the rally, when there had been so much to do. Now it was over. He strove to understand exactly what had happened that night. He could recall the meeting in the ring of stone, and the arguments amongst the crowd. He remembered being alone, far away from them all, hiding in the bush, surrounded by silence. And he remembered the bonfire, and a burning cross, rushing up over the hilltop. But was there something else? Why did the memory of fire feel so disturbing? Not the cross, not the bonfire, but a ghostly memory, dancing out of reach ... a shape, standing off in the darkness. A man, flame streaming over his face. But that was impossible. That must have been a dream.

And yet it had heralded disaster, he was sure of that. The burning man was a warning — but of what? About the way the rally would end, amidst fire? About what had happened to his uncle? The old man had almost died, and William knew that he had been defeated in some deeper way too. It was his rally, his League, his people, and yet they had abandoned him to follow the others — Terry and Henry and Kevin. And most crucially of all, where had those three committee members been when the white-hooded men appeared? William hadn't seen them anywhere, so the conclusion was inescapable: they were hidden under the robes. Was this what the fiery shape had come to tell William? That the rally would end in betrayal? But no ... in his memory that didn't feel right. There had been no urgency in the way the figure approached through the trees. It had seemed unhurried — profoundly so — and the little gathering on the hill had meant nothing to it at all.

Had it come to warn of the westerly winds then? There was no doubt that they were a disaster. William only had to listen to their hot breath curling about the House to know that. And he had heard the mutterings of Dr Moffat and Mr Drury, as they shook their heads and spoke of the worst drought in decades. Out west gigantic dust storms were raging, and back east bushfires were ravaging the mountains and forests. And so, William wondered, could it be that he had seen some harbinger of the drought that night, a personification of the sort of heat and fire the desert winds would bring? Did such visions always walk the land before evil days, like dire prophets? But he didn't think it was that either. The figure had shown itself only to William, so whatever warning it brought was for him alone.

But what did it mean?

No answers came, and the weeks passed in a blustery haze of boredom and foreboding. The news from upstairs was that his uncle's recovery had been slowed by serious complications with his lungs, and William still wasn't allowed to see him. For nearly two months the convalescence continued. The winds persisted, fitful and fretting, easing away for a day or two, or even longer, but always returning. The sky clouded over with dust and smoke. On the rare occasions that William ventured out into the yard, their hillside seemed to be floating — there was no horizon, the plains below were a blur, the mountains in the east could only be guessed at. Dead grass crunched under his feet, the wind plucked and scraped at his skin, and the sun shone a baleful red, glowing like sunset in the middle of the day.

And finally it seemed that Mrs Griffith had gone mad. William discovered the old woman one afternoon in his uncle's office, speaking on the telephone. He had never seen her use the phone before, but now she was bent around the receiver as if it was a cherished treasure, her eyes alight, and she was whispering, too low for William to hear. All the while she shot worried glances to the ceiling. She hung up with elaborate care, then started when she caught sight of William standing in the doorway.

'Get out,' she spat. 'This is your uncle's room.'

'I've been in here before.'

'Not alone you haven't.' She had hold of his collar now, and dragged him down the hall, glancing always towards the ceiling. 'The House isn't yours. Not yet. Oh no.'

'Let me go!'

They were at the foot of the central stairway. 'I've called her,' she said, poking his chest with a bony finger. 'So we'll just see now, won't we?'

She had to be crazy. But later that night, when William and his mother sat down for dinner, the housekeeper was back, rocking with some secret pleasure at her end of the table. She spoke not a word all through the meal, but when it was finished, and William's mother was about to take his uncle's food upstairs, the old woman made a gleeful announcement.

'She's coming, you know.'

William's mother hardly noticed. 'Who is?'

'I called her today. She gave me the number, years ago.'

'What are you talking about?'

'Ruth. I called Ruth.'

And to William's surprise, his mother faltered, put the plate down. 'You called Ruth?'

The housekeeper nodded, eyes glittering with vehemence. 'I told her about the heart attack. And she's on her way.'

William couldn't understand why his mother looked so stricken, or Mrs Griffith so triumphant.

'Who's Ruth?' he asked.

The housekeeper cackled. 'Doesn't he know?'

William's mother considered him bleakly, her hands still curled around the dinner plate. Then she sank back down into her chair, and began to explain.

Chapter Twenty-nine

THE NEXT DAY THE WESTERLY WINDS BLEW ON AS BEFORE, BUT everything else had changed now that William knew John McIvor had a daughter, and that she was on her way. The whole point of William and his mother being at the House was that his uncle had no other family. And yet now there was this woman, conjured up like a malign spirit by the housekeeper — not some distant relation, but the old man's own flesh and blood. It wasn't just the fact of her existence that was disturbing, it was that she had been kept so secret. There could be nothing good in a deception of that magnitude.

As if in response to the news there came a summons — the old man wanted to see his nephew.

'You're to go up,' said William's mother. 'On your own.'

There had been a defensive slump to her shoulders ever since the housekeeper's announcement. William recognised it from a hundred previous episodes, and knew what it meant — the world was hemming his mother in, and with it would return the migraines and the frightening spells of withdrawal. He hesitated, wanting to help, if only he knew how.

'Go on,' she snapped. 'Go and see him. For all the good it will do now.'

It was nothing like his first visit to the upper floor. Back then the House had been silent and still, wrapped in a cold winter's day. Now he ascended into a hot, airy space, where gusts of wind moaned and a thousand noises creaked and clanked from the roof above. He paused at the top landing and gazed along the central gallery. In his memory it had been a dank cavern of shadows, but now it was suffused with orange light — the colour of the haze outside, leaking in through the broken windows and doors. Everything was tinder dry and dust swirled in eddies.

William made his way along the hall. Empty chambers towered on either side. And there, at the end, was the padlocked door of the red room. An image came to him of the telescope, a hunched metal creature, as watchful as a vulture, guarding the remains of the dead explorer and an ancient policeman's uniform. His uncle's room of secret treasures. And yet there had been no sign of the greatest secret of all, no picture of a child or lock of her hair. What did that mean? And why had his uncle tested him and lectured him all this time, if in the end there was a daughter who could be called home?

'There you are,' rasped a familiar voice.

William stood in the doorway to the white room. He'd expected to find an invalid confined to his bed, but in fact the old man was sitting in an armchair, propped up by pillows, the remains of his lunch spread across a low table at his side. The typewriter sat there too, a sheet of paper in it.

'Well, come in boy, I'm not contagious.'

He still looked very ill. Dark circles surrounded his eyes, the stubble on his chin stood out from his sunken cheeks, and knobbly hands and feet protruded from the sleeves of his pyjamas.

The room was almost as William remembered, except that now the white walls had turned yellow in the dusty light, and the curtains flapped in the hot draughts that whistled through the cracks about the window frames. He took a seat across the table, aware of the old man's eyes upon him all the while. They were not the stern eyes of the prophet, nor were they the kindly eyes of the grandfather. They were something else again, something sickly and eager. From above came the sound of the tiles on the roof, scraping in the wind. William found himself staring at his uncle's leg, fascinated by a network of old scars that entwined one ankle, and rose up the shin.

'So how have you been, down there all this time?'

'Okay.'

'I told you, didn't I? A hot summer, I said.'

'I remember.'

'Good. Remember everything I taught you. Especially now.' The old man smiled, his lips faintly blue. 'I understand we're to have a visitor.'

William nodded, watchful.

'You know who she is?'

'Mum said she's my cousin, once-removed.'

'Yes ... I suppose that's right. But tell me this — you didn't know I had a daughter, did you, until now? Your mother — she never said a word?'

'No.'

'No, I bet she didn't.'

William only stared accusingly.

'But I didn't say anything either, did I?' His uncle's teeth gleamed. 'That's what you're thinking, I can tell. We both of us lied to you, your mother and I.'

William lowered his eyes.

'Ha!' But then the old man was coughing, thin and hoarse. 'Well,' he sighed at the end of the bout, rubbing at his lips, 'there are lies and there are lies. The truth is, I haven't seen my daughter for ten years.' He waited, gauging William's reaction. 'It's true. I haven't even spoken to her. This visit wasn't my idea, you know.'

'It wasn't?'

'You think I told Mrs Griffith to make that call? No.'

'Then why is she coming?'

'That's the question, isn't it?' The smile emerged again, hungry on the old man's thin face. 'Maybe Mrs Griffith said I was dying. My daughter would want to see that.'

'But you're not dying — are you?'

'Me? No!' The old man tapped his chest weakly. 'I'd be fine if it wasn't for this pneumonia. But I'm shaking it off. A month or so, I'll be back on my feet. Then you and me, we'll get back to normal. There's still work to be done. Lots of it.'

William felt a quiet relief. Perhaps then the daughter was no great danger after at all. Maybe nothing had changed. His gaze settled upon the typewriter. Work, his uncle had said, and that could mean only one thing.

'Is it time for the next newsletter?'

The old man turned cold. 'There won't be any more news-letters. I'm through with all that.'

William blinked in surprise. His voice fell. 'Is it because of the rally?'

'You tell me. You were there, up on that hill.'

'I ... I know that's when you got sick.'

'It's got nothing to do with me being sick. You saw what happened.'

And even though he knew the answer, William couldn't help but ask. 'Where were Terry and Henry and Kevin? When the men with the cross came? Where did they go?'

His uncle considered him for a long and silent time. 'They went their own way,' he said at last. But then he shook his head. 'Not even their own way, not really. Kevin and the rest, they're imitators, and that's the worst thing to be. They think people overseas know better than we do. They want guns and robes, they think that makes them big. The country could be falling apart, and all those idiots will ever do is dance around in white sheets.' He saw the unhappy look on William's face. 'Don't worry about them. Good riddance, I say.'

'But what about everything else? What about the laws we were trying to stop?'

'Ah ... well, the world hasn't been asleep these last months, more's the pity. We've lost too much time. The legislation is due before the Senate very soon now. Maybe it'll pass, maybe it won't. But it's too late for us to do anything about it.'

'But what will happen to the station?'

'The station?'

'Don't the new laws mean that people can come here, and you can't stop them?'

His uncle nodded in sudden approval. 'Good, good. You remember. And who is it who'll come here, whether I like it or not?'

'The Aborigines?'

'Yes, but we don't hate them, right? We aren't burning any crosses around here, are we?'

'No,' said William, confused.

'Good. It's right that you should be worried. Nothing good will come of those laws.' But then the energy faded. 'Still, I thought you understood by now. The fact is, we don't have all that much to worry about, even if the legislation passes. Native Title won't touch us. Not on this property. This is a perpetual lease we're on, Will. As good as freehold any day.'

'But I thought...'

'It was the rest of the country I was fighting for. Out west. The sort of land that some of those fools at the rally will lose. Pastoral leases. Crown land. Well, to hell with them.'

'The League can't stop it?'

'There is no League any more. Not my League anyway. The others can go by any name they like.' His uncle had shrunk back into his chair, curled around a knot of bitterness. 'I don't know if we could have stopped it anyway. But by Christ, at least we could've made a point. At least we could have shown the rest of the country just what's being threatened here.'

But William only heard that the League was lost. All those people on the hillside, all the cars and the campground and the games and 'Waltzing Matilda' floating into the sky, all the things that had happened before the shooting started — they were gone. Yet the League had seemed so strong, that afternoon, so right.

'Forget about those people.' The old man was watching him again, carefully. 'That isn't why I called you here. There's something else I've been wondering about. Something that happened up there on the hill, something you said.'

William felt himself go still.

'That night, I saw you sneaking away during the speeches. Where did you get off to?'

'I … I felt sick. I went for a walk.'

'Sick? Sick with what?'

'I don't know … I just had to leave.'

But his uncle was leaning forward now. 'No, Will. When you came back, just before everything went crazy, you told me you'd seen something. Off in the hills. What was it? What did you see?'

William pressed himself back into the chair. 'Nothing.'

'Don't lie to me, boy.'

'Fire. I saw fire.'

'That's not what you said.'

William felt a pit opening within him. He couldn't say something like this out loud, could he? Not in this hot, windy ruin of a room. It had been a madness that night, some sickness that had taken hold of him and made him see things that weren't there. To say it out loud could only bring the madness back, make it real. But his uncle's eyes were startling white in their black circles, irresistible.

'A man. I saw a man on fire.'

'Ah ...' William had expected laughter, a scornful dismissal, but instead the old man only nodded, strangely pleased. 'And you've seen him before?'

'No.' But he could hide none of the truth now. 'Maybe. Once, from a long way away. Before I came here.'

'And who do you think he is?'

'I don't know.'

'Your father?' The eagerness was awful. 'You know your father was burned. Do you think it was him?'

'No.'

'How can you be sure?'

But William only shook his head, wide-eyed. That was the worst possibility of all, yet he knew it couldn't be true, knew it with the certainty of old love. His father would never come to him in such a form, would never force his son to see something so terrible.

His uncle looked away, studied the rumpled bed thoughtfully. 'You weren't asleep? You weren't dreaming?'

'I don't think so.'

'We see a lot of things in dreams.' He glanced back to William. 'But I believe you. There's something about you, Will. Something a little touched. It's your eyes. They aren't always looking at what's in front of you.' He passed his hand before William's face, and William felt a dizziness as his eyes followed the long bony fingers waving back and forth. 'But we're blood, you and me. We must be. We share the same ghosts.'

The old man straightened, and William felt something pass, a shadow lift.

'Your mother though, that's a different story. She's no family of mine. Oh, I know — she's been busy up here. But you and I both know what that's really about, don't we?'

In a daze, William nodded.

'Yes … but I'm not going to hand this place over to her just because she's fed me a few meals, am I? She's not the important one, is she?'

'No,' echoed William.

'Watch her, Will. She's your enemy. She'd sell this property in an eye-blink, if it was hers to sell. You don't want that to happen, do you?'

William shook his head.

'Good. Mrs Griffith now — she's your enemy too. That's why she called my daughter. She's hoping that if Ruth comes home, then maybe I'll send you away. Why would I need a nephew if I have my daughter back? She isn't thinking straight, of course. If I had my daughter back, then I wouldn't need a housekeeper either, would I?'

The old man was coughing again.

'Don't forget it, Will. Two women in this House, and neither of them is on your side. And now there's a third one on her way. The worst of the lot.'

Abruptly he was standing, levering himself painfully from the chair. He swayed when he was upright, and William rose to support him.

'The bed,' his uncle instructed breathlessly, resting a hand hard on William's shoulder. Together they shuffled across the room, and the old man sat down carefully on the edge of the bed. For a time he gazed away to the curtained windows, pondering some thought. The sky out there looked as dark as if a storm was approaching, and yet it was only dust and smoke from far-off fires.

'Tomorrow, I'm told. She'll be here tomorrow.' He swung his legs onto the mattress and sank back against the pillows. 'Who knows. Maybe I'll ask her about her dreams too…'

An amazing thought came to William. 'Have *you* seen the burning man?'

His uncle only smiled, closed his eyes. 'Thanks for coming up, Will. You can send your mother to me, when you get downstairs.'

William almost asked the question again. Because what if it was true? But the old man looked serene now, ready for sleep. William backed away towards the door.

His uncle lifted a warning finger. 'Be careful of my daughter, when you meet her. Be careful of what she says to you. Don't trust her.'

'Why not?'

'She'll pretend to be your friend, that's why.'

Chapter Thirty

RUTH MCIVOR NEVER REALLY CAME HOME FROM BOARDING
school. Brisbane was too far away for weekend trips, so she
returned to her parents' house only during the longer holidays.
And even then, things weren't the same. The eager girl John
remembered was gone, replaced by a reserved young woman, a
stranger. She ignored the farm and spent most of her time in her
room, buried in books. In one sense that didn't bother John — she
was doing better than ever, academically. But there was a pang,
nevertheless, whenever he saw how little interest she had in
anything he said or did. Surely she understood he still loved her,
and missed her when she was away? Surely she understood that,
in the end, it was all for her benefit?

Perhaps Dudley was the problem. Inevitably, John and Harriet
had brought him home to live with them again, reinstalling his
camp bed in the office. Of course, they moved him back to his farm
when it was time for Ruth's visits, but she still knew. The smell of
rum, of unwashed clothes and hair, lingered in the house even

when Dudley wasn't there. The same smell must have embedded itself in her skin that night, never to be cleaned away or forgotten. But whatever Ruth thought about the situation, she said not a word. Not to her father anyway.

In 1962, having graduated from school with first-class results, Ruth enrolled at Queensland University to study law. John was impressed. Other girls her age were taking secretarial work or employment in dress shops, or doing nothing at all, simply waiting for a husband to appear and provide. But not his daughter. When it came time to assume her place at Kuran Station, she would have both a rich estate *and* a professional career. Even so, he felt some disquiet, for it was not as if Ruth sought her parents' approval: she simply declared her intentions and demanded their financial support. And she visited home even less frequently from that point on. In quieter moments, it struck John that if everything he was doing really was for Ruth's benefit, then it was odd that he never talked with her about it. But these concerns always passed. She was growing up, that was all, finding her own way. She would come back to him once Kuran Station was secured, and she realised just how much her father could do for her.

In the meantime, he was busier than ever. In 1958, in partnership with Dudley, he finally purchased a third property. It was the same size as the first two — a square mile selection of black soil on the Kuran Plains — and close enough for him to manage conveniently. Over the next few years his life consisted of little else but work. There were two thousand acres of prime cultivation to be ploughed, planted, tended and harvested. He hired men to help, of course, but still, he was hardly ever home, returning mainly to eat or sleep, or to rest his bad leg, which was still prone to give way when he was tired. But it was all paying off. Bumper season followed bumper season, and in 1962 the partnership purchased another three hundred acres, and then, in 1964, yet another three hundred.

But if the world seemed to be opening up at last for John, then it seemed to Harriet that it was shrinking down ever more tightly. Her daughter was gone. Her husband was a silent, driven man she barely saw. And her other suitor, from far in the past, had become her major care and burden. For it was also in 1964 that Dudley began to sink into what would become his final illness. His lungs were choked with emphysema, and the instability that had afflicted his mind for so long had developed into dementia. He was bewildered by faces he no longer remembered, by places he no longer recognised, and Harriet had to bathe, clothe and feed him. She knew full well that he should be in hospital. Not that there was any hope of a cure — Dudley was dying, and no hospital would change that. What she resented was that he had to die right in front of her, so slowly, in her own house. But John refused as vehemently as always to send him away.

So Harriet gave up her community work, withdrew into the invalid's isolation and sat by Dudley's bed through the long, last days. Her patient slept restlessly, often crying out from uncon- sciousness, and she stroked his greasy hair gently, her heart torn and bitter. She would strive to remember the young logger she had once known, and to pretend that it was him she was nursing, but all she really saw was the man who had raped her daughter, and the man who had chained her to this sickroom. There were moments, in fact, when she wished she had never met either Dudley *or* John. Her life might have been so different. But it was all too late now. Dudley finally passed away in early 1966, slipping off in his sleep. He was fifty-two years old. The war had inflicted wounds upon him that were mortal, sure enough, but it had taken him over twenty years to die.

The funeral was held in Powell. There was only a small crowd, including five middle-aged ex-servicemen from the Eighth Division. John would have liked to ask them about Dudley's war experiences, but at the wake the veterans gathered in a circle, looking inwards sombrely, and he found himself too ashamed somehow to intrude. An even more disconcerting presence was Dudley's aunt. She was a hale farming woman in her sixties, and seemed keenly interested to hear about her nephew. John tried to appear helpful, but knew that he sounded guarded and hostile. Nevertheless, when she asked to see Dudley's farm, he could not refuse. After the wake he drove her out and showed her over the house. It was obvious that it had been empty for some time, and when the aunt, surprised, inquired about Dudley's last years, John had to admit that he had lived with himself and Harriet.

So the suspicions were sown. In the following weeks, John heard rumours that the aunt was looking into her nephew's affairs. And when she did indeed challenge Dudley's will, he was enraged but not surprised. It only confirmed that he had been right all along. At least with Dudley dead, and his glaring disabilities buried with him, John was confident the situation could be saved. And so it proved. The McIvors won the court case, and were even commended by the magistrate for their solicitude. What they lost was the battle of public opinion, for the dispute made headlines in the Powell newspaper. The aunt's lawyer had not spared John and his wife, accusing them of manipulating a vulnerable ex-serviceman for their own ends, and of virtually imprisoning him in their house, away from the advice and succour of his family. And despite the verdict, somehow it was this uglier version that the townsfolk came to accept.

The gossip didn't much concern John. He had the land, secure in his own name at last, and as fate would have it, the following few years were golden. In 1967 he purchased another twelve hundred acres, bringing his ownership of Kuran Plains land to just on four thousand acres all told. He was now one of the largest grain-growers in the area. He was also one of the most unpopular. This was only partly because of the suspicions about Dudley. John was a demanding employer, paying poorly for long hours. He refused to serve on any grain boards or committees, as was expected of a farmer of his stature. He belonged to no church or club, and gave nothing to charity. Indeed, he was so mean, his neighbours muttered, that despite his riches he still lived in the tiny, dilapidated cottage he had bought in the 1940s. He hadn't even bothered to install proper plumbing.

All John knew was that, at long last, Kuran Station was within his sights. So let his neighbours sneer. They would still be digging away at their little blocks long after he was gone. Harriet, however, did not find things so simple. She had hoped that Dudley's passing would allow her to engage with the world again, but the rumours and innuendo that spread about town, and amongst her neighbours, humiliated her profoundly. It wasn't just the inference that they had exploited Dudley, or robbed him, or perhaps (who knew?) even hastened his end with neglect and alcohol. What was worse were the old stories that emerged about the three of them, from long ago, before the war. There were whispered speculations — exactly what had happened between the two men and Harriet? Exactly who had been whose lover? Did something scandalous lie at the root of it all?

In the years following Dudley's death, she abandoned her old pastimes. Her friends discovered a distance and distrust in her, and gradually they dropped away. John was no support. Her sorrows were an irrelevance to him. He expected nothing from her any more, beyond running the house and cooking his meals. (Not even physical contact — that had ceased, once and for all, the moment Dudley crept into their daughter's bed.) Indeed, Harriet was becoming the strange, reclusive wife of an even stranger man, her life hidden in his shadow. And looming over both of them was a darkness from the distant past — the name McIvor itself. The memory of John's father still lived in older minds, and so did the odium that went along with it. This sentiment was resurgent, now that John was becoming a large landowner in his own right. It was too much like history repeating itself.

In late 1968, after yet another splendid wheat harvest, and with a sense of momentous fulfilment, John began making discreet inquiries about purchasing Kuran Station. The owner was open to discussion. Maybe next year, the agent said, maybe the year after. But he had a warning. John knew, didn't he, that the old mansion on the property was a wreck? That it was abandoned, in fact, apart from an old caretaker woman, and should probably be demolished? He didn't expect to live in it, did he? John suppressed his impatience, and said nothing. The House would keep. And a small delay meant nothing when the great goal was so very close, after so many years.

But then, intruding on his satisfaction and anticipation, the dreams returned. The same burning figure, standing watchful and silent. What was it? *Who* was it? Oliver Fisher? A phantom, that was all. But John found, even after waking from the nightmares, that a fear still lingered. Often he was compelled to get out of bed and search the house, or to stand on the back verandah and stare into the night, looking for something or someone that might be there. One day, while he was in Brisbane on business, he saw a telescope in the window of a nautical antique shop. Almost without volition, he walked in and bought the instrument. He took it home and set it up on his back verandah. Late at night he would use it to sweep the plains, straining at the eyepiece. And every time he found a light, he waited breathlessly to see if it shimmered and moved and took shape. It was madness, he knew. There was nothing to see out there but the lights of cars and houses. And yet he felt helpless to stop himself.

Then there was Ruth. She had completed her studies, and was working in Brisbane, and that should have been pleasing. And yet it wasn't. With every visit home she seemed stranger, her ideas more alien, the distance between father and daughter more unbridgeable. For years John had ignored the warning signs as best he could, trusting that time, and the culmination of his own plans, would set everything right between them. But then in 1969, just as the negotiations for Kuran Station were firming up, Ruth returned for what would be her last visit.

She brought a man with her, and announced that he was her husband.

Chapter Thirty-one

ON THE DAY OF RUTH'S ARRIVAL, WILLIAM AWOKE LATE TO FIND
that the House had ceased to run before the weather. There were
no more creaks or groans from the timbers, no shudder in the
floorboards — everything seemed hushed. He rose and ventured
out onto the porch. A baleful sun glared through smoke that hung
motionless over the mountains, and across the plains the haze lay
like a flat sheet. Some time during the night, the westerly must
have frittered away and died. Now nothing moved anywhere.
Heat prickled on William's neck, and he felt a quiet thrill of
dismay. They were becalmed. It was as if the House had passed
through the outer gales of some great barren cyclone, and finally
reached the eye, a place of deathly stillness.

In William's ear, the ache pulsed anew.

He spent the morning roaming restlessly about the halls. It
was so silent that there might have been no one else in the
building. His mother was hidden away, sunk in gloom, and his
uncle was alone in the white room, brooding privately upon the

approach of his daughter. Finally, oppressed by this lonely waiting, William resolved to stand guard upon the porch. It seemed that *he* at least should be there when Ruth arrived. To greet her and, if indeed she was a threat, to show that he was ready to defend his territory. He donned his captain's hat, seeking reassurance from the authority of the metal badge. Then he set up a chair, deep in the shade of the verandah, and watched.

But no one came. Great gleaming black horseflies circled about the garden. The wind had driven them off in previous days, but here in the doldrums they had crawled forth, hungry and clinging. One of them alighted on William's ear and he batted it away. It kept coming back, crawling about on his lobe as if it wanted to burrow inside the canal. It was disgusting. And it seemed to bring with it the scent of rotting that William remembered from the rally — faintly revolting, but impossible to pinpoint. Time crept by. William sprawled in the chair, staring out at the shimmers of heat on the plains. He felt he was alone in the hot focus of nowhere, a netherworld to which the wind had driven him and then, satisfied with itself, abandoned him. His head sank to his chest.

And thus it was that when Ruth McIvor arrived, all she found amidst the junk on the porch was a thin, barefoot boy wearing a strange hat, fast asleep in the middle of the afternoon.

'Excuse me.'

William was dreaming of horseflies, giant ones that hummed like bees. When he opened his eyes a black car sat in the drive, and an unknown woman stood upon the steps, frowning at him.

'Who are you?' she asked.

'Captain Bill,' he said, still half in his dream.

She blinked. 'I'm here to see my father.'

William fought his way out of sleep. This was the daughter! She had caught him unawares after all.

She said, 'Can you tell me where I'd find Mrs Griffith?'

William continued to stare. She was so old! Older than his mother even, by far. He had expected someone younger. It was because of the word 'daughter', he realised belatedly. But this woman looked at least fifty, with a narrow face, deeply lined, and close-cut, greying hair. She was dressed in a dark suit, and radiated a tense severity.

'Mrs Griffith?' she repeated. 'Is she around?'

He spoke finally. 'I don't know.'

The frown turned quizzical. 'Do you live here?'

William nodded. 'With my mother.' He was puzzled. Didn't she know who he was? He had assumed that the housekeeper had told the daughter all about him.

'Your mother? What does she do here?'

He cast about for an answer. 'Uncle John said we could move in.'

'*Uncle?*'

'I mean, great uncle.'

'Oh.' Her eyes narrowed. '*Oh.*' She studied him with full attention finally. 'You must be my cousin's son. I haven't seen him in years. And your mother's name is Veronica, isn't it?' But the frown remained. 'I don't understand. I thought they had a farm.'

'Dad died.'

'Died?' She mused on this. 'I didn't know.' Then she glanced around again. 'I was really hoping Mrs Griffith would be here.'

No, William thought. The housekeeper had set her plans in motion, and now she would remain in the shadows to watch them unfold. She might be observing them even at this moment, from the corner of some window. But she wouldn't come forth.

Instead, William's mother appeared in the doorway, her face pinched unhappily.

'Ruth,' she said.

'Veronica,' returned the newcomer levelly. 'I'm sorry. No one told me my father had other people in the House.'

William's mother nodded, her eyes dropping to the front of her dress, where her hands clutched at the material. 'You'd better come in.'

They passed into the entry hall, and William followed. It was sweltering indoors. He watched as Ruth took in the shabby walls and cluttered passages of her father's home.

She took a deep breath. 'So how is he?'

'He's better than he was,' William's mother answered, wary.

'Better? Then he isn't...?'

'I don't know what Mrs Griffith told you.'

Ruth's shoulders stiffened. 'She said he was dying.'

'No ... not any more.'

'She said he was asking for me.'

'I don't know anything about that either.'

'I see.' The daughter flushed. 'There seems to have been a mistake.'

'I could find Mrs Griffith if you want.'

'No ... I don't really know her. She was just supposed to call me if...' She trailed off and glanced back towards the front door, tight lipped.

So the housekeeper had lied, and now the daughter knew it. William caught a furtive gleam of hope in his mother's eyes. 'I could tell him you called,' she said carefully, 'if you don't think you should stay.'

But at that, Ruth turned her head and studied the younger woman for a long moment. Then, strangely, she smiled, and for the first time William saw the ghost of his uncle in her.

'So how long have *you* been living here, Veronica?'

The gleam blinked out. 'Four months now.'

'And your husband was...?'

'Killed. In an accident.'

'And my father was kind enough to take you in.'

William's mother nodded, curling in on herself.

Ruth was still smiling. 'I'm glad. It must be nice for him, to have some company about.' She glanced down at William. 'Especially someone young. What was your name again?'

'William.'

'After your dad, of course. You like living in this big house, do you?'

'Yes.'

'Shouldn't you be at school? Or is it holidays?'

'He's sick,' William's mother broke in. 'He's got glandular fever.'

'It's nothing serious, I hope.'

'No. He'll be fine.'

A silence fell. William looked from one woman to the other, sensing an unspoken battle of wills, delicately poised. He was also uncomfortably aware of the contrast the two made, and that his mother came away the poorer. Maybe it was just her old floral dress, faded and drab against the visitor's more sophisticated clothes, or her wispy mouse-brown hair against the older woman's striking grey. But whatever it was, his mother looked insubstantial, a wan, weaker woman.

Finally, Ruth spoke. 'So ... he's in his room?'

William's mother hesitated, then gave a sullen nod of defeat.

'And where is that?'

'What?'

'I don't know the way. I've never been here before.'

'Oh,' William's mother stared in amazement. 'It's up the stairs. The west wing, last room on the right.'

'Thank you. I'll be fine on my own.'

'You should watch the floors.'

Ruth paused, an eyebrow raised.

'For holes,' William's mother concluded, faint.

'I will,' said the daughter, and began climbing.

William watched her until she disappeared through the partition. This wasn't what he'd been expecting at all. How could it be that Ruth had never even been inside the House before? Her father had lived on the property for over twenty years — had she never visited in all that time?

His mother looked away from the stairs. 'Come on,' she said, her voice flat. 'Let's leave them to it. They don't need you or me any more.'

Together they went back out to the front porch. His mother sank into the chair and William sat on the top step. They didn't speak for some time. The afternoon was lengthening, but the heat remained, stultifying, and still no breath of wind stirred the air. All was silent, a limbo world, miles from anywhere. Ruth's car crouched in the driveway.

'Should I get her bags?' William asked.

'She can get them herself, if she has any.'

'Isn't she going to be staying?'

'That's up to her.' His mother lifted her eyes to the second storey. 'And your uncle, I suppose.'

William thought. 'Do they really hate each other?'

'That's what I was always told.'

'Why?'

'Christ, I don't know. It was years ago. There was a falling out — I think she took up with some man your Uncle John didn't like.'

'Who?'

'Just some man. It doesn't matter. He left her, long ago.'

But there was another question, one William had been wondering about ever since he had learnt of Ruth's existence. 'Mum ... does Uncle John have a wife?'

'He did.'

'Where is she now?'

'Will, please! I can't explain everything. Not right his second.'

William subsided. His mother tapped a foot restlessly, her head on an angle. She was listening for noises from the upper floor.

William looked towards the ceiling. What was happening up there? What could they possibly be talking about, after so long apart? But the minutes inched by, ten, twenty, thirty, and still Ruth did not come down.

'She has her father's eyes,' his mother said hopelessly, to no one.

In the end it was almost an hour before Ruth came back out to the porch. She was fumbling in her pockets as she emerged, and brought forth a pack of cigarettes. She lit one up and sucked in the smoke with a long, shuddering breath. The time with her father had changed her — or maybe it was the heat of the upstairs rooms. She looked exhausted, her face sheened with sweat, her clothes wilted. She would go now, William thought. She would take out her keys and, without another word, climb into her car and drive off, never to be seen again.

'Is there a spare bedroom?' she asked hoarsely, staring out at the plains.

William watched his mother absorb the news. 'You're staying then,' she said.

'I don't know.' The words were bitten off. 'It's not my decision.'

William realised that Ruth was furious. And then, to his alarm, she turned her gaze to him, the cigarette clamped tightly in her fingers.

'My father said that I had to ask William. Apparently, it's his choice.'

In a horrified flash, William understood. They had talked about *him* — this nephew who had come into the House. And now the decision was his to make. The old man must have planned it all along. A lesson, for both nephew and daughter. A test for him, and a humiliation for her.

William was aware of his mother's wide stare, startled and hopeful, and knew what she wanted him to do. But what could he say? He was a nine-year-old boy, and Ruth was a grown-up.

It wasn't right that he could tell her what to do. For a long instant he hung on the horn of the decision, wondering if he actually dared ... but it was impossible. He could never say it.

'Well?'

'I dunno.' William's voice sounded small in his ears. 'You can stay if you want.'

His mother's face fell. He had failed her, he knew. And perhaps his uncle as well.

'Thank you,' said his cousin stiffly. 'Now, can someone show me to the phone?'

Chapter Thirty-two

WILLIAM WALKED THE RUINS OF THE GARDEN. IT WAS LATE evening, and he had come out there to escape the heat, but the darkness was just as heavy as the day, the air just as breathless. Overhead the stars were lost in haze, and a sombre glow on the eastern horizon spoke of fires in the foothills.

He was thinking about Ruth McIvor. His cousin had moved herself into one of the downstairs bedrooms of the west wing. William had overheard her on the phone, arranging extra time off from work, her voice tired and brusque as she explained that, no, she couldn't say how long she would be staying. But for William there was a bigger question. Why was she staying at all? Her father wasn't dying and did not need her. Indeed, the old man had only insulted her, thrusting his nephew in Ruth's face, the very boy who had supplanted her. So why was she still here?

He kicked about the garden beds, going nowhere. According to his mother, the answer was simple. It was all about who would inherit the station when his uncle died. Now that Ruth knew her birthright had been stolen away, she would not leave again until she had reclaimed it.

It made sense. And yet...

William looked up to the House, the prize in question. It hulked against the sky, ivy creepers dangling from its gutters like the shreds of torn rigging. He turned away and drifted across to the pool, gazing into its empty depths. He sighed, unsure about everything.

Close by, a naked flame flared to life.

'Don't fall in.'

He started. Ruth was sitting on the far edge of the pool, lighting a cigarette. He caught a glimpse of her grey hair, hands cupped close, her eyes watching him. Then the flame died, and she was only a pale figure in the night, exhaling smoke.

'I've been wondering,' she said. 'Why is this pool empty?'

William studied her doubtfully. 'There's a hole in it.'

'That's a shame. You must wish you had a place to go swimming.'

Her tone was friendly, nothing like it had been earlier. But then William thought of the water hole. He frowned. Is that what she meant? Was she hinting at something?

'Actually,' she said, 'I was hoping we'd meet up.'

'Why?'

'Just for a talk.'

Don't trust her, his uncle had told him. And yet it didn't seem to William that he could just walk away. He circled the pool warily, and then sat down on the edge, some distance from his cousin. She smoked in silence for a time, and the air was so still that William could see the smoke from her cigarette rising vertically into the night, an unruffled line.

'Just so you know,' she said finally, 'it wasn't you I was mad at this afternoon.'

William made no reply.

She blew out smoke and pointed. 'Look at that, even the diving board is broken. Everything is falling down around here. I don't know how you put up with it.'

'It's okay.'

'The House, the yard … you don't mind?'

'No.'

'Well, I'd want it fixed up, if I had to live here.'

William stared at her suspiciously, alert for a hidden attack. 'Uncle John said it would cost too much to fix up properly.'

'Is that what he told you?'

'He said it would cost a million dollars. Even more.'

'As much as that?' She was taunting him now, he knew, but then the smile in her voice faded away. 'Tell me, Will, have you ever heard of the Heritage Trust?'

'No.'

'It's an organisation that looks after historical buildings. Like this one.'

William glanced up to the House and its broken-back roof line.

Ruth was looking at it too. 'Ten years or so ago the Trust made an approach to my father. They wanted to restore this place. People in the district thought it ought to be done — the House used to be the centre for the whole region, after all, so they didn't like the idea of it just falling down. There was talk of fundraising and getting in volunteers. All they needed was my father's permission. And the only thing the Trust wanted in return was for the House and the gardens to be open to the public occasionally. Not all the time, just now and then.'

'He said no?'

'More than that — he took legal action against the Trust to stop them interfering in his business. So that was that.' She flicked ash away, turned her shadowed gaze to William. 'Believe me, my father has no interest whatever in fixing this place up.'

William looked towards the House again, its ruinous presence a mute witness. It wasn't that he didn't believe her, it sounded like something his uncle would do, it was just that …

Ruth laughed lowly. 'I know. Why should you listen to me?'

William thought in puzzled silence. 'How do you know this stuff?'

'About the Trust?'

'You said you'd never been here before.'

'I heard it from a friend at work. But the truth is, I have been here once before. Only I didn't go past the front door.' She inspected the stub of her cigarette, ground it out against the wall of the pool. 'I was just here to pick up my mother.'

Her mother. William hesitated, feeling that, out of respect for his uncle, this was not something he was meant to know about. And yet he did want to know.

'What happened to her?' he asked.

'She left him.'

'Why?'

'It was partly because of this place. I think it was 1970 when they finally moved in. My mother hated it. Dark little rooms, dark little hallways. She left after only a few months. Of course, leaving was the easy part. What she had to do then was build up the nerve to actually divorce him. That took her another five years.' She paused. 'He's never told you any of this?'

'No.'

'I wonder why.' For a moment it seemed that she would say no more. But then she shrugged. 'He didn't seem to mind so much, when she left. But divorce — that got him mad. Divorce involved money. He didn't want to give her a cent. We had to take him to court in the end. After all, it was her inheritance that got them started in the first place.'

She tilted her head ironically.

'It's odd, you know, but my father has always been lucky with inheriting things.'

She cleared the thought away.

'Anyway, we won, and he owed mum exactly half of everything. The problem was, all his money was tied up in this station. So he was left with a choice — either split the property and give half to her, or buy her out. It nearly killed him, I think, that decision.'

'What did he do?'

'The place is still in one piece, isn't it? But he had to go into debt to do it. He'd never liked loans, but this time he borrowed a lot. Obviously, after that, his plans to restore the House had to be put on hold. He hated us for that. Hated Mum, anyway. He was already long through with me.'

William sat up straight. 'Then it's not his fault.'

'What isn't?'

'He really couldn't afford to fix up the House.'

Ruth laughed again. 'That was eighteen years ago. He's got plenty of money now. No — he *likes* the House this way. So he can show everyone how badly the world has treated him.'

William slumped. It seemed that there was no safe ground between father and daughter. But Ruth was oblivious, lighting another cigarette.

'You see, after fighting so long to get his hands on this place, it all fell apart. His wife left him, he had no money, I suppose he felt robbed. And everything else was changing. The Whitlam government was in then — it was their new divorce laws that helped my mother win — and all the rules were being thrown out the window. People out here didn't like it, my father in particular. So he holed up in this terrible old building and sulked. Then he started up the League.'

'You know about that?'

'Know about it? I'm a member.'

William was speechless.

'It's true.' She considered him. 'Do you know what I do for a living?'

William shook his head.

'I'm a legal adviser. I work for the state government — in the Premier's Department. One of our jobs is to keep an eye on radical political organisations. One day someone was passing an Independence League newsletter around the office, laughing at this crazy little right-wing group from the bush. So I had a look. And there was the name on the letterhead.' She breathed out smoke in wonderment. 'My own father, chief proprietor of Fascists Incorporated. The weirdest thing is, take away the bogus patriotism and the inherent racism, and he's mouthing the same old anarchist shit he used to hate so much.' William was staring at her in bafflement, and she caught herself. 'Sorry ... It's all before your time. Anyway, I subscribed to the newsletter. Not under my own name, of course. But it was one way to stay in touch. Poor Dad. I gather the rally was something of a disaster?'

'You know about that too?'

'Oh, I know plenty of things. I know that my father has been dumped from the League's central committee, for a start. In fact, there *is* no League any more. Now it's called Unity Australia. I got their new magazine the other day. Nicely printed too. But otherwise, it's the same old names, and the same old policies. They've just tacked on a militia and a call to arms. Plus they're going to start running candidates in elections. The idiots are actually going to register as a political party.' She shook her head, disbelieving. 'I don't think my father would ever have stood for that.'

William had nothing to say. The way she spoke about the League was so bizarre. He had always known that his mother, for instance, didn't approve of his uncle's activities ... but that had seemed mostly because of the money the old man wasted. This was different. Ruth sounded almost amused by the League, in a cruel way. He found his eyes drawn to the flagpole in front of the House. And for the first time since the rally, he noticed that the Eureka flag was no longer hanging there.

'You actually liked all that League stuff, didn't you?' Ruth asked.

He could only nod.

'That's what I thought ... He's got you locked away with him in this House, and he's filling your head with all his crazy ideas. I don't know why your mother allows it, or why she even brought you here. Except, I do know.'

But that didn't seem fair. 'We had nowhere else to go.'

'There's always somewhere else to go.'

William shifted his legs uncomfortably. Her judgment was spoken with all the weight of her years, and he couldn't argue.

'Where's *your* mother,' he asked.

'She died,' said Ruth simply. 'She'd been living with me in Brisbane. I wasn't sure my father would come to the funeral, but he did. That was the last time we spoke. You know what he seemed most interested in? Who Mum had left her money to.'

'Was it you?'

'Of course it was me.' She was stubbing out her second cigarette, sparks showering down into the pool. 'And he was pleased with that. He thought it proved something.'

She fell silent. As it was, William already felt he'd heard too much, seen a hidden part of his uncle's life nakedly exposed. All the things he'd thought he understood, they sounded different when they came from her — twisted and strange. He remembered his uncle's warning. Maybe she was just trying to confuse him. But why? Indeed, why was she talking to him at all? If it was the station she wanted, then it was her father she had to deal with.

He realised she was watching him sidelong.

'So,' she said, 'will you fix the pool, when this whole place is yours?'

William went still. There it was. Spoken out loud. Now the attack would come.

Instead, she smiled. 'You don't have to worry, you know. I don't want it. Not the House. Not the property. Not any of it.'

He stared at her. 'You don't?'

'Not even if my father offered it to me. Which he never would. But what about you? Do you want it?'

Amidst his surprise, William wasn't sure what to answer. 'Yes,' he said at last.

'I thought so.' Ruth sounded almost sad. 'And to get it, all you have to do is be nice to your Uncle John...' Then, abruptly, she was standing up, tucking her cigarette packet away. 'Enough for one night.' She turned to face the plains. 'God, it's hot. And look at those fires, up in the hills. They must have burned out half the national park.'

William rose as well, still uneasy, yet relieved.

But Ruth was studying him again. 'It was a fire in the wheat, I'm told.'

William blinked at her.

'Your father, I mean.'

'Yes.'

'That must have been hard,' she said. And then to William's dismay she reached out a hand and rested it on his shoulder. 'Poor boy. I know what it's like.'

Then she set off back across the garden, picking her way with care in the darkness, while her father's House waited silent to receive her.

Chapter Thirty-three

By 1969, JOHN MCIVOR HAD TO ADMIT THAT HIS DAUGHTER baffled him.

He blamed the times. A new age had swept across Australia, and the decade seemed to belong to young people with wild hair and wilder clothes. These types were not a familiar sight around Powell, but they were everywhere on television and in the newspapers. And it wasn't just their appearance that John disliked — what grated most was their aggressiveness, all their marches and riots in the streets, their protests against the war in Vietnam, or apartheid in South Africa, or whatever took their fancy. But what did they know? Had they survived any great wars or depressions? Had they struggled to raise families and buy homes? No. And yet they felt free to cast judgment upon anyone older than themselves. It was a sorry state of affairs. And that wasn't even considering their pre-occupation with drugs, and their sexual immorality.

Worst of all, they had stolen his daughter away.

John had once thought that law would be a sensible career for

Ruth. But after finishing her degree, she joined a community legal centre in Brisbane's West End. Her work had something to do with women's rights, although she was never clear about what she did exactly, or whether she was even paid. Indeed, John was aware that Harriet often sent her money secretly. Of course, all his money was his daughter's to ask for, if she really needed it — but this was just subsidising her in folly. Who knew what she spent it on? Certainly not on her clothes or her appearance. The neat daughter John remembered had turned into someone scruffy, barefoot and careless. She talked of nothing but campaigns and rallies and protests. Closing his ears, all John could do was hope that inside her the old Ruth remained, ready to re-emerge one day, when reality sank in.

That hope was especially important now.

For in late 1969, at the age of fifty-five, John McIvor finally began proceedings to sell all his land and purchase Kuran Station. Nearly forty years had passed since the day he and his father had been banished by Elizabeth White. Forty years ... it was a span of time to be marvelled at. He had waited so long, and grown so old. But when the agent took him for an inspection tour of the property, John was overcome by the sight of it — so huge, so alive, so beautiful. And almost *his* now. He could feel the strength of the hills flowing into his limbs like youth. What then did age matter? He would have as many more years as he needed. A price was settled upon, and all that remained was the paperwork, then the sale would be official.

The moment was a culmination so sublime that John felt full to bursting with the desire to express it — but who was there to tell? Who could even understand his achievement? No one around him remembered his earlier days on the station, or the shame of his downfall. His father was dead, so was his mother. He hadn't spoken to his sister in decades. Harriet was coldly uninterested. Which left Ruth — and if only *she* could grasp the importance of what he'd done, then John would've been content. But on the rare occasions she deigned to visit, all he saw was a young woman who lolled about the house in torn jeans, obnoxiously bra-less beneath her T-shirt, spouting maxims from the lunatic fringe.

How was he to make her understand that all the grandness and stature of Kuran Station was ready for her now — that the whole life he'd always planned for her was ready. The picture of it was so clear in John's mind. With the station behind her, she could have her pick of the finest suitors in the country, she could find someone influential and rich, from a landed background maybe. The House would be hers and her husband's to live in, restored to its former glory. And when they had children of their own, the kids could be raised there on the property. Kuran Station would become a family seat once again, the foundation of a new dynasty, eclipsing even the Whites. And there at the head of family, the great patriarch, would be John himself. If only he could make Ruth *see*.

Just how vain were his hopes, and how totally deluded he was about his daughter, became clear the moment Ruth arrived home on what would be her last visit.

She appeared at the door with a man, and declared that they were married. But 'man' was too kind a word. In those first few hours of shock and anger, John saw him as the very worst example of everything he hated about the younger generation. His name was Carl, and his long dark hair and beard couldn't hide the fact he was only a boy, nor could the infuriating air of superiority with which he slipped into the house in Ruth's wake. Slim and pale, his clothes of tie-dyed cotton, it was obvious he had never laboured for anything in his life, and yet there was a persistent mockery to his smile as he looked over the farm. It was, Ruth told them, his very first trip west of Brisbane. He was the son of two university lecturers, and he was trying to become a playwright.

It only got worse over dinner. Carl announced that they should know he was a confirmed anarchist. He proceeded to lecture a silent, fuming John about what libertarian socialism really meant — implacable opposition to hierarchy, or any organisational structure that embodied authority, and hence oppression. Anarchists were not against order itself, but it had to come from below, directly from the community, and never from an institution artificially granted power over others. Like parliament, Carl offered helpfully. Did they understand what he was getting at? John understood all right — it was perfect idiocy. He loathed every word that came out of the boy's lips, shining pink and plump amidst the wispy hairs of his ridiculous beard. And yet Ruth sat by, nodding.

At the other end of the table, Harriet watched them all unhappily. Caught between father and daughter, she sought for a topic that might distract them both. She opted for Kuran Station, and the fact that John had made an offer on the place. It was the worse possible choice. Ruth greeted the news with a deliberate indifference, and John glared at his wife in rage. This was no time to be speaking of the House! Not with this intruder present. And yet Carl was the only one interested in the news. What was this Kuran Station, he wanted to know. And so, faltering under her husband's icy stare, Harriet explained a little about the station and its history. It set Carl off on another lecture. The grand homesteads, and the landed gentry who had owned them, were prime examples of an oppressive hierarchy. Land was inalienable from the people, he declared, a common possession, and should never be owned by any individual to the exclusion of others. And all along, Ruth smiled at her father.

John could think of nothing to say, his outrage so towering that it was all he could do to remain at the table. She had *married* this fool. When Harriet tried to divert the conversation by asking about Ruth and Carl's wedding, John's control almost fractured. How could she want to talk about it? Didn't she understand what Ruth had done to them all? But then, blessedly, came deliverance.

For it turned out that Ruth and Carl weren't married at all, at least not legally. An anarchist could hardly accept that any church or agency had the right to formalise a marriage contract, so they had devised a service of their own, and held it in front of a few of their friends in a park.

It was still a binding vow, Carl asserted. But John was so relieved he was barely listening. Maybe something could still be salvaged from the wreck. Ruth may have become almost fatally misguided, but so far there were no legal ramifications to her actions. That lone fact enabled John to survive the rest of the evening without exploding, and it also saw him through the awkward discussion about Ruth and Carl's sleeping arrangements. Even if they really had been married, the idea of them together would have disgusted him. But as it was, with only a narrow single bed in Ruth's room, there was nothing to argue about. Carl had to make do with the camp bed in the office. So John went to his own bed with a measure of calm. With sleep and time to think, perhaps things would improve. Time was the key. Time, more than anything, for Ruth to come to her senses.

But far into the night, John awoke from a dream haunted with flame and sensed, just as he had fourteen years ealier, that somewhere, someone was moving in the house.

The déjà vu was chilling and immediate. Only this time, he knew instantly what the half-heard sound must be. He rose anyway, and crept down the shadowed hallway. The camp bed in his office was empty, and so he came without pause to his daughter's bedroom. There was a light under the door, and a smell in the air that he didn't recognise, but which he guessed, despairingly, had to be marijuana. Yet far worse were the noises. He sagged against the wall, weak with anger and shame as, mere feet away through the thin wooden door, his daughter was violated by the man she called her husband. Images flooded John's mind and he was helpless to stop them — a thin white body heaving above

Ruth's; long, greasy hair hanging down across her face; those pink lips smeared on hers. Was it Dudley he was seeing, or the hideous boy? It didn't matter, his daughter was willing this time, he could hear with appalling clarity exactly how willing.

And yet in his vision she was joyless. She stared over the man's shoulder directly at her father, as if there was no wall between them at all, and there was only hatred in her eyes as his hips pumped and pumped. *I fuck him to fuck you, Father. This is what I learnt from you. This is what you allowed to happen to your daughter, and this is what I will go on doing forever and forever.* And when Ruth cried out in pleasure, John almost cried out as well, longing to fling open the door, tear the man from her, throw him to the floor and beat him, beat him ceaselessly ... but beat who? It wasn't Dudley in there, and his daughter didn't want to be rescued. He'd had his chance to do that years ago and had failed her. He had sent her away, and now she was avenged. All he could do was creep back down the hall, impotent and nauseated. His daughter's soft, fierce laughter chased after him, and he knew that she had wanted him to hear everything, that her hatred was unqualified and permanent, and that nothing could be saved after all.

The next morning, while Carl showered and sang in their bathroom, John told his daughter that if she insisted on staying with her husband, then he had no interest in seeing her again. The vindication in Ruth's eyes made it perfectly clear that she'd hoped for this. But just to make the cut as deep and fatal as it could be, John spelt out exactly what he meant — that she would be severed from them completely, there would be no more support, she would never be welcome home, and no matter what sort of wealth John accrued in the rest of his life, no matter what property, no matter the possession of Kuran Station itself, none of it would ever come to her. Not if it was be shared with this boy she had presented. And with a triumphant, shining anger, Ruth replied that such terms suited her exactly.

She and Carl were gone within an hour. It was left to Harriet, tearful and horrified, to follow them out, clinging to Ruth and whispering into her ear. Whispering what — pleas, promises, sorrows — John didn't know or care. He was aware of a vast hollowness opening inside him, and all the pain and rage was falling into it, to vanish forever. He felt nothing at all, only an exquisite isolation. Whatever he did from now on would be for himself, and that would be enough. When Harriet came back, her eyes red and her body jolted by shock, he said nothing, felt no need to speak. Instead he left her mourning in their little cottage, and went off to his work on the farm.

Two months later he signed the contracts, and Kuran Station was his.

Chapter Thirty-four

IN THE DREAM WILLIAM WAS WALKING THROUGH A BURNED-OUT wheat field, and he was aware that his father walked beside him. He could hear footsteps crunching in the stubble, and though he wanted to see his father again, he didn't dare look, because if he looked he would see the burning man instead. But when he finally did look there were no flames, there was just his dad. And he wasn't burned, he was the same as he had always been, whole and clean and smiling. William felt immense relief. But then he saw that his father's cheek was smeared with a streak of black ash. Sorrow welled up in him, and suddenly he couldn't see his father any more. His father was dead, and though in the dream William turned and turned, he couldn't catch sight of him again. He was alone in a terrible field of burned wheat and dust, and somewhere far away a monster trod the earth.

There were tears in his eyes when he woke. His ear throbbed as if someone had lanced it with a knife, and William curled up into a ball, waiting until the pain eased. And the other pain as well, from the dream. It was his cousin's fault — she had resurrected the ghost of his father. And so gently ... he should have been angry with her for even daring to mention the subject, angry with her pity and her hand upon his shoulder. And yet he wasn't. All he felt was lonely and unwell. He stared at the window. Red daylight glared out there — the sun, the haze, the torpid air, none of it had changed. He rose finally, his limbs sluggish and sore. In the living room he found his mother, slumped upon the couch, staring fixedly at the television, even though it wasn't switched on.

'Mum?'

Her eyes did not leave the blank screen. 'What?'

Vacant hostility dulled her voice. William became fully awake in recognition and alarm. Her bathrobe had fallen open to reveal the cleft of her thin chest, sweat sheened upon it. And lying nearby on the floor was a small bottle, empty of pills.

'Are you okay?' he asked.

'I took him his breakfast,' she said, her dead gaze finally drifting from the TV, up to the ceiling. 'He wouldn't eat it. He told me to get out.'

William's heart wrung with concern. He hadn't seen his mother like this in months — not since the days after his father's death. She was at a stage far beyond the migraines or the nervous hand-wringing. This was the mood of deep blackness that descended upon her at times, a dark river that swept her mind away and left her body behind.

'It's *her* he wants,' she said. 'I know it.'

'Mum...'

'She was here before.' Her slurred speech became bitter. 'Your new friend. Your cousin. She was looking for you.'

'Why?'

'I don't know.' She glared at William from under her puffed eyelids. 'Well? You're the one who let her stay. So if she wants you, go.'

'I didn't…'

'Go on!' Fury roused her momentarily. 'Before she throws both of us out on the street!' She lurched forward and her robe fell open further, revealing scrawny breasts. 'She'll do it! She's turned your uncle against us! That's why she's here!'

William fled in dismay.

He found Ruth on the front porch.

'Will,' she said gravely.

He squinted at her in the hot light.

'I saw your mother earlier. Is she all right?'

But he couldn't accept the sympathy in her voice. His mother was sick, that was all, she wasn't to blame. And it was no one else's business. 'Did you want me?' he asked.

Ruth nodded, seeming to understand. She brightened. 'Are you busy today? I thought you might be my guide.'

'Guide?'

'I want to see some of this station of yours.'

'It isn't mine.'

Ruth only smiled.

'Where do you want to go then?' he asked.

'Wherever you think.'

William thought wearily. His cousin was dressed in jeans and T-shirt and boots, as if she meant to go exploring far afield. And if she went far enough, she might come across the campground and the ring of stones. She might even discover the water hole. But those places were secret.

'I can show you the graveyard,' he said. 'It's not far. We can walk there.'

'A graveyard?' She considered the idea. 'Actually, I'd like that. Better put a hat on though. That sun is pretty fierce.'

So William went back to his flat. He could hear sobbing from the main bedroom. He blotted out the sound, grabbed his captain's hat, then returned to Ruth on the porch.

She was examining one of the pillars that supported the upper verandah.

'It's beautiful sandstone, this. They quarried it locally, you know. And all the timber was local too, red cedar and pine, from the mountains. The only thing they needed to import was the slate for the roof. The whole thing cost an absolute fortune.'

William stared for a moment, puzzled once more.

But they set out across the garden and over the crumbled section of the wall, then walked up through the paddock towards the crown of the hill. The heat was searing out there, the whole hillside dusty and dry, and grass crunched as brittle as glass under their feet.

'I've got a confession to make,' Ruth said.

He looked up at her.

'I know a little more about this station than I've let on.'

'Like how the House was built?'

She nodded. 'It's a funny thing. It's like — well, imagine you were married, and your wife ran off with another man, someone you'd never met. You'd be angry. But you'd be curious too, wouldn't you, about what this other man was like?'

William screwed up his face. 'I guess so.'

'Well, I was curious about Kuran Station. So I did some research. And it wasn't hard to find things out. You know that this place was quite famous once, don't you?'

'I know.' But he found her admission disturbing.

They came to the top of the hill, pausing to take in the view. There was little to see. Haze still masked the horizon, the plains were a blur, and smoke blanketed the mountains. It was a dreary world, a monotone of dead grass and scorched trees and bare earth. Droughts were pale brown, William decided. Not red or yellow or black, but the ugliest, drabbest brown imaginable.

'I've never seen it this bad,' his cousin sighed. She was a little breathless after the climb. 'I grew up on a farm out there, you know. Just like you did. We could see it from here, if it wasn't so hazy.'

'You could see mine too.'

She looked at him. 'Do you miss it? Your farm?'

'Sometimes,' he said, thinking of his mother in tears.

'I drove past our old place on the way here. It was all gone. The house, the sheds, knocked down and ploughed under. No sign we were ever there.' Ruth lit a cigarette, gazed around at the hills. 'My father never liked it anyway. This is what he always wanted.'

'It goes all the way to the mountains,' William offered.

'And the original station was even bigger, wasn't it? I've seen the old maps. It reached about as far as we can see in every direction from up here.'

'That's what the settlers did. They stood up here and everything they could see, that's what they got.'

She smiled. 'Your uncle told you that?'

'He said there was nothing here when they first came, and sometimes they died.'

'Yes, some of them died, true enough.'

But her agreement was offhand, and suddenly it seemed important to William that she understand what he was saying. 'The explorer who found Kuran Station, he died right here. There was a statue of him, in front of the House, in the fountain.'

She puffed on her cigarette. 'You know, no one really *found* Kuran. And it wasn't empty. Other people were already here.'

'I know that,' he insisted. 'They were the ones who killed the explorer.'

Her smiled had thinned. 'I'm sure my father told you that, too.' She studied the plains again. 'I was reading once about Allan Cunningham, the explorer. When he first saw the Darling Downs, it was in conditions like this — there were fires everywhere, and smoke.'

'Was there a drought?'

'No. It was summer, though. Cunningham thought that maybe the fires had been started by lightning strikes setting the grass alight. You know how this was all savanna, before it was settled? No forests or anything, just miles and miles of grass?'

William nodded, remembering. Grass as high as men on horseback.

'That's what the fires were really about,' his cousin said. 'The Aborigines lit them. Every summer, apparently, they burned the plains clean through. That way they had fresh green grass every year, and so more animals would come down from the hills for them to hunt. The Aborigines never let any trees grow. The last thing they wanted was for the plains to be covered in scrub. The problem was, they did too good a job. A hundred and fifty years ago, the squatters came along and saw all that beautiful grass. And they thought, wow, won't this be perfect for cattle and sheep. And aren't we lucky that all this pasture is just sitting here, with no one using it. So they marched on in.'

Ruth stubbed her cigarette out on her heel.

'Can't really blame the Aborigines for getting a little upset, can you? All that work they'd put in, year after year — gone. No wonder they speared the odd white man.'

William blinked in uncertainty. His uncle had said that there were no trees on the plains because the black soil couldn't support them. He hadn't said anything about fires.

Ruth turned eastwards. 'So where's this graveyard?'

They broached the rise, and then tramped down towards the church. It looked even more ruinous than normal, now that all the grass and weeds about it had died. Ruth barely glanced at the little building, passing straight on to the cemetery. The headstones reared up starkly from bare earth. William followed her from stone to stone, staring at the worn inscriptions.

'The Whites,' she said, oddly satisfied. 'I was hoping they'd be here.'

'You know about them?'

'Oh yes. Do you?'

'I know they built the House.'

'That's right, the great homestead. Their finest memorial.' She kicked thoughtfully at the dust. 'I'll make another confession, Will. I actually agree with your uncle about one thing. I don't want the House fixed up either. I wouldn't care if it fell in a heap tomorrow.'

'But you said—'

'I said the Heritage Trust wants it restored. I didn't say I did. Oh, I know, it's a pioneer landmark. And I'm sure you've heard how important the Whites were, carving out a station in the wilderness, and how that means we should preserve their House. But all they really did was get here first, grab as much as they could, and then keep everyone else away. When other people came out here, looking for a bit of land, there wasn't a scrap left. Just 'No Trespassing' signs for twenty miles in every direction. Those people would have looked up at the House and hated it.'

'But the station got broken up,' William protested. 'It's all little farms now.'

'Now, yes. Not before a lot of misery, though.'

They came at last to the biggest tomb, with its crumbling angels standing guard. William saw that the hole beneath the gravestone was still there, only now it looked like an empty crack in which nothing lived. Ruth shook her head, smiling tightly.

'And here's the great man himself — the last of the Pure Merinos.' She crouched down before the tomb. 'It's strange — everyone thinks Edward White was so impressive. But I've read some of the speeches he gave in parliament. He was as slimy as they come. He lied and cheated and bribed, anything to protect his property. He held up development in this region for thirty or forty years. The best thing the old fraud ever did was die and get out of the way.'

William stared at the grave in perplexity. His cousin was

confusing him yet again. Why was it that nothing seemed simple or straightforward around her?

Ruth had picked up a chunk of stone: a carved hand, from one of the angels, snapped off at the wrist. 'I'm surprised my father has left this such a mess. He always admired Edward. I think he wanted to be like him. And I guess he is, now. Another old man, clinging on to this bloody station for dear life.' She glanced wryly at William. 'Sorry, I know you've been told how wonderful Kuran and its history is. But I really don't like the place.'

William watched her uneasily.

'I was supposed to like it, you know. My father wanted all this for me, once. Or at least, that was his excuse. He never asked *me* about it though. And, in the end, when I told him I wasn't interested, he threw me out of home.'

She tossed the angel's hand aside, and it cracked in two against the tomb.

'That's what happens when you don't agree with him.' Something cold danced in her eyes. 'Lucky that he found you then, isn't it? You'll always agree.'

William felt his face reddening.

'It's all right, Will. What else could you do? But just remember, he's not really doing you any favours. Or your mother. This inheritance business is for his sake, not yours. So that his precious station survives after he's gone.'

Ruth lifted her gaze once more to the hills, and the coldness faded.

'But maybe it shouldn't survive. I don't think this piece of land has ever brought anyone much happiness. Not the Aborigines. They just saw it get taken away. Not the Whites. It only made them hated. Not my mother. It cost her a husband, and me a father. I don't think it's even made Dad happy. Not really. Just look at him.'

She stood up, dusting off her hands.

'In fact, if I were you, I'm not sure I'd be so keen to take what he's offering.'

And, finally, William understood.

His mother had it wrong — Ruth didn't want to turn her father against them, or to throw them out on the street. It was the other way around. She wanted to turn *William* against her father.

Chapter Thirty-five

THEY STRUCK BACK TOWARDS THE HOUSE.

William walked in sullen silence. He felt tricked. All Ruth's talk, all this time she had spent with him — he saw now that it was just to make his uncle sound hateful, and the station too. She was trying to convince him that the inheritance wasn't worth accepting. He even guessed her deeper purpose here. What she really wanted was for her father to be left to die alone, without anyone to follow in his footsteps, or to keep his station alive. Because that was exactly what *she* had done, long ago. It was a terrible thing to want. And she pretended to be so kind!

They crested the hilltop, and there was the House below them again. This was the worst angle from which to see the building, with the swayback roof revealed, ill-patched with tin, and the walls scabrous with ivy that had died and shrivelled and turned brown. But it had been beautiful once, William knew. It didn't matter who had built it or what those people had been like. It was his home now. Ruth had no right to make it sound like something shameful.

They walked down and climbed over the wall. Finally they stood before the fountain, its truncated pedestal sticking up from the empty bowl.

Ruth considered it. 'An explorer you said?'

'He's buried under the House. Mrs Griffith told me.'

'Mrs Griffith? I wouldn't put too much stock in that, then.'

'Uncle John said they found the bones.'

'Maybe. There are probably a lot of bones around here — but mostly they'd be black, not white. And you don't see any memorials to *them*.'

William had had enough. The ache in his ear was back, and all he wanted to do was get away from the heat and the sun. And from his cousin.

'Can I go inside?'

'No.' The friendliness was gone from Ruth. 'I see your face, Will, whenever I mention Aborigines. It closes right up. So you're going to hear this. God knows, no one else in this House will ever tell you.' She settled herself on the lip on the fountain. 'When I was a girl, I used to help my father on our old farm. Sometimes the plough would dig up sharpened stones. But what were they doing in the middle of a black soil plain, where there should be no stones at all? My father said they were axes. The Aborigines had carried them there — from the mountains perhaps. But he didn't seem very interested, so neither was I, at the time. Did you ever see anything like that on your farm?'

William shook his head stubbornly.

'Well, they're quite common. Now a stone axe would have been important to its owner. They didn't grow on trees. They took time to make. And yet they're lying all over the plains, as if they were just thrown away like Coke cans. Why do you think that is?'

'I don't know.'

'Because their owners died, that's why. No one knows for sure how many Aborigines lived here on the Downs. Maybe three thousand, maybe six thousand. No one bothered to count. At least, not until about fifty years after Europeans arrived, when the government did a survey. By then, in the whole region, there were just over one hundred Aborigines left. The government gathered the last of them up in 1911, packed them off to the Cherbourg mission, and that was that.'

Impatience simmered in William. He didn't care about any of this. And anyway, nothing she said could be trusted.

But his cousin wasn't finished. 'The same thing happened on this station — for all that my father would like to forget it. This land belonged to the Kuran people. No one knows how many of them there were either — but after a few decades of settlement, they numbered less than twenty. The survivors used to live right here around the House, and if they were lucky they got blankets and flour. But by 1911, time was up. They were shipped off with all the others. And that's why, to this day, you'll barely see a black face in this part of the world.' She eyed him knowingly. 'And my father is lucky it happened that way, otherwise he might really have a Native Title claim to worry about.'

William stayed silent.

'Come on. I've read your uncle's newsletters, remember. Don't try and tell me you don't know about Native Title. What do you think that whole rally was for?'

He spoke at last, out of resentment. 'It was about stopping a bad law.'

'A bad law?' She appeared to ponder the notion. 'Maybe it is bad. Most likely it's unworkable. Black, white, no one's really happy about it.' Her eyes were on William again. 'But I'm interested — why do *you* think it's a bad law?'

'It's unfair.'

'Unfair? To who?'

William felt the importance of the question. She was

challenging him, and his uncle too, so he strove to be defiant. 'People will lose their farms,' he said.

'Rubbish.'

'They will. Out west.'

Ruth shook her head patiently. 'You're talking about pastoral leases. And this new law actually rules out claims on those sorts of properties. Of course, the Aboriginal land councils won't stand for that, they'll test it in court, so who knows — but at most, it's only about sharing access. And only if the tribes can prove that they've had a continuous connection with the land in question, which is going to be a big problem. But no matter what, absolutely no one is going to get kicked off their farm.'

William knew that he was missing some vital point of the argument, but he was becoming furious with her. 'It's a stupid law. It's just what people in the cities want. They don't care, because nothing will happen to them.'

She shook her head, disappointed. 'That's your uncle talking.'

He dredged his memory. 'The blacks are gone. You just want to rewrite history.'

'And those racist idiots in the League...'

'They're not idiots!'

'Of course they are, and rednecks too.'

'Australia is our place now! You can't make us give it back!'

And he noted with satisfaction that she was finally struck silent. But he felt so dizzy and hot, and Ruth was studying him now with distaste.

'Jesus,' she breathed, 'just listen to what my father's got you saying. You're all caught up in this idea that the station will be yours one day. And then he tells you, look out, the evil Aborigines are coming to steal it away, so you better start hating them.'

But William was ready for that. 'He doesn't hate them.'

'No, of course not. I'm sure he respects their culture. That's the way he likes to put it, isn't it?'

'He doesn't even care about them. He knows they can't claim this property anyway.'

For a moment Ruth seemed on the verge of disputing this. Then she sank back bitterly. 'No, they probably can't. But Christ, it would serve him right if they could.'

Relief ran through William. He felt that he'd won something. And he had made it clear that he was siding with his uncle, not with her. 'This is the wrong sort of land,' he said. 'It's not like the stations out west. It's perpetual.'

Her eyebrows lifted. 'Perpetual?' And to William's alarm she sat forward again. 'You mean a perpetual lease? Is that what your uncle said?'

William blinked. He could barely remember. 'It's safe, that's all...'

'A lease,' she wondered. 'I always thought it was freehold.'

William didn't understand. Had he said something wrong?

But his cousin had forgotten him. She was looking up at the House. 'Well, well. That changes a few things, doesn't it?' And suddenly she was standing. 'Thanks for the tour, Will. But you should get out of this sun. You look a little flushed.'

And with that — as if they had been discussing nothing of importance — she hurried up the steps and disappeared into the darkness of the House.

William slumped against the fountain, his thoughts a wretched quagmire. *Everything* he'd said had been wrong. He only knew that he'd needed to defend himself. But some of the words that came out of his mouth had sounded horrible, and the way she had looked at him...

His ear throbbed and the sun hurt his eyes. He lifted his gaze and stared out over the plains. Everywhere he looked there was haze and smoke, vague shifting shapes that could have been anything. Towns that became farms that became empty grassland set on fire. Nothing was solid, not the land, and even less so its history. He had been told so many stories — but which ones was he to believe? He had seen none of these events with his own eyes, walked none of the world with his own feet.

He retreated to the safety of the House. Just inside the doors he found his mother. She was standing at the bottom of the central staircase, staring up. William could hear raised voices from somewhere above, distant and unintelligible.

'They're fighting up there,' she told him, hushed. 'Ruth and your uncle.'

Her eyes were still red and swollen from the morning's tears, but now her face was lit with hopeful expectation, and William could not stand to be near her. He found his way to his bedroom and cast himself upon the bed. He shut his eyes and saw swirling patterns, felt nausea roiling in his stomach. The foul smell was with him again, and he knew that something was profoundly wrong.

He woke much later in the afternoon. Someone was entering his room.

'William?'

He dug his face deeper into the pillow. It was his cousin again. Her voice sounded hoarse. 'You uncle has asked me to leave.'

He opened his eyes, but did not roll over to face her.

'I've just come to say goodbye.'

But she didn't go. Instead, he felt her sit down on the edge of the bed.

'Is it just me,' she asked, after a time, 'or is something dead in here?'

William said nothing, his eyes wide.

'What *is* that smell?' she repeated.

'You can smell something?' William asked.

'I'm not sure … I thought there was something … or is it just this thing?'

William rolled over. His cousin was holding his captain's hat, and sniffing it curiously.

'Is it? No...'

She sniffed the air again, and then her shoulders sagged. William studied her in amazement. She looked so old. And had she been crying?

She handed the cap to him. 'Why do you wear this anyway?'

'I like it,' said William.

But he examined the hat closely. Had this been the source all along? And indeed, the material was pungent with age ... but it wasn't the rotten smell. That was something much stronger, and it seemed to come from everywhere and nowhere.

'Where on earth did you get it?' his cousin asked, watching him.

'I found it,' William said. 'I thought it was from the army. But Uncle John said it's only an old police hat.'

'It's old all right.'

'He said it was his father's.'

That caught her attention. She peered at the cap again. 'I didn't know my grandfather was ever a policeman.' She touched the brim. 'So that's a police badge?'

'I guess so.'

'QMP,' she read. 'Queensland something Police? Queensland Mounted Police?' She shook her head and pushed back her grey hair. Her eyes were dry now. 'Maybe I'll ask my father about it, next time I see him.'

'You said you were leaving.'

'For now. But he's not rid of me yet. Once I've checked into some things, I'll be back.'

And William couldn't decide any more if that was good or bad. He had been so angry at her that morning ... but she had smelled the rotten thing, when no one else had.

She smiled at him. 'I'm sorry if I upset you before. I know it can't be any fun, caught between two old people like me and my father.'

And her concern only confused William more.

'Are you sure you're okay?' she asked. 'You really don't look very well.'

'I felt dizzy before.'

She slapped her forehead. 'Oh ... of course, I'm sorry, your glandular fever, I forgot all about it. You're sick and I've had you tramping all over the hills.'

There was nothing he could say to that.

'Well, you just rest. I'll be off.' She stood up, looked down at him one last time. 'Listen, Will. Whatever happens, my father won't give you this place for free. He'll make you pay a price. So be careful of what he tells you to do.'

And she was gone.

There it was — another attack, just when William was changing his mind about her. And yet he knew that the old man really was strange sometimes, and frightening. But what was he supposed to do? He could never turn against his uncle. The old man needed him.

He rose finally, and went out to the front porch, standing alone on the steps. The afternoon was fading into a lurid orange haze. His cousin's car was gone, and only the dead world of the drought remained. He imagined Ruth rolling away towards Powell, conditioned air wafting from the dashboard, cool and delicious. And suddenly he wanted to be anywhere but where he was, to be escaping to somewhere green and wet and far away. A place where there were people, and schools, and back yards with grass to play on, and other children ... not these deserted hills all around, and the loneliness of the House at his back.

A movement caught his eye as he turned towards the front door. Mrs Griffith hovered there, peering out from the interior darkness. The housekeeper grinned her toothless, mirthless smile at him, victorious. Then she slipped away.

Chapter Thirty-six

FOR WILLIAM, RUTH'S DEPARTURE MARKED A POINT WHERE
somehow the real world began to slip away, and where his illness
began to consume him. It was the same malaise that had over-
whelmed him at the rally — the dizziness, the ache in his ear, the
sense of creeping dislocation — only this time there was no
remission. Over the next four days it grew steadily worse, until a
furnace seemed to burn in his head, and his surroundings shrank
away, pale and detached. And with every breath he took, the evil
smell that clung to him became more sweet, and more sickening.

Yet no one took any notice of him. The House had more
pressing concerns, for on the night that his daughter left, John
McIvor suffered a second heart attack. An ambulance raced out
from Powell, but as gravely ill as he was, the old man refused to go
to hospital. Dr Moffat was called in to attend him daily, and
William's mother, miraculously revived by the disaster, returned to
her nursing duty upstairs. In all the tumult, William's condition was
dismissed as nothing worse than a late bout of flu. He spent the days

alone, in bed or curled up on the couch, watching television. Sometimes his mother would bring him meals, but she never stayed long enough to see that he threw away most of the food.

Her firm belief was that Ruth had caused the second heart attack. 'This could be the end of him. His own daughter!'

But William, watching from far inside himself, saw that the outrage was only a pretence. Instead, his mother was happy — Ruth was gone and could do no more harm. He didn't have the energy to tell her that, in fact, his cousin had already done all the damage necessary. She had tainted the prize, and ruined every certainty. Even the House didn't seem the same to William. Once, he had been able to see through the thin walls to discover the grand building of long ago. But now, with his sickly thoughts full of Ruth and her stories, he felt that he was being suffocated by decay. He saw on television that the school year was over, that in another world entirely children were heading off with their families for Christmas holidays. But not William. He was trapped here.

They all were. The House still drifted in a zone of murderous calm. At times William would sit hunched in a chair on the front porch, his arms wrapped about himself. There was nothing to see but glare and haze. The smoke had grown thicker every day, an immense pall that was blotting out the world. There was not a breath of wind to disturb it, and yet to William's eyes it moved and revolved — with infinitesimal slowness, but with a sinister purpose all the same. Gathering, and thickening, and bearing down upon the plains, the pressure of it mounting and mounting until William, sitting rigidly, had to fight not to scream. But the nights were the worst, when the darkness closed in, and the light in his bedroom appeared to burn too dimly, as if through a fog. He couldn't sleep, but nor was he quite awake, and the House was unquiet around him, full of subtle creaks and groans, as if sharing the agonies of its master.

On the fifth night William slept finally, from sheer exhaustion, but he dreamt of a voice calling his name, louder and louder, until he awoke with a violent trembling. Bewildered, he realised he was not in his bed. Looming shadows surrounded him in a bizarre, alien space. Then, to his dismay, he recognised the hallway of the upper floor. He must have climbed there, walking in his sleep. Through a doorway, jagged moonlight grinned at him from the tiles of a bathroom, but even worse was the memory of the voice that still rang in his ears, as if someone had bellowed at him in a last extremity of rage and pain. And then, turning reluctantly, he saw that far away, at the end of the gallery, there was a dim glow. It came from the doorway of his uncle's bedroom.

William made a hopeless sound, but his feet were moving, drawn forward. His ear pounded painfully in the silence, and the hallway seemed to lean and veer about him. What was he going to see when he reached the room? Why had he been called? A few feet from the door, the answer came to him. His uncle must be dead. The old man must have died this very minute, and through some link that existed between them, William had been summoned to witness his end. The thought almost stopped him short. Should he run and fetch his mother? Wake the household? But then he was at the door.

The bedroom was a dim cavern. In a small pool of light cast by a lamp, his uncle lay unmoving upon the bed. Was this what death looked like? An old man propped up against a pillow, wrapped in the shroud of a single sheet? William crept towards the bed. His uncle's head hung forward, sightless white slivers under his eyelids. There was no rise and fall of his chest, and William was at the bedside now. He reached out a hand to touch his uncle's cheek, to feel the lifeless flesh, to know for sure.

'Ah,' the old man whispered, 'William.' Strangely calm, neither relieved nor disappointed, William drew back. His uncle's eyes fluttered open, blinked slowly. 'I was dreaming of you.'

And fleetingly, William saw himself in his uncle's dream,

climbing unaware through the darkness of the House, to this bed-side. One dreamer calling to another.

The invalid did not speak again for some time. Then his throat worked, and gave a rattling laugh. 'Come up to watch me die, have you?'

William shook his head.

'It's all right. I don't mind. We'll watch together, and see if it comes.'

They waited in silence. The room, for all its gaunt size, felt as confined as a closet. The windows were closed and the curtains were drawn. The clock at the bedside told that it was four in the morning. It ticked the seconds away, pulsing in time to the pain in William's ear.

The old man licked his lips. 'I can smell burning. All the time.'

William swallowed. 'There's a fire in the mountains.'

A faint frown. 'You know that's not what I mean. We've both seen him.'

William said not a word.

'And now you've met my daughter.'

'Yes.'

'Well? What did you think of her?'

But he couldn't speak about his cousin. 'I don't know.'

'You don't?' A tremor of anger ran through his uncle's voice. 'She had plenty to say about you.'

William closed his eyes, forced the words out. 'She told me things.'

'About me?'

'About you. About the station, too. I don't know if they were true.'

'She tells lies, Will. And they're clever lies. I warned you.'

William opened his eyes again. The old man was gazing dreamily at the ceiling, his head sunk deep in the pillow. It wasn't enough, William thought. It wasn't enough just to say that she lied. The doubts were embedded in his mind now. They were one and the same as his illness, and could only be driven out by something certain and clear.

William spoke. 'She said the League was stupid.'

A flicker of pain crossed his uncle's face.

'She said you were wrong about the new laws.'

But the old man shook his head, slowly, fighting against the stiffness in him. 'None of that matters any more. Not to you and me, Will. It's out of our hands.' He seemed to be looking far beyond the walls of his room. 'I listen to parliament on the radio. They're sitting late, night after night, trying to get the legislation through before the end of the year.'

An image came to William, as if transmitted from his uncle's mind, of the parliamentary building in Canberra, and of hundreds of men in suits, gathered deep underground within the hill, as the night and the moon rode silent above them.

'It's bad a thing, isn't it,' William asked, not knowing what he hoped for.

'It's bad,' his uncle agreed, 'but it hasn't passed yet. The vote will be close.'

'Ruth said...'

'I don't want to hear her name.' The old man breathed fitfully for a moment. Then his head tilted towards William, oddly gentle. 'You talked to her, didn't you? You told her about this property being perpetual lease-hold. She got that idea from you, didn't she?'

'I'm sorry...'

'You gave her a weapon, Will. She's a lawyer, remember. That perpetual lease has got her thinking. She's gone to stir up trouble.' And to William's bafflement the old man sounded almost fond. 'She wants to frighten me with Native Title. But you don't have to worry.'

'The lease is okay?'

'Forget about the lease. There can never be a claim on Kuran Station regardless. There's nobody who can lodge one.'

A vision of the plains joined the tumble in William's thoughts, of grassland afire from horizon to horizon. 'Nobody?'

'Only traditional owners can lodge a claim, Will. And none of them are left, not from this part of the world. They're all dead, or they were taken away long ago.' The old man might have been recalling a pleasant story. Then his teeth were bared. 'There's only me left. I've been here all along. So *I* claim Native Title. I claim it for both of us.'

A chill ran through William. This wasn't the solution. Something crucial was being warped here, bent into a shape it wasn't meant to be. It was too heavy, and out of balance. And it would be crushing when it fell.

His uncle was turning his head from side to side, drawing in ragged breaths. 'Are you sure you don't smell burning?'

'No.'

'You don't smell anything?'

William whispered his deepest truth. 'I smell something dead.'

The old man's gaze locked onto him, intent suddenly. 'Yes.' His body shuddered, and a hand crept across the sheets to clutch William's arm. 'Yes, I smell it too.'

'You do?'

'Something rotten. Something rotten and burned.'

'What is it?' William pleaded.

Madness ignited in the old man's eyes. 'A sign, boy, it's a sign. It's my death you can smell.'

'No…' William moaned, trying to tug his hand away.

His uncle wouldn't let go. 'We're blood, remember, you and I. I can feel it in you. You're an open door. The world talks to you. You see things.'

'No, I don't.'

'You mustn't say that. It's a good thing. It's why I chose you.'

'Chose me?'

'When I die, Will, all this will be yours.'

'You're not dying.'

'It's the only way. You can't own this House until I'm dead.'

'I don't even want it!'

'What?' The old man withdrew his hand, aghast. 'What are you talking about?'

'I don't know!' William cried miserably. And then, more softly. 'I thought I did … But everyone keeps telling me different things.'

His uncle sank back, staring. 'Ah … I see.'

William turned his face to the floor, abject. He rubbed the skin of his arm. It radiated heat from where the old man had touched it.

'Was it that easy for her, Will? Has she set you against me?'

But William didn't know what had happened to him any more, or who had done it. All he longed for was to feel normal again.

'Listen.' The command was urgent, and William looked up to see his uncle heaving his body forward, straining to sit higher against the pillow. 'Listen. I was born here. And then I was sent away. Forty years it took, to find my way home.'

'I know …'

'Yes, but before that there was one time I came back. I never told you.' The old man's gaze was alive now with the memory. 'I went to the water hole … and it spoke to me, Will. The hills, the mountains, the station — they *spoke* to me. And in that moment, everything about my life changed. There was never any doubt about what I had to do.'

William stared, caught by a force that seemed to reach out like enfolding wings.

'This country will speak to you too, if you listen. The blacks say it flows into you through your feet, and they're right. But it's not an Aboriginal thing. It's not a white thing either. It's a human thing. Not everyone has it. But I do. And you have it too.'

His uncle had hold of his arm again, and heat was streaming through the old man's hand. 'I don't have anything,' William said, afraid.

'You say you don't want the station any more?'

'I don't know...'

'Well, it wants *you*.' And the eagerness in his uncle was insatiable. 'You can't lie to me, Will. You feel this country calling. I know you do.'

'I feel sick, that's all.' It was a despairing plea.

'You're fighting it, that's why. But it's out there, William. Out there in the hills. That's where it happened to me. At the water hole. That's where you have to go too.'

And suddenly a vision exploded in William's mind. Water. Cold and dark and deep. Surrounded by cool shade and dripping rock. And for an instant he saw himself plunged into the depths of that water, a freezing relief from the heat, from the confusion, from the fever in his head.

His uncle's eyes were wide. 'You see it, don't you, right now.'

William nodded in amazement. It was the answer. The disease in him could be extinguished and washed clean. Why hadn't he thought of it before?

'Alone,' the old man insisted, his hand clutched still tighter. 'You have to go there alone. You can walk it in a few hours. Take food. Take water. Leave right now.'

William's wonder faltered. 'Now?'

'It's almost dawn. You know the way — I showed you. You know the places, the powerful places. Forget me, forget my daughter, go and learn for yourself.'

William struggled with the insanity of it. The water hole was ten miles away at least. 'I can't go on my own.' And yet, he could feel the conviction in his uncle's touch, the utter certainty of it, seeping through his body. 'Mum wouldn't let me...'

'I'll look after her. I'll tell her you went exploring. I'll tell her to pick you up at the water hole tonight.'

Could he really do it? He would be alone out there for a whole day. But if he dared … he would be immersed at last in water so deep and dark it would be like oblivion. He wouldn't have to worry about anything ever again. And the old man's breath was hot on his face.

'You have to do this now. Before my daughter gets back. So we can face her together, show her that she's lost, once and for all. Say you'll do it. Say yes to me. Then all these last months will have been worth it.'

It was as if his uncle's mind had become one with his own, a whirl of fear and hatred and flame, and William saw that the old man was right about everything. The decision passed between them in the beat of a heart, and the old man's face lit with triumph. He flung William's arm away.

'Now! Before your mother wakes up!'

And William went. He backed away from his uncle's bed, withdrawing from the pool of light, leaving his uncle illuminated there alone, crazed eyes burning, waving a bony arm.

'Go on. Stick to the track. Go!'

Then William was in the darkness of the hallway. The shadows didn't matter — the old man's certainty blazed within him, and he knew exactly where he was going. He slipped back to his bedroom, dressed silently, and gathered up his old school backpack and his captain's hat. Then he stole into the kitchen. Prying open cupboards and the refrigerator, he collected random items of food — biscuits and bread and cheese. He filled a plastic bottle with water, jammed it into the backpack.

The front doors waited open for him. A pale light was growing in the sky, the world warm and quiet, hushed before dawn. The certainty still burned in his mind. He crossed the garden, climbed the wall, and set off eastwards into the hills.

Chapter Thirty-seven

Sunrise found William in a strange land.

He had already passed by the church and the graveyard — the broken tombs of the White dynasty watching on silently — and was further away from the House than he had ever been on his own. The haze and smoke gathered low to the ground like a mist, and there was a darkness above that might even be clouds, promising rain. Birds called in mournful hope, and William strode forward eagerly. The water hole was still a sparkling vision in his mind, his body felt as light as paper, and it seemed that he could walk there in no more than an hour.

But gradually the light strengthened. The sky revealed itself, pale and empty as ever, and when the sun finally lifted above the mountains, William felt heat prickle upon his face. He had been carried this far by the force of his uncle's hand, gripped about his arm, and by the conviction that had possessed them both. But now, as he stumped towards the sun, he felt something shrinking inside, something that the old man's touch had left swollen and inflamed. He realised that, in fact, he had covered hardly any distance at all. Taking a drink of water, he considered the bottle. It would have to last him until he reached the campground, where the windmill and the water tank waited. As far as he could recall, that was about halfway to the rock pool.

He strode on, labouring a little on the upwards slopes. Walking the track was nothing like rolling along it in a car. In a car, the miles slid by with the pleasant crunch of gravel under the wheels, and the track itself seemed to curl tightly about the hills like a wandering stream. On foot, it was a longer road of slow, sweeping curves, in which he could see every rut, every jagged stone, and feel them too, biting at his feet. There was little shade, and ahead of him the sun blazed in a hard white sky, all vestiges of the misty morning long gone. The hills were naked brown, and the only sound was the occasional croak of a bird. The station felt abandoned to drought. He was completely alone out there, every step taking him further away from home.

The water hole, he reminded himself. All that mattered was that he get there, then dive into its depths and ... and do what? It had all seemed so clear in the old man's room, but William found he was struggling to remember. Illness was seeping back into his head, muddling his thoughts. Some understanding was supposed to come to him out here, some voice was supposed to speak — his uncle had made all sorts of promises. But they seemed faintly ludicrous beneath the glare and heat of the day, with the hills dozing in stupor and flies droning in the grass.

The sun climbed steadily towards midday, and William could feel the beginnings of sunburn on his arms. The track had become hot, scalding his feet through his shoes. Flies began to cluster on his back and whine about his face. He flapped his hands at them futilely. At one point he caught a glimpse of something dark as it slipped into the grass, and he knew, with a flicker of fear, that it must have been a snake. Still later he saw a crow, pecking and digging at something on the track. It flew away as William approached, and when he arrived at the spot all he saw were stiff remnants of blood-stained fur. He could smell that the animal had been dead for days ... or was it only the smell he already carried with him? He stared at the remains for some minutes, uneasily fascinated.

By midday he was trudging along with his head down. There was still no sign of the campground, although surely he had walked far enough. Could he be lost? He was following the track, but the hills all looked the same, and with the sun overhead in a featureless sky, even north and south were gone. He stopped in a tree-lined gully that offered shade, and sat on a log to rest. He ate some biscuits, even though he still had no appetite, and saw that he'd already drunk most of his water. He watched ants swarming in the red dust, devouring the crumbs he had dropped. He looked up at the trees hanging above him, their branches drooping low, the leaves shrivelled and cracked. He gazed back along the track, wondering if perhaps his mother might come for him early. But there was no sign of her or the car, only the hum of flies, and his ear throbbed relentlessly.

He waited there for perhaps an hour, or even longer — but time had begun to telescope. Abruptly, he shook off the lethargy, drank the last of his water, and set off again. His pace was steady for a while, but the heat was stupefying, burning through the dark material of his captain's hat and setting his head afire. The glare narrowed his eyes into slits. Fatigue set in, and thirst, and still the hills refused to form themselves into a pattern he recognised. Eventually he dropped back to a slow march, his eyes fixed upon the ground. There was nothing to see anyway, only his own shadow lengthening before him as the sun began to descend westwards. When he glanced up blearily and saw the windmill, off to the left of the track, for a moment he could only stare at it in surprise. Then he was stumbling towards the water tank. He turned the tap at its base, and drank.

The water was tepid and sour, but that didn't matter. He stuck his head under the tap and flooded water all down his back. The fever in his head receded. He sucked in deep breaths and looked about the campground. It was nothing like he remembered from the rally, just a dusty hillside of brown grass, scuffed here and there where cars had parked, or a tent had stood. He lifted his eyes and saw, on the hilltop, amidst the trees, the shapes of standing stones. They seemed smaller than he recalled. But he remembered what they had looked like under the stars that night, in the darkness and firelight. He left his backpack by the tank, and climbed up through the grass.

There were signs that people had gathered here — the remnants of campfires, a lone shoe that had belonged to a child, a pile of empty beer cans, their bright colours already fading. Then he came to the stone circle. At the edge of the ring he saw a blackened pile of ash that had been the bonfire. Beyond that, in the middle of the circle, were two angled lines of charred wood and burned grass. The shape they formed was marked in his mind, billowing smoke and flame as white robes danced madly. And yet the memory didn't seem so terrible now. He gazed around at the stones in puzzlement. Had something changed, or was it that on a hot, airless afternoon, the whole mystery of the circle was hidden? Perhaps it needed the old man's presence, and the hypnosis of his voice, to bring the place alive. But the ring no longer felt powerful, just drab and empty, and the patches of ash gave it a leftover appearance, like a rubbish tip.

He descended the hill, studying the sun in the western sky. Perhaps he should stay here by the water tank and wait for his mother. But as he reached the bottom he remembered that there, on the other side of the track, where the land fell away into a gully, was where he had seen the burning man. And that memory, unlike the others, had not faded. He couldn't stay here — he had to move on or go home. Weariness assailed him at either prospect, but he thought about water, dark and deep and glimmering, and he remembered the stone seat beneath the willow tree. Maybe it wasn't so far. It would be a fine thing if he could be sitting there when his mother arrived. He would have swum in the pool by then, he would have purged his body of heat and dust and disease. And there was his uncle too, who wouldn't be pleased if William gave up just because he was hot and tired.

He refilled the bottle and gathered up his backpack. The road beckoned, and he set his feet to it, marching eastwards, the sun burning on his neck. But his progress remained slow. The track climbed more steeply than before, across hills that reared ominously high, and the sick feeling, relieved momentarily by the water, came stealing back. Time fled by. All around him the trees were casting longer and longer shadows as the afternoon deepened towards evening, but the heat did not abate. He had been walking almost an entire day. Surely he should have covered ten miles by now. But then it occurred to him that while the station was indeed ten miles in length, the track would be longer because it wound about the hills. How much longer? Twelve miles maybe? Fifteen? And even as he added the numbers in his head, he realised he had come to a halt, swaying back and forth on his unsteady legs.

He pushed on, but the bottle was already half empty again, and the surrounding hills had become unrecognisable once more. He didn't think he was anywhere near the water hole. Finally, his legs gave up on him. Looking back, he saw that the sun was slipping behind a western ridge. Out on the plains there was maybe another hour yet to sunset, but in the hills, evening lowered across the slopes. Enough was enough. William limped to the side of the road, looking for somewhere to sit and watch for his mother. He had come to a small field between two hills, and there was a lone tree not far from the track, its branches spread wide over the grass. Beneath it a few ancient posts leant, all that was left of a long forgotten fence or shack. He unloaded his backpack, sat down against the tree, facing the road, and waited.

The last crows of the day were calling their farewells. The buzzing flies were finally gone, but other insects whirred in the grass, and the reedy shrill of cicadas sprang up as the shadows deepened. The sky turned from pale blue to dusty red, and somewhere, hidden behind the ridge, the sun sank below the horizon. William strove against a growing unease. It was not night, not really. His mother would be leaving the house right at that moment, or maybe she was even closer. But the light continued to fade, and gradually the world was slipping away, the haze deepening into gloom, the hills melting into vague shapes that loomed on either side. A few lone stars glowed above, and in the west the last hints of red sky were turning yellow, and then the faintest of greens. Still, it was not night, he told himself, not proper night. But finally William saw the moon lifting above the eastern slopes, and he could deny it no longer. It *was* night, and his mother had not come.

Panic fluttered at the back of his mind. What was she doing? His eyes darted back and forth, probing the darkness. The moon was only just past full, but it was sickly yellow, and seemed to cast no light. All he could see were the tangled shadows of the tree above him, and the line of the hills against a slightly paler sky. He realised that he had not brought a torch or matches. What was he to do? Should he begin walking home? But his legs still ached and twitched, and the mere thought of all those miles was anguish. Besides, he would have to pass by the campground, and the gully waiting below. He was better off where he was. His mother had to come eventually. But still the minutes raced by, and with every one of them he felt more afraid and wretched.

He huddled against the tree, chill despite the warmth of the air. The moon rode well clear of the hills now, and the evening shrill of cicadas was fading away. His mother wasn't coming.

Something had gone wrong. Had his uncle forgotten to tell her? And then a truly horrible thought struck him. What if his uncle had died? Before telling anyone? No one would know where William had gone. He stared at the darkness, despairing. Shapes seemed to form in the night, and approach, and then dissolve away into shadows. Everything was merging into blackness ... and suddenly William snapped his head up from his chest, blinking in astonishment. He had almost fallen asleep. That mustn't happen. He had to stay awake. He propped himself up against the tree and rubbed his eyes.

He was face down in the dirt when he woke again.

Something was tickling his cheek. William lay unmoving, his eyes closed. He could feel the ground beneath him, and the itch of grass on his legs, and then the feather-light touch came again, legs creeping across his face. A spider, he thought, and yet stayed still, as if this was a dream, and any movement would break the spell. The touches crept across his neck and then disappeared. William opened one eye, the other pressed against the ground. It was deep night.

He heard a low, snuffling grunt. His single eye went wide, and the grunt came again, nearer now. A shadow moved. It had arms and legs. It was a man.

He was hunched low, dragging something with great difficulty across the ground, a large and ungainly object. With the same dreamlike calm, William realised that it was the body of a second man. The shapes paused not ten yards from where he lay. Then the figure on the ground stirred slowly and groaned. The first man gave a snort of displeasure and stood upright for a moment. William caught a glimpse of a ragged broad-brimmed hat and a lean, bearded face. The man held something in his hand, something with a long handle. Steel glinted, then the man lifted the axe and swung it down. The body on the ground went still. But the axeman laughed, and brought the weapon down again. And again. He circled the corpse in a shuffling dance as William watched with his one staring eye.

The axe paused in mid-stroke.

The man stood motionless, his head tilted alertly. He sniffed the air, this way and that. Then he looked directly towards where William lay unmoving beneath the tree.

William shut his eye. It was only a dream. There was nothing there. He would wake up again and it would be dawn and his mother would arrive with the car.

Footsteps crunched in the dead grass.

What have we here?

It was a voice and no voice, hoarse and breathless.

I know you're awake, boy. Something shifted closer, greedy and pawing at the ground. *It's into the tucker bag with you.*

It was upon him now, hovering eagerly above. And still William felt no fear, but his skin went cold as a hand seemed to skim along his body, not touching him, but only inches away. The hand came to his head, and then there was an angry hiss of surprise.

Oh-ho. Up jumped the troopers. The presence drew back, and the voice went sullen. *I was hungry, that was all. They sent us here and forgot us.*

There were more scuffling sounds. It seemed to William that the figure had turned away. But then it was close again, bent low over him. William heard harsh panting, right in his ear, felt hot air against his face, and there came the smell of sweat and hair and rotting meat.

You're a long way from home, boy, it whispered, all fury and hate. *But not far enough. This isn't the place.*

It strode away. Something heavy thumped and shifted in the grass, then there was silence. William found that he could move. He sat up at last. Almost unconsciously, his hand went to his head and found his captain's hat still perched there. He stared in every direction, wondering.

But the night was empty.

Chapter Thirty-eight

SUNLIGHT WAS BURNING THROUGH WILLIAM'S EYELIDS.

He opened them and saw that it was full day. The sun was already high and hot. He lifted himself painfully, looked around at the tree and the leaning posts and the little field. There was no sign that anything had been there, no footprints in the dust, no marks of a body having been dragged through the grass. Of course not. It had never happened.

He fished in his backpack for the water bottle. It held two or three warm mouthfuls. He drank them down, felt his thirst awaken, and knew that there was no more.

He turned his gaze to the empty road. A full day and night, he thought resentfully. Why wasn't his mother looking for him? It didn't matter if something was wrong at the House — even the death of his uncle — she should have come searching by now. But then his anger died. He had to get more water, and that meant either returning to the campground, or pushing on to the water hole. He looked eastwards, and to his surprise realised that he could see the balding peaks of the Hoop Mountains. They were tinged blue with drifting smoke, but perhaps the fires up there had burned themselves out, for the haze had definitely cleared a little. The lower slopes were no more than a few miles away. He took heart. If the mountains were close, then so was the rock pool.

William set off, limping doggedly as he climbed out of the valley. His mind was curiously languid, random thoughts rolling about it. He remembered a story his uncle had told him, about two shepherds who had worked in these hills, long ago. Hadn't one murdered the other with an axe? Yes ... the dream was just one of his uncle's stories, all twisted because of the fever in his head. As soon as his mother came for him, he would demand that he be taken to a doctor. And not Dr Moffat either, a proper doctor in Powell, in a proper surgery that was clean and shining. He thought of the main street of the town, busy with cars and people. He remembered green parks, and the swimming pool, long and wide, glittering with blue water. It smelled of chlorine, and there was a canteen there too, that sold cold drinks from a refrigerator with condensation dripping down the glass doors...

William stumbled, and was back on the dusty road. Why was he thinking about Powell? His uncle had taken him away from things like parks and cold drinks. The hills were his only world now, and his duty was to walk them from end to end. No, not his duty, his punishment. For daring to think that he could ever own something as huge and harsh as the station. His uncle was teaching him a lesson. The old man would never tell William's mother where he had gone. Even if he found the water hole, he would have to turn around and walk all the way back. And by then his mother would have disappeared, and his uncle too, and there would only be Mrs Griffith in the House, and she would not let him in, she would say that there had never been any little boy living there...

William stopped short, shook his head wildly. He saw that he had actually wandered ten yards or so off the road. He had to be careful, he had to concentrate. Ahead of him, the track rose towards a high stony ridge. He studied the slope wearily. It looked cruelly steep, but then at the crest he saw a single tree, bent into a familiar shape. William searched his memory. Was this the hill he had come to with his uncle, on that first tour of the station, where they had stopped and looked at the view? If it was, then from the top he would see the mountains directly before him, and below would be the creek, the border between the station and the national park. There would be no water in the creek, of course, but from there it was no more than a few miles south to the water hole.

Energy came from somewhere, and William bent his back to the climb. But when he broached the rise there was no valley waiting on the other side, no creek, there was only a wide saddle between this hill and the next, and beyond that, more hills. The mountains looked no closer. His legs buckled and he sat down, rocking back and forth in frustration. He would sit here until his mother came, no matter how long she took. And it would be her fault if the heat and thirst killed him. But eventually his rocking slowed, and reason took hold. He couldn't stay here. The track did not extend forever, even if it seemed that it did. He rubbed his eyes, felt how raw they were. He looked eastwards again, saw the sinister way shimmers of heat rose in the distance. But it was no use sulking. He had made the decision to grow up months ago. Tottering, he climbed back to his feet.

At some later stage it was noon. The planet, rolling with its vast slowness in space, had exposed its brown hide directly to the full fury of the sun, and William felt that he was a tiny figure crawling naked across its surface. He could see himself from far above. And he had been wrong about the track — it really was endless. This wasn't even his uncle's property any more. He must have strayed into some other place, a maze of blank hills and dead grass and scrub. He walked, but nothing got closer, and nothing fell further behind. He was pinned to the spot in a hot void. The mountains had vanished again, and on far-off ridges trees danced mockingly in heat waves of distortion. Time and time again his legs stopped, and he would gaze back along the road, waiting for the car that *had* to be coming for him. But there was never any car, and he would turn and stumble on into a world of shimmering mirages.

And out of those mirages, his second vision came.

It appeared on a ridge ahead — a misshapen thing, a tangle of arms and legs, like some giant, gangling insect. William gazed with mute disbelief as it descended towards him. It was the evil spirit-shape of the drought itself, he decided. Its limbs were knobbed sticks, its elongated head leered and glared, and its touch would surely be poison. But as the figure approached, he saw it sway and stumble, and he realised that it was really two beings, not one. There was a man, and he was leading a horse — a lean, ragged beast, laden with gear. The man was limping, head down, but he tugged obstinately at the horse, and metal clanked with each step.

Don't speak to him, William thought. The vision would continue on its way, pass him by and disappear again into the heat waves. He shut his eyes, as he had the night before. But the clank of metal came close, and then stopped.

Ahoy there, rasped something awful.

William moaned, opened his eyes. The man loomed tall before him, a figure of bone and rags. His face was ravaged by starvation, a leathery skull with terribly protruding eyes.

Found you at last, the figure whispered. He was peering eagerly at the cap on William's head. Then his blackened lips curled open to show white teeth from which the gums had peeled, and he lifted a gaunt hand to his brow, in salute. *My inland sea.*

'Go away,' William croaked.

The man shook his head, his stare unblinking. The horse waited behind him, a skeletal thing, its head bent, abject, to the ground.

'You're not here,' William insisted, convinced that he was standing alone under the noon sun, and talking to empty air. 'You're not real.'

A hollow laugh came. Then, still grinning, the man began to grope through his clothes. He was bedecked with thin straps that seemed to hold a multitude of items — water bottles, satchels, watches, tin cups, notebooks, an impossible array. But everything was frayed and rusted, as if from a century of wind and rain. The objects clinked and clanked together, and a dark, unpleasant memory stirred in William. He thought of walls painted red. And then he saw, with despair, that while the man's right foot was encased in a worn boot, his left was bare, the toenails blackened, the heel bloodied and bruised.

'You're dead,' William said.

The man paid him no heed. He pulled out a battered compass and peered across its face to take a bearing from a horizon that pulsated with heat. Then he lifted a bony arm and pointed, away to the southwest, his head inclined in silent invitation.

'No,' William said, 'that's the wrong way. I have to get to the water hole.'

The man rolled a swollen tongue over his lips, as if the mention of water had awoken a forgotten desire. His horse shuddered. It was stooped under the weight of its saddle, which was piled high with tripods and wooden frames and rifles and rolls of canvas. The beast's ribs stuck out from its sides, and gaping sores yawned on its legs, thick with dust and flies.

William knew that he must not follow, not at any cost.

'I can't leave the track. I have to wait for my mother.'

The spectre's lips curled again. *Your mother's not coming.*

'She has to.'

She won't ever come.

William turned away, looking for the road. But some blindness was upon him. He could see nothing, only waves of mirage. Where had the track gone? He smelled dust and leather and oil, felt his resistance crumbling away, and the voice was in his ear.

It's not far now. The sound was hissing sand. *It's been waiting for you.*

William choked on dry tears. 'What has?'

The rains have failed, boy. The rivers have run dry.

'I don't understand.'

You will.

William surrendered. He was too weak, he had fought madness as hard as he could, it was so much easier now to let go. He stumbled forward, he didn't know to where, the road and all suggestion of direction were gone. But the explorer was at his side, dragging the horse along by its rope. Metal clanged discordantly, the sound of water tins long since empty.

'You died,' William said, desolate. 'They killed you with spears.'

There was no response, and William said no more. His legs moved automatically, and his sanity retreated to some inner place. For what seemed like hours, they crept forward through a land demented by heat. Hills streamed into the sky. Oceans of water beckoned and then melted into nothing. Trees broke apart and floated away. William would close his eyes at times, and know that there was no explorer and no horse, that he was crazed with thirst and sickness, a little boy wandering in circles in the hills. But then he would open his eyes again, and the ragged figure would be there beside him.

What were they searching for anyway? There had been something important, it seemed to William, that he had been sent out here by his uncle to find. But it was at the water hole, he would never get there now, and he could not remember what it was anyway. His mind crept back from its refuge, and he stared through grainy eyes. Somehow the explorer had got far ahead of him, and was looking back. Bizarrely, the sky was aglow behind him, and his face was in shadow.

'Wait...' William complained. It wasn't fair. He had surrendered, hadn't he? He had let the apparition take him where it would. So how could it leave him behind?

Walk south, boy.

'You tricked me,' William declared hotly. 'You said you'd show me the way.'

You'll find it there.

A slow, orange blaze filled the entire horizon. An immense burning. The explorer had hold of the rope, and was leading his horse into the flames. Fear woke William from his long stupor at last.

'Wait!' he cried again.

Then he realised he was staring directly at the sun. It hung low upon the horizon, swollen and crimson in the haze. He blinked at it, appalled. He had walked the entire afternoon in his delirium. Walked in the wrong direction completely. And he had left the road. The track was nowhere to be seen, there were only hills and scrub, already dark with long shadows, and there was no landmark that he recognised, nothing that could tell him where he was. The water hole could be miles away, in any direction at all. And even if his mother was searching, she would never find him now.

Bits of metal clinked somewhere, then fell silent.

And William's second evening alone drew on.

Chapter Thirty-nine

THERE HAD BEEN A MOON, WILLIAM REMEMBERED.

He was stumbling through dead grass, gazing upwards, his head lolling back and forth as he studied the night sky. On the previous evening, he was certain, there had been a moon. So where was it now? The hills were pitch black without it, and he tripped constantly over invisible tree stumps or holes. Sometimes he fell, and it was hard climbing to his feet again. He was walking south, just as instructed. At least, he hoped he was. He'd started out with the setting sun on his right, but in the darkness he had probably veered off in some other direction entirely.

He was so thirsty. He thought feverishly of the water hole, the goal he had failed to reach, relishing memories of a stream trickling over stone. He was hungry too. There were biscuits and bread in his backpack, but the backpack was gone. At some stage during his march with the explorer he must have shrugged it from his shoulders and simply thrown it away. So he reeled on and at last the blunted moon rose in the sky. He paused then, gazing up, sensing the great weight of it from infinitely far below, his blood responding like a tide. And beneath the moon floated the pale line of the mountains, seemingly detached from the earth, and yet achingly close. They were on his left, so he had kept his bearings after all. He lurched forward again.

But the ground still tricked his feet. Inky blots of darkness warned of trees, or a shadow would loom sharply and he would flinch away, only to look again and find nothing there. His pace slowed to fitful bursts of a few steps, after which he would stop and gaze at the moon. It was almost over, he decided. Sooner or later he would have to lie down and sleep. Two days of walking and pain and thirst — and what had he discovered? Nothing. There was no great secret out here, waiting to be told. The station had an empty heart. What would his uncle think of that?

William blinked, suddenly fully awake.

A sound had penetrated his daze. He stared about at the night, listening. And then he heard it again, a noise that diminished, and then returned. It was the distant growl of an engine — a car, somewhere in the hills. His mother! It had to be. She was on the road, searching for him. William's exhaustion vanished. He had to attract her attention, he had to get to the road somehow. But which way? He kept turning as the sound rose and fell. It echoed in the hills, deceptive, impossible to pinpoint. He strained his eyes to see the headlights, or even the faintest reflected glow of them in the sky. But there was nothing, and the sound seemed to be fading.

'Mum!' he called, the effort tearing at his parched throat.'Mum!'

The car was moving further away, the echo of its engine dwindling.

He ran, a dozen yards, twenty, calling all the while. The shadow world leapt and jagged about him, but there was no light, no road, and his cries were swallowed by the night. He stopped finally, gasping, and when the heaving of his lungs was still again, the sound was gone.

'Mum,' he whispered.

For a moment William thought he might drop to the ground in despair. Instead, he remained upright, and went very still. Some inner sense was coming alive in him — a warning of imminent danger. He listened. Without the car, there were just the normal night noises to hear — the flitting of insects, the shrill of cicadas. And yet he stared about, his alertness growing for no reason he could name. It was as if in his haste he had blundered too close to the edge of a cliff, and was now only a step from plummeting over the precipice. But in fact he stood at the foot of a low hill, and the moonlight showed him only grass and bushes and a few very weary trees. It was a patch of scrub as unremarkable as any other on the station. And yet there was a weight upon him, a deep vibration in the air of this spot that rang with foreboding.

The heaviness increased, until William found it was hard to breathe. What was it? What was here? Every second it only became more unendurable. He began backing away, he didn't know from what. Every pale tree trunk, every half-guessed clump of grass, even the chorus of cicadas — they were nothing, and yet they were something unspeakable. He was trembling now, his teeth clenched. Another step backward, and another. How far did he need to go? More steps, slow. And still there was no visible sign, no marker to show the boundary he had crossed, only the sense that he was withdrawing from somewhere he was not supposed to be. He turned, ready to flee.

The shape was waiting for him there, dark against the sky.

It seemed to William that he had an hour of thought in which to consider what it was, and his first certainty was that it was not remotely human. The thing half stood and half crouched, its hulking body towering above him. Moonlight gleamed on a shaggy, slimy hide, and William smelled mud and rotting leaves. An enormous head was tilted to the night sky. It might have been the head of a horse, or of a lizard, or of some giant predatory bird, depending on the way the shadows took it. When the creature shifted on its slow haunches, it became a multitude of shapes, and no shape at all. Tendrils of lank hair dripped from it like a mane, and from its skull two huge eyes bulged, white and terrible.

William shrank away. He knew this thing. His uncle had told him about it on the night of shooting stars. It was a beast that lived in caves or bottomless pools, it stalked hills and mountain ranges, and left broken trails through the forests.

The wild eyes regarded him.

This is the place, child.

The creature did not speak, it was a sound only in the mind, the crack of old stone, the groan of timber in the wind. William stared, unable to move. Was he really awake? He felt that he was, but it was impossible, this had to be another dream, another ghost, like the man with the axe, or the lost explorer. But the shape knew his thoughts, and exuded scorn.

White men dreamt those spirits. The black men dreamt me, long ago.

It was true, William thought, through his fear. He had heard other stories about this thing, even before he met his uncle. The Aborigines had warned the early settlers of its presence — an animal that was never seen, that could be known only by its tracks, and by its cry, heard in lonely places at night. The settlers in turn had passed the story down to their children, and so on for years. But no one believed it was real. And the Aborigines were gone.

The creature's great eyes held the memory of all this, and of far more.

Old things still wait. In the special places.

The cicadas shrilled madly, and William was shivering. The monster emanated a deep cold. But other things came from it as well. Images of age, of time flowing like water, and the stars wheeling rapidly above. It stood guard here, William realised, and had done so for thousands of years. But why? What was special about this place? William had *felt* something — but there was nothing to be seen. No ring of standing stones, like his uncle had shown him, no ancient meeting place.

Contempt flowed chill from the creature.

Dead stones on a hill, and little fires. The old man is blind.

Understanding shook William. The hilltop at the campground was not a meeting place, and the stones there had no meaning. *This* was the only place, and his uncle had never found it. But somehow, through all his wanderings, William had.

The monster nodded its huge head.

You bear the mark, boy.

More images pervaded William's mind, a confusing rush of violence that he could not grasp, but his hand lifted, and his fingers touched the badge of his captain's hat. Dread flooded into him, for he understood now that he had been called here for a purpose. He could feel an old rage within the creature, a long patience that was nearly at an end.

The eyes glared affirmation.

The rivers have run dry. Caves have opened to the sun.

The shape shifted its bulk closer, and the stench of mud was overpowering, a reek of hatred and pain, staggering in its force.

The dead are ready for you now.

Then it reared above him, a mountain building itself against the sky, its wild mane shaking, its great talons clawing the air. William fell back in terror, but too late.

The bunyip called.

It was a piercing, grating, tearing cry — the sound of death and cold and age, and of long, intolerable loneliness. The earth froze and the stars dimmed. William ran — through the night and the tumbled shadows, echoes chasing after him like the rumble of thunder as birds awoke from their sleep, chattering in alarm. The whole bush was suddenly alive. Onwards he fled, unseeing, until his lungs stabbed in agony and his legs burned. Then he tripped and rolled down an earthen bank. His head slammed against stone. Fire exploded in his skull, and everything went black.

The sky was grey when he woke, and the moon was gone. He shifted his limbs and sat up. Dawn was near. He saw stony banks rising on either side of him, and a channel winding away. Rubbing his head gingerly, William remembered. He'd fallen into the dry bed of a creek.

The creek! He climbed dazedly to his feet. It could lead him to the water hole. Lifting his gaze, he saw the dark line of the mountains against the faded sky. The bed of the creek climbed towards them in a series of shallow ledges. So upstream was eastwards. But that made no sense ... And then, through the thumping pain in his skull, he understood. Somehow he had come all the way across to the southern boundary of the station, where the creek ran east to west, along the side of the spur. Which meant that if he walked upstream towards the mountains, he would find the pool.

Thirst awoke in him, raging and insatiable. He lurched forward, giggling wretchedly as he clambered upwards across boulders and the scraggling roots of trees. His body protested, strained beyond its limits, but he did not stop. The sky was turning pale pink, and he could clearly see the hills about him now, cool in the hour before dawn, robbed of both the shadows of night and the shimmering delusions of full day. The land was empty. He had brought the visions with him, phantoms of his disease. He was filthy with it, but the water hole was near now, and it would wash him clean.

He scrambled over a low shelf, and found himself facing a higher shelf further ahead, sheer sandstone. He would have to go around it. He shambled forward, and then stopped, for he was looking at a terrible thing. Atop the rock wall bowed a willow tree, and beneath it sat a stone bench. William gazed around in horror. It couldn't be. But it was. The creek bed spread out about

him, the banks rising high to form a wide, deep bowl. The floor
was rocky in parts, sandy in others. He was standing in the water
hole, and it was completely dry.

But his uncle had *promised*. The pool never ran dry. There
was a spring that fed it, no matter how little rain might fall.
William stumbled towards the base of the cliff. There! The ground
fell away and he saw a dark hole waiting. He sank to his knees and
clambered down. The cave was deep; the last remnants of night still
lurked in there, hiding at the back. He crunched over dead leaves
and twigs, the brittle branches of fallen trees, some grey, some starkly
white in the dimness. All the flotsam of the pool must have collected
here when the water level sank. None of it was even damp now, and
beneath, where the cave narrowed to a crack, there was only sand.
His fingers scrabbled in the earth for any hint of moisture, but it was
as dry as if water had never flowed there.

William was moaning. Darkness swept down on his mind, the
heavy beating of wings. The energy drained out of him like the
sand slipping through his fingers. It was all he could do to back
painfully out of the hole before it became his tomb. At the lip of
the cave he raised himself to his knees and stared bitterly at the
sky. The sun was coming, bringing the furnace of another day.
He was at his end, he could walk no more, think no more, believe
no more.

He sank down into the sand and curled himself into a ball.

The world spun on its axis, and birds sang for the new day.

The morning grew full. Ants crawled across William's legs, but
he did not move. His mind was far away. When he heard the sound
of a car approaching, still he did not stir. The noise of the engine
swelled, and then stopped. From above the cliff came the slam
of a door, and footsteps on the gravel. There was a pause, and then
a woman's voice, swearing. A scrambling amidst the rocks
followed, and finally two hands were on William's shoulders,
turning him over.

'Mum?' he moaned.

'No,' replied his cousin. 'It's not your mother.'

Then she was lifting him. William gazed at her, not under-standing, but not caring either, as long as it wasn't another dream.

Ruth's face was black with anger.

'Take this fucking thing off your head,' she said, pulling his captain's hat away. 'And let's get you home.'

Chapter Forty

William floated in dreams for most of the day. He knew he was in his bed, and intermittently he was aware of people around him, and of soup being spooned into his mouth. Each time he surfaced, however, an irresistible drowsiness would drag him back under. When he finally awoke, Dr Moffat was there, packing gear away in his black bag. William shifted slightly, and the doctor smiled at him.

'Well, you've been in the wars.'

William stared up at the man, not knowing what to say.

'Thirsty?'

He nodded.

'Sit up then.'

William obeyed. Dr Moffat helped, propping up pillows behind him, and then pouring a glass of water from a jug on the bedside table.

'Take it easy now. Don't gulp it.'

William sipped. The water was slightly warm, but it soothed

his cracked lips, and eased the raw feeling in his throat. He finished the glass, held it out for more.

Dr Moffat shook his head. 'That'll do for now. Too much will only make you sick. You've also got a nasty sunburn, some blisters on your feet, and a giant lump on your head — but you'll live. Lucky thing, too. It could have been a lot worse.'

'Thank you,' said William, his voice coming out in a whisper. He touched his head carefully, explored the swelling there. Confused images flickered in his mind. Had he fallen somewhere? His whole body was sore, muscles, bone and skin. The water sat uneasily in his stomach. His ear throbbed monotonously and, worst of all, a foul smell rose from his pillow.

'My ear hurts,' he said.

'Still got trouble with that? Didn't the antibiotics clear it up?'

'There's a smell...'

'A smell?' The doctor leant across the bed, sniffing, and William was almost overcome by the sour exhalation of alcohol. 'I don't smell anything.'

'It's something rotten!'

Dr Moffat stared in surprise, then patted the bed. 'Look, I'm sure everything will hurt for a while, and things will look strange and maybe even smell strange too. You're not yourself again yet. We'll just wait a few days, and then we'll see how you feel.'

William sank back helplessly.

The doctor snapped his bag shut. 'Now, let's get your mother in here. She's been worried to death about you.' And he bustled out.

It was only then William remembered that it was his cousin who had rescued him, not his mother. His mother, in fact, had left him out in the hills for two whole nights, and into a third day. Anger and resentment awoke in him, and self-pity, and the memory of gazing along the track, amidst all the heat and mirages, waiting vainly for a car to appear. So when his mother entered the room, he turned his face away, even when she sat down by the bed.

'Awake at last,' she said, sounding falsely bright. 'You certainly gave us a scare.'

He didn't answer.

'Dr Moffat says you'll be okay,' she carried on. 'We found you before any real harm was done. All you needed was some water and food ...'

The brightness trailed away, and still William would not look at her. *We*, she'd said. But there was no *we*. There had been only his cousin.

She bore his silence for a moment longer. Then abruptly she was angry. 'What on earth were you doing out there, anyway? Why didn't you tell me where you were going?'

The injustice of this made William roll over. He was the one who should be furious, not his mother. But her appearance gave him pause. She looked exhausted, hunched at his bedside. Her hair was tangled, her eyes were red and swollen. And her anger, he saw, was a facade. Beneath it, she was wretched with unhappiness. But he couldn't forgive her, not this time. It had hurt too much, the sight of that empty road, hour after hour.

His voice was an accusing croak. 'You were supposed to pick me up.'

The facade crumbled. She shook her head frantically. 'No, that's not true. That's not what your uncle said.'

'You were supposed to come and get me at the water hole.'

'No, no. Your uncle said you didn't want me to come. He said you'd gone camping, that you had food and everything. He said I had to let you be. He got so mad, and you know I can't afford to upset him. I didn't have a choice.'

She looked pathetic and defiant, all at once. William could even imagine how it must have been for her, how torn she must have felt. But she was his mother. Nothing should have stopped her looking for him. Not his uncle, not anything.

She gripped his hand. 'I did go looking. Once. Yesterday afternoon. I drove out along that track, no matter what your uncle said. But you weren't there.'

Uncertainties assailed William. 'I ... I wasn't on the track by then.'

'Why not?' She was gazing at him in confusion. 'What were you doing?'

William shook his head. There was no way he could tell her. But now resentment came again. His uncle had lied. The treacherous old man had abandoned him out there deliberately. William thought about the hole under the cliff, the hateful feel of it, the dry sand in his fingers, down there amongst the sticks and rubbish. And then — hands, rolling him over.

'When did Ruth get back?' he asked, wondering if it had really happened.

'Last night.' His mother pulled away nervously. 'She went looking for you, as soon as she heard. And then again this morning.'

William stared at her, and the question hung between them.

She was abject now, slumped in misery. 'It should have been me that found you. I can't explain it. I'm sorry. I just didn't know what to do.'

'It's okay,' William said, his voice hollow.

'No, it's not. I was wrong.' It was the shameful truth for once, stripped of all pretences. 'Everything I've done here has been wrong.'

For a moment, William dared to hope. 'Mum, my ear hurts. All the time.'

She seemed bewildered. 'Your ear?'

'And there's a smell.'

'But you took the antibiotics.'

'They didn't work.' He considered her sadly. 'Dr Moffat — is he a good doctor?'

She began to answer, but stopped herself. Her shoulders sagged. 'No, I don't suppose he is.'

'Can I go to a real doctor?'

'Right now?' She bit her lip as she thought, and William hated the indecision he could see in her. 'It's just that … well, maybe, if you don't feel any better in a day or two. We'll go into town. Okay? But not right now. We have to clean you up a bit first. Otherwise a doctor might wonder why you're all battered and bruised … Do you see?'

William saw. And the last remnant of faith he had in her died. He nodded, but it was only to himself, a confirmation that his mother was incapable of helping him.

'Good.' She smiled weakly. 'You know, it's only a week until Christmas. That'll brighten things up around here. I'll have to go and do some shopping.'

Christmas. The notion was inconceivable to William, there in the House. But it meant that the end of the year was close. And five months ago, his uncle had said that he would decide by year's end, about whether William and his mother would go or stay. And about who would get the station. William turned his gaze to the ceiling. He pictured the old man waiting up there. And he knew why his uncle had sent him to suffer alone out in the hills. It was the last test before the decision was made.

'What are you thinking about?' his mother asked.

William blinked. 'Is Ruth still here?'

She nodded, her Christmas smile fading. 'She's been fighting with your uncle. Something about that hat of yours, I think. I don't understand it.' Her haggard face set hard, and William saw the old fear. 'I don't know what she wants. I don't know why she can't just leave us alone.'

When William woke once more the room was empty. He lay motionless for a time, staring at the window. It was getting dark —

and yet it was still the same day. Only this morning he had been at the water hole. It didn't seem possible. Finally he threw back the sheet and swung his legs out of bed. Dizziness took him, but he waited until it eased. He dressed stiffly, then went out through the dim halls. No one was about, and he came to the front porch.

The sun had set, but the heat was still oppressive, the sky as cloudless as ever, and a smoky haze hung brooding upon the horizon. Nothing had changed. In fact, it was worse, for now William knew what it was like out across the station when night fell. He could remember the shifting shadows, and the moon, and silent, watching hills. Those things would always be with him. Nor was the ordeal over, because sooner or later his uncle would call him upstairs, eager to hear all that William had seen and learnt. And yet what could he say? What had he really discovered in those three days? Nothing. Only dreams and delusions.

Except ... there *was* one thing he had found, of which he was certain his uncle had no knowledge. That place, that unremarkable patch of scrub he had stumbled across, where something invisible had made the air too potent to breathe. Even now, William could remember the cicadas singing and the terror that had gripped him. A presence dwelt there, some cold and ancient secret of the land itself, faceless, but imbuing the very trees and grass with dreadful meaning. And it was a power that wasn't to be found high on a hilltop, marked with tall stones, where anyone could see it. It was hidden away, in surroundings so anonymous that those without the right eyes would simply pass it by.

His uncle had passed it by. And somehow that disturbed William more than anything else. For if his uncle did not know that such a place existed — if instead he had been fooled by an empty stone circle — then what did the old man really know about the property at all? And yet everything William had ever believed about Kuran Station was based on what his uncle had told him. All those tales about the people who had discovered the plains, about the men who had built the House, about shepherds and stockmen and explorers — those stories were what made the station so precious.

Were they all a lie? The beings William had met in the hills — they were not the figures of which his uncle had spoken. Some of them were deranged things, wrong things. They were from a different history altogether, a history Ruth might have told, harsh and ugly. He thought again of the old man up in his bedroom, brooding over the great gift that was his to bestow. But if Kuran Station was none of those things William had been taught, if the truth was thirst and heat and twisted ghosts, then Ruth was right, and the inheritance was no gift. It was a burden.

He looked up. The House waited behind him, huge and timeless. The last glow of the sky was reflected in the windows, so that no lights were visible from within, and William could imagine that the building was deserted. That his uncle was dead, and no one had followed him, and this was the House in twenty years time, neglected and forgotten. Its rooms were stripped bare. Mildew mottled the walls. Vandals had smashed the windows. The roof had collapsed and the upper floor was an open gulf where green things grew. Passers-by would shake their heads, remembering the old man who had lived there alone for so long, and before him, the great and glorious figures of the House's past, all come to nothing. And the property that surrounded it, the remnant of a vast station, would be broken up at last and sold off in small lots to this person or that, or simply left to run wild.

It could end that way, if William so chose.

And he would have to choose soon.

He gazed out at the plains. It was almost fully dark now, a dusky, somehow expectant night. From below on the hill came the sound of a man whistling. Presently the station manager, Mr Drury, appeared, walking up from the sheds. He passed by the front gate and lifted a hand, cheerful.

'Heard the news?' he called.

He didn't wait for an answer, disappearing around to the back of the House. The whistling faded away, and the silence of the evening bore down on William.

What news?

He went back inside. His mother was not in their apartment, but the television was on, the flickering screen bright in the dimness. William saw a satellite map of Australia. It was a weather report. Then suddenly he knelt before the TV, staring. For the northwestern edge of the continent was hidden under a swathe of cloud, a giant white swirl feeding in off the depths of the ocean. As William watched the map changed, and the clouds were replaced by a pattern of deep blue, shot through with intense pulses of green and orange. In time lapse animation the sheet of colour was moving slowly southeast across the continent. The weatherman chattered on excitedly, but William didn't need to listen. He knew what the tide of blue, and the blazes of green and orange, signified.

The rains have failed, the visions had told him. *The rivers have run dry*.

But rain was coming now.

Chapter Forty-one

In bed that night, William rolled miserably for hours, unable to sleep. His whole body was aching, and every time he closed his eyes he saw the lurid colours of clouds on a weather map. Why did that picture disturb him so much? Rain was a good thing — he knew how desperately the station needed it. And yet, after sleep finally came, those same colours pulsed ominously in his dreams. When he woke next morning he was almost afraid that rain would already be whispering on the roof. But when he climbed painfully out of bed and looked at the sky from the porch, the day was still hot and fine and crackling with sterility. Nor was there any hint of a change on the horizon.

But William's unease remained, as did his illness. He had no appetite for breakfast, and spent the morning lying in front of the television, drifting in a low fever. Waves of nausea came and went. His mother was getting ready to go to Powell, to do the Christmas shopping.

'I'll get decorations,' she said, mustering a wan smile, belied by her eyes. 'And a little tree. We can't do up the whole House, but we can make it nice in here.'

William nodded, barely listening.

'Will...' she began helplessly, then gave up and departed, purse in hand.

At midday, the weather report came on. The satellite image showed the great sheet of cloud crawling across the map. It was still a vibrant mass of blue and green and orange, and the foremost fringes of it had already touched the western border of Queensland ... but that was still hundreds of miles away. The whole system was moving slower than expected. 'Late tonight,' said the weatherman, 'for those watching in southeast Queensland. Or perhaps early tomorrow.'

William closed his eyes and tried to imagine puddles in the yard, the rattle of water in the drainpipes. He couldn't do it. Instead he was haunted by the visions he had seen in the hills. They had not spoken of rain falling, but of the drought, and of the rivers drying up. It had sounded like a warning, as if there was something urgent they wanted him to find, something that the drought had laid bare. *Caves have opened to the sun.* And yet William had found nothing. Unless it was something he had missed. Or something he had seen, but failed to recognise...

'Your uncle wants you.'

William opened his eyes. Mrs Griffith stood in the living room doorway. He sat up, disorientated. The housekeeper never came into their apartment.

'Upstairs,' she said. 'Now.'

The summons was upon him.

William stared hopelessly. He still had no idea what he could say to satisfy the old man, or if he even wanted to try. He was confused about so many things. But the call could not be refused. He rose and followed Mrs Griffith through the hallways, watching the bitter hunch of her shoulders. At least he understood *her* a little now. It was the House and the station that had made her the way she was. The lure of them, eating at her mind. William had felt the same thing happening to himself — and he had suffered it for only a few months, not an entire lifetime.

They came to the stairs, but William paused, for at the end of the hallway the door to the office opened, and Ruth emerged. She had a pen in her mouth and a sheaf of papers in her hand, and her grey head was bent, reading. She looked up and saw them there.

'Will,' she said, sounding surprised.

He had forgotten all about her.

She came down the hall, her eyes serious. 'Should you be out of bed?'

'I'm okay,' he said. But her presence threw him off balance. He realised that he had not even had the chance to thank Ruth for saving him.

'You don't look okay.' She glanced disapprovingly at Mrs Griffith.

The housekeeper returned the glare. 'His uncle wants to see him.'

Ruth ignored her. She squatted down to William's level. 'You don't have to do anything he says, you know. Not after what he's done.'

'He ... I wasn't supposed to get lost.'

'It doesn't matter what was *supposed* to happen.' Her gaze held his, until William had to look away. 'Okay,' she decided. 'But I'll come with you.'

William looked up at the housekeeper. Her eyes darted back and forth between them, the daughter and nephew. 'It's none of my doing,' she declared, and made off towards her own apartment.

Ruth watched her go, shaking her head. 'Come on.'

But she led William back down the hall, not upstairs. He felt swept away. His uncle was waiting, but his cousin had intervened and the day was veering off course.

'Thank you for finding me,' he mumbled.

She waved a hand. 'I don't blame you. I blame my father for sending you out there in the first place. And your mother for letting him.'

'She had to,' William broke in. 'She has to do what he says.'

'And how much longer would she have left you there? A week? A month?'

They had reached the office. It was even more of a shambles than usual. William could see that Ruth had ransacked the drawers and cupboards. Piles of yellowing papers and maps were spread across the room. She cleared some space on a chair for him, returned to her own behind the desk.

'Sorry about the mess. There were some things I wanted to make sure of, and I didn't have much time.' She paused. 'Have you seen the news on TV?'

'About the rain?'

'No, not the rain — the Native Title legislation. Remember? The Senate has almost finished debating. Parliament rises for the Christmas break tomorrow, so the vote is set for tonight. The minor parties are making their last-ditch amendments right now. It's close. It's literally down to a vote or two.'

William was nonplussed. What did it matter? His uncle had told him that the station was safe, whether Native Title was law or not. But Ruth was watching him, aglow now with some suppressed excitement.

'Believe me, Will, if it does pass, nothing is going to be the same around here.'

William's brow wrinkled in puzzlement. 'Why?'

'Information has come to light, that's why. I've been doing some checking in Brisbane. And then on my way back here, I stopped in at Cherbourg.'

He stared at her blankly.

She smiled. 'It's a small town a couple of hours from here, on the other side of the mountains. It used to be an Aboriginal mission. These days it's an all black self-governing community. I told you about it, remember? It's where the last people from Kuran Station were sent to in 1911.'

William felt an abrupt shifting of the ground.

'It's a strange place to visit — off away on a dead-end road, and you can still see the gates that would have been shut when it was a reserve, to keep whites out and blacks in. But in other ways it's quite nice. There's a cultural centre now. That's where I started asking. I wanted to know if anyone in town could trace links back to Kuran Station. They got all suspicious. Who was I and why did I want to know? It seems that all sorts of people have been visiting the community lately, asking questions about who came from where originally. White people, worried about land claims.'

Her smile had gone sharp.

'The folk at Cherbourg thought that I was trying to *stop* a land claim, you see. Once I cleared that up, they were more helpful. But getting answers still wasn't easy. After all, families from right across Queensland ended up at that mission, and everything is mixed up now. But they asked around, and finally they brought in an old woman, and she said yes, she knew a bit about Kuran Station in the old days. What's more, she could name other people who did too.'

William listened through his growing uncertainty. 'She came from here?'

'Not just her. There were six or seven old women in the end. Of course, none of them had actually grown up on the station. It was over eighty years ago, after all. But their mothers came from here, or their grandmothers, and stories had been passed down. What stories, I wanted to know. But then they went all quiet and careful again. Why was I asking? What business was it of mine? They thought I was just prying where I shouldn't be. But I wasn't just prying, Will. It *is* my business, as much as it is theirs. And this is the proof.'

She picked up something from beside her chair, dropped it on the desk.

'My hat,' said William, startled.

The smile was gone. 'It isn't yours. It belonged to my grandfather.'

'I know,' he said. 'But Uncle John said I could wear it.'

'Indeed. What was it you told me — you thought it was an army hat?'

'I knew it wasn't, not really.'

She was holding up the hat, so that William could observe the badge. 'You see the letters? QMP? I was right, they stand for Queensland Mounted Police. So I looked up the records. They're sketchy, but yes, a Daniel McIvor is mentioned. He joined the force in 1888, when he was very young. He served for seven years and then left. And that was it. No big deal. Except that he wasn't just an ordinary mounted policeman. He was part of a special detachment.' She cast the cap aside. 'They were called the Queensland *Native* Mounted Police. And that hat is a rarity. No complete uniform from the detachment survives. Not even the Police Museum has one.'

William frowned. He already knew that her grandfather had been a policeman. Did it matter exactly what sort of policeman?

Ruth was considering the painted walls.

'You have to understand, Will — the history of Queensland settlement was a little different from states like New South Wales or Victoria. One of the differences was that there were more Aborigines in Queensland than down south, and so when white people tried to move out and settle the bush, there was more trouble. The tribes were warlike, and they weren't going to stand aside and lose their land. They killed quite a few whites in the more remote areas. At times it got so bad, especially up north and out west, that whole white communities went into a panic and evacuated. The government decided they had to do something, so they set up a special troop. The Native Police. There were over one hundred of them, at their height. Quite an army for those days. And their job was to make sure that the Aborigines didn't bother the white settlers. Their orders were to "disperse" any troublesome blacks. And the thing was, no one ever really defined what "disperse" might mean.'

William too looked at the walls, at the faded images of old England, and then at the ghostly riders in Australia, trailing after their sheep.

'The word itself means to break up, to scatter, to chase away. And sometimes that's all the Native Police did. Ran the blacks off, or arrested them. Other times, however, they just shot them all. No one knows how often exactly, because the Native Police didn't keep official records. The old reports speak only in euphemisms. "We dispersed this tribe, we dispersed that tribe." It could mean hundreds of dead, it could mean thousands. But the Native Police operated all up and down Queensland, and they went on "dispersing" for over thirty years. It got so awful that it disturbed white people, even back then. There were complaints and inquiries. But that didn't stop the killing.'

And inevitably, William found his eyes drawn to that corner of the mural where the dark faces huddled. Were they lying in wait for the white men, he had always wondered, or were they hiding in fear? And now that he looked more attentively — were there rifles in the riders' hands?

Ruth's voice was flat. 'My grandfather was one of them. He slaughtered blacks for a living, and wore this hat while he was doing it. It's an officer's cap, by the way. The officers were the only white men in the Native Police. The private troopers were all Aborigines from New South Wales and Victoria, trained and armed. Who better to hunt down and kill blacks than other blacks, right?'

Wide eyes stared out from the walls, and the glimmer of teeth.

'Is that what happened here?' William asked faintly.

Ruth gave an odd laugh. Then she shook her head. '*Officially*, the Native Police never had anything to do with Kuran Station. The first troop was only formed around 1860. By then, there was no need for them on the Darling Downs. The real troubles were further out on the frontier. As far as I can tell, my grandfather was stationed mostly in the far north, where the blacks kept causing problems right into the late 1890s. But after that the Native Police were disbanded, and he was out of a job.'

She fixed William with her stare.

'He kept hold of his gun, though. He used to carry it with him, when he worked here. And obviously he kept that hat. I know you don't really understand, Will, but my father's had you dressed up in the Australian equivalent of an SS uniform.'

William studied the cap. No, he didn't understand her, but it seemed darker now, and heavier. And yet he remembered the feel of it on his head, the pleasant weight of the badge. And he remembered the men from the League, Terry and Henry, and the way they had laughed and saluted and called him Captain Bill. They had thought it was all for fun.

But then another memory came, of night, and of cicadas shrilling, and of a shapeless creature with glaring eyes. *You bear the mark, boy.* Yes ... he had borne that hat like a beacon the whole time he was in the hills. The murderous shepherd had recognised it, and drawn away. The explorer had saluted its authority. And the bunyip had regarded it with ancient hostility. But why? The Native Police had never been on the station, his cousin had just told him they hadn't. Whatever her grandfather had done with his black troopers, it had happened miles away from here, in some other part of the state.

Ruth was gathering her papers.

'So, those women at Cherbourg, I said to them, "You bet it's my business. My grandfather was out there wading in Aboriginal blood." That got through to them. But I didn't tell them the very worst thing about my grandfather. I haven't told you yet, either. I'm saving that for your uncle. He's the one who needs to hear it first.'

William gazed at her, shaken by doubts.

'Do you still want to go up to see him?' she asked.

He didn't know. He felt dizzy again, half drawn back into the dream-world of the hills. The things he had seen and heard, the messages, the warnings, the hat, the coming rain — they were all linked somehow. And the answer seemed to dance tantalisingly close.

His cousin held out a hand. 'C'mon then. Let's go up.'

Chapter Forty-two

HIGH IN THE WHITE CHAMBER, JOHN MCIVOR FOUGHT AGAINST delirium as he waited for his nephew.

A fever throbbed within him, mirroring the heat of the room, and he could feel his twice-scarred heart beating febrile in his chest. He was seventy-nine years old, and he was probably dying. Not his mind — his mind was alive in a way it had seldom been before. Oh, but his body…

Pain flared, and he strove to shift his limbs, sweating with the effort.

He was so weak. How he hated the indignity he had suffered these last months, having to be fed and nursed like an infant. And by the boy's useless mother, no less. In fact, he was surrounded now by women he did not want. Veronica, and the old housekeeper, they were vultures the both of them, circling, eager to pick at his carcass. But worse by far was his daughter, the poisonous child. If only he could rise from his bed and physically cast her out. Cast all of them out.

He groaned, rolling his head across the pillow.

And for a bewildering instant it seemed as if his father was there in the room with him. A stern, silent, giant of a man, his gun at his side, and dressed in a uniform.

That was Ruth's fault as well. This fuss about William's hat. In some ways, she had seemed angrier about the hat than she had about William being sent out alone. You'd think he'd given the boy a snake to play with. And yet, there was no denying the rest of it — his daughter's revelation had been an unpleasant surprise. John had never known the details of his father's police career, until now.

'You didn't tell me,' he complained to the empty room.

And for a moment, something inside John quailed. The Native Police — was that the taint that had smeared his father so long ago?

He banished the doubt. Of course not. It was no shame to have served with the Native Police. They had performed a necessary duty, that was all. Did his daughter think that Australia had been claimed as easily as walking onto the land and taking it? No, it had been fought for, like land anywhere in the world. Declarations of war and treaties meant nothing in the end. There was only the reality of occupation, and it was a brutal business.

'Whites were dying too, remember,' he muttered.

And if it happened that his father was part of it all, so what? It didn't make the man a murderer or a monster. The history was there to be read — lives had been saved, settlement had been assured. So what did it matter where William's hat came from? It couldn't do the boy any harm. There was no evil genie hiding in an old police badge.

But his daughter wasn't finished with him, he knew. She was rummaging through his papers downstairs in the office, searching, no doubt, for details about the station's lease. Well, let her look. The only document that mattered was his will, and it wasn't in the office, he had it there in the bedroom, beside him in the cupboard. He had typed it himself only yesterday, forcing his trembling fingers down on the keys. And there was no mention of Ruth, nor of the other two women. Let them guess and wonder and plot to usurp him. And let them perish with frustration in the end.

'I have the boy now,' he told the room, grinning hotly at the memories.

True, he had doubted William at first.

He recalled his initial sight of the lad, moping about on the day his father died. (What luck, that harvester catching fire.) There hadn't been much promise to see in him then, but John had persevered. And on that dreadful night of the rally, William had proved that he was the right choice. For the boy had seen it too! Not for real, of course, his childish imagination must have plucked the image from a dream. But it was the *same* dream, John's own dream, and surely that was the point.

The room waited silently.

'Yes,' he explained, 'but I had to know for sure.'

And if the boy wanted Kuran Station, then he had to discover the answer for himself. Ownership could not be shared. Not the power of it, and not the weight of it either. It could be crushing, that weight, encompassing all the history that the land had ever witnessed, the summation of the lives and deaths of all those who had walked it before. But William barely even *knew* the station — he hadn't smelled it or touched it or felt the terrible age of its bones. John didn't remember what he had said to the boy to launch him out into the hills, he remembered only his certainty that William had to go.

And there had never been any question of his mother picking him up. The child was afraid, and it was fear that he needed to master. He would have to find his own way there and his own way home. It didn't matter that Veronica had been frantic, or that Ruth had interfered. The women weren't important, they would never grasp the truth. Perhaps, John considered, ownership was fundamentally a male concern. He had always known that the boy would survive. If he was worthy. If not, then better the fact be known now, before it was too late.

'It's not my fault the water hole was dry,' he complained.

Anyway, the thing was done. Once William reported what he had seen and learnt, then the matter would be sealed and there would be nothing anyone could do — not Ruth, not Veronica, not even Mrs Griffith. John would have his heir.

And it was right! The vindication came every time he closed his eyes. Awake, his mind swarmed with thoughts, but ever since he had sent William into the hills, his sleep had been blissfully calm. The past no longer stalked his dreams. There were no more visions of the House as it had been when he was a child, with all its lights and sumptuous crowds, no more phantom appearances of Elizabeth White, always aloof and mocking and out of reach. He no longer dreamt about his time in the mountains, of great dark forests and balding peaks. He no longer dreamt of Dudley, with his sad tortured face, or of the hideous sight of him, stretched naked across a crying girl. He no longer dreamt of Harriet, or of that single perfect moment they'd shared, amidst the rock and the water.

Most crucially of all, there had been no more nightmares. Not one glimpse of that familiar figure standing patiently while it burned. Perhaps it was Oliver Fisher, perhaps it wasn't — John had stopped pondering the question years ago. But ever since the day of Oliver's death, John had known that there was a price he must pay to achieve his ends. Friends, family, wife and daughter — he had surrendered them all. And that, he had come to believe, was what the nightmare really signified. The burning man was his reminder of things lost, and his accuser of things done.

But now it had vanished, and John knew why. It had moved on to William. All unknowing, the boy had assumed the burden, and John was free of it at last. He dreamt of nothing now, as if he was a man without history or memories. There was only an empty, silent place in his sleep, where his mind hung in soothing darkness.

John blinked, stared into the corners of his room.

There was no one there.

Beside him, the radio whispered stories of rain sweeping across the country, and of fierce debate raging in the Senate. The world spun on, and now Native Title loomed, the final decision hanging in the balance. Did he care any more? No ... all of that was gone with the League and white robes dancing around stones. Still, the vote was approaching, and if the new laws passed, then it was fitting that William should witness the moment, here at his side. *See*, he would say to his nephew, *with one hand I give you the property, and with another they begin to take it away. Not with this law maybe, but with the next, and with all the others that will follow.* The boy would know he had been betrayed, even before the inheritance was his, and the seed of a lifelong hatred would be planted.

Rightly so.

John McIvor smiled. He moved the radio dial, let his fingers fall drowsily.

What was keeping the boy?

Chapter Forty-three

WILLIAM AND RUTH FOUND THE OLD MAN FAST ASLEEP.

His arm was draped across the bedside table, fingers upon the radio dial. Static crackled, and the room was stifling, awash with an angry red light that told of faraway fires and smoke, but to William, his uncle looked at a peace, lost in a deep, sweet dream, his head thrown back in abandon.

But dreaming of what?

Unaccountably, William shivered.

Then Ruth switched off the radio, and the old man's eyes flickered open. He focused disapprovingly on his daughter.

'I didn't ask for you.'

'I know.'

The two considered each other, the daughter looking down, cold and without pity, the father looking up, frail and bedridden, and yet with rage smouldering. Was there any real resemblance between them, William wondered? No … and yet they were palpably not strangers. They were bound by a thousand unseen things, hatred not the least among them. Strangers didn't look at each other that way, it was something much closer, something to do with family. It occurred to him that it was only within families, between parents and their children, that a hatred so profound was even possible.

His uncle shrugged minimally. His gaze moved away from his daughter, towards William, and the anger softened into a smile. 'So. You made it back after all.'

'After you almost killed him,' Ruth said.

'Rubbish.' The old man's eyes didn't move from his nephew. 'She doesn't know half of what she thinks she knows. You're the one that's been out there, Will. You and me both.'

And again, William felt the ardent touch of his uncle's mind, the madness in it, and he knew how easy it would be for his own control to slip loose, teetering as it already was.

'You saw what you needed to see?'

'Yes,' he said, not knowing if it was a lie or the truth.

His uncle's hand fluttered from the bedside table to William's shoulder. 'I knew it.' And the fingers gripped there a moment, a flush of heat. 'It's what I said. The blood is in you.'

His daughter snorted. 'Is there anything you won't do to warp this child?' She sat down by the coffee table. 'I told him about the hat.'

'It's his grandfather's,' said the old man, serene. 'That's all he needs to know.'

Ruth looked up sharply. 'Not *his* grandfather's. *My* grandfather's.'

The old man blinked. 'Go away. Will and I have to talk.'

But she wasn't going anywhere. 'I brought these for you,' Ruth said, spreading out her sheaf of papers upon the table.

'And what are they supposed to be?'

'Photocopies. I got them in Brisbane. I was looking up records about property transfers. The tricky part was trying to work out exactly what deal was made between the White family and the government, when this station was transferred from leasehold to perpetual lease. The official records are vague, which is interesting in itself. So I thought, who else might know?'

The old man's smile was mocking. 'No one.'

'No? What about the White family themselves?'

'The Whites are all dead.'

'Elizabeth isn't.'

Forgotten, William had backed up to the wall, his hand spread against it to steady the vertigo in his head. He watched a wary stillness grip his uncle.

'She's old,' Ruth continued, 'she's into her eighties, but she's fit enough. She lives in Brisbane. I went to see her. I found her number, right there in the phone book.'

A grin flared, skull-like. 'And does she know who owns her House now?'

'She didn't. But I told her.'

'Good!'

'She doesn't care. She never did.'

The grin grew vicious. 'You two got on famously, I suppose.'

'She didn't even want to talk to me at first — she's got no liking for the name McIvor. But when I told her what I was after, she was more cooperative.'

'I bet she was.'

'So I found out what I needed to know about the property transfer. And trust me, this perpetual lease is open to interpretation. But that wasn't the really interesting thing. We talked for quite a while. About the station and the old days. Even about you.'

The old man only stared.

'Yes, she remembers you. But mainly we talked about your father. This was the day after I'd found out about him being in the Native Police. So I mentioned it to her, and she went very quiet. Then she said she had something to show me.'

William's uncle hunched himself against the pillow, his eyes lidded with suspicion. 'She hated my father. I wouldn't believe a thing she says about him.'

'She didn't say anything. All she did was bring out some old notebooks.' Ruth held up the photocopied pages. 'They were journals. They belonged to *her* father.'

The old man's eyes narrowed. 'Malcolm?'

'He was the useless one, right? The drunk and the womaniser, the one who threw all those scandalous parties here.'

'He was a fat fool.'

'So I'm told.' Ruth was the serene one now. 'But he was religious about writing in his journals, and Elizabeth still has them all. It was the mention of Native Police that got her attention. It chimed with something of her father's that she'd read.' She held out the papers. They were covered with dark, cramped handwriting. 'Do you want to the see it?'

'Nothing that man wrote is of any interest to me.'

'Then maybe Will wants to hear it?'

And she glanced William's way, questioning, but he saw that she was barely aware of him. This was for her father, and only her father.

'Do you remember going on any picnics as a boy?' she asked the old man.

'Picnics?'

Ruth consulted the documents. 'Around Christmas? Say late December, 1917? You would have been three years old.'

'Is that all that idiot wrote about? Picnics?'

'Malcolm wasn't there. He only heard about it later.'

'Heard what? What picnic?'

Ruth explained it calmly. 'Your father took your mother and you, and a few of his men and their families, on a day out. At that water hole. You're sure you don't remember it?'

'No!'

She shifted the papers. 'Of course, you wouldn't remember the station Aborigines either.'

The old man was caught off-guard. 'What?'

'In fact, they were taken away before you were born.'

'I know that,' he snapped. 'My father told me all about them. They used to get free blankets and flour. The Whites treated them damn well. Too well, if anything.'

'Your father didn't approve?'

'He knew they'd be better off somewhere else. They were just a nuisance around the station. There were only a few old men and women and some kids.'

William could see that Ruth's hands were trembling now, whether with excitement or anger he didn't know. But her voice was steady. 'And so in 1911 they were shipped off to Cherbourg, and that was the end of the problem. Except it wasn't. Not according to Malcolm's journal. Two years later, they left the mission and came back. Not the women, just the men and the boys. Only six or seven of them, but that was the tribe's whole male population by then. Your father caught them wandering about the station and reported them to the police.'

The old man was watching his daughter very closely now. 'So? Those were the rules back then. Blacks had to stay where they were sent.'

Ruth wasn't listening. 'Two years later, in 1915, they did it again. No one knows why. But your father caught them again, and handed them over to the police again. Only this time, apparently, he beat some of them first, quite badly. To teach them a lesson. Or so Malcolm says. He was no friend of the blacks, but he was uneasy about it, all the same. I think to him it was like a man beating a horse or a dog. It was in bad taste.'

'If my father did anything like that,' said William's uncle, his expression venomous, 'then he did it because they had no right to be here.'

'Oh, I don't know. It was nothing new for him, was it? We know that. It used to be his job. Chasing blacks about, roughing them up. Dispersing them.'

'He was enforcing the law.'

'Well, it didn't work. Two years later the blacks were back yet again. This time your father didn't spot them, not straightaway. And one day, around Christmas 1917, you were having a picnic with your family at the water hole. At some stage, it seems, you wandered off on your own, just a little boy, exploring down along the creek bed. And then your father heard you screaming. Maybe he thought you'd come across a snake. Or a wild dog perhaps. Either way, he went running to find you. And of course he always had his gun with him. You really don't remember any of this?'

'Remember what? A snake? A dog?'

But his daughter was far away. 'No one knows exactly how many of them there were. But when your father arrived, you were standing there screaming at them, scared out of your wits by the black men. They were naked, someone told Malcolm, and all painted up. I guess they were the first Aborigines you'd ever seen. But your father knew them, it was those same damn trespassers again, all naked and wild, threatening his boy. And he had his gun. It's no surprise what happened. Some of the other men even joined in. But everyone agreed Daniel McIvor started it. Habit dies hard, I suppose.'

'Is that it?' William's uncle was laughing. 'It's a fairytale.'

'Oh no,' Ruth smiled, 'it happened. Afterwards, they burned the bodies. Because times had changed a *little* — you couldn't just leave black corpses lying around like in the old days. So they burned them. Or charred them at least — apparently they couldn't get a proper fire going. And then they just dumped the remains in the creek.'

'Rubbish. If there was any truth in it at all, my father would have gone to jail.'

'Who would tell? His own men were terrified of him. Edward White didn't care, and Malcolm was too weak. Your father knew he was safe. He'd disposed of the bodies, so there was no evidence. And anyway, it was only a few blacks. The authorities would have assumed that they'd just run away from their mission and disappeared. It wasn't unheard of. So no problem.'

'It's a lie. A slur. Malcolm made it up.'

'It wasn't just Malcolm. Word got around, quietly. Elizabeth remembers the rumours herself. People suspected, and a lot of them were appalled. It was harmless old men he'd killed. Boys.'

The old man was shaking his head stubbornly, back and forth, back and forth.

'And in places like Powell ... Well, Powell liked to think it was a civilised community. Elizabeth said that, from then on, they made your father an outcast.'

William saw his uncle's head-shaking abruptly cease.

And for John McIvor, time stopped.

An outcast?

The denial died on his lips. John found he couldn't speak. For with that one word, the great enigma of his father was suddenly laid bare. A man always so reviled, so distrusted, so dogged by whispers and frowns. And now, at last, John had a reason. Could his daughter's story really be true? It *must* be true. What else explained so much? An atrocity had taken place, and as the dark rumour of it spread, the people of Powell had turned from Daniel McIvor in disgust.

And from his son.

John felt he was drowning, that the room had been robbed of air. Memories tumbled through his mind remorselessly, every slight and setback he had ever received, each one irrefutable. The whole tenor of his life, all the bitterness and hardship, everything had been preordained by this one action of his father. And the incident had happened when John was only a child. An innocent, wailing in fear.

And that was like another gulf opening beneath him. For if his own cries had initiated the slaughter, then he was his own prime cause, the unwitting mover of his own downfall. How could that be borne? And then the ground was falling away yet again, he was in an abyss of memory, far, far back in the recesses of his existence, and most terribly of all he could smell smoke. The room and the bed were gone, his feeble body was gone, the recollection was complete, he was living in it. He was smelling smoke and crying and he was only a little boy, clutched tight in his mother's arms, so tight he was almost suffocating, and she was crying as well, her breast heaving against his face, as somewhere men yelled and laughed and flames crackled.

From far above he heard his daughter's voice, cool and detached. 'The question is, why do you think those men and boys kept coming back here? They must have known, after the first time, that they weren't welcome.'

'Lies,' he whispered in the blackness.

'Did they just miss their country? Or was it something more than that? What was so pressing that they had to return at around the same time every two years, at such risk to themselves? Was there some sort of initiation rite or corroboree they had to hold? A sacred site they had to visit? I don't suppose we'll ever know. But whatever it was, they died for it.'

But to John her words were meaningless.

'Uncle John?'

And the concern in the voice brought him back. It was the boy, at his bedside. Not Ruth, not the viper of a daughter who had brought this horrible enlightenment to him. He could see again now, and she was smiling still, her obscene papers before her. And at the sight, pride stirred in him, reviving. Nothing she had told him mattered. Kuran Station was his, won by his own hands.

Nothing she could say could rob him of that. All she could do was frighten him with ghosts. William's hand was on the bed, and John clutched it, drew strength from it. Yes, the boy was his, the boy had come to his aid. He levered himself up against the pillows, felt the blood pumping in his veins again.

'I'm fine now, Will,' he said, squeezing the boy's fingers. 'It was just a bit of a turn.' And he was staring squarely at his daughter.

'They died trying to keep alive their traditions,' she said.

'Who cares?' John felt strong again, his certainty returned. 'It was eighty years ago. It doesn't matter to anyone now.'

'It might matter a lot.' Ruth nodded towards the silent radio. 'It might change everything. If Native Title becomes law.'

Chapter Forty-four

WHY DID THOSE MEN AND BOYS KEEP COMING BACK HERE?
It was Ruth's question, and when William heard it, something blazed in his mind. He saw a three-year-old child, wandering down the creek bed, to find the black men waiting there. It was the same area that he himself had clambered and scrambled across that last tortured morning. And there was nothing in the creek bed itself, no reason for men and boys to gather.

But not far from the creek...

A sacred site they needed to visit?

Darkness rushed into William's head. He was standing in a moonlit landscape, where cicadas sang madly and shadows played across grass and trees, and where an unreasoning fear had possessed him. A site of secret power. And standing guard there, a blunt figure, leaning against the sky.

The black men dreamt me, long ago.

'Lies,' William heard his uncle whisper.

It was only then that William turned to the bedside and

clutched the old man's hand, to tell him that it wasn't lies, that he knew why the Aborigines kept returning, and why they were so close to the creek on the day of the picnic. It was because of that place. *Their* place.

'Uncle John,' he said. But his uncle gripped so hard it hurt William's fingers. Then the old man was propping himself up, drawing the vitality from somewhere, and William tugged his hand away.

'Let the damn law pass,' the old man was saying now. 'We've been through this before.'

His daughter shook her head. 'Have you actually read the draft legislation?'

'I've read it. It can't touch me.'

'Don't be so sure. The perpetual lease on this station was arranged in very dubious circumstances. It was a hushed-up deal between the Whites and the government. No one will know exactly how that stands until it's tested in court. But believe me, this place might still qualify as Crown land. In which case, it'd be open to a Native Title claim.'

'A Native Title claim,' William's uncle mimicked. 'Lodged by who? You can't do it. There's no one left who can.'

'Really?' Ruth's smile was tight. 'I've been to Cherbourg. There are people in that town who came from this property. Six people at least who I spoke with.'

'They were *born* here?'

'No — but their parents and grandparents were.'

'Ha! Exactly!'

'Exactly what?'

'I don't know who you talked to, but they've never set foot on Kuran Station. Not in the twenty-three years I've lived here. And not when I lived here before, either. So what could they claim? They have to prove a continuing presence on the land.'

Andrew McGahan

'How could they? The Kuran people were taken away by force.'

'The legislation is perfectly clear. If they left, for whatever reason, then they lose all rights of appeal.'

'Oh yes, it's a nice legal trick. But in this case they kept coming back, didn't they? Year after year. Until your father killed them.'

'Even if that were true, how does it give them a case now? Where's the continuing presence since then?'

'Continuing presence might not mean what you think it means.'

'It damn well means something!'

William was leaning up against the wall once more. He looked from father to daughter as they argued, and he realised that they didn't really care about what had happened at the creek. This was about something else. The ownership of Kuran Station, yes, but mostly it was about the unending war between these two. And now they were coming to the heart of the matter.

'They continued their presence as best they could,' Ruth insisted. 'It was so important to them that they broke the law repeatedly to return. They made every effort humanly possible to stay in contact, and got slaughtered for their trouble. *Then* they stopped coming.'

'It doesn't matter why they stopped. They stopped. It's over.'

'It isn't. This law is brand new, it has to be interpreted by judges. Maybe the Kuran people haven't kept up a continuing presence, but if they argue that eighty years ago their entire male population was killed off while *trying* to — then what? What humane person isn't going to consider that a reasonable excuse, no matter what the letter of the law might say?'

'And how do they know anyone was killed?' the old man sneered. 'Those people at Cherbourg didn't see it. What proof do they have that it ever happened?'

'There's Malcolm's journal.'

'No court would accept that. Malcolm didn't see it either. It's hearsay.'

'No criminal court maybe. But a Native Title tribunal? That's a different thing altogether. Old letters, old journals, old stories — that's exactly the sort of evidence they're going to have to accept. If we're talking about Aboriginal history, what else is there? And those old women haven't forgotten. They know that those men and boys never came back. They know what must have happened.'

'They can't know for certain!'

'They will when I tell them. I've already told them about your lease, and the loopholes in it. So sooner or later, they'll lodge a claim. And when what your father did comes out, I think they actually might win.'

The old man's jaw worked in rage, unable to find words.

Ruth leaned forward. 'I'll make *sure* they win. One day, you're going to have to share this place with those people, whether you like it or not.'

And looking on, William could sense the chaos that raged inside his uncle — the frustration and bitterness, the hatred of so many things and so many people, lawyers and politicians and governments, all of them interfering endlessly in his affairs. And now he was trapped, hounded into this corner by his own treacherous daughter.

'You'd do it, too,' the old man shouted, his last restraint giving way, a bony finger pointed. 'You'd help them, just to get to me. Anything, to steal what's mine. But where's the proof? You show me the bodies. You show me the bones of those people. You can't, can you? I know this land better than anyone. And there's nothing out there.'

Ruth was remorseless. 'You don't need bodies to make a claim.'

'It's insane!'

'It's the law. Or it might be, by tomorrow.'

Huddled against the wall, William trembled. It was not the yelling that shook him, or the unveiled loathing between father and daughter. It was a sudden memory from his time in the hills. Not a vision or a hallucination, but something real. Something he'd seen and touched.

His uncle had said he wanted *proof.*

'Uncle John,' he started to say.

But just then there came a cry from below. It was Dr Moffat's voice. 'Hello? Hello up there?'

The old man's eyes lit with manic decision. 'Moffat!' he roared, 'Get up here!' He was possessed, scrabbling through the drawers of his bedside table. 'It's time you saw,' he said, spitting the words at his daughter, 'You won't get one more scrap from me.'

Then Dr Moffat was at the door. He glanced at them all in surprise. 'What's everyone doing up here?'

William's uncle had a sheet of paper in his hand, jabbed it towards the doctor. 'Moffat, you're a Justice of the Peace, right?'

'That's right.'

'Then notarise this for me.'

The doctor looked at the paper, bewildered. 'What?'

'Sign the damn thing! Make it legal!'

Dr Moffat took the document. 'But what is it?'

'My will, you fool. What else?'

The will, William thought, gazing at the paper. Finally, there it was. A single page. The reason behind all these long months that he had lived at the House, striving to please his uncle, his mother, his cousin. And now that the moment had arrived, he found he didn't care. All he could think of was the proof, the thing he had seen, out there in the hills.

Show me their bones, his uncle had said.

Across the room, Ruth rose to her feet. 'The will doesn't change anything,' she said. But her father didn't even glance her way.

Dr Moffat was studying the document. 'So it all goes to the boy...'

'Yes,' the old man echoed, 'the boy.'

And all eyes in the room were upon William. He could only blink back. They didn't understand. He was seeing a gleam of white, deep at the bottom of a cave.

'Sign it,' his uncle told the doctor. 'Sign it and it's done.'

'You're sure of this?'

'I'm sure.'

'It doesn't change a thing,' Ruth repeated.

But Dr Moffat had placed the will on the coffee table and was scribbling with his pen.

The old man rocked with pleasure. 'Take the station from me now,' he gloated to his daughter. 'I dare you. Only you won't be taking it from *me*. It's all Will's now. It's all on his shoulders. So go ahead and help your friends with their claim. It won't be me you're hurting.'

She looked at William, then back to her father. 'He's only a boy!'

'I know,' the old man grinned. 'But he's mine, not yours.'

Ruth shook her head, so repelled she couldn't speak. Then with one sweep of her hand she gathered up her documents. 'You can't put it all on him,' she said. 'You're the one who has to pay for this, and in the end, you're the one who will.'

And with that she was gone, her father's laughter pursuing her down the hall.

Dr Moffat was finished. 'There.' He held up the will. 'What do you want me to do with this?'

William's uncle stretched out a hand. 'Give it here. Then get out.'

'I still need to examine you, John, you shouldn't be getting so excited.'

'Get out!'

The doctor glanced at William. 'C'mon, son, let's leave him to it.'

'William stays.'

Dr Moffat considered his patient for one last, doubtful moment. 'Ruth's right, you know. He's just a child. And he should be in bed.' Then he was gone too.

Andrew McGahan

The old man was hunched over the sheet of paper, glorying in it. He beckoned to William. 'Come over here, boy. Look at this.'

William came, the secret swollen inside him.

His uncle held out the will. 'Isn't it beautiful?'

William took it, glanced at the typed words and the signatures below, his uncle's and the doctor's. It should have been heavy, such a thing. It should have weighed as much as the stone of the House and rocks of the hills combined. Instead it might have been made of air.

'Your name, Will,' his uncle sang softly. 'See your name there? You know what that means?'

William nodded. He knew. He was the only one who did.

'Forget my daughter. Forget what she said. That was all between me and her. But it's yours now, Will. The House and the station, all of it. And that robs her of everything. There'll be no claim. She won't bother with any of that, not if she can't get to me. We fooled her.'

William handed the paper back. 'Uncle John,' he said, 'the water hole. It was empty.'

The old man was studying his testament again. 'I know.'

'There was a cave. I thought there might be water in it.'

'I know, I know. Under the cliff, where the spring rises.'

'There wasn't any water. But I saw...' He hesitated, abandoned to the memory again. He understood now how it must have happened. They had burned the bodies, Ruth said, but they hadn't burned them completely. Then they had thrown the remains in the creek ... but that part of the story was wrong. The water was too shallow in the creek, or maybe there was no water at all. And this was a crime, it had to be kept secret. So instead they'd hidden the remains where they would never be seen again, where there was always deep, deep water. 'I thought they were sticks,' he said. 'I thought they were dead branches from trees.'

His tone made the old man glance up. 'Sticks?'

William nodded. 'But they were white.'

His uncle's eyes were intent on him now, a suspicion blooming deep within them, down where his sanity and reason still survived.

A desperate sadness engulfed William. 'You said there had to be proof. Proof that it was all true. The thing that happened out there. You said there had to be bones...'

'The water hole,' the old man breathed.

And for an instant John McIvor was suspended in cold, clear water, diving deep, his lungs aching. The sky was a shrunken blue bowl above, on the rocky bank a woman was waiting, and he was young, swimming for the sheer pleasure of it, before it all went wrong, before he emerged from the water and took her and conceived a daughter and destroyed everything. None of that had happened yet, he was still innocent, and he was diving down, down into the darkness, and there, in the furthest recess, where the icy water oozed out of the rock, he had glimpsed a whiteness.

The will slipped from his hands. He gripped William by the shoulders. 'Bones? You saw them, right down there at the bottom?'

'I thought they were sticks,' William moaned. 'Sticks and rocks. They weren't. They were bones. The bones of those people. They were thrown in the water hole.'

'You don't know that. You can't...'

'They told me,' William wailed. 'The things out in the hills. They said I'd find it!'

John let go of him, staring.

A shiver flowed through the House, and a mutter and creak came from the roof. John looked up. The windows of his room were closed, but he knew that after so many days of heat and stillness, the air had finally stirred out there.

'Rain's coming,' he said to the boy. 'Coming tonight.'

John thought of storm clouds over the hills, of cold water tumbling down rocks and along creek beds, and of pools filling slowly, hiding what lay in their depths. But not hiding it forever, and worse, not destroying it, as his father should have destroyed it, so long before, when John had been only a child and cried in his mother's arms as the fires burned.

'Listen,' he said. 'Tonight, after all the others have gone to sleep.'

William looked up at him. 'Yes?'

'I want you to find a shovel, Will. And some sacks. Look in the shed out back. And get some torches. We'll need light.'

The boy only stared in perplexity.

'Load them all in the utility,' John told him. 'And when everyone's asleep, I'll come for you.'

Chapter Forty-five

It was the last hour before midnight, on December 21st, 1993. William rode with his uncle, driving out to the water hole.

They'd had to wait until William's mother went to bed. All evening she had floated around her little flat in a bright bath of joy, putting up Christmas decorations. She'd been transformed by the news of the will, hugging William so tightly that she lifted him from the floor. Then she threw herself into the decorating, stringing tinsel about the dark walls, convinced that the House was beautiful, that it was a palace, now that it had been conferred upon her son. William took no part. A piece of paper had been signed, but for him the inheritance had been darkened by the shadow of a malevolent history. A history with one chapter left to write. And his sickness only made it worse. His ear pounded, and the smell of rotting flesh came and went, dizzying.

But when all was silent and still in the House, his uncle had come creeping into William's room, as promised. How was it that the old man could even walk? He had not risen from his bed in weeks, but somehow he was upright, a limping skeleton in a bathrobe, clinging to the wall for support. And there was no sign of weakness in his eyes, no acceptance of defeat, only the madness burning.

Now they drove through the hills. The dust raised by their passage was blown ahead of them to herald their way. The air was vibrant out there, alive with fitful winds, and a pitch black shadow had risen in the western sky, swallowing the stars. There was no lightning, no flicker of storms, but the winds told their own story. Rain was close. From time to time William tilted his head through the window and gazed upwards. The great sheet of cloud sailed steadily east, far above, and the atmosphere was pregnant with moisture, setting the skin alive, the flesh singing with expectation. But when he pulled his head back into the cabin, all he smelled was his own scent of rotting. His uncle was hunched painfully over the steering wheel, his lungs labouring as he struggled with the gears. He did not speak, and William had nothing to say to him. Their course was set.

The moon had risen and was riding above the mountains, but it was shrunken and shed no illumination. William could recognise none of the places along the track where he had walked or slept. He thought of his visions. They were the ones who had set this night's work in motion. Were they still out there in the darkness, beyond the reach of the headlights? Did they turn as the utility drove by, their eyes gleaming with dead thoughts? Did they understand what was going to happen, and did they approve or denounce? Either way, William felt that something in the night was following them. That the shepherd had lowered his axe, and that his companion had risen from the ground, and together they walked in the utility's wake. That the explorer had turned his weary horse, metal clanking, and was bent now on their trail. All of them coming to bear witness to this final indignity. And waiting somewhere ahead was an ancient creature without shape, silent beneath the stars.

Suddenly the track was gone and there, at the limit of the headlights, stood the willow tree, with the stone bench beneath. Beyond it a rocky shelf dropped away into blackness. Then William's uncle switched off the engine and the lights, and the night rushed back.

The old man gasped for breath, reached for the door. 'Bring the gear,' he said.

William climbed out. Looking up, he saw that the ragged edge of cloud was closing upon the moon. A questing gust of wind came, and the shadow of the willow tree danced. With it muttered something that might have been thunder, vastly distant, but still there was no shimmer of lightning, only an inky darkness sweeping towards them. William shuddered, and reached into the back of the utility for the equipment. His uncle had already disappeared into the night. William hurried after him, dreading to be alone even more than he feared their purpose here. He found the old man shambling across the rocks, a wild figure with his bathrobe flapping. They had to work their way around to the far side of the water hole, where the banks were lowest.

'Some light,' his uncle demanded, hoarsely.

William switched on the torch, played it downwards. The dry floor of the water hole sprang into view, sand and stones and dead branches. They descended, the old man clinging to his nephew, and then crept across the stones, back under the lee of the shelf. The willow tree bowed above them, tendrils undulating in the wind. But beneath the swaying tree a hole opened at the base of the cliff, and down there nothing moved. At the brink, William aimed the flashlight, and they peered in.

White bone shone in the beam.

'William,' the old man moaned, clutching. 'William.'

But William didn't answer. The rank smell of rotting had returned, as if the cave was filled with it, even though he knew that the bones were dry as the dust.

'No one must ever know. You understand, don't you? They must never have the proof they need. They must never take this land from me.'

William looked up at the old man's face and saw an immeasurable misery etched there, hollow and wretched and beyond hope.

'Give me the light, boy. It'll have to be you. I can't get down there.'

And as William descended into the hole, the world became a dream to him. He felt the sacks in his hands, he felt the awkward weight of the shovel, but they were meaningless things. Light shone from above, but he had forgotten about air and sky and his uncle. He was deep within the earth, surrounded by rock. He watched as his hands picked at the bones. Some of them lay loose on the sand, others were half buried, and others again crumbled at his touch. He did not allow himself to recognise them as human, not even the white domes with holes that gazed darkly, not even the rows of pebble-like teeth. He refused to count, to ever know or remember how many bones there were, or how many people they represented. He acknowledged nothing at all, working in silence and putting whatever he could recover into the sacks. When the ground was bare he heard a voice from above, telling him to dig. The shovel scraped and bit at the earth and he was hardly aware that he himself moved it. Then there were more white sticks and shards of bone, and the dream went on, darker and deeper and without end.

Finally his uncle was calling his name, telling him that it was over. The beam of light wavered and disappeared, and William rose again to blackness, dragging the sacks behind him. He was filthy. Dirt was in his hair and caked under his fingernails, as if he had clawed his way from the grave. There were no stars in the sky now, no moon. The old man was rattling the sacks, and the flashlight flickered back and forth. William could see tiny droplets of water falling in the beam, drifting slowly downwards, like snow. There were cold pinpricks on his face. He almost laughed. The rain had come too late. Too late to refill the pool and hide its secret, too late to wash him clean. He would never be clean.

His uncle was still urging him fervently — their work wasn't done. Numbly, William took hold of the sacks and carried them back towards the utility. Was the night full of watching eyes, were his visions still with him? He felt he was one of them now, that his own ghost would eternally haunt this place, bearing its burden back and forth amidst the shadows. Then the utility was loaded, and his uncle was behind the wheel, steering them away, back around to the road. In the headlights William could see white drops floating, still only the merest mist of rain, spiralling in flurries. They sparkled on the windscreen, until his uncle swore, turned on the wipers, and the windscreen became a blur. Dizziness claimed William in the darkness, and something hot and awful was dripping from his ear.

When he looked again they were pulling into the driveway. The House rose in the headlights, a wall of ruined stone and clinging ivy, and a cold drizzle was falling.

'Now for the finish,' his uncle said.

The old man was dragging the sacks towards the front door, limping drunkenly. William circled around to the back of the House, his face to the sky, feeling the dirt on his skin turn into mud. He knew what his uncle was going to do, had known all along. The things they had dug up could never simply be hidden again. The threat had to be eliminated completely. He came to the woodshed, and groped about in the darkness, picking up splinters of timber from amidst the sawdust. The rain whispered on the tin roof. His arms full, he stumbled back across the yard, bent over the wood to protect it, and on through the rear entry of the House. It was dry and still inside, the warmth of the day lingering. The hallways were lightless, but he knew his way, and he knew where his uncle would be. When he came to the office he found the old man kneeling before the fireplace, stacking wood in the hearth.

'More,' his uncle demanded. 'Pile it on here.'

William heaped on the wood while his uncle clutched newspapers from the piles around the room and jammed them in. Then the old man was fumbling at a box of matches. The fire caught in moments, and flames crackled and leapt. His uncle opened the sacks and began casting their contents upon the blaze, his withered face aglow, fervid with triumph. He might have been laughing, but William heard only the fire, raging high now. The hunger of it throbbed with the pain in his head, as if the disease in him too had finally been unleashed. In a daze he raised his hand to his ear, felt something wet. He lowered his fingers and saw blood on them, black, clotted blood, shot through with white streaks of pus. It was hideous and it stank, and it had come from within him.

There was a voice at his back, crying out a question. He turned and saw Ruth, her hair tousled from sleep, her eyes wide.

'Gone,' John McIvor cried back, his hands full of bones. 'You're too late. They're all gone. They were never here.'

Ruth stood aghast.

The old man was hurrying now, before his daughter could act. He snatched up the last bag, turned towards the flames — and his bad leg crumpled beneath him. He swayed, and in the final instant Ruth reached out for him. Then he toppled forward into the fireplace. Smoke and ash billowed into the room. Ruth screamed. She grabbed at her father's bathrobe and pulled him back, burning wood and bones scattering everywhere. Taking up a sheaf of newspapers, she started swatting at his clothes, pounding furiously as the old man writhed.

She shouted to William. 'Get help! Get a blanket!'

Already the flames were spreading greedily amongst the rubbish. William fled, aware that he was yelling, but not hearing the words. A blanket, he had to find a blanket. He dashed to his bedroom and pulled one from a cupboard. His mother appeared in the living room, sleepy and confused, and he shouted at her before running back. But it was such a long way, the passages twisted and turned, and then there was the doorway to the office, a fiery rectangle from which thick smoke poured. Ruth came staggering out, slapping at her own smouldering clothes. She fell to her knees, coughing uncontrollably, but William stopped short, the blanket tumbling from his hands.

A burning shape walked through the door.

It was wrapped in smoke and flame — bathrobe, pyjamas, they had all been transformed into streaming sheets. And it was silent. Or perhaps William's hearing was stricken along with the rest of him, for he was aware of no sound. The thing came down the hallway towards him. Ruth fell away before it. The figure didn't reel or stumble, it seemed possessed of a calm and terrible deliberation. Dark hollows among the flames suggested eyes and a mouth, and its head turned slowly, searching, just as it had been searching the first time William had seen it. Then its gaze fell upon him, and it paused, grave, and yet somehow horribly eager at the discovery. The mouth opened, a black hole, guttering smoke. In the depths of his horror William was sure that it would speak, that it would utter the question it had carried with it for so long. But instead the head tilted upwards slowly, beseeching, its question unasked and unanswered, and then something within the shape gave way.

John McIvor fell headlong at his nephew's feet.

The roar of fire shook the House, the office wildly ablaze. William was pulled backwards suddenly, and his mother was there, pushing him further away. He saw Ruth lurch to her feet and stumble down the hall, staring in disbelief at the burning corpse of her father. And then everything descended into chaos, a blur of smoke and fire and panic. William was pushed this way and that, faces loomed through the smoke, and he was fleeing along the hallway towards the front door. He could see spurts of flame licking along the ceiling, jetting ahead of him, faster than he could run. Then he was out in the night air. It was delicious and cool upon his face, and the rain was falling softly.

For a time he was alone, standing stupefied at the bottom of the steps, gazing up at the House. Already the entire western wing seemed to be alight, flames flaring from the windows, the crumbling verandahs catching fire with a savage glee, the dead ivy igniting in a fiery wall. No rain would help, not even a deluge. Flames raced across the facade and whipped up over the roof. William heard the crack of the slate tiles as they shattered, he heard a series of explosions and knew that the ammunition in the red room was detonating in the heat. Burning debris tumbled down about him, and he retreated beyond the fountain. From the front doors his mother and Ruth emerged, supporting Mrs Griffith between them, the housekeeper white and half naked and barely recognisable. They staggered away from the building, and Mrs Griffith sank to the ground.

Then amazingly William saw that his mother was heading back towards the House. Ruth went after her, and the two women were arguing, gesticulating, and William could only watch numbly. His mother looked like a stranger to him, a madwoman streaked with ash, screaming crazily at the fire. She broke away from Ruth and dashed back through the front doors, disappearing into the smoke and glare. Ruth followed her as far as the top step, but then she hesitated, turned and came back. William saw then that his cousin's face was livid, her hair singed, her eyebrows reduced to powder.

'Upstairs,' she shouted over the roar of the flames. 'She's gone upstairs!'

William stared. The House was swollen with fire, as if the great walls were bulging outwards. Why had his mother gone in there? Then he remembered his uncle's bedside table, and the document the old man had hidden away in it. He remembered his mother's joy at the news. All she had ever wanted, for herself, for her son, was contained in that one piece of paper. But the old man's room was deep within the House, far away up the staircase and down the empty halls where the fire now walked. William's whole world had shrunk to the single focus of the doorway. But the front of the House was ablaze from end to end, and Ruth was dragging him backwards. He felt her fear, and worse, her horror and pity. He was frantic now. His mother, where was his mother?

In answer the great House groaned, a long anguished sound, the wrenching of timber and stone. And then, with slow majesty, the blazing line of the roof began to sag inwards. For a tortured moment it held, and then thunder filled the air as it collapsed from one wing of the House to the other. Flames exploded from the windows, and a great fireball belched out through the front doors and across the garden, black with smoke and flying debris. Then only a great bonfire remained, roaring within the roofless walls, towering up into the night, and defying the rain-drenched sky.

It was the last William saw of his inheritance. Ruth turned him away from the sight, set his face to the south. He felt cold droplets upon his face. Shrugging free of his cousin's hands, he walked into the rain. He made it as far as the empty pool. Beyond it, he could see that the whole hillside was lit by the blaze behind him, the trees lurid against the greater darkness of night, sentinels of the station bearing mute witness to the fall. He was incapable of any tears of his own, but the scene before him was misty, blurred by mournful sheets of rain. Far out upon the plains there were lights moving, a file of them with revolving points of blue and red, distant rescuers racing along the Powell road. The pool waited like a grave to receive him, and his ear pulsated as if the fire was inside his head. Blood trickled down his cheeks and the night began to spin. William laid himself carefully down on the ground. It was already muddy from the rain. He stretched out, turned his head, and sank his ear into the cool earth. For a moment he knew relief.

Then the ground opened beneath him, and he fell into blackness.

Epilogue

RAIN DRUMMED DOWN FROM THE BRISBANE SKY.
Ruth McIvor sat motionless in the hospital chair and gazed at the newspaper on her lap. She had found it discarded in the hallway. It was a copy of *The Australian*, dated December 22nd, 1993. One story dominated the front page.

MABO WIN FOR PM AT LAST
By Lenore Taylor

The Prime Minister, Mr Keating, declared yesterday the beginning of a 'new deal' for Aborigines after the West Australian Greens finally agreed to support the Government's Native Title Bill, ensuring it passed the Senate early today.

After months of uncertainty, torturous negotiations over amendments and 41 hours of debate in the Senate, the Greens announced yesterday they would support the Bill, which was put to the vote right on midnight.

Andrew McGahan

Moments after their announcement, Mr Keating held a press conference to say the Bill's passage marked 'the end of the great lie of terra nullius and the beginning of a new deal ... a turning point for all Australians'.

'At the start of the debate I was told by a great many people that this could not be done, that the interests were too conflicting, that there was not sufficient good will,' he said. 'The passage of this legislation will demonstrate that this generation of Australians would not buy that sort of bigotry...'

The Leader of the Opposition, Dr Hewson, said that it was 'a day of shame for the Australian people' and vowed the Opposition would 'make the Government's unjust, divisive and damaging Mabo legislation a major issue right up until the next election...'

Dr Hewson said the Bill was 'an unprincipled piece of legislation which has lost sight of what Australia is all about — a united, democratic country in which all our people are equal before the law'.

Ruth let the paper slide from her knees. With her hands the way they were, she couldn't open it beyond the front page anyway. For a time she stared through the speckled windows, watching grey sheets of cloud drift low above the city skyline. It was getting dark out there. Lights gleamed in high-rise apartments. She could hear the swish of peak-hour traffic on the wet streets below, the clatter of horns, and the hissing air brakes of buses and trucks. But the sounds were faint, dulled by thick panes of glass and the whisper of air-conditioning. She shifted her body carefully, still in considerable pain. Both her hands were heavily bandaged, and her face, bright red and peeling, was slathered in ointment. But worse than the pain was the smell of smoke. She couldn't rid herself of it — it was in her hair, embedded in her skin, and her throat was layered with soot and grime, making her cough periodically.

Still, she knew she was better off than the boy.

William lay sleeping in front of her, the bed curtained off from the other end of the room. It was only an hour since he had been moved there from the post-operative ward, and he was not expected to wake for the rest of the night. The upper half of his head was swathed in bandages, and a great lump of padding was situated over his right ear. His face, thin and pallid, looked absurdly small underneath it all.

Ruth sighed, and it became a slow, hacking convulsion. Spots swam before her eyes. She had not slept since the fire, and the day stretched out behind her in a blur of hospital rooms and doctors. The paramedics attending the blaze were the first to realise that something serious was wrong with William. He was unconscious and blood was oozing from his ear, thick and smelling of rot. Ruth rode with him in the ambulance to the district hospital in Powell. But specialists were needed, so at dawn William was in another ambulance bound for Brisbane. Again, Ruth went along, for who else was there to go with him? By nine o'clock they had arrived, and more doctors were examining the ear. They declared an emergency, a theatre was cleared, and by eleven, William was undergoing surgery.

The disease was called a cholesteatoma.

According to the specialists, it was a tumour that grew in the lining of the middle ear. It usually began when some minor injury created a perforation in the ear drum. Foreign tissue from the outer ear was then able to invade the middle ear cavity, where it could latch on and develop into an abnormal growth. This tumour itself was not malign, said the doctors, but as it grew it distorted the cavity, shed dead skin, harboured bacteria and, worst of all, released an enzyme that ate away at the bone. The cavity would thus fill with necrotic tissue, some of which would leak back through the perforation in the drum, resulting in a foul-smelling discharge. The odour was what usually alerted the patient to seek treatment. In William's case, though, the tumour

Andrew McGahan

had been left to rage unchecked, eating its way from the ear right through the bone of his skull. Abscesses had then formed on his brain.

The surgeons were confident, however. They had relieved the pressure in his skull cavity, and excised the tumour. Unfortunately, it had been necessary to also remove most of the inner canal and the remains of the bone structure, so he would lose all hearing in his right ear. The doctors also noted that the boy was malnourished, dehydrated, extensively bruised and badly sunburnt. They would have referred the case to a social worker, on the suspicion of parental neglect, if not for the regrettable fact that the child's mother was recently deceased.

Ruth had listened to all this in a daze. She was in shock, and her own burns were serious. She had mumbled something about glandular fever, but the doctors only shook their heads, studied her curiously, and then left her alone.

Rain sheeted down outside the window.

Ruth was coughing again. She should go home and rest. The boy would sleep through, and there was so much for her to arrange in the coming days. Her father's funeral. And maybe even the funeral of William's mother, for Ruth was aware of no other family to take on the task. Then there would be the investigations into the fire, by the police, the fire brigade, insurance companies. And after all that, weeks from now, there would be the question of the inheritance to be settled.

Suddenly Ruth could have laughed, if the skin of her face had not been so tight and sore. Because, after everything, her father had died intestate. The only copy of his will had burned along with the House. Kuran Station belonged to no one.

There would be trouble about that, of course. Her father had made his last wishes clear enough, but with nothing in writing, the property lay open to any number of claims. Mrs Griffith, for instance. Ruth had seen the old woman in the Powell hospital, where she was being treated for smoke inhalation. Despite her condition, the housekeeper had lost none of her grim tenacity. She was already telling anyone who would listen that John McIvor had exploited her for decades, that she had cooked and cleaned for him for over twenty years without being paid a cent, and now was owed compensation. And Ruth did not doubt that she was serious.

Then there was William. The station belonged to him now, if her father's last acts meant anything at all. But he was only a boy, and not her father's direct descendant. Ruth could dispute William's claim, if she wanted, and inherit the property herself. And perhaps she should really do it. But the thought roused no feelings in her, sitting there in the hospital room. When her father was alive it had seemed important that she ... that she what? Take the station from him? But now he was gone, and all her arguments felt empty. She remembered, shamefully somehow, the old women she had met in Cherbourg, and the way they had watched her, as she talked eagerly of leases and land and rights. The look in their pale eyes. Measuring. And, despite all her promises, unconvinced.

But couldn't she prove them wrong? If the property was rightfully hers, then why couldn't she give it away? She could go back to Cherbourg and hand over the deeds. But she was lawyer enough to know, perfectly well, that it would never happen that way. Mrs Griffith would fight it. Or maybe the boy. Or if not them, someone else. A long forgotten relation would appear; maybe even the state government would intervene, disputing the validity of private deals made decades ago, and leases that were supposedly perpetual ... No, if anyone from Cherbourg really wanted the place, they would have to lodge their claim, along with everybody else. It was fifteen thousand acres of prime grazing country. In this world, something like that wasn't just given back. It had to be fought for.

Her thoughts tumbled to a halt.

It was something her father might have said.

She gazed down at William. Such a sad and silent child. She didn't think she had ever seen him smile. Pity bit at her, and a weight settled against her heart. Was he her responsibility now? Oh ... but she was too old. The burden couldn't fall on her.

It was time to go. Her hands and face hurt, and every bone ached. She would leave the boy to his sleep, and then maybe later they would talk and see what needed to be done. She turned, towards the door. Just then William stirred, moaning incoherent words. She hesitated. But he was sedated, she knew, and too exhausted, surely, for bad dreams.

She glanced once more at the rain against the windows. A memory came. The smell of earth, and of wheat, and the feeling of a familiar hand upon her head, rough with calluses, and so strong. All of it wasted, all of it ruined.

Ruth fought the tears, for her bandaged hands could not brush them away.

Then she returned to the chair, and the long vigil of the night.